"Come—I'll race you back to the stables."

Grant's eyes twinkled roguishly and his mouth curved in a devilish grin. "I'll beat you."

Adeline tossed back her head and threw him a confident smile. "I don't think so. You'll have to be content with second best."

"Never," he declared with laughing certainty.

"You're very bold with your challenge, sir," she said, a flicker of mischief in her eyes.

"When I'm allowed to be I'm not easily dissuaded, and I usually take the initiative when I know I can win."

"So it would seem with a race."

His eyes glowed and he smiled at her. "With everything, Adeline."

Adeline did not dare to contradict him or ask him to enlarge on his statement. "When you lose I'll be magnanimous in my victory, I promise."

"Adeline," he threatened, in a soft, ominous tone, while his eyes danced with amusement, "if I lose you'd better ride for your life in the opposite direction."

* * *

Wicked Pleasures
Harlequin® Historical #873—November 2007

Wicked Pleasures

HELEN DICKSON

TORONTO • NEW YORK • LONDON
AMSTERDAM • PARIS • SYDNEY • HAMBURG
STOCKHOLM • ATHENS • TOKYO • MILAN • MADRID
PRAGUE • WARSAW • BUDAPEST • AUCKLAND

ISBN-13: 978-0-373-29473-2
ISBN-10:   0-373-29473-5

WICKED PLEASURES

www.eHarlequin.com

Printed in U.S.A.

Chapter One

From where he stood, leaning gracefully against a silver birch tree, allowing his mount a moment's respite after the long ride from Sevenoaks, Grant Leighton was taken by surprise when two horse-riders—a man and a woman—came thundering past him like the Light Brigade hurtling into the Valley of Death.

Utterly transfixed, he heard the woman's joyous laughter as her horse's competitive spirit flared; it seemed determined to keep ahead of its mate. Its mane and tail flying, legs flailing, the horse, setting a cracking pace, was galloping its heart out. From what Grant could make out, the other horse was beginning to tire and didn't stand a chance.

Looking through his binoculars, he watched them, filled with admiration for the woman's ability and daring. It was clear that she was utterly fearless. It was unusual to see a woman riding astride, with her mane of hair like polished mahogany flying behind, a tangled pennant of glossy waves. He could see buff-coloured breeches and riding boots beneath the skirts of her dark brown riding habit spread out over the horse's rump.

The man was riding a chestnut mare and the woman a grey

stallion—a huge beast, a thoroughbred and no mistake—which would take some handling at the best of times and would challenge even his own.

Wide and emerald-green, the field stretched before them. Giving up the chase, the man slowed to a canter, but the woman carried on, riding beautifully, her slender and supple body, arresting and vigorous, bent forward, her gloved hands almost touching the horse's flicking ears, urging him on. Leaping a gorse hedge and landing soundly, she then soared over a wide ditch like a white swan and rode on, following the field round and down the other side, her body moving with her horse like a lover's, encouraging him every step of the way. Coming to the far end of the field, she slowed him to a canter. Riding through an open gate, with a backward look and a wave of her hand to her companion, who seemed in no hurry to follow her, she disappeared from sight.

Long after he could no longer see her Grant continued to stand and stare at the spot where she had vanished, half expecting—and hoping—to see her appear once more. Never had he seen a woman ride with so much skill. By God, she was magnificent. Deeply impressed, he was curious as to who she might be. He hadn't seen her features, so he would be unable to recognise her again, but he would dearly like to meet her.

The early morning was cool and crisp—unusual weather for early August—but Adeline, riding back to the stables, favoured it over the sticky heat of midsummer. As always, she had enjoyed her ride on her beloved Monty enormously, feeling those splendid muscles flexing beneath her. Pausing to retrieve her bonnet from where she had left it hanging on a fence, and hurriedly arranging her hair into a demure bun at her nape, she secured the untidy mess and tied the ribbon under her chin. How she would love to toss the bonnet aside and feel the wind tear through her hair once more—but that would never do. Not for the demure and prim Miss Adeline Osborne.

Now she was close to the house there was the possibility that she would be seen and her father informed, and he would chastise her most severely for riding with such complete abandon.

Horace Osborne was a strict authoritarian, and expected little of his daughter except that she behave as a well-brought-up young lady should. Adeline thought about her father as she followed the path. She was an only child, her mother deceased, and one would have thought she would be his golden child—the adored centre of his life—but he was indifferent to her. It was as if she was some kind of reject, and she was convinced that the reason for this rejection was her lack of beauty—which her mother had possessed in abundance.

As soon as Adeline had come out of the schoolroom, and her governess had been dispensed with, she had taken on the business of running the household—instructing servants, entertaining neighbours and her father's business colleagues, making things comfortable for him.

To her surprise and dismay, Paul was waiting in the stable-yard when she rode in, his presence reminding her of the importance of the day ahead. Later there was to be an 'at home' at Rosehill, to celebrate their engagement.

The sight of him put a dampener on her ride. Paul Marlow, a widower, and twenty years Adeline's senior, was distinguished-looking rather than handsome—of slender build, with fair hair peppered with white. Women were generally drawn to him. He moved carefully and spoke carefully. He was impeccable, and his clothes fitted him in a way that only the best tailors on Savile Row knew how to fit them.

A friend and neighbour, and a close business associate of her father, he was pacing the stableyard impatiently, with both hands thrust deep into his trouser pockets, his stern features set in an unsmiling expression of disapproval as he regarded his future wife. She knew he didn't like the way she rode astride like a man, or the breeches she wore beneath her skirts, but until they were married there wasn't a thing he could do about it.

'Why, Paul!' she exclaimed, dismounting and handing the reins to a stable lad. 'This is a surprise. I didn't expect to see you so early. Are you here to see Father?'

'He invited me over for breakfast. Adeline, it is most unbecoming for you to be riding unattended,' he said with cold reproof. The ride had given her cheeks a delightful red glow, but Paul failed to notice. 'A groom should be with you at all times.'

Adeline felt herself flushing at his strict censure and began to walk to the house. 'He was—Jake—but I left him in the big field. He stayed to further exercise one of the horses. I really don't know why it should bother you so much. I have always ridden unattended. Besides, at this time of day the grooms are far too busy with the horses to waste time riding out with me.'

'But I insist. I cannot have my future wife behaving in a manner that is less than circumspect. It's bad enough you wearing those infernal breeches without that.'

'There is nothing wrong with my behaviour, Paul. I have ridden alone all my life, so it's a bit late in the day to start being concerned about appearances. A chaperon is quite unnecessary—and as for my breeches, I find them both comfortable and practical.'

Paul's brows drew together and he shot her a surprised look—Adeline rarely spoke sharply to anyone. 'There is something else to consider,' he continued, in a more tolerant tone. 'I am thinking of your safety, too. There is every possibility that you may take a tumble, and with no one on hand to assist you, where would you be?'

'I never fall off. I am an accomplished horsewoman, as you well know. However—' she turned and smiled at him '—I am touched by your concern, Paul.'

'When you are married to me I will be prepared to allow you a certain amount of freedom, but I shall insist you are accompanied by a groom at all times, or you wait till I am free to ride with you.'

'Very well, Paul. As you say,' she murmured, having no wish to argue. 'Now, I think we had best hurry lest we are late for breakfast. We don't want to keep Father waiting, and I have to change.'

'There is one more thing, Adeline. Lady Waverley has kindly invited us to her house party next weekend. That should leave you adequate time to prepare for it.'

'I see.'

She looked straight ahead. The general tedium and vacuity of Saturday-to-Monday country house parties held no appeal for Adeline, who often went unnoticed. Diana Waverley was everything Adeline was not. Adeline was as plain as she was beautiful. Diana was also a popular socialite, free and easy with her modern manners, and her house parties were said to be fast and furious—which Adeline was sure she would find highly disagreeable.

'It would be good manners to reply, but how can I when I have received no invitation? It really is most unusual. You have accepted for us both, I take it?'

'Of course. An invitation to spend a weekend at Westwood Hall is not to be turned down, Adeline,' Paul told her starchily. 'Lady Waverley is renowned for her hospitality, and it is a heaven-sent opportunity to have our engagement made public.'

'I would have thought the announcement in the papers and this afternoon's gathering should take care of that.'

'It will, my dear. But a little extra exposure will not go amiss. Of course there will be society people there.' His eyes did a quick sweep of her riding habit, and Adeline was sure his lips curled with distaste. 'You may want to visit the dressmaker, to avail yourself of a new habit. Some of the ladies are fanatical about the correct riding clothes, and I know how much you will want to join in.'

'Yes, I will. But there's no time to order any new outfits. What I have will be perfectly adequate.'

As Adeline climbed the stairs she thought of the day ahead and the forthcoming house party with little enthusiasm. She always dreaded parties, and usually spent the entire evening in a corner, playing whist with some of the more sedate elderly ladies. She had met Lady Waverley on a couple of occasions, but she had never been to Westwood Hall. If she could have refused to attend she would have. No doubt there would be a wearisome procession of tennis, garden and dinner parties, and boating parties. Thank goodness Lady Waverley kept a good stable and she would be able to escape to indulge her passion for riding.

Adeline wasn't in love with Paul any more than he was with her, but she respected his ability at managing his affairs. Seldom courteous, often impatient, and occasionally quite cruel, he appeared actually to dislike her much of the time— returning her smiles with scowls and greeting her conversation with a request for silence while he read his newspaper. He made no attempt to flatter or please her. He admired her stoicism, and the way she got on with things on the hunting field as deeply as he deplored her passion for it, and he was always quick to criticise her imperfections.

Fastidious in his habits—which quietly irritated her—he liked a well-ordered life, and while she often chafed at his high-handed manner towards her she was willing to honour her father's wish that they marry, despite it having been decided without any consultation with her. Horace Osborne was keen to see his only child wed to such an estimable gentleman. It would be an advantageous marriage.

Sons were bred to continue the line and enter the family business—but unfortunately Horace had not been so blessed.

Daughters were bartered and married young, while still malleable, passed like possessions from father to husband. They were expected to obey and be happy with this change in guardianship, and Adeline would be. Her father's word was law. But it saddened her that he saw her more as a commodity than a daughter.

Uncommonly tall and straight, and with a whipcord strength, Grant Leighton emanated an aura of carefully restrained power. He was a man of immense wealth. A great deal of his fortune came from land, taking no account of his industrial interests—which were considerable—and the London properties he owned.

He was admired and favoured by women, who liked the dominance of his arrogant ways. For years gossip had linked him to every beautiful, unattached woman in society, but marriage had not been an offer he'd made to any of them, and he had left a trail of broken hearts in his wake.

At twenty-nine, he had a handsome and intelligent face, lean and brown like a gypsy's, and eyes that were silver-grey. His hair was a shade between brown and black—thick, with a side parting, and combed smooth from his brow. He had a strong mouth with a humorous twist and was inclined to smile—but not just then.

His anxiety about his mother was at the forefront of his mind. She was the most precious person in the world to him, and at present she was recovering from a serious bout of influenza. After he had found her message, on his return from Sevenoaks, his worry that her request to see him must be bad news had made him urge his mount up the narrow drive to Newhill Lodge. The square, stonebuilt, ivy-clad house stood sedately in its neatly enclosed gardens, with tall trees casting shadows on its frontage.

As he approached and dismounted, a groom appeared to take

his horse. The door was opened by a fresh-faced young maid. She smiled, bobbing a polite curtsy as he entered the house.

'Good morning, sir.'

'Good morning, Edith. Is my mother in her room?'

'Yes, sir. She's expecting you.'

'Then I'll go straight up.'

Carrying his riding whip, he strode across the hall, smiling when his eyes lit on a vase of newly cut, beautifully arranged pink roses. His mother loved flowers, and insisted on a constant supply of fresh blooms to be picked from her garden or sent over from his own hothouses at Oaklands, just half a mile away. He proceeded up the stairs.

Light fell through the lead-paned windows in bright shafts upon the polished floor, casting a warm glow on the fine mahogany staircase and the crimson and gold carpet. On the landing he knocked gently on his mother's bedroom door. It opened and Stella, his mother's maid and her companion of many years, bade him enter.

'How is she, Stella?' he asked in a low voice, lest he disturb his mother if she was sleeping.

'Tired. She had visitors earlier, and she is quite worn out, but she's eager to see you. Can I get you some refreshment?'

He shook his head. 'No, thank you. If Mother is tired my visit will be brief.'

Stella went out and closed the door quietly behind her. Grant approached his mother where she was resting, propped against the cushions on a chaise longue. A book and her knitting lay discarded on the small table beside her. Sunlight filtered through the lightweight curtains, bathing the room in a soft, golden glow. Her eyes were closed, and she looked frail and drained by her illness. There were deep hollows in her cheeks and her face was starkly white. Bending over, he placed an affectionate kiss on her forehead.

'Grant?' Hester Leighton opened her eyes and held out her

hand to him. It was thin and deeply veined. 'I'm so glad you have come.'

He sat down in a chair facing her, his eyes clouded with concern as he touched her cheek with caressing fingers. 'I got your message. What is it that is so important you had to send for me? Are you feeling worse? Is that it?'

She offered him a thin, tired smile. 'No, Grant. Don't concern yourself. I'm feeling very much the same—perhaps a little better. There is something I want you to do for me.'

'And what is that?'

'No doubt you will think I'm mad, and that I'm a selfish old woman, but I've heard Rosehill is coming onto the market. I want you to buy it back for me.'

Grant's dark brows drew together. 'It's the first I've heard of it. Where has this information come from?'

'Mrs Bennet, the vicar's wife, told me yesterday when she came to visit. It was mentioned to Reverend Bennet when he was attending a parochial meeting at Sevenoaks. Apparently Mr Osborne is considering moving to London to live.'

'But that doesn't mean to say he will sell Rosehill.'

'Mrs Bennet seems to think he will. He spends so little time there, and his only child—a daughter—is to be married shortly, and will surely move out to live with her husband.' Her lips trembled. 'I rarely speak of your dear father, Grant. I find it extremely painful. It's been five years now, but I do still miss him so very much. Contrary to what people say, I find the dulling of grief and the passing of time have very little to do with each other.'

Grant smiled with soft understanding. 'The doctors can only find cures for afflictions. We can hardly expect them to find a cure for a broken heart, can we?'

'I suppose not—which is why it is so very important for you to buy back Rosehill for me. It was my home—my family's home—for generations. I loved it so. It broke my heart when it was sold to Mr Osborne to pay off those debts, but things are so very different now. If he is to sell it, then I want it back.'

For a moment Grant regarded her steadily, and then he said, 'You've thought hard about this, I can tell.'

Tears came to her eyes. 'I have. Please go and see Mr Osborne, Grant. It is so important to me. I would like to end my days there. Afterwards—when I'm gone—you can do what you like with it. That will be up to you. But I want it so very badly.'

Unable to deny his mother anything, Grant nodded. 'I'll make some enquiries, I promise. Have you spoken about this to Lettie?'

'No, but she'll understand. I know she will.'

'Where is my dear little sister, by the way?' he asked, sitting back and crossing his long booted legs.

'In London, staying with that friend of hers—Marjorie Stanfield. I'm expecting her back sometime tomorrow.'

'Is she behaving herself?'

'I certainly hope so—but you know Lettie. She does keep me informed of most of her activities—although I have to say that perhaps I'm better off not knowing about some of them. Ignorance is certainly bliss where Lettie is concerned.' She smiled, indulgently. 'But I know she would never do anything to disgrace herself or the family.'

'Don't bet on it,' Grant said dryly. 'My sister is both spirited and fearless, and she will not rest until women are completely liberated from the tyranny of man.'

Hester laughed lightly. 'She always puts forward a passionate argument.'

'Which will get her arrested if she's not careful.'

'Not Lettie. I am always interested to hear about her activities with the Women's Movement—or Suffragists, as they like to call themselves. I offer advice where I can, and I accept her many extended absences. I am immensely grateful to Lady Stanfield for letting her stay with Marjorie—she is such a placid young woman, and I hope she has a calming influence on Lettie.'

'Be that as it may, Mother, but it's time she thought of settling down and finding herself a husband.'

'Maybe—but you are extremely fond of her, and for good or ill she is your sister. There's not a thing you can do about it. And, speaking of settling down, I have been hearing gossip about you and a certain lady of late. Grant, I know that in the past there have been rumours linking you to several young ladies—some of dubious reputation,' she pointed out with quiet censure, 'and until now I have never asked you to verify or deny them.'

'Then why now?'

'Because of *this* rumour—about you and Lady Waverley.'

Something in the soft romanticism of her words irritated and irked Grant. He did not like being the subject of gossip and speculation. 'I can see word of my recent visit to Westwood Hall has reached the ears of your visiting ladies. Really, Mother. I credited you with more sense than to listen to gossip.'

'Can you blame me?' She smiled. 'When I hear that my eligible son—a man who seems to avoid young ladies of impeccable background as if they have some kind of dreadful disease—is suddenly seen visiting a beautiful socialite? And on more than once occasion, it would appear.'

The Leighton brow quirked in sardonic amusement. 'At twenty-eight, and a widow of five years, Diana can hardly be classed as a "young lady", Mother.'

'Then at fifty-five I must seem positively ancient to you. You know nothing would please me more, Grant, than to see you settle down with someone who will make you happy.'

'I will—in time. But not with Diana. Six years ago I might have, but she chose to marry Patrick Waverley instead.' He spoke dispassionately, giving away nothing of his feelings. 'The idea of being Lady Waverley outshone that of being plain Mrs Leighton. But I am still fond of her, and enjoy her company from time to time.'

'I only met her on one occasion, and I was not in her company long enough to form an opinion. Did she hurt you?'

Grant shrugged and smiled wryly. 'I was young, and easily drawn to a pretty face. I think I was more angry and humiliated by her rejection than anything else.'

Hester studied her son intently. 'And now you're not— drawn to a pretty face?'

'Now I tend to look beyond the pretty face. It's what's on the inside that determines a person, not what's on the outside. Diana is beautiful, intelligent, well bred and well connected. But— and you said it yourself—she is a socialite. She is an appalling flirt who likes to play hard. Her husband left her well provided for, but Diana is a spendthrift and will soon have nothing left if she doesn't curb her spending. Money is important to her. She would sell her soul to have more.' He grinned. 'I soon realised she did me a favour by marrying Patrick. Believe me, Mother, you would not want Diana Waverley as a daughter-in-law.'

Hester sighed and rested her head wearily against the cushions. 'Oh well, that's a pity. But if she is as you say, then you must avoid her. You are in a position to choose better.'

She gave him the beguiling smile that, ever since he was a boy, had been able to get him to do almost anything she wanted, but on the subject of marriage he remained unmoved. 'When I choose a woman who is most suited to be my wife in every way, there will be affection and respect. When I finally settle down I expect to be made happy by it. Marriage to Diana would ensure nothing but misery.'

'And love, Grant? Does that not come into it? It is necessary if you are to have a good marriage, you know.'

Standing up, he laughed and kissed her forehead. 'I might

have known that would concern you. You always were senti-
mental. When I decide to settle down you will be the first to
know. I promise you.'

On arriving back at Oaklands—the magnificent Leighton
residence situated in a verdant valley in the heart of the Kent
countryside, so large it made Newhill Lodge look like a
garden shed—carelessly dismissing his mother's desire for
him to settle down, Grant thought seriously about her other
request. He would write to Horace Osborne and request to see
him—perhaps stay overnight with Frederick.

Grant had never met Horace Osborne, but he knew him to
be a shrewd, hard-headed and self-made businessman. He
was a parvenu, but he had been accepted by the leading
members of established society with far more favour than
most of the newly rich.

The Leightons were 'old money', and because Grant
seemed to have the golden touch when it came to making investments they still had plenty of it. For his mother's sake
Grant would ask that Mr Osborne give the proposition he
would put to him serious consideration. Not for one moment
did he think Horace Osborne would refuse his offer—and if
he should prove difficult Grant didn't have the slightest doubt
of his own ability to negotiate and persuade him.

The gathering later that day at Rosehill was a quiet and dig-
nified affair, attended by elderly relatives from both sides and
a few business associates. As Paul and Adeline were con-
gratulated on their engagement on this day, which should have
been the happiest day of her life, Adeline felt as though she
was standing at the bottom of a high cliff, on top of which a
huge boulder teetered.

Everyone complimented her on how she looked, but she
knew they were only being polite.

'Too thin,' Paul's elderly Aunt Anne said. 'Too tall,' said another. 'Too plain,' someone else commented.

But what did any of that really matter when her father was a wealthy businessman and respected in the circles in which he moved?

Adeline knew she didn't make the best of herself. Her deep red hair was usually fashioned into a bun, and she wore dresses in varying shades of brown, beige and grey that did nothing for her colouring and made her look like some poor relation. Her eyes were foreign-looking, and in her opinion her cheekbones were too high and her mouth too wide. As a rule men took one look at her and didn't look again.

But if anyone had been inclined to look deeper they would have found that behind the unprepossessing appearance there was a veritable treasure trove. Twenty years of age, and formidably intelligent, Adeline had a distinct and memorable personality, and could hold the most fascinating conversations on most subjects. She had a genuinely kind heart, wasn't boastful, and rarely offended anybody. She was also unselfish, and willing to take on the troubles of others. She never showed her feelings, and she seemed to have the ability to put on whatever kind of face was necessary at the time.

She was also piercingly lonely. Her maid, Emma, was her only companion, her only source of love and affection since her mother had died, when Adeline had been ten years old.

A knot of people crowded the platform. Between them, Emma and Paul's valet took charge of the luggage—Paul was talking to the stationmaster. As the train to take them to Ashford pulled into the station, in a cloud of smoke and soot, Adeline stepped forward and watched as it came to a stop in a hiss of steam. The passengers began to get off. Pushed and jostled as people seemed to be going in all different directions, she dropped the book she was holding, which she had brought to read on the journey.

Suddenly one of the passengers who had got off the train stepped forward.

'Allow me.' The man, taller than Adeline, and dark, bent and retrieved the book before it was trampled on and handed it to her.

Adeline took it gratefully. Looking up, she met a pair of silver grey eyes. There was no overlooking the sensuality in the mould of his mouth, even when it had a sardonic twist, as it did now. 'Thank you so much. That was careless of me.'

He smiled. 'These things happen.' He tipped his hat. 'Good day.'

Without a second glance, and dismissing the incident from his busy mind, Grant walked away. Frederick was to have sent his carriage to meet him. He was to stay overnight with Frederick before going on to Rosehill tomorrow—where he had arranged to see Horace Osborne.

What an attractive man, Adeline thought as she watched him walk towards the exit with long athletic strides. She wondered who he could be. There had been a cool purposefulness about him a confident strength that emanated from every inch of his body.

Feeling a hand on her elbow, she turned to find Paul beside her.

'Come alone, Adeline,' he ordered briskly. 'We don't want the train to go without us.'

On arriving at Ashford, they found Lady Waverley had sent her carriage to the station to meet them. When they reached Westwood Hall, Emma and Paul's valet disappeared to see which rooms had been allotted to them.

Westwood Hall was a large, sprawling half-timbered Tudor structure, and so beautiful that when Adeline first set eyes on it she temporarily forgot her reluctance for this weekend party.

The lawns had been mown to resemble smooth velvet, and the terraces all around were ablaze with trailing roses in various colours, and pots of flowering shrubs.

Most of the privileged, rich and well-connected guests had already arrived. Swarms of titled, wealthy and influential people invaded the house, lawns and terraces, their colourful gowns, jackets and painted parasols echoing the bright colours of the flowerbeds and the graceful sculptures.

Lady Waverley, widowed after just five years of marriage, was flitting among them like a butterfly. With her confident manner she presented an imposing figure.

On seeing Paul, she made a beeline for him, her red lips stretched over perfect teeth in a welcoming smile.

'My dear Paul. What a pleasure it is to see you. It has been altogether too long. I trust you are not too fatigued after your journey?'

Looking distinguished in an elegantly tailored tweed jacket, Paul smiled at her and stooped politely over her hand. 'Not at all. It's good to see you again, Diana.' Taking Adeline's hand, he drew her forward. 'Allow me to present Miss Adeline Osborne—my fiancée.'

Lady Waverley received Adeline with noticeable coolness. But she was also curious, and Adeline was uneasily conscious of being measured up. She decided there and then that she didn't like Diana Waverley. There was a cloying scent of musk about her, which Adeline found sickly sweet and unpleasant. Not unaware of the woman's exacting perusal, of a sudden she wished she had taken more care over her appearance. The dark brown hair of Lady Waverley was exquisitely coiffed, and she was gowned with costly good taste in a high-necked russet and gold-coloured dress, offset by ribbons and flounces.

'I appreciate your invitation, Lady Waverley,' Adeline said, determined to be polite.

'Well, now, I could hardly invite Paul without you, could

I? You must call me Diana, and I shall call you Adeline. Still, I like the title, and it is one of the few good things—this house in particular—that my late husband left me. Any feelings I had for him I left at his graveside five years ago.'

Adeline's raised eyebrow betrayed some amazement, but out of good manners she didn't dare question a woman on such brief acquaintance.

Diana laughed at her expression. 'Oh, it's no secret—please don't look so shocked. Everyone knows about my marriage to Patrick Waverley. He was a gambler and a drunk, but he died before he could gamble away all his wealth, thank God. Still, I make the best of what he left me. You will find my house parties are very informal. I must congratulate you on your engagement, by the way. Do you have a date set for the wedding?'

Paul shook his head. 'Not yet—perhaps early spring.'

Adeline's eyes shot to him. This was the first she'd heard about it. But, as with everything else that concerned her, she was never consulted by either Paul or her father.

Diana nodded and looked at Adeline. 'It's a shame you have not been to one of my weekend parties before, Adeline. They are an experience to be enjoyed—is that not so, Paul?' Her full lips curved in a smile and her eyes were half closed as they settled on Adeline's fiancé. '*You* never fail to miss an invite.'

Adeline already knew that this was not the first function Paul had attended at Westwood Hall, and she did not like being reminded so blatantly of the fact.

'I've been in London for several weeks,' Diana continued, 'but with too many parties behind me I have removed my aching feet from the city's cobblestones and settled for the calmer joys of the country. However, I do make Westwood Hall quite lively when I'm here, and surround myself with company. I do so hate an empty house. Now, I will have you shown to your rooms, and afterwards I will introduce you to my guests—I insist on you enjoying yourself to the full while you are here.'

Westwood Hall was as elaborate inside as out—ornamentation, decorative scrollwork, heavy furniture, gas and lamplight on polished panelling. There were so many guests it was impossible to be introduced to all of them. Some Adeline knew, some she didn't, and she quickly lost interest in them. There was one person she *was* pleased to see, however, and that was Frances Seymore. She had been invited along with her older brother, Mark.

Frances was older than Adeline but just as plain, deemed to remain a spinster, unlike her three sisters—all sweet-faced, plump-breasted and coppery-haired—who had made splendid marriages. Frances was very dear to Adeline. The whole family was dear to her. They had befriended her when her mother died and had been very kind. She also suspected they felt sorry for her—motherless, and living with an arrogant, authoritative man who seemed to be indifferent to her.

Relieved that Adeline had found someone to talk to, Paul quickly excused himself. Adeline watched him heading Diana off in the direction of the terrace. She saw him slide his arm about the waist of their hostess, saw his head bend towards her upturned face, and with a stirring of irritation sensed that what they felt for each other was more than friendly regard. When Paul dropped his arm Diana took it, and pressed her breast against his sleeve. The contact was evidently intentional, for Paul did not draw away.

Feeling that she had witnessed something she had not been meant to see, Adeline turned away to accept a glass of spiced wine. She was embarrassingly conscious to find that some of the other guests were giving the couple a second glance, too. It seemed their closeness was too conspicuous to be ignored—and the weekend had only just begun, Adeline thought. More annoyed by the scene she had just witnessed than hurt, she turned to Frances, who was looking at her with quiet understanding.

'Diana has a penchant for handsome men, Adeline. Paul is no exception, and I suspect his maturity appeals to her gregarious nature.'

'I see.' And she did see. Quite clearly.

'In fact if you and Paul hadn't recently become engaged I would have said Diana Waverley has set her cap at him. I've been here twice before—I always seem to get invited with Mark. I only come along because I have nothing else to do—and it can be quite entertaining, I suppose. Diana goes to great pains to see that her parties are highly pleasurable to those who have a taste for sexual intrigue and illicit liaison. She is always an ever-willing and resourceful collaborator.'

Adeline raised her brows, quite shocked. 'Are you saying that she *encourages* that sort of thing?'

'Oh, absolutely. When an illicit couple come to an understanding, it is usually agreed that something is left outside the lady's bedroom door to signify that she is alone and the coast is clear.' She laughed, vastly amused by the whole thing. 'When you hear the stable bell ring at six o'clock in the morning—providing a reliable alarm, you understand—there is always such a rushing about on the landings as everyone returns to their respective rooms and their own beds.'

'Goodness! If that is the case then I shall be sure to lock my door—and I hope that Paul does likewise,' she murmured as an afterthought.

Frances studied her thoughtfully. 'You know, I must say that I have misgivings about your engagement, Adeline. You deserve better than Paul—someone with a more generous nature, with passion in his veins. Someone who will care deeply for you.'

Adeline gave her a wry smile. 'You always were too senti-
mental, Frances. I don't require passion in a husband.'

'Of course you do—every woman does. Beware the perils
of a pompous husband.'

Later, sitting under the trees where tea tables had been
laid, Adeline sat drinking tea out of china cups and eating
dainty cakes with Frances.

The afternoon was hot. With the sun shafting through the
trees, the noises from the tennis court as background, people
laughing, people talking, birds singing, it should have been
perfect. But it wasn't. Adeline wished she could feel the happiness such a lovely day demanded instead of being alter-
nately angry with Paul for neglecting her and miserable,
exhausted and bored with the sheer physical effort of smiling
and chatting to people she didn't know. What she really
longed for was Monty, and to ride away like the wind.

Dinner was a long drawn-out affair, and everyone could not
have been more gracious in their compliments. The food was
sublime, the wine superb, but the choice of conversation was
different from what Adeline was used to.

As the meal progressed, and more wine was consumed,
cheeks grew florid and talk raucous. Few remarks were addressed directly to her, and when they were she replied with
a murmur or a smile or a nod. Most of the time she was
unhappy with the trend of the conversation—its content
became shallow, and leaned towards the vulgar—so she kept
quiet, for fear of making a fool of herself, and then began to
fear that her silence was creating precisely that impression.

She was appalled when Diana suddenly looked down the
table and spoke to her.

'You are very quiet, Adeline. I suppose as the proper, dutiful
daughter of Mr Horace Osborne you don't find the conversa-

tion as interesting or as stimulating as it is at Rosehill—perhaps you find all this superficial social chit-chat rather boring.'

Adeline stared at her. Was she mocking her? She saw no sign, but she sensed it. Her quietness had been misinterpreted as intellectual boredom. She didn't intend to alter that impression, but nor was she about to forget that she was at Westwood Hall on Diana's invitation. She would not be rude, but she would be the butt of no one's joke—especially a woman who was making a play for her fiancé, however subtle her methods.

Adopting a pleasant smile, she said slowly, and with great restraint, 'You're quite right. It isn't easy to work oneself into a passion over who is having an affair with whom. And with so many doing so surely they must be at the point of exhaustion in their search for pleasure for much of the time?'

There was a moment of silence before the laughter came.

'Bravo, Miss Osborne!' a gentleman across from her called out. 'Your fiancé can be amusing—but you must know it is only play.'

'I know my fiancé plays as well as any man. In fact I often think it is his—playfulness—rather than his search for pleasure that so exhausts him.' She had the courage to look directly at Paul. He looked back at her, his face set in the kind of frozen disapproval he seemed to reserve just for her.

'Why, my dear,' Diana said, her eyes full of mock consolation, 'and here was I thinking you were shy.'

Adeline smiled back at her. 'If I am, then please don't mistake it for lack of backbone.'

'No, I wouldn't dream of it.'

The dinner was over and the guests settled in the large drawing room for talk and music. Green-jacketed servants passed among them with more champagne, brandy and fortified wines.

As the evening wore on, and Adeline sat engrossed in a

game of whist, partnered by Frances, from the corner of her
eye she watched Diana making a play for Paul across the
room. Responding to her blatant attention—his chest puffed
out like a stuffed peacock, his natural arrogance greater than
ever—Paul raised his glass and bowed briefly to his hostess.
Adeline saw the subtle, conspiratorial look that passed
between them and witnessed the imperceptible inclination of
Paul's head in reply.

Seeing Adeline's interest, Lady Waverley drew away—but
not before her eyes had met Adeline's, with that same challenging, mocking look she had bestowed on her earlier.
Adeline knew Paul was physically attracted to their hostess.
She also knew when they each left the room by separate doors.

Anger surged through her. Damn him! How could he do
this? Was he so insensible to her feelings—to her as a woman?
Perhaps if she cared more for him it would hurt, but as it was
all she could feel was anger. She thought of him with cold
distaste—and a sense of wonder that she had allowed herself
to be bullied into marrying him by her father.

She would have to be stupid and fairly thick-skinned not
to see what was going on right under her nose. But what
could she do about it? Confront him? Make a fuss? Make
herself look silly and childish? For after all Paul wasn't the
only one doing it. To this smart gathering of supposedly civ-
ilised beings at the party adultery, intrigue and sexual liaison
were an amusing fact of life. The women, with their jealous-
ies and quiet war-mongering, wove webs of deceit, and the
men were just as bad, with their love of competition and of
bettering the next man.

Adeline really should have declined her invitation to the
party—not that she'd received one personally, she thought
bitterly. That was how little she was thought of—how unim-
portant she was. She would go to bed and pretend she hadn't
seen her fiancé leave the room with Diana. She told herself

she could manage—that no one need ever know about her humiliation, her rejection.

When she heard the six o'clock stable bell ring the following morning she stood in the shadow of a huge jardinière that held an elaborate array of ferns and watched Paul scuttle out of Diana's bedroom.

Afterwards she had no idea how long she stood there, gazing at Diana's bedroom door, for her gaze was turned inwards, on herself. It was as if she were witnessing a different creature being born anew out of these frightening emotions. The force that was rising within her was horrifying. All she wanted to do was go into that room and vent all her fury on Diana Waverley—to strike out at her again and again.

It was several minutes before she could move and blindly make her way back to her own room. She was determined to carry on as if nothing had happened, to get through this unpleasant time until it was time to return to Rosehill and she could decide what to do about Paul's sordid affair.

One thing she was sure of: she would not be made the object of censure, gossip and ridicule. But she had one more interminable day to get through—and one more night. How was she going to stand it?

Chapter Two

When Grant went to Rosehill to meet with Horace Osborne he didn't know what to expect, never having met him. But each man knew of the other, and both were admired and respected for their business acumen.

Horace had made himself what he was, and had spared himself nothing in a mighty effort which had brought his father's business back from near bankruptcy to marvellous prosperity. So it was not to be wondered at that he looked older than his fifty years. Grey hair was swept back from his forehead, and below it his narrow face was deeply lined, his cheeks sunken.

He greeted Grant cordially, curious as to the reason for his request to see him. His eyes swept over him, seeing a man reputed to have the same ruthlessness as himself, but taller, darker, and with a lean, powerful face.

'You wanted to see me about something important?' he said, ushering him into his study and offering him a chair before seating himself behind his richly carved desk.

'Yes. I want to buy your house,' Grant said, coming straight to the point.

Horace looked at him hard. 'Then I'm afraid you are going

to be disappointed. Contrary to what you might have heard, Rosehill is not for sale.'

Not to be deterred, and with the impudence of the devil, confident that he could make him change his mind, Grant offered him a sum that would have made any other man's eyes water. But Horace Osborne would not be moved.

Horace sensed that he had met his match in Grant Leighton. The penetrating power of his eyes indicated his swift and clever mind, and Horace decided he would rather have him by his side than as his adversary. But he would not let him have Rosehill. He had more money than he knew what to do with, and, yes, he was to move to London to live, but this house was to be given as a wedding present to his daughter and her fiancé.

Grant hadn't reckoned on this, and there wasn't a thing he could do about it. He sat a moment in silence, and with shattering certainty he knew his mother was to be denied her wish. He also knew what this would do to her—what it would mean to her.

Dear God! How was he going to tell her?

Putting off the inevitable, and in need of an immediate outlet for his disappointment, instead of going home to Oaklands, Grant went to Westwood Hall—and Diana.

Adeline got through the day as best she could. After breakfast she went to church with Frances and Paul—who looked no different than he always did, which was surprising after his night spent in Diana's bed. Any other woman would have taken him to task over his behaviour, and Adeline would have—had she loved him. As things stood she was like an empty shell, senseless to pain. What tomorrow held for her she could neither fathom nor rouse a care for.

After luncheon they went for a drive, then it was tea and bridge, and after dinner more bridge.

Frances and Adeline had gone out onto the terrace, where they sat idly flicking through some fashion magazines in quiet conversation, content to watch the sun go down over the landscape.

It was his voice that first attracted Adeline's attention—deep and resonant. She could hear him all the way from the small private sitting room. She could not hear what was being said, but the voice was raised in anger.

Adeline turned and frowned, and said to Frances, 'I wonder who that can be? He sounds extremely vexed, whoever he is.'

At that moment a tall, dark, incredibly handsome figure with a face like thunder came striding out onto the terrace. Long-sighted, Adeline took off her pince-nez, dangling them from a narrow ribbon around her neck, and looked at him. His head jerked in her direction, and her breath froze at the hard anger flaring in his piercing silver-grey eyes. For a brief second their eyes clashed, and then he looked away.

Adeline felt an unfamiliar twist to her heart—an addictive blend of pleasure and discomfort, and also recognition—for it was the gentleman who had come to her aid on the station platform.

With long, athletic and purposeful strides he made his way in the direction of the drive.

Frances lifted her lorgnettes and peered after him. 'I can't say I've seen him before—I'm sure I'd remember someone so terribly good-looking. But he does seem to be in a bit of a temper. I wonder why they were arguing.'

Adeline shrugged. 'Who knows?'

Their heads turned simultaneously to the doorway as their hostess appeared. She was scowling after the departing man—then her eyes lit on Adeline. She became thoughtful and then, as if something of a humorous nature had suddenly occurred to her, she smiled and went back inside.

* * *

After another couple of hours, pleading a headache and seeking the sanctuary of her room, on passing the library Adeline heard voices from inside. The door was partly open. Not wishing to eavesdrop, she was about to go on her way when she heard Rosehill mentioned. Burning to appease her inquisitiveness, she paused and glanced inside, seeing the same man who had stalked out of the house earlier. The other person was Diana.

Having discarded his jacket over a nearby chair, the man had unbuttoned his white shirt halfway to his waist. With his hair falling in disarray over his brow, his profile was hard and bitter. Adeline gazed at the recklessly dark, austere beauty of his face, at the power and virility stamped in every line of his long body, and her pulse raced with a mixture of excitement and trepidation.

Indeed, it looked as if he had been partaking rather freely of Diana's liquor for some time. A glass with some brandy left in it dangled loosely from his fingers. Lifting it up, for a moment he stared at the remaining brandy, then he tipped it up to his mouth and drained it. From the way he swayed to stay on his feet, it was obvious he was well on his way to becoming blind drunk.

'I omitted to ask you earlier if you'd got that business arrangement settled?' Diana asked, seeming unconcerned about his condition.

The man glanced at her briefly, unable to defeat the scowl that creased his brow. 'No. Osborne refused to sell.'

Diana's smile was ironic. 'Did he, now? I congratulate him. I'm glad there is someone who has the courage to say no to you when others wouldn't dare. Failure is not a word in your vocabulary. You must have met your match. What will you do now?'

A muscle moved spasmodically in his throat, but he made

no effort to defend himself. He shrugged. 'Nothing. There is nothing I can do. I have to accept defeat. I have done everything that can be done, and only hope my mother will not be too disappointed.'

'Well, it was nice of you to come and tell me. I appreciate that, but there really was no need. It has nothing to do with me. Do you want to stay the night?'

'If you'll have me.' Reaching out, he caressed her cheek with the backs of his fingers. 'Don't be angry with me, Diana. You've always been a friend when I needed one. I'm sorry about earlier, and I will give your proposition some thought, I promise.'

Diana gave him a wry smile. 'Since Mr Osborne has turned your proposition down, could you not redirect the money you would have spent in bailing me out of a tight situation which has become quite desperate. The bank has refused to extend my credit.'

'I'm hardly surprised. Perhaps you should curtail your extravagances? I mean, was this weekend party absolutely necessary?'

'No, but I like parties.'

'Which has much to do with the mess you are in. So the answer is still no. However, if there's anything else you ever need, don't hesitate to call on me.'

Diana straightened her spine and did her best to smile. 'I'm afraid what I need most you can't give me—and you know I'm not referring to the business matter that got you so riled up earlier. You've made your feelings quite clear—unless you've had a change of heart.'

His face was wiped clean of emotion, and his silence was an eloquent declaration that he hadn't.

Obviously deflated, Diana sighed. 'I see. Well, now—if you'll excuse me, I must return to my guests.' She regarded the empty decanter. 'If you intend cauterising your wounds

I'll have some more brandy sent in. You can't drink yourself into oblivion without it.' She walked towards the door, where she turned and looked back at him. 'Oh, and if you intend joining me in my room later, it's on the landing to the left of the stairs. Look for the door with this ribbon tied around the handle,' she said, indicating the scarlet ribbon about her waist.

'Diana, are you involved with anyone?'

'I might be. If the ribbon isn't on the door, you will have to sleep on the couch.'

In danger of being discovered eavesdropping, Adeline knew her situation was extremely precarious. Moving away from the door, she hurried up the stairs, wondering what possible business the man could have with her father.

After Adeline had prepared for the night, and Emma had left her, it was a relief when, just before midnight, she slipped between the sheets, knowing that in the morning she would be leaving for Rosehill. She had left the curtains partly open, so she could watch the moon steadily arch its way across the sky. Closing her eyes, she gradually settled her mind into the haven of sleep, and dreamed of herself as a beautiful woman in a beautiful gown, with a man holding her in a close embrace as they danced a waltz together, his eyes gleaming with warmth into hers.

Floating on the edge of sleep, she didn't know how late it was when she awoke, sensing a presence in her room. Staring into the gloom, she could make out the figure of a man, trying to stay upright as he removed his clothes. Struggling with the buttons of his shirt, he sounded a low curse. She recognised the voice as being that of the man she had seen in the library— the same man who had referred to Rosehill and her father. Gripping the sheets beneath her chin, she stared in total horror when, totally naked, he fell full-length upon the bed beside her. With a sigh he lay still.

After a few moments of listening to his heavy breathing, in desperation Adeline slowly slid out of bed, so as not to disturb him, and crept to the door. Thankfully it opened soundlessly. Bright moonlight streamed in through her windows, lighting the broad landing off which were most of the bedrooms. A table had been left with a lamp burning—no doubt for the benefit of those with a taste for illicit liaisons, she thought bitterly.

The house was silent and there was no one about. Hopefully no one had seen him enter her room. She was about to close the door when, looking down, her eyes were riveted on the scarlet ribbon tied around the handle. Recalling the conversation she had heard between Diana and the man in her bed, she froze, staring at the offending ribbon, knowing that for some sick and sordid reason of her own Diana intended to humiliate not only the man but her, too.

Anger coursed through her. Did Diana consider her so chaste and easily shocked that she would scream and create a fuss, thus adding to her humiliation, knowing that the ensuing furor would be disastrous for all concerned? If so Diana Waverley did not know her. Untying the ribbon, she closed the door and flung it into the nearest chair, before turning and looking at the man lying on the bed.

She shivered, but it was not from the cold. Suddenly she was warm—far too warm. Something was happening to her. It was as if a spark had been lit that could not now be extinguished. A need was rising up inside her—a need to be close to this stranger, to wallow in the desire that had suddenly taken hold of her, to saturate herself in this newfound passion.

She pulled her nightdress over her head, her hair tumbling down to her waist and her heart pounding in her breast, and, completely naked and carried away by her desire, returned to the bed and lay beside him. Coming into contact with his flesh, she felt something stir within her—something she had never felt before. A flicker, a leaping, a reaching out.

Even as Adeline had closed the door, through the lingering essence of the brandy clouding his brain, Grant had been aware of the blurred shape of a woman walking across the carpet and getting into bed. His mind felt slow and listless, but he had no reason to believe the woman was anyone else but Diana. Now as she lay beside him her nakedness whetted his appetite, and he realised with a surge of desire that he wanted her—wanted to fill his mouth with the taste of her and draw those inviting hips beneath him.

When he reached for her, Adeline relaxed against him with the familiarity of the most successful courtesan, little realising the devastating effect her naked body had on him. He was so different from her—earthy, vital and strong, all rippling sinews. His mouth, hard and demanding, tasting of brandy, was on hers, kissing her lips, her shoulder, her ears and her neck.

'You are wanton, Diana—and how perfect you are. I must have you. Thank you for not shutting me out.'

'Shh,' Adeline whispered against his lips in the warmest tone, thankful for the shadows that covered them both. 'Don't talk.'

She did not care that he thought she was Diana. Her body was burning and she wanted more of him. She knew deception would be easy when the bold, insistent pressure of his body made her realise that the path she had chosen was where he wished to go. He cupped her breast in his hand. She had never been touched like this by a man before, and the feel of his hand almost melted her bones. He crushed her to him, and her mind reeled from the intoxicating potion of his passionate kiss.

It was when her thigh brushed the scorching heat of his manhood, throbbing with life, that she was suddenly made aware of her innocence. Suddenly primeval fear mixed with the awesome pleasure of his hard body. Less sure of herself, she felt fear take over and panic set in. She couldn't do this. It was wrong—totally wrong. She felt her body tightening, and she felt cold, as though her blood had turned to ice. She wanted to cry out, to tell him to stop, but his lips were on hers and her throat was constricted.

In desperation she tore herself free and rolled away from him. But, not to be cheated out of what he desired, he laughed and shot out his hand, catching her arm with a strength she had not thought possible. Though she prised at his fingers she could not escape. He pulled her back downward and covered her with his body, growing more purposeful, his hungering lips insistent. With his mouth against her flesh his tongue teased the soft peak of her breast, his hand spreading, caressing the soft flesh of her inner thigh that began to tingle and to glow.

Her fear was gone. Incapable of reason, she felt her body respond as if she were another person. And though her mind told her this was wrong, her female body told her mind to go to the devil—for this was what she wanted. There was nothing she could do but let go of herself. What was happening to her? What was he doing to her? Every fibre, every pulse, every bone and muscle in her body came alive. A shuddering excitement swept through her, and the strength ebbed from her limbs as his lips travelled over her flat belly, and hips and thighs.

She strained beneath him. They were entwined—and a burning pain exploded in her loins.

Joined with him in the most intimate way imaginable, crushed beneath his strength, Adeline became aware of a sense of fullness as he plunged deep within her. With lips and bodies merged in a fiery fusion, she gasped. His hungering mouth searched her lips and he kissed her with a slow thoroughness, savouring each moment of pleasure before beginning to move. And then she felt something new and incredible, and it all seemed so effortless as she began to respond to his inner heat.

Never would she have believed that she could feel such fierce pleasure, nor that she could respond so brazenly as she yielded, giving all her desire and passion, as if an ancient, primitive force were controlling her, driving her on. Then his control shattered, and as though he were seeking a much-needed release for his mind and body he claimed her fully, filling her with an urgent desire until he collapsed completely, his shuddering release over.

Still in a state of intoxication, and unable to keep at bay the oncoming forces of sleep, with his rock-hard body glistening with sweat Grant drifted away into a heavy slumber, losing all contact with reality and the young woman in his arms.

Adeline was aware of nothing but an immense, incredible joy, beyond which nothing was comparable. Sated and deliciously exhausted, her body and lips tender from his caresses, she nestled against her lover's warm, hard body, closed her eyes and slept.

A hint of dawn fell on the slumbering forms. Grant emerged slowly from sleep. His eyelids, feeling like sandpaper, flickered open—and closed immediately to ease the throbbing ache that shot through his head. He groaned and tried to move. That was the moment he became aware of the warm, sweet-smelling form cradled against him, and the vibrant mahogany-coloured hair spread over his chest.

Diana! He smiled, although the remembrance of the woman who had been so warm and vibrant beneath him brought confusion. He found difficulty in equating it with Diana. Opening his eyes, he was relieved when the pain in his head began to ease a little. He frowned, feeling an uneasy disquiet. Something was wrong. Looking down, he disentangled himself from the long limbs entwined with his—limbs that were surely longer and shapelier than Diana's. Carefully pushing back the hair that covered the woman's face he stared in disbelief. It wasn't Diana. Who was it—and how the hell had this happened?

Without the warmth of his body, Adeline half opened her

eyes and, remembering the night, smiled and stretched her long slender form, reaching high with her arms above her head and emitting a deep, contented sigh. Her heart skipped a beat as she gazed up at the powerful, dynamic man looking down at her. Masculine pride and granite determination were sculpted into every angle and plane of his swarthy face, and cynicism had etched lines at the corners of his eyes and mouth.

Grant looked at her naked, luscious shape in appalled silence. Her face was not beautiful in the classical sense, but it was attractively arresting and he was drawn to it. Her lips were soft, full and sensuous, her eyes—heavy with contentment, fringed by thick black lashes—were almond-shaped and clear, and a sparkling shade of green. An abundance of dark red hair framed the flawless, creamy-skinned visage. His breath caught in his throat. And, dear Lord, what legs—what a body! He must have been drunk out of his skull to have thought she was Diana.

Drawing himself up, he tightened his mouth. 'Good God! Who the hell are *you*?'

Adeline opened her eyes wider and met his gaze. 'I might ask the same of you,' she retorted, her voice quite deep and disturbingly delicious in its shadowy luxury.

Though she shrank before him, her eyes never left his—which were wide and as savagely furious as a wild, wounded animal. He was six feet three inches of splendid masculinity, wide-shouldered and narrow-hipped, his chest covered with a light furring of black hair. Without haste she sat up and pulled the sheet into place, running her fingers through her wildly disordered hair. Disconcerted, and embarrassed by the way the sight of his naked body was affecting her, she lowered her gaze. Last night, when he had been in his inebriated state, she had for a time felt confident and in control. Now she felt confused and strangely vulnerable.

'Do you mind telling me what happened here last night?'

'I think we both know that.'

'I thought you were—'

Her eyes met his. 'Diana?'

'She said she'd—'

'What? Hang a scarlet ribbon on her door so you would know where to find her?' Adeline's lips twisted wryly. 'How appropriate. A scarlet ribbon for a scarlet woman.'

Ignoring her sarcasm, Grant rubbed a hand between his brows, making an effort to recall the last few hours and failing miserably. 'How do you know that?'

'I think the ribbon tied to the handle of my door speaks for itself.'

Grant looked stunned. 'Are you saying that Diana set this up?'

'That's precisely what I'm saying. And I ask you not to give her the satisfaction of letting her know that her sordid attempt to embarrass us both has worked.' Adeline tilted her head to one side and slanted him a quizzical look. 'Now, I wonder why she did that? Perhaps you know?'

Grant scowled, beginning to dress with feverish haste. 'I have an idea.' He paused while pulling on his trousers and shot her a look. 'I must have been very drunk.'

The lean, hard planes of his cheeks looked harsh in the watery dawn light. 'You were. Blind drunk.' Adeline watched his expression harden, and at the same time his voice became chillingly polite.

'For that I apologise. It is not my habit to drink to excess. Did you have no control over what so obviously happened between us?'

'Perhaps.' A little smile played on her lips. 'You can be very persuasive,' she murmured softly.

'You could have cried rape.'

'No, I couldn't—not without waking the entire household, which would have proved embarrassing for both of us. Besides, it wasn't rape,' she confessed quietly.

He stopped and looked at her. The grey eyes seemed sheathed in ice, fury and horror, and his mouth was fixed in a stern line. 'Did you plan this?' His voice was quiet, controlled.

'Certainly not. The first I knew was when I awoke and found you getting into my bed. I can see that you're angry—'

His eyes slashed her like razors. 'How very observant of you,' he mocked scathingly. Frowning, he peered down at her, trying to read the quicksilver light in her eyes. 'Did I hurt you?'

Adeline considered his question. Her body was limp and aching, and still throbbing with a strange kind of tenderness. But she had wanted him to make love to her and he had granted her request—even if he couldn't remember any of it. 'No, you didn't hurt me.'

Grant's gaze went to the dark flecks of blood marring the stark whiteness of the sheets, which told their own story. He was incredulous. The evidence was overwhelming—damning. He couldn't deny what he had done, and the inevitable consequences of it hit home. When he spoke again the husky savagery of his voice shocked Adeline into intense awareness.

'You were a virgin. I have ruined and ravaged a virgin.'

Adeline winced at the fierce accusation in his tone. 'Yes. Does it matter?'

A muscle flexed in his jaw and the metallic grey of his eyes was dim as he buttoned up his shirt. 'Yes—and if you have any measure of self-respect it should matter to you.'

'Please don't feel any sense of guilt,' she said, tossing her hair over her shoulder.

'How do you expect me to feel? I have wronged you—dishonoured you.'

'I don't feel wronged or dishonoured. If you feel that way then that is unfortunate, and for you to deal with. Your dishonour is not mine. Whatever happened between us, I did it on my terms.'

'Because I was drunk?'

'Yes. Oh, you needn't worry. I have no intention of demanding that you do the honourable thing.'

He froze. Slowly he leaned forward, his hand reaching out and grasping her chin so that she was forced to look into eyes that blazed with white fire just inches from her own. 'Lady, let me assure you that you don't want to be my wife,' he gritted through his teeth. 'Let's not play games. I've already played them all, and you wouldn't enjoy them even if you knew how to play. Unlike other men, who enjoy bedding innocents, I prefer the women I take to my bed to be experienced and knowledgeable—women who know how to please a man, sensual and willing.'

Adeline tried turning her head, but the strength in his fingers held her chin firm. 'I believe the word for a woman like that is prostitute.'

'Aye, lady, and if you go on behaving as you did last night you are going the right way about becoming one yourself.'

The blood drained from her face. 'I am not a whore.'

'You have all the makings of one. Women like that are ten a penny. They are expendable.'

'Why—how dare you?'

'I do dare.' His eyes were two slits of hard, unyielding steel. 'It isn't the first time an innocent young woman has insinuated herself into my bed with marriage as her goal. Most of them are out of the door on their backside before they can take their hats off. I am experienced—as you clearly are not—so it is useless to try extracting money out of me, if blackmail is what you have in mind.'

Insulted to the core of her being, Adeline shot him an angry, indignant glare. 'I am no scheming opportunist. You seem to forget that this is *my* bed and it was you who insinuated yourself into it.'

Releasing his hold on her chin, he stepped back, his look one of cold contempt. 'Whatever. I will not marry you. Crude as this may be, there is only one thing I would be interested in—and it's a lot safer for me to find it in a brothel.'

'And I would not marry *you*—besides, I am hardly in a position to do so. Despite the attraction you seemed to have for me last night, you do not know me—so how can you care for me in any sense that would result in a happy union? I would appreciate it if you would refrain from mentioning what happened to anyone.'

'You can be assured I won't mention it. I'm not that much of a fool. Can you assure me I won't have an angry father challenging me to pistols at dawn?'

Adeline lifted her gaze to his. 'I don't intend to tell him or anyone else. What is done cannot be undone, but I do ask you to forget it happened.'

'Of that you can be guaranteed. I'm glad we have an understanding. Do you care nothing for your reputation? Do you hold yourself in such low esteem that you thought nothing about giving yourself to a complete stranger?'

Those words, uttered with such biting contempt, hurt her. Stunned and stricken, she looked away from him, beginning to resent his effect on her, the masculine assurance of his bearing. She would never forgive him for turning something that had been so wonderful into something quite ugly.

'You have said quite enough. Please get out of my room.'

He raised one well-defined brow, watching her. 'There is just one thing I would like to ask you before I go. Could you have stopped me?'

'Perhaps. I don't know.'

'Then why didn't you?'

'I had my reasons.'

'Do you want to tell me? I've been told I'm a good listener.'

Uncomfortable with both the question and the penetrating look in his steely grey eyes, Adeline averted her gaze, fixing it on a rather fancy ornament of a spaniel on the dressing table.

In spite of her prior intimacy with this man, he was still a stranger. How could she tell him about Paul's betrayal with the woman this man had wanted to spend the night with?

'No, I don't think so. I am not obliged to share them with you.'

'And did you enjoy what I did to you?'

Despite having willingly participated in her own seduction, she flushed and found it impossible to lie. 'It was the most wonderful thing that has ever happened to me.'

Shrugging on his jacket, he gave her a long, assessing look. When he next spoke his tone was sarcastic and cruel. 'Good. I don't like to leave a woman unsatisfied. I have my pride to consider.'

'I'm sure you have,' she whispered.

His attitude to what had happened between them made her feel worthless, so cheap and so ashamed of herself. It seemed incredible now that not only had she allowed him to make love to her, she had instigated it. Bright flags of humiliated colour stained her cheeks and tears stung her eyes.

She pointed across the room. 'There is the door. Please— just go, will you?'

He stared at her in silence and then, with nothing further to say, turned on his heel and walked out, without so much as a nod to her.

A feeling of anger, frustration and a profound sense of shame raged through her. She meant nothing to him. How could she when he didn't know her? When he had never laid eyes on her before? He had been drunk and, roused by a temporary passion, had taken his pleasure where he found it— with a willing body. Instant gratification. To be forgotten and discarded afterwards.

She thought of Diana Waverley with shame, and knew she could never equal *her* sexual experience. She could not believe the ease with which she had given herself to a stranger—a man whose name she didn't even know, who would scorn her, laugh at her. She had behaved so out of character. Now, in the cold light of day, it was so ugly—so horribly shocking. What she had done was sordid. She was corrupted and beyond forgiveness. And to humiliation and her sense of guilt was added the fear of pregnancy. Dear Lord, don't let it be so.

When Emma came in Adeline appeared composed, and put on a cheerful face, while in truth she was struggling with shame and mortification. For now she'd had time for calm reflection she greatly regretted her rash behaviour. Throwing away her virginity because of a childish desire for vengeance hadn't solved her problem with Paul; it had simply created another. As for his affair with Diana—what could she do? Besides, wasn't she guilty of the same?

Thinking how her time at Westwood Hall had changed everything, she realised that she would still have to face Paul and deal with the situation. Of course she would have to marry him—pretending that all was well, playing out a polite farce for the rest of her life—but she realised that pretending nothing had changed in their relationship would prove a severe strain.

Grant left Westwood Hall for Oaklands—no more than three miles away—before the other guests were stirring. The ride helped clear his head, but he was unable to shake off the memory of what had happened. It hadn't occured to him until he'd left Westwood Hall behind that he didn't even know her name, but he was unable to shake off the feeling that he had seen her before.

He was consumed with a bitterness that was directed not at the young woman but at himself—he was a man who could usually hold his liquor. Embarrassed and shamed by his temporary lapse, and his lack of proper decorum, a wave of guilt washed over him. Miss Whoever-she-was had told him she had known what she was doing, but he could not escape the fact that he had taken her without the slightest courtesy or endearment, with less feeling than a dog for a bitch—and what made it a thousand times worse was that he couldn't remember a damned thing about it.

A memory of the young woman flicked across his mind—a mercenary little flirt with a body that had drugged his mind. He could not rid himself of the image, or of the hot, smothering desire that coursed through his body, and it shocked him to think how much he still desired her.

He knew he could find her if he wanted to—he had only to ask Diana—but since she had engineered the whole sordid episode, in excruciatingly bad taste, he refused to give her the satisfaction of letting her know he had fallen for her ploy, hook, line and sinker. Diana was intelligent and direct, and she wanted more from him than he was prepared to give. But it was too late—six years too late—and there was no going back. But that did not stop him enjoying her company now and then.

Hopefully he would never cast eyes on the young woman again. And, dismissing her from his mind, he concentrated on how he would break the news that he had failed to buy back Rosehill to his mother.

On the train taking them back to Sevenoaks, Paul and Adeline were alone in the carriage. Paul glanced across at his fiancée. With her lips compressed in a thin line, her glasses on the end of her nose, she had her head bent over her book. He realised she had not spoken to him directly all morning, and she seemed to find it difficult meeting his eyes. And had he imagined it, or had she shrunk from his hand when he had offered to assist her onto the train?

'Have you enjoyed the weekend, Adeline?'

'It wasn't what I expected,' she answered, without raising her head.

'Why? What did you expect?'

Her face was shuttered. Paul never knew what she was thinking—and in this instance if he'd been made privy to her thoughts he would have been both shocked and appalled.

Adeline was trying to feel abused and furious about what had occurred, but the memory of the stranger making love to her stirred something more akin to warmth and passion, a feeling of wanting to sample what he had done to her more fully. It was wrong what she had done—she knew that—and she knew she had sinned far more devastatingly than she had ever done. But it had felt wonderful, too—and important. How could anything as wonderful be so sinful?

Resting her book in her lap, she looked at Paul as she would an annoying, persistent fly she wanted to swat away. This man she had pledged to marry had an odd mixture of high intelligence and an almost total incapacity for laughter. He also had a gravity that was totally without delicacy or tenderness. Now she saw him as he really was—a weak, shallow, horrid individual. This time forty-eight hours ago she would have thrust such thoughts deep down into her mind, there to stay out of respect for her fiancé. But by his own actions Paul had killed all respect in her.

'I saw little of you, Paul. You spent a lot of time with Lady Waverley.'

'Diana?'

'Yes, Diana.'

'I was being sociable—which is more than can be said of you.'

His deprecatory tone stirred Adeline's ire. 'Please explain what you mean by that.'

'You really should try to be more outgoing, Adeline—more convivial. You spent the entire weekend with Frances Seymore to the exclusion of everyone else.'

'Perhaps that was because my fiancé was too busy giving

all his attention to someone else,' she responded tersely. 'I *did* notice.'

Paul was taken aback by the sharpness of her tone. 'What's come over you, Adeline? It isn't like you to criticise.'

'I'm not criticising. It's just that you were with Diana for most of the time.' She looked at him with an unusually defiant expression. 'Are you carrying on an affair with her, Paul?'

His eyebrows shot up. 'Now you are being ridiculous.'

Adeline looked at him direct, and he had the grace to look away. 'Am I? I don't think so.'

Her bosom rose and fell, and her eyes darkened with anger. Nothing was more sure to upset Paul than the discovery that he had been caught out in an indiscretion. It might be that it was merely one of those affairs that distracted men from time to time—a sudden appetite that once sated lost its hunger— and after being made love to by an experienced, incredibly handsome stranger, Adeline now knew what that hunger could do to a person.

She told herself not to torture herself about last night, and to further insulate herself against going mad decided to firmly put an end to her thoughts about him. But, feeling badly done by, she was out of sorts, and it gave her satisfaction to stand up to Paul for once.

'I may have been tucked out of the way in a corner at Westwood Hall for most of the time, but I do have eyes—and so has everyone else. Don't embarrass me, Paul—or my father.'

'Really, Adeline,' he snapped, shifting his position uneasily. 'You read too much into my friendship with Diana. It is you I am to marry, after all. I am very fond of you, you know. You accuse me of neglecting you, but you could try showing me more affection.'

She merely looked at him. Her face was inscrutable. How could she show what she didn't feel? The thought of all the days and nights of her life being so soft and impassive while he carried on one intrigue after another enraged her beyond measure.

'Now, if you don't mind, my dear,' Paul said, unfolding his newspaper and beginning to scan the columns, 'it is a subject I prefer not to discuss.'

Lowering her head, she looked at her book, but instead of the print she saw Diana as she had looked when she had come into the breakfast room earlier. So brazen, so self-assured and smug, Diana had settled her shrewd eyes on Adeline, trying to gauge the effect of her machinations—but to no avail. Having already decided to behave as if nothing untoward had happened, and keep Diana wondering, Adeline had smiled pleasantly, said good morning and hoped that she had slept well, and without giving Diana time to respond lowered her gaze and attacked her boiled egg.

She resumed her reading. Having always been conservative in her choice of authors, when others could have enlightened her more fully, she now told herself she was no longer ignorant of the ways of the world and men. Her two days at Westwood Hall had furthered her education in such a way that she would never feel the same again.

That same evening, Adeline and her father had finished their evening meal—eaten in silence for the main part—and retired to the drawing room. Adeline poured them each coffee. Her father never drank alcohol—he said it clouded the mind, loosened tongues and made fools of men, and following Adeline's encounter with the handsome stranger at Westwood Hall she now realised how much sense there was to his words. The whole episode seemed unreal to her, and she looked back on what had happened with total disbelief, but nothing could take away the memory of what it had felt like, and she was discomfited by the warm rush of feeling that accompanied the memory.

Her father seemed quieter than usual, more subdued. He

had presence, and he made himself felt by his temper and sharp tongue. He was both respected and feared by every member of his household, but Adeline had lost her fear of him. His temper no longer affected her, but she always felt duty bound, and would never disobey him.

With his stern grey eyebrows drawn together, Horace looked at his daughter. She was composed, but she looked different—older, a woman. Having been married to a beautiful, warm and giving woman, he was disappointed in Adeline. She managed his house as efficiently as a wife, but she had always been devoid of womanly attraction. He didn't imagine that marriage to Paul Marlow would improve matters in that direction, but there was a change in her.

'Have you enjoyed your weekend at Westwood Hall?' he asked now.

'Yes—it—was pleasant,' Adeline replied hesitantly.

Horace nodded, not particularly interested, and didn't ask her to enlarge on it. 'We've been invited to spend a weekend at Oaklands—which isn't far from Westwood Hall.'

'Oaklands?' Adeline put down her cup and stared at him. Not another weekend house party, surely?

'Mr Grant Leighton's place.'

'Who is he? I do not believe I've heard of him.'

'That's hardly surprising,' Horace said brusquely. 'He came to see me recently—made me an offer for Rosehill.'

Adeline stared at him. His pronouncement rang a bell in her mind, and she recalled the conversation she had overheard between Diana Waverley and the gentleman in the library at Westwood Hall—the man who had later made love to her. But she didn't put any importance on it just then.

'He did? Why? I didn't know you wanted to sell it.' Her father wouldn't have told her if he did anyway.

'I don't. I bought the house from his mother's family— they hit on hard times and were forced to sell. Rosehill was in her family for generations and she has fond memories of the place. Somehow it's leaked out that I'm moving out to live in London. She wants to buy it back. I refused Leighton's offer, of course. I intend to make it over to you and Paul as a wedding present.'

Adeline stared at him. This was the first she'd heard about it. 'Why, that's extremely generous of you, Father.'

'I want you to have it. I don't need it—I'm always happier in town—but nor do I want to part with it. Besides, Paul will be looking for somewhere to live when you're married. Can't live with your in-laws. Wouldn't be right.'

'And Mr Leighton?'

'He thinks that by inviting us to Oaklands he'll get me to change my mind.'

'And you won't?'

'Absolutely not. But it may prove to be an interesting and enjoyable weekend. I liked Grant Leighton. He's got sound business sense and mature judgement, which brings confidence. You need confidence to run a business of any kind. Reminds me of myself when I was that age.'

'Is it necessary for me to go?'

Obviously disappointed in her lack of enthusiasm, her father said irritably, 'We are all invited. It would be discourteous of you not to come along.'

Adeline sighed, resigned to spending another interminable weekend in someone else's house. Unfortunately there would be no Frances to help see her through. 'Then I suppose I'd better go.'

The Leighton family had a long and distinguished history. It had been Grant's great-grandfather who had bought the extensive Oaklands estate in Kent and settled his family there.

The original house, built in the mid-eighteenth century, had been old-fashioned and cumbersome, and he'd lost no time demolishing it and building anew. The present house was built in a restrained Italianate style, the main block long and two-storeyed. Its classical style, the simplicity of its form, the way it sat solidly in its own secluded woodlands of oak, beech, lime and yew, hiding the house from all unwanted views, and its formal gardens, drew admiration from all who visited the house.

As the coach proceeded along the winding tree-lined drive, Adeline looked out of the window at the façade of the great house. She couldn't help but be impressed. She fixed a smile on her face as servants rushed forward to assist the new arrivals, and they were shown into a memorable entrance hall—Mr Leighton's impressive collection of Italian white marble sculpture, reflecting one of his abiding interests, standing out against the different-coloured marbled walls.

Suddenly a man appeared from one of the rooms and came striding across the hall to greet them. In Adeline's mind a bell of recognition rang.

'Mr Osborne! I'm delighted you could come.'

At the sound of his voice—the deep, well-modulated tones of a gentleman—Adeline stood stock still. Thunderstruck, she stood as one paralysed. Then she lowered her head blindly, her breath coming so rapidly she feared the lacings of her corset would burst. How dreadful! What a terrible thing to happen!

Ever since she had lain with him she had remembered what it had been like to wake up to his manly, shadowy form, standing tall and silent at the side of her bed, his furred chest and broad shoulders void of shirt. She'd had dreams about him—dreams about him kissing her, making love to her— dreams that made her wake up feeling hot and confused. She had thought never to meet this man again—the man she remembered her father telling her wanted to buy Rosehill. And here he was, taller and more elegant than she remembered, and ruggedly virile. And she had to spend two days in his house!

She could only stand and stare as Grant Leighton shook her father's hand. For what seemed an eternity she waited, existing in a state of jarring tension, struggling to appear calm, clinging to her composure as if it were a barrier she could hide behind as, with dread, she waited to be introduced.

'Allow me to present my daughter, Adeline. Paul you already know.'

Adeline was thankful the brim of her bonnet kept most of her face in shadow. If he was taken aback by her rather dour appearance he was too polite to show it. He stooped courteously over her hand and then, as if she were of no importance, turned to Paul and shook his hand.

'Good to see you again, Paul. Glad you could come.' Grant found Paul Marlow irritating, and didn't particularly like him, but seeing as he was his invited guest he forced himself to be civil.

'Your invitation surprised me,' Horace commented.

Grant grinned broadly. 'I knew it would. But I don't give up easily.'

Horace gave one of his rare smiles. 'I knew that from our meeting. How is your mother—forgiven me, I hope?'

'Not a chance. She's more determined than I am.'

'Really? She strikes me as being a remarkable woman. I'd like to meet her.'

'You will. She's determined on it.'

'And I am intrigued.'

'Come—I care little for standing still. Come and sample my brandy.'

'Tea will do. I don't drink. Never touch the stuff.'

'Then I'm sure Paul will appreciate it. I've invited just a few friends to stay. You may know them—or some of them.' He turned to Adeline. 'I'm sure you would like to freshen up after your journey, Miss Osborne. Your maid has already arrived—along with your father's and Paul's valets. Mrs

Hayes, my housekeeper, will show you to your room,' he said, with a gesture to indicate the hovering housekeeper.

Adeline couldn't hide her face away any longer. Taking the bull by the horns, and fully expecting the worst, she lifted her head and turned the full force of her gaze on him. Recognition was instantaneous. She saw his reaction go from surprise to abject horror and cold, ruthless fury. His jaw clenched so tightly that a muscle began to throb in his cheek. Thankfully he had his back to her father and Paul, so they couldn't see that anything was amiss.

Meeting his eyes in absolute complicity, she said quietly, 'Thank you, Mr Leighton. I would like that.' Bestowing a smile on Mrs Hayes, she moved away from him and followed her up the stairs.

Chapter Three

Adeline couldn't believe this was happening. It was like reliving a nightmare, and trying to escape it was pointless.

As she followed Mrs Hayes her knees were shaking so violently she was afraid she'd fall. She tried desperately to keep her emotions under control so that she could think clearly. Little had she realised, when she had climbed back into that bed for a night of passion with a complete stranger, the consequences of her actions. She had been a naïve and gullible fool. Now she could not believe she had been so reckless.

The thought of going downstairs and having to behave as if everything was all right filled her with dread. She considered pleading illness, but that would be no good. It would only be putting off the moment. She had to face him sometime.

By the time she went downstairs some sanity had returned, but panic was heavily mixed with it. When she reached the hall she saw he was waiting for her in an open doorway, like a guard on sentry duty, his presence potent and powerful, undermining everything honourable she had ever thought about herself.

How she wished she could sink into the ground and disappear.

Attired in Norfolk jacket and tweed trousers, he had the stamp of implacable authority on his stern features. He really was the handsomest man she had ever seen, but there was no softness in the lean, harsh planes of his cheekbones, the long, aquiline nose and the implacable line of his jaw. He was every inch the aloof, elegant gentleman—the master of all he surveyed.

'Miss Osborne—I would like a word with you in private, if you please.'

Encased in a tight ball of anguish, Adeline paused and looked at him. It was important that she remain calm. In tense silence she moved towards him. He stood aside, and when she had swept past him into the room he closed the door. She was in a library, but she took scant notice of the magnificent leather-bound tomes that lined the walls from floor to ceiling. It seemed like an eternity before he finally spoke.

'Please sit down.'

'I'll stand, if you don't mind.' That way he wouldn't seem so tall and intimidating.

'As you wish. This is unfortunate, Miss Osborne.'

She faced him fully. In place of the cold animosity she had expected his tone was polite and impersonal, his features hard and implacable. 'I agree, I had no idea who you were. If I had I would not have come.'

'And if I had known who you were I would not have invited you.'

'Well, you did. So we'll just have to make the best of things, no matter how unpleasant the situation is for both of us.'

'I agree. So if you are wise, Miss Osborne,' Grant said in a chilling voice, 'you will be careful to avoid me while you are in my house.'

'I have every intention of doing so, Mr Leighton. Believe me, there is nothing that disagrees with me more than having to spend time with you.'

'Then we understand each other perfectly.' Looking at her

now—dressed with a sobriety which bordered on the austere—he couldn't believe that anything of an intimate nature had happened between them. With his hand behind his back he moved closer, his eyes like two shards of ice as they fastened on hers. 'Now, listen to me very carefully and heed me well. One way or another we will get through this weekend, and when it is over you will leave here with no one any the wiser. We will not meet again.'

'I sincerely hope not.'

'In the meantime, to allay any suspicion, we will be polite and amiable towards each other. I hope that will not be too difficult.'

'Contrary to your low opinion of me, I have no desire to see either of us disgraced. I shall try to be a good actress.'

'I am certain that among your other brilliant talents is the ability to act. In fact when I recall your past performance I'm sure you will succeed admirably, Miss Osborne,' he commented wryly.

'And how can you know that when you had drunk yourself senseless, Mr Leighton?' she countered, with biting sarcasm.

'That, to my shame, I cannot deny. I am not proud of myself. However, it will not be in either of our interests to let our sordid secret out. How do you think your fiancé would react,' he taunted lightly, 'if he were to learn of—what shall I call it?—your indiscretion?'

She was reluctant to speak of the matter in such a blatant manner, and embarrassment and anger brought a bright flush to Adeline's cheeks. 'I must confess that I really have no idea. But that is for me to worry about, not you.'

'Then let us hope for both our sakes that Paul doesn't find out. When you took it into your head to admit me into your bed instead of kicking me out—which is what I deserved—you placed us both in a difficult situation.'

Anger blazed hot and fierce in Adeline. 'You really are the

most loathsome, hypocritical, conceited man I have ever had the misfortune to meet. How dare you have the gall to criticise my behaviour? The fault lies with us both, so don't you dare shift the blame onto me. I have tried to blame you, but my conscience refused to let me. If I am guilty then you are equally so,' she declared wrathfully.

Grant raised a dark brow and considered her flushed cheeks, her green eyes sparking ire with icy arrogance. 'What happened between us was unfortunate. I'm convinced you did not expect a proposal of marriage, financial gain and a life of luxury from what you did—so we will put it behind us.'

'I am not interested in luxury,' Adeline snapped.

'Of course not. I realise your father is an extremely wealthy man. Although I have always harboured the delusion that all girls yearn to snare wealthy husbands, regardless of their upbringing and background.'

'Plain and serious, and with no feminine appeal whatsoever, Mr Leighton, I am not like other girls.'

'No—I realised that when I woke up in your bed.'

Adeline heard the insult in his smoothly worded comment, and almost choked on her anger. 'What you or anyone else thinks of me does not matter. I learned to live with and accept the way I am a long time ago.'

Her admission struck Grant, and brought a strange ache to his heart. Momentarily distracted by the myriad of emotions playing in her expressive eyes, he was staring at her in utter astonishment as he recalled with vivid clarity all the womanly attributes concealed beneath her shapeless, unfashionable brown dress. He recalled seeing her stretched alongside him, as naked as a babe, and he remembered how white her high young breasts were, well-rounded, the nipples as wide and pink as rose petals. Why on earth she chose to wear her glorious wealth of hair in that unflattering, hideous bun at her nape he could not for the life of him imagine.

'You may not make the best of yourself, Miss Osborne, but when I awoke in your bed I did not see you as plain, and you certainly did not lack feminine appeal—and I am prompted to say that despite our differences I suspect we were compatible in bed.'

Adeline stared at him, unable to believe he could describe the passion they had shared with such clinical calm. She failed to notice he had just paid her a compliment, for her fury was so great it was uncontainable.

'You have no idea how hard I have castigated myself for not "*kicking you out*", as you so aptly put it. It would have saved me all the misery I have endured since. You cannot possibly know how I have hated myself for my own lack of character and restraint for actually being tempted by you. I will never be able to forgive my stupidity.'

Grant put his hands on his lean hips and regarded her coldly. 'I had no idea you would be so hard on yourself,' he said sardonically, raising one dark brow.

'That, Mr Leighton, is putting it mildly. For one night of illicit sex I behaved no better than all the other vacuous women who were guests at Diana Waverley's party, and I cannot deny the awful truth that I sacrificed my principles, my virtue, my honour and my morals.'

'You knew what you were doing.'

'Yes—and unlike you I blame no one but myself. I made you a gift of my body and you can't even remember. How do you think that makes me feel, Mr Leighton? I will tell you—insulted, dirty and defiled are the only words I can find to describe it. You are heartless, and I cannot believe I let you touch me. It is a shame I will have to live with for the rest of my life.'

Without further ado she turned on her heel and strode to the door, where she turned to deliver her parting salvo. 'One more thing. Just in case you are wondering—although somehow I doubt it's even entered that arrogant head of yours—I am not pregnant. So that's one concern taken care of—and I hope the last.'

Grant watched the door close behind her. My God, she did have a way of knocking a man between the eyes. Devil take it, how had he ever got himself into this situation? Try as he might, he could not completely blame or acquit her. That there might be a child as a result of his stupid, irresponsible behaviour *had* bothered him. Thank God she wasn't pregnant. He stood perfectly still, bemused and unable to shake off what had just transpired—or to believe that the beautiful creature he had made love to had quite unexpectedly turned up at his home when he'd thought he would never set eyes on her again.

Ever since that night his mind had been tortured by her. He could not forget even the smallest detail of her glorious body. Why she chose to dress the way she did, as if for some reason of her own she wanted to make herself inconspicuous, was a puzzle to him. Women with such courage and daring and fire in their veins as Miss Osborne possessed did not try to hide themselves away.

The weekend had lost its shine. Shutting out the reality of Miss Adeline Osborne's presence under his roof was going to be impossible.

Adeline paused at the other side of the door and tried to compose herself before facing the other guests. She was trapped in this house, therefore she was going to have to find some way to remain here in relative harmony for the duration. In order to survive the ordeal she would simply have to ignore Grant Leighton's inexplicable antagonism and take each moment as it came. She would be poised and polite and completely imperturbable, no matter how coldly or how rudely he behaved.

With that settled in her mind, she went to join Paul and her father.

* * *

Oaklands was made for grand occasions. By six o'clock the huge table in the dining room was laden with an impressive array of silver cutlery, Crown Derby and exquisite crystal glassware. There were few table decorations, and what there were created a light and graceful effect. Vases were filled with blooms which had been grown in Grant's own hothouses.

Well-presented delicious food would be served, along with many various wines. No guest ever left the table at Oaklands with less than complete satisfaction.

Two beautiful crystal chandeliers were suspended from the high ceiling in the large drawing room. One wall was a wide sweep of windows, with French doors thrown open to the scented breezes of the garden and a broad stone terrace ablaze with pots of flowering shrubs, affording breathtaking views of the manicured lawns, the magnificent gardens giving way to a lake and surrounding countryside.

Grant moved among his guests—twelve in all—with the confident ease of a man well assured of his masculinity and his own worth. He conversed politely, seeming to give each his full attention, but the major part of it was concentrated on the door, as he waited for Miss Adeline Osborne to make an appearance.

Adeline entered the room feeling more than a little trepidation. Directly ahead of her was the impressive figure of their host, and he was looking straight at her. With a defiant toss of her head she lifted her chin and walked forward between Paul and her father.

Grant disappeared for several minutes, and when he returned had an elderly lady in turquoise silk on his arm. They circulated, laughing and chatting to guests, and eventually crossed the room to where Horace Osborne stood with a rather stiff-looking Paul and an apprehensive Adeline. When Grant introduced the lady to Horace she eagerly extended a thin hand in greeting, giving him all her attention.

Small, trim and white-haired, Hester Leighton gave the physical impression of age, yet her twinkling blue eyes and easy, willing smile were the epitome of eternal youth.

'I am so pleased to meet you, Mr Osborne—and Mr Marlow and your charming daughter.'

Horace bowed politely over her hand. 'Likewise, Mrs Leighton.'

She smiled sympathetically at Adeline. 'How young you look, Miss Osborne. I'm afraid you're stuck with a lot of old fossils for the weekend. I don't think there's anyone here under the age of forty—excluding Grant, of course,' she said, smiling fondly at her son.

'Oh, I'm sure I'll survive, Mrs Leighton,' Adeline replied, for the most part keeping her gaze averted from their host.

'Less of the old fossils,' Grant chided mockingly. Speaking to Horace, he said, 'Mother is still youthful, despite having raised four children.'

Horace arched his brows, seemingly surprised. 'Four? And are they all present this evening?'

'No,' Hester replied. 'Just Grant—and my daughter Lettie will be along later. My youngest son Roland is in India with his regiment. I had a letter just last week, informing me he will be coming home for Christmas—as will my daughter Anna and her family, from Ireland. It's all very exciting—a Christmas to remember. It will be the first Christmas we have been together as a family for many years. Do you have other children, Mr Osborne?'

Horace shook his head. 'Sadly, no. My wife died when Adeline was a child. I never remarried.'

Hester smiled at Adeline. 'It's a pity Lettie isn't here—but she will be later on. At least I fully expect her to be. She's only just arrived home from London, so she will miss dinner, I'm afraid.' Her gaze was drawn back to Horace. 'I really am so glad you came.' She turned to Grant. 'You have seated me next to Mr Osborne at dinner, I hope, Grant?'

He smiled indulgently. 'As you requested, Mother.'

'Good. We have so much to discuss.'

Horace smiled. Her light-hearted charm was infectious. 'I hope you don't hold a grudge because of my refusal to sell Rosehill?' he questioned.

'Of course not. I'm disappointed, naturally, but I never hold grudges.'

'I'm relieved to hear it.'

Mrs Leighton was as gracious and kind as she was witty and warm. Adeline was surprise to see that her father was captivated. Her surprised deepened as his face took on a rare sparkle of humour.

At that moment the butler announced that dinner was about to be served.

Mrs Leighton turned at Horace. 'Will you be so kind as to escort me into dinner, Mr Osborne?'

He offered her his arm. 'It will be my pleasure, Mrs Leighton.'

'Oh, you must call me Hester. We are very informal at Oaklands, you know.'

Horace's eyes twinkled. 'And I would like it if you would call me Horace.'

The rest of the evening passed in a relaxed and congenial atmosphere. Adeline listened, and conversed when spoken to, and smiled when it was appropriate. Often when she looked in Grant Leighton's direction she found him watching her with a strange sort of intensity she could not define—as if he were making a study of her person.

After dinner everyone gathered in the drawing room to partake in various amusements. Grant leaned on the piano, listening to Mrs Forrester play some Chopin nocturnes—both she and her banker husband were his guests from London. She was a clever, interesting woman Adeline had conversed with at length at dinner, and she was extremely proficient on the keyboard.

Adeline surreptitiously watched Grant's tall, lounging figure. His head was bent low as he listened attentively to the music. Without warning he turned, and Adeline was caught in the act of staring at him. His gaze captured hers, and a strange, unfathomable smile tugged at the corner of his mouth. Immediately she jerked her gaze away and looked down at her book.

Unable to resist speaking to her, Grant went and perched on the arm of the sofa where she sat, looking down at her. He had noticed that her face in repose had a vulnerability to it that was startling, as if pain were familiar to her. She could not have been aware of her expression or she would have been more guarded. Now she peered up at him in surprise through her spectacle lenses.

'I think you may have lost your way, Mr Leighton. Please don't feel you have to speak to me.'

'I don't. I suppose we must play out the farce to its conclusion.'

'It looks like it. But do you have to be so disagreeable all the time?'

'I intend to continue being disagreeable while you are in my house.'

Adeline sighed and closed her book. 'It might please you to know that I am paying dearly for my lack of judgement—which is only right. And even though I am now in the most dire straits because of it, I suppose that, too, is justice.'

'Exactly what do you mean by that?' Grant asked, in spite of himself. 'Something to do with your lack of loyalty to your fiancé, perhaps?' he mocked lazily, watching tension and emotions play across her expressive face.

'Either that or his loyalty to me.' She grimaced. 'Paul doesn't know the meaning of the word.'

Her tone was scathing, and her reply left Grant puzzled.

Despite his resolution not to give a damn what her problems were, he was a little disturbed by her answer—but he didn't want to enlarge on it.

Sensing he was softening a little, Adeline dinted her pride and presented her advantage. 'Mr Leighton—'

'Grant.'

'What?'

'Please feel free to call me Grant. Everyone does. It will seem odd if you don't.'

'Very well—then you must call me Adeline.'

'Please continue—Adeline. You were about to say something?'

'Yes. Surely nothing that has happened between us should make us behave badly towards each other?'

Grant lifted an arrogant sleek brow. 'No?'

'Neither of us were hurt.'

'We weren't?'

'No. So there is no reason why we can't be cordial to one another—for the time I am here.' She gave him a small beguiling smile and, removing her glasses, looked at him directly. 'Believe me, if I could I would leave. But I can't—so we are stuck with each other.'

Her smile was so disarming that Grant experienced the first crack in his defence. Her clothes may be severe—almost puritan—but her face threw out a challenge. It was a face with a capacity for merriment and cheerful cynicism, and there was impudence in the tilt of her nose. Suddenly he was surprised to find he wasn't nearly as immune to her as he wanted to be.

'It seems like it,' he replied. 'You know, you look so much better without your spectacles.'

'So do you,' she replied with a trace of sarcasm.

Grant laughed, not in the least offended. Without her spectacles to distort his view, he thought how beautiful her eyes were—green and large, and surrounded by thick black lashes.

When he had first seen her earlier he had thought how unattractive she was, and had found it difficult to believe he had found anything striking about her when he had awoken in her bed. But looking at her now, bathed in a golden light, her lips—sensitive lips, full, sensuous and sweet—her expression soft and alluring, and looking very young, he was forced to revise his opinion.

'I would also like to remind you that like everyone else I am your guest, so I would appreciate being treated like one and not as an intruder. You have hardly been the soul of amiability towards me.'

Grant tilted his head to one side, studying her. He was considering whether or not there would be an advantage in putting their hostility aside. Concluding that there would, he nodded in agreement. 'Very well. I want the time that you are here to be pleasant for both of us, and for the weekend to run smoothly for all concerned. I will make every attempt to be civil.'

'Are you sure you're up to the challenge?'

'I shall prevail.' Suddenly he smiled at her, and that smile was as bright as the sun coming out from behind a cloud.

Completely caught up in the heady power of that smile, Adeline warmed to him, appreciating the considerable charm he could wield without any effort at all. 'Thank you.'

'It may interest you to know that Mrs Forrester has been singing your praises. It would appear that you have hidden talents, Adeline. She says you are an extremely knowledgeable young woman who can converse on most subjects. She was delighted to find herself in the company of another clever, intelligent woman.'

'That's nice of her.' Adeline's smile became mischievous as she gave what he'd said some thought. 'Clever and intelligent? Oh, dear—for an intelligent woman I'm not doing very well. Look at the mess I made of things at Westwood Hall. My life hasn't been the same since.'

'It's a little late in the day to start thinking about that, but you'll soon get it back in order—when you marry Paul Marlow.'

Adeline looked at him and tried to feel some enthusiasm, but failed. 'I suspect you don't like Paul.'

'You suspect right.'

'Then why did you invite him?'

'Because I was afraid your father wouldn't come otherwise.'

'So you could try to persuade him to sell Rosehill?'

Grant nodded.

'He won't, you know.'

'I know that. He was most definite about it. But it means a lot to my mother,' he said, with a teasing twinkle in his eyes, 'and I couldn't deny her the opportunity to use her persuasive charm on him.'

'Father never succumbs to charm.'

'And he's not an easy man to live with I imagine.'

'Not really. He's always worked hard, and he has become set in his ways—he always believes he's right.' She smiled, then looked away. 'He's terribly strict, but not cruel. He's the kind of father who allows me every indulgence, except the freedom to choose my own husband. Not that there's anything unusual in that. Most fathers are stiff and virtuous, and keep a very short rein on their daughters, regardless of how plain they are.'

Grant lifted an eyebrow, surprised at her outspokenness. 'And do you regard yourself as plain?'

'Oh, absolutely. Still,' she said, laughing softly, 'since Mrs Forrester says I am intelligent and clever, I don't suppose I can have everything—and if I had to choose between the two then I would choose intelligence over everything else.'

'Then I must introduce you to my sister Lettie. I think you will find you have much in common. Speaking of which—' he said, looking beyond her towards the door, where there seemed to be some kind of a disturbance. He rose to see better the cause of it.

Lettie's entry was like a whirlwind coming through the door—a fresh, airy breeze sweeping through the house. Adeline saw a slim young woman clad in rose-coloured satin. Bestowing smiles on everyone she passed. The new arrival made a beeline for her brother, and with her came a freshness and vitality that shone.

Grant smiled tolerantly as she threw her arms around his neck and hugged him tightly. 'Dear Lord, don't throttle me, Lettie,' he complained, but his firm lips were stretched in a grin as he held her at arm's length and surveyed her. 'You're looking well.'

'It's been a whole month, and I've been working very hard, I'll have you know, so I must look a sight—but bless you for the compliment. It's lovely to see you again—and Marjorie sends her regards, by the way. I've missed you. Have you missed me?'

'Like a bad headache,' he drawled, pleased to see her nevertheless.

Adeline was more than a little charmed by Lettie. She smiled a great deal, and her bodily movements were as lively as her expression. Dark haired, with deep blue eyes, a pure complexion, a waist the requisite handspan and a dazzling smile, there was no doubt in her mind that this was Grant Leighton's sister. They were so alike.

'I'm sorry for the disturbance. I do hope you'll forgive me for being late.'

'You're always late, Lettie.'

'I only got back from London tonight, and I've had simply heaps to do. You're not cross with me, are you, Grant?'

Grant grinned at her, slipping an arm about her narrow waist and hugging her close. He was clearly very fond of his sister.

'I was none too pleased that you missed dinner, but at twenty-three years old you're a bit too old for me to take you across my knee, Lettie.'

'You always were a tyrant,' Lettie teased, laughing gaily.

The love in Lettie's voice was discernible to Adeline. It was clear to her that Grant and his sister enjoyed a warm family relationship of a kind Adeline had never known and never would.

Grant turned and looked down at Adeline. 'Lettie, this is Adeline Osborne. She is here with her father and her fiancé, Paul Marlow.'

Adeline stood up and smiled at Grant's sister, finding a pair of fearless sparkling eyes scrutinising her curiously. Then a delighted smile dawned on her pretty face and she clasped Adeline's hand in a warm gesture of greeting.

'I can't tell you how pleased I am to meet you—or how relieved I am that I will have someone nearer to my own age to talk to. Grant has a disagreeable habit of inviting people to his parties who are either too long in the tooth or have nothing of interest to talk about—although to be fair to them I have known nearly every lady and gentleman present for most of my life, and they are all extremely nice people.'

'My sister is a rebel, Adeline,' Grant provided with mild humour. 'Liberal and free-thinking, and she has strong opinions about most things. She is an independent young woman who flouts convention disgracefully. She argues passionately about rights for women and she has a habit of championing the unfortunate.'

'Really?' Adeline smiled, glancing at Lettie with something akin to admiration. 'How commendable.'

'You may think so. Mother is remarkably tolerant of her earnest convictions—me less so. Take care not to offend Adeline, Lettie,' Grant warned with mock gravity. 'She is a gently reared young lady who spends most of her time buried in the country and has probably never heard of the Women's Movement and Suffragists.'

His words were highly provocative to a sensitive Adeline. Her eyes snapped to his. 'On the contrary. Because I spend most of my time "buried in the country" it does not mean that I am stupid. I have heard of the Women's Movement and I am full of admiration for what it is trying to achieve. As for myself, I have many accomplishments. I am well read, and conversant in several languages. I am also a capable horse-woman. I swim and fish, and I excel at fencing—a talent you might like to test some time, Mr Leighton.'

He smiled broadly, his strong white teeth gleaming from between his parted lips. 'I might consider it,' he replied, open to the challenge and deliberately baiting her. 'But are you good enough, I am prompted to ask?'

She raised an eyebrow. 'As to that, I invite you to be the judge.'

'Then I shall look forward to disarming you.'

Lettie laughed good-humouredly. 'You'd better watch out for Grant, Adeline. He's quite a ladies' man.'

Grant gave his sister a dark look. 'And your only diversion is to shock and annoy me, Lettie. I'm seriously thinking of putting a muzzle on you. Your manners are atrocious. That said, I will leave you two to get acquainted. I've neglected my other guests long enough.'

Lettie placed a restraining hand on his arm. 'Grant— wait.' He paused and glanced at her. 'Will you be riding in the morning?' He nodded. 'Good. I'll see you at the stables at seven.' She laughed when he raised a dubious brow. 'I won't be late, I promise.'

'I'll believe that when I see it. You're always late.' His gaze shifted to Adeline. 'What about you, Adeline? If you ride as well as you say you fence, then perhaps you would care to join us? Most of the guests will be along, and I have several splendid mounts.'

'Thank you. I'd love to join you.'

He nodded, and after excusing himself went to circulate among his other guests.

Immediately Lettie pulled Adeline down onto the sofa and began chatting animatedly.

Adeline found the conversation extremely stimulating, and joined in with an enthusiasm that surprised her. She listened in fascination to Lettie's visionary ideas about how one day the dark days of repression would end for women and they would overcome the stigma of inferiority and become completely liberated. Adeline didn't believe it, of course, but she liked to think Lettie was right.

When Lettie accused most men of being tyrants, Adeline found herself glancing across the room at Paul. In conversation with an elderly gentleman, he looked morose. Meeting her gaze, he regarded her with the air of an inquisitor. Looking away quickly, Adeline was inclined to think Lettie was right in her assertion, which boded ill for the future.

Suddenly Paul appeared in front of her. She hadn't even seen him approach.

'Paul—I believe you are acquainted with Grant's sister?'

Paul bowed his head politely. 'I am. It's a pleasure to see you again, Miss Leighton. Adeline, have you forgotten that you promised to partner me at bridge?'

'Bridge?' Lettie remarked amusedly. 'Oh, but Adeline and I are just getting to know each other, and we have much to talk about. I'm sure you can find someone else to partner you, Paul.'

Paul was not amused, Adeline could tell. He had been cold, distant and argumentative ever since they had arrived, which she put down to the company and lack of female attention.

A hardness entered Paul's eyes, and they narrowed on her with censorious annoyance. 'Adeline, are you coming?' he persisted.

'No, Paul. Suddenly I have an aversion to the game.'

He looked most put out. 'You never have before.'

Her smile was defiant. 'I have tonight,' she replied, reflecting that she would need to be prepared for a scolding from him later.

Normally Paul would have insisted, and she would have relented—but, not wishing to make a scene, he had to accept it. He thought—quite correctly—that she had come under the influence of Miss Leticia Leighton—for it was well known that she held some ridiculously extreme radical views regarding the rights of women. Although he had also noticed of late that Adeline seemed to have developed a subdued aversion to him, which was both a mystery and a source of irritation. Because he had never had any difficulty getting on with the opposite sex, he was forced, therefore, to set the blame entirely down to her, and hope things would improve when she became his wife.

'Very well. Will you be riding in the morning?'

'Yes. I'm looking forward to it enormously. Will you?'

'Of course.' So saying, he excused himself and walked away.

'Dear me,' Lettie murmured, her eyes following Paul across the room. 'Why on earth are you marrying him?'

Normally Adeline would have been uncomfortable with such a pertinent remark, yet she was so amazed at Lettie's outspokenness that she wasn't offended by it in the least. 'You don't like Paul, do you, Lettie?'

She shrugged. 'Not much.' Lettie glanced at Adeline with concern. 'I hope you don't mind me speaking my mind. I always do. Mother says it's one of my bad points.'

'Not at all. But do you mind if I ask why you find him disagreeable?'

'Well, for a start he's absolutely convinced of his own superiority. There's also something secretive about his manner which makes me uneasy—and besides, he's much too old for you.'

Adeline sighed. Lettie was right, of course, but out of loyalty and duty—more to her father than to Paul—she made no comment. 'Father doesn't think so. He considers it a suitable match.'

'And you go along with that?'

'It's easier than arguing with him.'

'Really, Adeline! My first impression of you was that you are a fighter. You must stand up for yourself.'

Adeline was amused by this. She was completely taken with the easy friendliness of Grant Leighton's sister, and accepted the feeling as mutual. 'Are you saying I should disobey my father?'

Lettie seemed to give it some thought before saying, 'Yes—yes, in this instance I am.'

Feeling restless and despondent, and unable to sleep, and being a great reader, Adeline looked for her book. When she was unable to find it she realised she had left it on the sofa in the drawing room. The hour was late and, thinking that everyone would have retired to their rooms long since, she pulled her robe over her nightgown and left her room. The house was deathly still, and only the chimes of a distant clock tolling one o'clock broke the silence. She glanced about her, peering into shadows and dark recesses as she went down the stairs.

Grant was in the drawing room, enjoying some time alone before going to bed. The room was in semi-darkness, with only a couple of lamps left burning. Having removed his jacket, he was seated before the dying fire with his legs stretched out in front of him. Looking through the open door and into the hall, he was amazed to see Adeline move smoothly down the stairs, looking like a fantasy—flowing white in ribbons and lace.

Immediately he was on his feet and moving quietly to the door. Adeline turned and gasped when he suddenly stepped in front of her. His bold silver-grey eyes raked her quite openly.

'Ah, another night owl.'

His voice, as soft and smooth as the finest silk, stroked Adeline like a caress. She felt its impact even as she realised how intently he was studying her face. His potent virility made her feel entirely too vulnerable.

'Oh! I'm sorry. I didn't mean to disturb you.' Adeline flushed. 'I came to look for my book. I believe I left it on the couch.'

Grant stepped back and swept his arm inward in a silent invitation for her to proceed. Adeline complied, and Grant watched in fascination the play of firelight through her clothing. His breath caught in his throat as the outline of her long, lithe body was subtly betrayed through her flimsy nightdress. His mind returned to the memory of that night, and her beautiful figure and glorious long legs. He was quickly brought back to the present when she retrieved her book from where it was in danger of disappearing behind a cushion and came back to him.

Adeline was uneasy. As he dragged his eyes upward from her body to her face his gaze was far too intent, thoughtful and serious. He was too close and too masculine. She averted her gaze, hot-faced and perplexed.

Grant knew enough about Adeline Osborne to know that she spelt trouble to him, but there was something unusual and provocative about her—something that stirred him and drew him to her. Reaching out, he ran a finger lightly down the curve of her cheek. Pausing at her mouth, with his thumb he traced the soft fullness of her lower lip.

Sensations of unexpected pleasure stirred within her. She trembled, and could almost feel the bold thrust of him between her thighs. Uncomfortable at the knowing look in his eyes, and sensing he was on the verge of kissing her, in order to retain her sanity she took a step back.

'Please don't,' she whispered.

'Why? Does my touch offend you?' He smiled knowingly. 'Spare me your maidenly protests. It didn't, as I recall, on one occasion.'

'An occasion we both agreed never to speak of.'

'There's nothing wrong with talking about it between ourselves—although you have the advantage.'

'I do?'

'You remember everything we did, whereas I...'

'You were completely foxed,' she reminded him sharply. 'That is your problem, not mine.'

'Are you not curious to find out if what you experienced is still as good as it was then? Didn't you say that it was the most wonderful thing that had ever happened to you?'

'Perhaps it was the danger...the risk that made it so exciting,' she whispered lamely, in an attempt to find an excuse to explain why she had told him that.

'Whatever it was, I am curious to discover what I missed.'

What he was suggesting startled Grant, and made him doubt his sanity. Although, having made the suggestion, he was beginning to see no great harm in it.

To Adeline, his statement confused her. She stared at him in dazed wonder. Self-conscious, she let her gaze dwell on his finely moulded lips, watching as a faint smile, a challenging smile, lifted them at the corners.

'What do you say, Adeline? Are you afraid to find out?' he asked, his voice low and husky. Reaching out, he fastened his hands on the curve of her exceedingly trim waist and drew her close. 'Finding you floating through my house at this late hour looking as you do, you are too tempting by half.'

In her confused state of loneliness and longing it was all too much. She made no protest when he bent his head and took her lips in a feather-light kiss, warm and inviting her to respond. Paralysed, she felt all the passion he had shown her before sear through her body. She couldn't believe it was happening again. She felt that familiar burst of exquisite delight as she let him hold her in the complete lassitude of surrender.

Raising his head, Grant looked down at her upturned face.

It was soft in the lamplight, her eyes large and dark. His lips lifted lazily. 'Is that how you remember it?'

Unwilling to surrender her secret memories of tenderness and stormy passion, she kept her gaze on his lips and murmured, 'Something like that.'

'Care to try it again?' Grant invited, still willing to indulge in a few more pleasurable moments—so long as there was no pretence that it was anything but that. 'Why don't you show me how you remember it?' he teased as his lips came closer. 'Show me…' His hands slipped beneath the heavy wealth of her hair and moved round her nape, sensually stroking it as his mouth felt the softness of her cheek and the disturbing lasciviousness of her lips. She was a woman of such contrasts.

Seduced by his kiss and caressing hands, Adeline clung to him, sliding slowly into a dark abyss of desire as once again she felt the wanton, primitive sensations jarring along her nerves. The feeling suddenly frightened her. She drew back, her heart beating sickeningly fast.

'I think you forget yourself,' she whispered. 'You shouldn't be doing this—not again. Do you forget that my father and my fiancé are guests in your house? What you said to me that night at Westwood Hall led me to presume you are not so fussy over where and when you accept favours from a certain type of woman. I am not like that. Despite what happened between us, my father brought me up decently. I am nothing like the women of your experience—like Diana Waverley.'

A sensual smile played about his lips. 'How quickly you become defensive. It is precisely what *did* happen between us not so very long ago that makes you not so very different. You can't change that, nor what you are, Adeline,' he said lazily, his arms still encircling her, not letting her go. 'A decently reared young woman would surely have been scandalised on finding a strange man about to get into bed with her. She would have shouted for help, alerted the rest of the household. You did not react that way, however hard you protest.'

Adeline gasped at his arrogance. 'And what am I?' she said bitterly. 'Do you see what I did as an open invitation to seduce me whenever you get the opportunity? Believe that because I gave myself to you once I'm fair sport to be ravished when the fancy takes you?' And with his expertise Adeline had no doubt that he would succeed, feeling as she did about him. She was drawn to him, and felt unwilling to resist.

'I've no intention of taking you here and now. But don't doubt my needs, Adeline,' he murmured softly, drawing her closer. 'Or my intention of repeating what we did. But not here. Not like this. When the opportunity arises it will not be a quick lift of your skirts in a dark corner—delightful though that prospect might be.'

Adeline stared at him, registering all that he implied. His handsome face was all planes and shadows and his eyes glittered sharply. 'You shouldn't be speaking to me like this,' she whispered. She knew it was wrong, and yet she could not deny that it was so wickedly exciting.

Pleasurably wanton feelings rippled through her at the memory of how she had felt when he had made love to her, her eyes glazing slightly as she conjured up the magic of his hands on her soft flesh, cupping her breasts. Instead of trying to stifle her feelings when he bent his head to cover her lips once again, she allowed them to flood through her. She received his kiss with innocent passion, and the offering of her mouth caused Grant to seize it in a kiss of melting hunger that deepened to scorching demand.

Lust roared through him, and he splayed a hand across her spine, forcing her into contact with his own hard, aroused body. Automatically his hands pressed her buttocks against his arousal, and then, suddenly aware of what he was doing, he tore his mouth from hers and stared down at her as he tried to regain control of his senses.

'Well? Was it the same as the last time I kissed you?'

She nodded. 'And some more.'

They pulled apart and stood facing each other, Adeline still clutching her book to her chest. Grant was debating whether to kiss her again, or try to pass the matter off as some light occurrence, when a male voice suddenly erupted from the doorway.

Chapter Four

'**G**ood Lord, Adeline! What's going on?'

Adeline spun round in mindless panic, her gaze flying to Paul. Mortified to the very depths of her being by the realisation that he had almost caught her in Grant's arms, she braced herself for a tirade on the subject of what Paul would consider to be her disgraceful behaviour. She stood and looked at him, rigid with shock. Meeting his eyes, somehow she managed to calm herself. Afraid of rousing some conflict between the two men, she could not let him see the flush of passion on her cheeks, or the warm light of desire in her eyes.

Paul's alert, suspicious gaze moved from Adeline in her night attire to Grant.

'Paul—I—I was just…' She cast a nervous, pleading look at Grant and found him regarding Paul not with shame but with irritated amusement. Paul's face hardened and he threw her a reproachful glance. Dear Lord, she thought, if he were to know the truth… But, no matter what was going through his mind, the last thing he would want would be a scene—he hated the vulgarity of scenes. As long as you didn't put a thing into words, it didn't exist.

'Adeline came to retrieve a book she left in the drawing

room earlier,' Grant said, in a voice that struck Adeline as amazingly calm, considering what had just transpired between them. 'She was just returning to bed.'

Paul looked sternly from Grant to Adeline. 'That is no excuse. You should not be wandering about in your night attire.'

'I was unable to sleep, and didn't think anyone would be about at this hour.'

'Then you were wrong,' Paul retorted stony-faced as he glanced at Grant. 'Excuse us, will you? I'll escort Adeline back to her room.'

Bidding Grant goodnight, Adeline left the room without a backward glance. Not until Paul had left her outside her door and she had closed it did she lean against it and close her eyes, her mind racing beneath the force of what had just occurred.

Grant stood for several moments after they had left, thinking about Adeline Osborne and the impact she had made on him. She was a young woman of many contrasts. Possessed of a bright and brittle intelligence, stunningly direct, polite but candid, she also had a provoking sensuality and was brimming with deeply felt emotions.

Despite having lost her virginity to him, there was no disguising the fact that she was still an innocent girl whose life was slowly pushing her out into the heady stream of sexual maturity—like a boat on the Thames River. She had no idea how desirable she was, how captivating—for, unlike Diana, she had not learned—nor ever would—how to use her attraction cruelly or cynically, simply for the pleasure of seeing her admiring swains dancing on a string.

Adeline rose early the following morning. It was a fine, sunny day. Wearing a tweed riding jacket over a silk shirt, and a bowler clamped to her head, her hair secured at her nape by a red ribbon, she went to the stables with a spring in her step.

Apart from the grooms saddling horses, few people were about. She was pleased to see Lettie, who had ridden over from Newhill Lodge, where she lived with her mother.

'Glad you decided to join us,' Lettie said, striding across the yard, her dark blue riding habit flattering her trim figure.

'I always like to ride early when I'm at home. Have you seen Paul, Lettie? He said he would be riding.'

'About ten minutes ago. He was already mounted and ready to go. He rode off on his own towards Ashford—which isn't half as pleasant as riding through the park.'

Adeline's head jerked up. 'Ashford? Oh, I see.' To hide her suspicion and sudden anger, she turned away. To her knowledge Westwood Hall was between Oaklands and Ashford, and she strongly suspected that Paul was calling on Diana. Deliberately shoving the matter to the back of her mind to be dealt with later, she determined not to let thoughts of Paul spoil her ride, and concentrated all her attention on the next hour.

Her eyes lit on the rather splendid chestnut stallion with a black mane one of the grooms was leading out of the stalls. The horse whinnied as she approached him with her hand out-stretched, and nuzzled her with affection, blowing his warm breath onto her cheek.

'What a magnificent animal,' she breathed, running her gloved hand over his coat, which rippled like satin. Eyes aglow, she turned to Lettie with unconcealed excitement. 'Please say I can ride him?'

'If you like—but I must tell you that he's highly strung and not easy to handle—he'll also bite you as soon as look at you. His name's Crispin, by the way.'

'He won't bite me—will you, boy?' Adeline whispered, rubbing his nose. 'I'm not afraid of him. I'm sure we'll get along nicely.' She turned to a groom. 'Saddle him for me, will you? And I don't ride side-saddle,' she was quick to add.

The groom gave her an appalled look before turning to Lettie for permission.

Seeing Adeline was determined, and that it was plain she was comfortable with the horse, Lettie laughed and nodded. 'Do as she says, Ted. I'm sure we don't have to worry about Miss Osborne falling off.'

When the horse was saddled, Ted linked his hands to receive a well-polished boot and give her a leg up. She was up in a flash, her feet feeling for the stirrups. Ted's eyes almost popped out of their sockets when he saw she was wearing buff-coloured breeches beneath the skirt of her riding habit. He'd never seen anything like it.

'You won't mind if I ride off by myself, will you, Lettie? I'm dying for a good gallop.' Feeling the thrill of excitement, the throbbing expectancy of the ride to come, Adeline was unaware that Grant had just entered the stableyard, and had paused in astonishment on seeing Adeline being hoisted onto the huge stallion.

With no idea where she was going, except that it was away from the house, and oblivious to the hush that had descended on the stableyard, putting her heels to the stallion's sides she was away.

'Did my eyes deceive me, Lettie?' Grant murmured, coming to stand beside his sister, his eyes glued to the disappearing speck moving across the park.

'No. That was Miss Adeline Osborne. She insisted on riding astride—and she was wearing breeches beneath her skirt.' Lettie smiled, unable to hide her admiration. 'There's nothing commonplace about *that* young lady. She certainly doesn't conform to the usual mode of riding. She was eager to be away—as you will have seen for yourself.'

'Without a groom?'

'The way she was riding that horse, she'd leave him standing.'

'I am intrigued by our Miss Osborne, Lettie—intrigued and

fascinated. I must see which way this phenomenon has taken.' Without more ado Grant shouted for his horse to be saddled immediately.

The stallion was fresh, his spirits high. Adeline set an easy pace, but she had her hands full for the first ten minutes. When he settled down, she bent to his ear. 'Now, let's see what you can really do.' And she gave him his lead.

Nostrils flared wide, Crispin swiftly exploded under her. Sure-footed, he moved like a dream, easy and fluid. Adeline laughed, the trees becoming a blur as they fairly flew over the ground. Her skirts ballooned over the horse's flanks, to reveal her long breechered legs, and her mane of deep red hair flew out behind her, her red ribbon flapping like a kite. Cresting a hill, she slowed him to a canter, exhilarated by the ride.

Hearing hooves thundering over the turf, she paused and looked back to see who it was. Recognising Grant, perched atop a great black horse which showed all the compressed power of good breeding, she waited as he approached. He looked so dapper in his tan coat, fawn breeches and waistcoat. He wasn't wearing a hat, and his hair flopped over his brow. Recalling what had passed between them the previous night— the way he had held her and kissed her, and how her body had responded just like that other time—she felt her spirits soar as she looked at his darkly handsome face.

Drawing rein beside her, Grant smiled broadly, his white teeth gleaming from between his parted lips. He'd watched her ride across the park, seen she was light in the saddle, handling the usually difficult mount with expert skill. His eyes appraised the long, lean legs encased in breeches astride the stallion. She was full of energy and emotional vigour, her cheeks poppy-red and her eyes sparkling green, and in that moment he thought she was the most striking-looking woman he had ever seen in his life. He was fascinated by this extraordinary young woman.

'Well, young lady, you are full of surprises. If my eyes do not deceive me, there is not much anyone can teach *you* about a horse. One can tell a born rider by watching the way he…' He paused and smiled. 'Or she. After watching you ride, I can see you certainly speak their language.'

Seeing the way Grant controlled his animal effortlessly, without thought, as fluidly and as softly as the horse himself moved, Adeline was thinking the same thing about him. She returned his smile, and for a moment there seemed to be only the two of them in the whole world.

'Thank you. I'll take that as a compliment—although he is a splendid horse, almost as fast as my own beloved Monty.' From beneath carefully lowered lids, Adeline slanted him a long, considering look. 'Shouldn't you be with your other guests?'

'Lettie will take care of them—although most of them won't surface until mid-morning. When I saw you riding out on Crispin I couldn't resist coming after you.'

'I love riding.'

He quirked a brow in amusement. 'Oh, I can see that. Do you hunt?'

'Absolutely.'

He grinned. 'A girl after my own heart.'

She darted him a sideways glance. 'Really? And I was sure you were wishing you'd never laid eyes on me.'

'Shall I tell you when I did first set eyes on you?'

'I already know. It was when I was boarding the train to Westwood Hall. You got off at Sevenoaks. When I dropped my book you picked it up.'

His eyes widened with surprise. 'I remember. Was that you?'

She nodded, giving him a puzzled look. 'If that wasn't the time you were referring to, then when *did* you first see me?'

'When I was staying with an old schoolfriend of mine— Frederick Baxter. I saw you out riding early one morning—

dressed as you are now. I'd no idea who you were—until now. You were riding a grey stallion. I remember it was a huge beast—I thought at the time it was too big and spirited for a woman to ride, but you soon put me right. You are one of the most skilled riders I'd ever seen mounted. I can see you are no ordinary young woman. I'm impressed by your prowess.'

'I had no idea I was being watched.'

His grin was boyishly disarming. 'How could you? You were flying like the wind at the time.' A crooked smile curled his lips as he let his leisurely perusal sweep over her. 'Nice breeches, by the way.'

Grant's smiling eyes captured hers and held them prisoner until she felt a warmth suffuse her cheeks. 'I always wear them when I ride. They're so practical.'

'I'm sure they are. I also remember what you look like without them.'

Her flush deepened and she lowered her eyes, seeing the hard muscles of his thighs flex beneath his own tight-fitting breeches as he sat his horse. 'You do remember something about that night, then?'

'I never forget what a woman looks like when she is naked in my bed, Adeline.'

'My bed,' she was quick to remind him, the light of mischief dancing in her eyes.

'Very well—your bed,' he amended with a low chuckle. 'Where's your fiancé this morning, by the way? I thought he was to join us.'

'Paul rode out early—in the direction of Ashford.' Briefly their gazes met, and Adeline wondered if he knew the nature of the relationship that existed between Paul and Diana. The direct look he gave her told her he did.

'Ah—I see.'

'Yes, so do I.' She wondered if he minded, and decided not to ask.

Grant's horse was becoming restive. 'Come—I'll race you back to the stables.' His eyes twinkled roguishly and his mouth curved in a devilish grin. 'I'll beat you.'

Adeline tossed back her head and threw him a confident smile. 'I don't think so—you'll have to be content with second-best.'

'Never,' he declared with laughing certainty.

'You're very bold with your challenge, sir,' she stated, a flicker of mischief in her eyes.

'When I'm allowed to be I'm not easily dissuaded, and I usually take the initiative when I know I can win.'

'So it would seem—with a race.'

His eyes glowed and he smiled at her. 'With everything, Adeline.'

Adeline did not dare to contradict him, nor ask him to enlarge on his statement. 'When you lose I'll be magnanimous in my victory, I promise.'

'Adeline,' he threatened, in a soft, ominous tone, while his eyes danced with amusement, 'if I lose you'd better ride for your life in the opposite direction.'

'You'll never catch me.'

Grant gave a shout of laughter as he kicked his horse into action. 'If that's your game, Miss Osborne, lead on. I will welcome your attention and the challenge—and I'll make you eat your words.'

Together their horse's hooves thundered over the hard green turf in long, ground-devouring strides as each fought to take the lead. They vaulted a low hedge effortlessly, then another with flourish. At one point Adeline gained a lead on Grant, but he soon closed the gap.

They rode at a breakneck pace. Leaning forward, Adeline felt exhilaration and jubilation, at one with her mount. Her hair, losing its ribbon, became unbound, and the glorious tresses unfurled like a pennant behind her. They soared over a ditch in perfect unison, and then turned their mounts at full speed towards the open stableyard gates.

'Good God, what a ride!' Grant exclaimed with an admiring laugh, his horse having finished alongside Crispin. Swinging his leg over the horse's back, he dismounted and strode to Adeline as she landed on both feet in front of him. Her colour was gloriously high and she had a wide smile on her full lips, her eyes liquid-bright. The sight of her almost stole his breath.

'Miss Osborne, you are quite the most outrageous, outstanding rider I have ever had the privilege to ride with. A draw,' he declared.

'No, it wasn't,' she objected laughingly, determined not to let him off. 'I beat you by a head and you know it.'

'A nose?' he beseeched, looking almost humble.

Adeline's eyes gleamed with laughter. 'Very well, a nose it is—but I still beat you.'

They were both breathing hard, the exhilaration of the ride still flowing through their veins. Removing her bowler, Adeline threw back her head and her hair rippled and lifted on the breeze. A strand wisped across her face and caught in the pink moistness of her lips. Reaching up a hand, she brushed it away. She looked into Grant's face, into his bright silver-grey eyes, and felt again the heat, the rush of sweet warmth she'd felt in his arms. Embarrassed by her thoughts, she took Crispin's reins.

'I'd better go,' she said, beginning to lead him into the stableyard, where she would hand him over to one of the grooms. 'I promised I'd have breakfast with Father, and I have to change.'

'I'll ride out and join the others. I'll be along later.' When she turned to walk away, he said, 'Adeline?'

She turned and looked back. His face, devoid of laughter, had taken on a different look, more serious.

'Thank you. It was a pleasure riding with you. We must do it again.'

'Yes—yes, we will.'

Later, when Adeline had changed and entered the breakfast room, she found her father alone.

Horace glanced at his daughter as she helped herself to bacon and mushrooms from the large silver dishes on the sideboard, kept heated by rows of little spirit lamps underneath. As well as hot food there were cold hams, tongues and galantine laid out on a separate table, along with porridge, coffee, and Indian and China tea—China indicated by yellow ribbons and Indian by red. Adeline chose the Indian, which was more to her taste.

'I didn't expect to see you—thought you'd have gone on the ride,' Horace remarked as she came to sit down, observing her still-shining eyes and flushed cheeks.

'I did—and most enjoyable it was, too. Have you seen Paul this morning, Father?'

'No. I thought he was with you.'

'He rode off early—by himself.'

The harsh tone of her voice brought a frown to Horace's forehead. 'There's nothing wrong between the two of you, I hope?'

'No, of course not—at least nothing that can't be put right when he condescends to show his face.'

It was almost lunchtime when Paul arrived back. Partnering Lettie, Adeline was just finishing an enjoyable game of croquet when she saw him ride up the drive and disappear round the house to the stables. He found her in the conservatory ten minutes later. The building had been added to the house in recent years. With its glass walls and high dome it was filled with rare, exotic plants—an explosion of flowers, colour and fragrance. There were others sitting around in white wicker chairs, gossiping quietly and drinking tea, but Adeline sat away from them in a quiet spot, looking out over the gardens.

On Paul's approach she rose, annoyed to see there was a jaunty spring to his step. Suspicions dancing along her raw nerves, when he bent his head to peck her cheek she turned her head away. Although she was quaking inside, she rose and drew him to one side, out of sight and earshot of the few people present, who were too engrossed in their own conversations to pay them any attention anyway. She faced him with outward calm, not having realised until that moment how much she disliked him.

She had changed physically. Having tasted passion, she would want the same again—and Paul wouldn't be able to give it to her. Grant Leighton might as well have branded her. When she had been with him earlier her heart had swelled, yet she had been forced to rein in her feelings. When she married she would want a declaration of unconditional love—it was a declaration she would insist on—and she would love in return. She would settle for nothing less.

Now the moment of confrontation with Paul was at hand she was strangely relieved. His sordid affair with Diana Waverley had given her adequate reason to break off their engagement.

'Here you are. I've been looking for you.'

'Have you, Paul? Why?' She noted that he seemed more relaxed than he had been last night. Suddenly, above the scent of exotic plants, there was the smell of musk. She looked at him accusingly. 'So my suspicions were correct.'

He glanced at her sharply.

'I believe you've been well occupied at Westwood Hall, haven't you, Paul?'

He paled visibly and averted his gaze, pretending interest in a rather splendid bloom growing out of a large terracotta pot. 'Westwood Hall?' he asked, his tone guarded. 'Why do you say that?'

'You've come straight from Diana Waverley to me.' Adeline's lips curled with sarcasm. 'Her perfume is distinctive.'

Paul's face stiffened with anger. 'Adeline, do not continue with this. It is nonsense, and you are not yourself.'

'I have never been *more* myself, Paul. I am neither stupid nor a fool. I have known about it for some time. Do you deny it?'

He shrugged. 'No, but she means nothing to me. It was just a moment of weakness—nothing more than that.'

Her eyebrows rose. 'A moment of weakness? I have not the slightest doubt that it is a "moment of weakness" that has attacked you frequently for a long time past, and will continue to do so in the future.'

'When we return home we will talk about it—decide how to deal with this. But not now.'

'No, Paul,' Adeline replied unsteadily. '*I* will decide how to deal with this now. When we were at Westwood Hall I knew you and she were… Well, thinking it would blow itself out, I tried to ignore it. But I can't. I consider our engagement at an end. I will not be played false. I will not marry you.'

Paul, his face suddenly ashen, and a pulse beginning to throb in his temple, could not believe what he was hearing. 'Don't be ridiculous, Adeline. Of course we will be married. It is what your father wants. What we all want.'

'It's no longer what I want. It never was. Father has strong principles regarding moral conduct, and he will be the first to understand. I will not marry a womaniser,' she upbraided him coldly.

Paul rounded on her, his face a mask of indignation and malice. 'And you, I suppose, have no deficiencies? Look at you, for God's sake. You have a lot to learn about your own limitations, Adeline. You have hardly been inundated with admirers, have you? If it were not for me you would remain a spinster for the rest of your life, and you know it.'

Enraged by his insult, but managing to remain self-contained, without taking her eyes from his she moved closer. 'And so I should be grateful to you? Dear God, Paul, I no more want to marry you now than I did in the beginning. Better to be a spinster than married to a man who has so little respect for his future bride. I had no idea you saw me in such an unfavourable light. But I am not as pathetic as you so obviously think I am.'

'What does that mean?' Paul demanded. For the first time he saw something in those eyes of hers—a fire that promised vengeance.

'Just this. Since you require a chaste little virgin for your wife, you should know that if I did marry you, you wouldn't be getting the virgin bride you expected.'

Paul's eyes narrowed, and he looked at her hard. 'What are you saying?' he asked, in a voice that had suddenly turned ominous.

Adeline checked herself abruptly, realising that in her furious state she had said more than she ought.

Paul read into her words and her expression exactly what she meant. His face darkened.

'You slut,' he breathed. 'You damned slut.'

And before Adeline could move, losing his gentlemanly control, he raised his hand and slapped her across her cheek and jaw. The impact sent her reeling. She staggered wildly, but regaining her balance she managed to whirl around, facing him in expectation of another attack.

Paul would have struck her again but, because he hated violence in any form, Grant reacted, quickly and deadly, and the cold, biting fury of his voice checked him.

'If you strike her again, Marlow,' Grant said, his expression savage, 'I swear it will be the sorriest day of your life.'

Paul's face froze into a mask of disbelief, as did Adeline's, when they spun round and saw Horace and Grant standing just behind them. Until then neither of them had realised they were present. Horace's expression looked far more ominous than amiable, and Paul was concerned with the tangible danger emanating from Leighton.

'And I second Grant.' Horace's voice was low and horribly calm, like the eye of a hurricane.

Adeline stood mute and unmoving before her father's accusing, unwavering stare, realising that he might have heard too much. He certainly looked his fiercest. His face had turned crimson; his sideburns were almost bristling.

Feeling himself pushed beyond the bounds of reason, Adeline's outrageous outburst having humiliated and diminished him in the eyes of Grant and Horace, Paul gave a snarl of fury. 'You whore.'

'Watch your tongue, Marlow,' Grant growled. He looked at Adeline. 'Are you all right?'

She nodded. The sudden blow had caused a tenuous strand of her hair to come undone from the bun at her nape and frame her cheek. It coiled down across her bosom and curled up provocatively at the tip. Despite her haughty stance, her eyes were glittering with unshed tears.

Horace looked from his daughter to Paul. 'Is it true what I overheard? Are you having an affair with Lady Waverley?'

Clearly embarrassed at being caught out, Paul flushed and shifted guiltily beneath the older man's hard stare, his fury diminished. 'I'd hardly call it an affair.'

'It makes no difference. Good God, man—you've been carrying on a relationship while engaged to my daughter. I would not have believed it of you. I thought better of you— thought you had more sense and self-restraint—and more discretion. You have made an unforgivable public exhibition of Adeline's virtue.'

'I can see that I owe you an apology, Horace,' Paul said, the rough edge of nervousness now tingeing his voice as he tried to bring all his faculties to bear, 'but I hardly think that a meaningless dalliance can be construed as a capital crime.'

Horace was rigid. His features were grim, his mouth set into a tight hard line. 'When it involves my daughter I regard it as serious. You have shamed her. I like to think I am a forgiving man, as well as a stern one. But I am not an idiot. I have never been an idiot and I never will be—and you won't make me one, I promise you. Our families go back a long way, and we have been friends and business associates for a long time, but what you have done is unacceptable.'

With that, he turned to Grant. 'I think enough has been said for now. I think we should discuss this matter further when we have all calmed down. I apologise for this unpleasantness, and do not wish to draw you into a situation that is none of your affair.'

Paul's face darkened, and he was trembling slightly as he glanced from Adeline to Grant and then sliced back to Adeline, comprehension dawning. 'Last night when I caught you swanning around in attire designed for the bedroom, you went looking for more than your book, didn't you?'

Adeline shifted uncomfortably, careful not to look at Grant. 'No! Of course not! That was precisely what I was doing— looking for my book.'

Paul turned to his host. The look on Grant's face caused a frisson of fear to trickle through him. He had thought his host completely malleable, but now he read a hardness of purpose and a coldness of manner beyond any previous experience. Strange and explosive emotions lurked in the hard, glittering silver-grey eyes. Pent-up fury crouched, ready to leap and destroy him.

'You will say no more, if you know what's good for you,' Grant said, aware of Paul's train of thought and of his silent accusation. His words were low, barely heard, but menacing enough to stop Paul from saying more.

Horace, his sharp ears attuned to what was going on, was fully aware of what Paul was implying—which was in all probability the reason why he had struck Adeline. He was unable to believe the situation could get much worse, but it appeared it could. When he looked directly at his daughter, all she could do was look back at him mutely.

There was a moment of unexpressed emotion which Adeline would never forget. Her father stared at her with such anger that she almost believed a fork of lightning would flick from his eyes and strike her dead.

Horace turned to Grant. The two men stood without moving, staring at each other. 'I am compelled to ask you, sir. Is it true what Paul is implying?'

Grant nodded, trying not to show the self-disgust welling in him. He tried telling himself that Adeline wasn't his problem or his concern, since it had been her decision to allow him into her bed while she was engaged to Paul, but he could not escape the fact that it was his ravishment of Adeline that had precipitated this mess.

'Yes, it is.'

Horace looked at Adeline coldly. 'I am disappointed in you. It seems I do not know my own daughter. Not only have you concealed what you have done, you were prepared to enter into marriage dishonestly. I don't want to hear the details of what you've done. I haven't the stomach for it.'

Shock drained the blood from Adeline's face. Somehow she managed to find the strength to control herself. 'Father, I am sorry.'

'And so you should be. You are twenty years old, and until you are married you are answerable to me, your father. I thought you understood your duty to me—that you would cleave to it no matter what and conduct yourself properly. Can you imagine how embarrassing it is to announce my daughter's engagement one minute only to discover the next that she's been carrying on with another man? The humiliation to me and to Paul's family, after spending so much time and energy in bringing about a union between the two of you has ended by making us a laughing stock.'

'That's the trouble,' Adeline complained, her courage reasserting itself. 'It's what it means to *you*. But what about me? Why didn't you ask me if I wanted to marry Paul? You just took it for granted that I would comply—which is what I have done ever since Mother died. My marriage to Paul was like a—a merger—it was business—cold and dispassionate—and that's not what I want.'

'What are you trying to say?'

'What I should have told you at the beginning. That I do not want to marry Paul. I will not marry him. Not now—not ever.'

The outburst surprised even her. But it was said now, and she was glad.

'Whether it's true that Adeline and I have a special regard for each other hardly matters now—nor does why Marlow found her in the drawing room looking for her book after midnight—and that was the real purpose for her being there, whatever interpretation he wants put on the incident.' Turning to Adeline, his jaw set in a hard line, his grey eyes like slivers of steel, Grant took her hand and drew her to his side. He glanced down at her pale face before fixing his gaze on Horace. 'I have asked her to end her engagement to Paul and do me the honour of agreeing to become my wife.'

At that blatant falsehood Adeline stared at him in confused shock. His announcement had rendered her speechless. He had spoken calmly, and held her hand almost lovingly, but Adeline was close enough to detect the underlying currents in his tone and in his body. He was seething with anger.

At length, Horace asked, 'And what is her answer?'

'I'm still waiting.'

Grant's revelation was too much for Paul. His eyes fastened malevolently on Grant, and his voice was incongruously murderous. 'So I was not mistaken. I knew it.'

Towering over him, Grant spoke, his voice like ice. 'What's the matter, Marlow? Can't you accept the fact that Adeline doesn't want you—that she might prefer someone else? If you find the concept impossible to understand or accept, that's for you to deal with. Get over it. That's the way the world works. And it's simply too bad if you don't like it.'

Horace turned to his daughter. 'You really have decided not to marry Paul?'

She nodded. 'Yes.'

Horace stood unflinching. Every trace of emotion had drained from his face. When he spoke, his voice was devoid of feeling. 'Very well. But I would not have believed it of you.'

Adeline sighed and turned away. 'No, Father. I don't suppose you would. Please excuse me.'

'Where are you going? We have to talk about this.'

'There's nothing more to say. I'm going for a walk.'

Grant looked at Paul, 'You are no longer welcome in this house. I would like you to leave as soon as you have packed your things. A carriage will take you to the station. I don't want you here.'

'Save your breath. I'd already decided to leave.'

Grant smiled tolerantly. 'No doubt Diana will be pleased to see you at Westwood Hall—and will help you lick your wounds.'

As Adeline walked, with nowhere particular in mind, she began to feel that something momentous had happened and that her life had changed beyond recall. The sudden breeze that rose and stirred the grass, swayed the trees and went searching and whispering through the branches and leaves, was like a secret message, telling her it was time to be free.

* * *

Back at the house, Grant was facing Horace Osborne alone, forced to listen while the older man delivered an eloquently worded blistering tirade concerning his unacceptable behaviour towards Adeline.

'I cannot condone or excuse what you have done. Because of you my daughter will be made the subject of public censure, and her engagement to Paul is off.'

'I think Paul has much to do with that,' Grant pointed out firmly, angry about being taken to task over his behaviour, and yet at the same time admiring everything about the man doing it—a man with strong principles about what was acceptable and what was not. A hard man, yes, who saw his daughter as little more than a commodity, but also a man of honesty and integrity, who expected the same behaviour from those around him.

'Do you deny that you seduced Adeline?' Horace demanded.

'No,' Grant admitted, without trying to defend himself.

'And did it not concern you that she might be pregnant?'

'She isn't.'

As Horace digested this some of the hostility went out of his voice. 'Thank God for that. But you did this despite the fact that she was engaged to Paul at the time—a man from a fine and decent family, with principles.'

'Paul is no plaster saint.'

'No man is that. At least you didn't try to shirk your duty to Adeline. You say you have proposed marriage?'

Grant nodded, watching Horace warily. 'As yet she hasn't given me her answer.'

'She will. Marriage is a foregone conclusion.'

'Assuming she agrees. Adeline may have other ideas.'

'My daughter will do as she is told,' Horace said curtly. 'Under the circumstances it is the right and proper thing to do. This dreadful business will make things very unpleasant for her. It is always uncomfortable to be closely connected to a public scandal, and vulgar curiosity will set people staring and talking, if nothing worse.'

'Adeline is an intelligent young woman. She has the right to make up her own mind.'

Horace's gaze was direct. 'Her wishes count for nothing. I shall insist on it. When the time is right you will announce your engagement, and after a suitable length of time you will be married. Until that time there will be no intimacies between the two of you. If the sacrifice of physical satisfaction is too much, then—'

'It won't be,' Grant bit out.

'Fine.' Horace's countenance suddenly relaxed, and his smile was almost paternal. 'Then everything's settled.'

Surfacing from his private thoughts, Grant wondered how the hell he had managed to let himself be coerced into this situation, thinking that an hour ago something as outrageous as tying himself to Miss Adeline Osborne for life would have been absolutely out of the question. He nodded.

'I'll speak to Adeline.'

Horace nodded, too, satisfied that the matter had been settled to his satisfaction.

Chapter Five

Grant found Adeline sitting on a stout fallen log at the edge of the wood, some considerable distance from the house. She didn't turn when he approached but, seeing her back stiffen, he knew she was aware of his presence. Shoving his hands into his trouser pockets, he propped his back against a tree, his narrow gaze trained on her. Having half expected to find her in a distressed state, he was surprised to find her looking un-ruffled and as cool as a cucumber.

Adeline saw Grant was wearing the same grim expression she had seen when she had left the house. He looked strained with the intensity of his emotions, but slowly, little by little, he was getting a grip on himself. His shoulders were squared, his jaw set and rigid with implacable determination, and even in this pensive pose he seemed to emanate restrained power and unyielding authority. There was no sign of the relaxed, laughing man she had ridden with earlier—no sign of the passionate man who had kissed her so ardently last night.

Where he was concerned her feelings were nebulous, chaotic—yet one stood out clearly: her desire for this man. She hadn't known herself when she had been in his arms, and last night she hadn't wanted him to stop kissing her. He was weaving a web about her and she could do nothing to prevent it, to deny the hold he already had over her senses and her heart. She wanted him with a fierceness that took her breath, wanted to feel again the depths of passion only he was capable of rousing in her. But she was determined not to let him touch her again.

While she had been sitting there thinking, a strange calm had settled on her, banishing even her shame. She had left Grant to argue it out with her father, and whatever decision they had come to she was resolved to do things her way from now on. It was her life, to do with as she pleased, and no man would order her to do his bidding ever again.

Raising her brows, she gave him a cynical smile. 'What a strange turnabout this is,' she said, in a flat, emotionless voice, giving no evidence of how the mere sight of him set her heart pounding in her chest, how the thought of never seeing him again almost broke her heart. 'Don't you agree?'

'I have to admit they're not the most romantic of circumstances.'

'No.' She let her eyes dwell on his face. How well he shielded his thoughts. 'I expect you are feeling a bit like a rabbit caught in a trap.'

'I wouldn't put it quite like that.' Grant lifted one hand and massaged the taut muscles at the back of his neck. His mind was locked in furious combat about what he was about to do. All the way here he had been straining against the noose of matrimony he could feel tightening about his throat. What had possessed him to announce that he'd asked Adeline to marry him? Now that he had, he was honour-bound to abide by his declaration, and there was no going back. 'Your father certainly knows how to make a man feel small.'

'I thought he only did that to women.' Adeline knew Grant would surmise that she was so weak and malleable that she would gratefully accept anything he had to suggest, but she was determined to have some control over this. 'Thank you, by the way. It was chivalrous of you to say what you did.'

'I wasn't being chivalrous.'

'Nevertheless, I didn't ask you to. In the view of conventional morality the loss of my virtue can only mark my downfall.'

He was frowning. 'I take full responsibility for all of this.'

'Why? You weren't the one I was engaged to, and nor were you having an affair with Diana Waverley—well, you might have been, but that is beside the point and has absolutely nothing to do with me.'

'Diana and I might have married once,' he told her tersely, 'but she married someone else instead.'

'And now?'

'Now we're—friends—of a peculiar kind.'

Adeline tilted her head to one side and looked at him. Not for the first time did she wonder what their bitter argument had been about when he had stormed out on Diana at Westwood Hall. 'By "peculiar" do you mean that now she is a widow she would like to be Mrs Leighton?' The look he threw her told her this was exactly as it was. 'And that is not what you want?'

'No,' he gritted. 'I don't give second chances.' Grant looked at her coolly.

'And how do you feel about her affair with Paul?'

'I don't feel anything. It won't last. Diana soon tires of her lovers. But enough of her. It's you and me we have to worry about.'

Adeline raised her eyebrows in question. 'You and me?'

'You have no need to worry about your future. It will be taken care of.'

'Really?' Adeline was quietly infuriated. It was as if she had no say in the matter. 'Grant,' she said, laughing lightly, 'you're not telling me that when you told my father you'd asked me to marry you that you actually meant it?'

'I never say anything I don't mean—and your father insists on it.'

Adeline felt an uneasy disquiet settling in. She could not believe what Grant was saying. He looked and sounded so cold, so dispassionate. 'Does he, indeed?'

'He has decided that our engagement will be announced when this unpleasantness has died down. We will be married following a decent interval of time.'

'That's a bit extreme.' She gave him a quizzical look. 'I'm sorry, but I seem to have missed something. I don't recall you asking me to marry you, Grant.'

'That's because I haven't.'

Adeline's expression dared him to attempt control of herself. 'Now, why do I feel this has happened to me before?' she retorted, her voice heavy with sarcasm.

'I apologise if that's how it seems to you. My only regret is that it was my intoxication which led to this.'

'And you are one of those men who has to do something noble in life?'

'It's not noble. We have no choice. You must see that.'

'No, as a matter of fact I don't.'

'Well, we haven't. I took that away when I announced to the world that I had asked you to be my wife.'

'And I recall you saying I had not given you my answer. I simply cannot believe that you want to marry me—a woman you hardly know, a woman you have no personal regard or respect for.'

Shoving himself away from the tree and running an impatient hand through his dark hair, Grant began pacing to and fro in frustration. 'How can you know that?'

'Because last night you accused me of being little better than a harlot,' she reminded him coldly.

He stopped and looked at her, his expression one of contrition. 'I'm sorry if I implied that. But that was last night.'

'And nothing has changed. To my mind all this talk about marriage and doing the honourable thing is wholly unnecessary. You are under no obligation to marry me.'

He stopped pacing and glared at her. 'Dear God! I appreciate the wrong I have done you, and that compounds my obligation to marry you.'

No longer able to contain her temper, Adeline shot to her feet in angry indignation, her hands clenched by her sides. 'And you assume in your arrogance that I am so pathetic, so desperate for a husband now Paul and I are no longer engaged, that I will accept you—me, plain, serious Adeline Osborne, who by all rights, as Paul so cruelly pointed out, should remain a spinster because no man unless he were blind would want me.'

'I think you undervalue yourself.'

'Perhaps you're right. But what a weak-willed idiot I must seem to you. Despite all my diligent efforts throughout my life to be the model of propriety, I let a total stranger—a handsome, inebriated stranger—make wonderful love to me—a man who wouldn't have given me a second glance had he been sober.'

'Now you insult me. I am ashamed of what I did to you. I can't blame you if you hate me for it completely, but it cannot be nearly as much as I hate myself.' This was true. Grant *did* despise himself for what he'd done to her—and the mess she was in because of it—and for the unprecedented weakness that made him want to repeat the act. 'Damnation, Adeline, can't you see that I'm trying to do the right thing by you?'

Fury flared in Adeline's eyes. 'How dare you say that to me? Don't you dare pity me, Grant Leighton.'

'I don't pity you. That's the last thing I feel. But you must realise that because of this, and what Paul might disclose, you will become the subject of gossip, your reputation in ruins.'

'And marrying you will shift the sentiment, I suppose, and find general favour?' she mocked. 'Given an interval of time

I shall produce an heir for Oaklands and cause no further scandal—which will in turn bring redemption through association, all my transgressions forgotten.'

'Something like that.'

Adeline drew back her shoulders and lifted her head, the action saying quite clearly that she knew her own mind. 'Do you know, Grant, I don't care a fig about any of that? What people think of me no longer matters. I've got a broad back. I can endure the slights and slurs. Besides, I certainly don't see a husband as the solution to my problems. You're not required to marry me. If I agree to this mockery of a marriage you will hate me for ever and I will be miserable for my entire life—as I would have been if I had married Paul—and no doubt longing for release in an early grave.'

'Now you exaggerate.' His biting tone carried anger and frustration.

'I don't think so,' Adeline bit back. 'My reputation is already besmirched, I agree—but do you know I don't feel guilty or ruined? Yes, the future is an uncharted path, and will possibly be filled with censure, but for the first time in my life I feel completely at peace. When you came to my bed I knew what I wanted and I took it. If I don't marry you nothing will change—at least not immediately. But given time any scandal will be forgotten.'

When realisation of what she was saying dawned on him, Grant stared at her in disbelief. 'Are you saying you don't want to marry me?'

'Yes. I don't want to be any man's wife.'

Placing his hands on his hips, towering over her, he glared down into her defiant face. 'You might at least show some gratitude. You are behaving as though I've suggested we commit murder. I'm offering to deliver you from a barren future—a way out—an answer to your dilemma.'

'How do you know I want one? You did a noble thing by

offering, but it was spur-of-the-moment—a moment of madness—an absurd compulsion. Once said, you couldn't in all honour retract it, but I have no intention of holding you to it.'

The corner of his mouth twisted wryly in a gesture that was not quite a smile. 'No? I'm surprised.'

'Why? Because I melted in your arms like the naïve and silly woman that I am?' She smiled. 'You are persuasive, I grant you that, but I don't know you and I don't trust you.'

'But you *do* want me,' he said, with a knowing light glinting in his eyes.

'That's beside the point, and has nothing to do with marriage. Men are the cause of my troubles—my father, Paul, and now you. As far as I am concerned men make excellent dancing partners, but beyond that are no use at all to me. In fact, the more I think about them the more depressed I become.'

'Now you're beginning to sound like Lettie.'

'If I am then I consider it a compliment. Your sister talks a great deal of sense.' She moved close to him, and suddenly he seemed enormous, his powerful body emanating heat, reminding her of what could be hers if she complied to his will and that of her father. But she would not back down. Meeting his gaze directly, she said, 'Let's stop all this nonsense, shall we? Be honest about it, Grant. You don't want to marry me any more than I want to marry you.'

With his face only inches from hers, his eyes boring ruthlessly into hers, he ground out, 'You're absolutely right. I don't.'

'And you agree that the whole idea is absolutely ludicrous?'

'Right.'

'I've decided that I'd make an exceedingly poor wife, and on reaching that conclusion I consider it wise to avoid that particular state of affairs. That is my final resolve.'

Her rejection of his proposal put her beyond his tolerance, and his voice took on a deadly finality. 'That's extremely wise of you. I'd make an exceedingly bad husband.'

'Good. I am glad we are in agreement. Then it's settled. We won't marry. Your duty, obligation to me—call it what you like—is now discharged.' Stepping away from him, she raised her head haughtily. 'And now, if you will excuse me, I will go and tell my father.'

Grant stared after her, feeling bewildered, misused, furious with himself and with her, and seriously insulted—for what man who had just offered a respectable marriage proposal expected to be rejected? What was he to do? He supposed it had been rather arrogant of him to assume she would fall in with his plans—and her father's—but damn it all, he was asking her to be his wife—a position he had never offered to any other woman. So it wasn't conceited of him to expect her to accept. Was it?

In his anger he had tried to blame her for what had transpired at Westwood Hall. He shouldn't have. She was proud, courageous and innocent. He knew damned well she wasn't promiscuous, shameless or wanton, but he had implied that she was and then treated her as if she was, and she had endured it and let him kiss her again.

Furious self-disgust poured through him. Bullied by her father, taken for granted, treated as less than a second-class citizen by Paul Marlow, and then told that she would have to marry him, Grant, little wonder she'd had enough of men and wanted her independence.

But none of this lessened the fury that ran in his veins. By making their sordid night of passion common knowledge and then turning down his offer of marriage she had humiliated and shamed him voluntarily, and no one did that. He hoped that when she left Oaklands on the morrow he would never have to set eyes on her again.

With courage and determination, Adeline sought her father out in his room. When his voice barked out for her to enter, she set her teeth on edge, inwardly trembling but outwardly calm, and entered his presence. She knew that he would have plenty to say when she told him she would not marry Grant Leighton, and she was not disappointed. He broke out into such a fury of anger that Adeline thought he might actually strike her.

What had possessed her to behave so wantonly? Had she no morals, no grain of sense or the slightest feeling of gratitude for all he had done for her? And if Adeline thought she had heard the last of it, she was very much mistaken.

And so he ranted on.

Adeline merely stood and felt the fierce scolding beat her like a stick. And yet, despite her wretchedness, she could not help noticing his own suffering at knowing all he had hoped for for his only daughter had crumbled into dust. Curiously enough, Adeline felt sorry for him, and with some degree of self-control she was able to apologise. She begged him to forgive her, and to try to understand why she could not marry either Paul or Grant. She had behaved extremely foolishly, and would never again be so selfish as to forget all he had done for her.

Her sincerity was as evident as her determination to stand firm on her decision. When her father realised this and spoke to her, at last his voice had lost its anger. On a sigh, his shoulders slumped with dejection, he told her that they would leave Oaklands for Rosehill as planned the following morning, where they would discover how seriously this unfortunate incident would affect her future.

Later, when Adeline was preparing for dinner, she sat in front of the mirror and looked at the image staring back as if she were seeing herself for the first time. When she had left her father, for the first time in her life she had begun to feel alive—but when she stared at the face looking back at her now, she knew she was in danger of losing her fragile newfound courage.

Attired in a plain beige dress, which seemed to drain the colour from her face, expensive though it was, never had she felt so drab. It did absolutely nothing for her. The fashion was for pastel silks offset by contrasting ribbons, beading, fringing, tassels and lace, in a style of gown that gave more emphasis to the back of the flat-fronted skirt, with complex drapery over a bustle trimmed with pleats and flounces.

As she surveyed her reflection she was far from satisfied with what she saw. On a sigh, she turned away.

Answering a knock on the door, her maid Emma opened it to admit Lettie, who breezed in and swept across the carpet to where Adeline was sitting. She perched on the end of the dressing table.

'Ooh, why the frown, Adeline? Why so pensive? Do you not like your gown?'

'Since you ask, no, I do not. But it's one of my best.'

Lettie was wearing a forget-me-not-blue taffeta with trailing skirts, and she looked radiant. 'You, Adeline Osborne, need taking in hand very seriously.'

'I do?'

'Most definitely. A visit to the dressmaker is what I advise—and someone to arrange your hair into a more flattering style.'

Adeline had the miserable notion that Lettie was right. She cast a surreptitious glance at the fashionable woman. Did she dare ask for guidance from her? Yes, she did—and she was willing to listen to any suggestions that would improve her looks.

Reading Adeline's mind, Lettie laughed softly. There was an ease in their communication, as if their friendship were natural. 'I will look forward to accompanying you to the shops, if you like. You must come and stay with me in London. I should love it if you could. You would be such good company for me, and I could introduce you to all my friends— when we're not visiting the fashion shops.'

'And I always thought feminists dressed in practical, un-adorned clothes. You certainly don't look like a Suffragette.' This was true, and it was a conflict these women faced between the desire to be feminine in appearance and decrying what this entailed.

'I always try to make the best of myself, and I see no point in denying the side of my nature which adores finery. I enjoy wearing glamorous clothes, and refuse to be ashamed of the feeling—nor to agree that wearing nice clothes is only to please men. Not for one minute would I think of donning any kind of feminist version of sackcloth and ashes just to resemble a ca-ricature of what a feminist is supposed to look like.'

'And do people take you seriously—looking as attractive as you do?'

'Some don't—especially people in authority. I confess that to look attractive is both a weapon—which I use to excess when necessary—and a hindrance. To be feminine is to be thought frivolous and empty-headed, and in my case,' she said, her eyes dancing with mischief, 'more than possibly wicked.'

'I suppose if I wanted to make a mark at all it would not be for my beauty but my individuality.'

Lettie's expression became serious. 'There's no reason why you can't have both, Adeline. But, you know, beauty isn't everything.'

Adeline smiled ruefully. 'Beautiful women always say that.'

'But you are a very attractive woman—Grant must think so, too, considering the intimacies you've shared. If there's one thing Grant's not, it's blind.'

'But we're not—I mean…' Adeline hesitated, knowing she was blushing to the roots of her hair and wondering who could have told Lettie. She didn't know how to say this. 'We—we aren't sharing a bed,' she managed to whisper, thankful that Emma had disappeared into the dressing room.

Lettie frowned in puzzlement. 'But when I spoke to Paul

as he was leaving—and he was most irate, I must say—he accused you of doing just that. And when he told me that Grant had asked you to marry him—well, I assumed you were—conducting an affair, I mean.'

'Well, we're not.'

'Adeline, I'm not trying to pry, but I know there must be more to this than meets the eye.'

'Oh, Lettie, I just don't know what's going on.' Adeline briefly described the circumstances of her involvement with Grant, omitting—for her pride's sake and Grant's—the fact that Grant had been blind drunk at the time.

At the end of the tale Lettie stared at her with a combination of mirth and wonder. 'Goodness!' she exclaimed. 'It's too delicious for words. The two of you—and under Diana Waverley's roof at that. How intriguing. And are you going to marry Grant?'

'No, I'm not going to marry him, Lettie. It was a mistake. We both agree about that. And what he said about having asked me wasn't true. He thought he was doing the honourable thing, that's all.'

'Knowing my brother, he will be filled with remorse for what he did while you were engaged to Paul.'

'He did ask me—after he said what he did in the conservatory—but I said no. I told him my future from now on is my own affair.'

'I see. Loss of respectability can be unexpectedly liberating, you know—although I'm sorry to hear you turned Grant down. I would love to have you as a sister-in-law. But if you're not in love with him then you did right to refuse him.' Glancing at her obliquely, she said, 'You're *not* in love with him, are you, Adeline?'

Adeline's flush deepened and she averted her eyes. 'No, of course I'm not.'

Lettie wasn't at all convinced by her statement. 'But you

can't admit to a supreme indifference to him, can you?' she persisted. 'It's written all over your face.'

'Am I really so transparent?'

Lettie smiled with gentle understanding. 'I'm afraid you are.'

'I only hope this unpleasant business soon blows over. The last thing I wanted was to involve your brother in my break up with Paul. The gossip will be dreadful.'

Lettie gave her a mocking sideways glance. 'Grant won't care two hoots about that. What he *will* care about is having his offer of marriage turned down. As far as I am aware he has only ever proposed marriage once before, and when the lady married someone else he vowed he would never again offer marriage to any woman.'

'Was the woman Diana Waverley?'

Lettie nodded. 'Grant was deeply affected by it. Hardening his heart, he became cold and distant, killing whatever feelings he had for her. He cut her out of his life without a backward glance—until Lord Patrick Waverley, Diana's husband, died. After that Grant began seeing her again, but he'll never marry her. Diana burnt her bridges when she rejected Grant for a title. He never gives anyone a second chance.'

Adeline recalled Grant saying the same thing to her. 'She must have hurt him very badly.'

'She did—although I think his pride was hurt the most. And, knowing my brother like I do, this latest will have left him seething. Grant is quite awesome when his anger is roused.'

'Then I shall endeavour to stay out of his way until it's time for us to leave. After that I doubt we shall see each other again.'

'Men can be difficult enough without marrying them—and you must remember that no one can force you to marry Paul, Grant or any other man, come to that. Even the smallest steps in a woman's life are guided by and controlled by the men around her—father, brother and husband—who think women should be passive and inactive except in matters concerning the home.'

Adeline liked Lettie enormously, but she doubted she would ever get used to her candid way of speaking.

'I can see I shock you. I am a feminist, but I am also a realist. I like having my independence—I also like having a good time. For myself, I want everything: career, husband, or lover—' her eyes twinkled '—which is so much more exciting—and children. My husband must back everything I do, and believe my work to be as important as his.'

'And do you have a gentleman in mind?'

'I do have someone—but I will never marry him.' Sadness clouded Lettie's eyes and she turned her head away, but too late to hide it from Adeline. 'I do not see marriage as an element in a love affair. But we're madly happy, of course.' She laughed—rather forced, Adeline thought—and, getting up, went to the door. 'I'll see you downstairs.'

As she went in search of her mother, Lettie considered her conversation with Adeline. Although she had told her that her future from now on was her own affair, Lettie thought that perhaps she could make it her affair as well. She knew her brother to be a man of passionate feeling, despite his outward demeanour. Having seen the way he had looked at Adeline in the stableyard, and the unconcealed admiration in his eyes when he had watched her ride hell for leather across the park, she just knew he was attracted to her.

And Adeline had confessed she had feelings for Grant. She was also a young woman who'd had the temerity to stand up to him. That boded well for the future. How wonderful it would be if they could be brought together. She was sure they would make each other happy.

Ten minutes after Adeline had left him—in high dudgeon and frowning like thunder—knowing how concerned his mother would be by Paul's sudden departure, Grant found her in a small sitting room, away from the guests.

As soon as Grant entered she arose, her face strained with anxiety. She studied her son for a moment, noting his narrowed eyes and the grim set of his mouth. Even to her, it was a little intimidating.

'Horace has informed me of all that has transpired, Grant. You cannot mean to go through with this? Surely not?' she said without ceremony.

'You will be relieved to know Miss Osborne has turned me down,' he informed her brusquely, pacing up and down in agitation.

'Oh, I see.'

'But I should tell you that if she hadn't, I intended to marry her.'

'But why?' Hester demanded. 'You hardly know the girl—unless what Horace says is true and the two of you have been conducting an affair.'

Grant had the grace to look contrite. 'Not an affair, exactly.'

'But the two of you were involved in a relationship of—an intimate nature?'

'Yes.'

'While she was engaged to Paul Marlow?'

'Yes.'

'Oh, dear!' Sitting back down, she folded her hands in her lap. 'Then perhaps you ought to marry her.'

'I've told you, she won't have me.'

Hester seemed to find his dry comment amusing. Grant sounded outraged—baffled, too—without any comprehension as to why Adeline had turned him down. 'I can scarce believe it.'

'Believe it, Mother. It's true.'

'Why did you offer to marry her?'

'Because I felt sorry for her,' Grant replied with brutal

frankness. 'And, like it or not, I'm also responsible for what has happened. It's as simple as that.'

Hester frowned. 'If what I've heard is correct, isn't Paul Marlow equally to blame? Has he or has he not been conducting an affair with Diana Waverley? Your—mistress, I believe, Grant?' she said, her eyebrows raised with knowing humour.

'Yes,' he said, trying to keep his voice calm, while irritated that his mother seemed to take some quiet delight in reminding him of something he preferred not to think about just then.

'How extraordinary.' Hester smiled. 'You do seem to be quite put out. Although I fail to understand why you should be if, as you say, you only asked her because you felt sorry for her. You should be relieved.'

Grant was clearly not amused. 'I am. Immensely.'

'In which case there is nothing else to be said on the matter, as I see it, so there is no point in beating yourself up about it.'

'I'm not.'

'Paul and Adeline are responsible for the break-up of their engagement, and if Adeline doesn't want to marry you then so be it. Although I have to say there is something about that young lady that I like. She seems such a serene, steady sort of person.'

'Appearances aren't always what they seem.'

'No—well, where Adeline is concerned you would know all about that, wouldn't you?' Hester said, giving him a meaningful glance. 'I really can't imagine why she refused you…' She paused, and her eyes narrowed on Grant. 'Did you *ask* her, Grant, or tell her? Which—however much I have come to like Horace—is what he would do. Is that how it was? No doubt that is the reason why she stuck her toes in—so to speak.' She laughed lightly. 'Good for her is what I say.'

Grant frowned. He found his mother's amusement at his expense irritating. 'I can see you're enjoying this, but you are supposed to be on my side.'

'I'm on no one's side, Grant, but I'm beginning to admire Adeline more and more. She is a young woman who deserves to be courted. You cannot expect her to obey an order to marry you—which is what she must have done when she became engaged to Paul Marlow.' Lowering her eyes, she said, 'At least Horace seems to have taken it in his stride.'

'When I left him he was reconciled to Adeline's change of husband. How he'll react when she tells him she doesn't intend marrying either of us, I have no idea.'

As if the incident in the conservatory had never happened, dinner was a relaxed, convivial affair. Grant fulfilled his role as host with careless elegance, but beneath the polite façade, as Lettie had predicted earlier, he was seething. Adeline's refusal to marry him, when he'd made the gesture against his will and to make things easy for her, had placed her beyond recall.

Later, when she was leaving the drawing room to fetch her book from her room, Adeline watched in astonishment as her father led Mrs Leighton off in the direction of the conservatory. She suddenly realised they had spent a good deal of time together, and that a singular affection was growing between them—which she suspected might have something to do with why her father had decided not to cut their visit short. She saw his hand slide about Mrs Leighton's waist, saw his head lean towards her upturned laughing face, and Adeline knew that what they felt for each other was in danger of becoming more than friendly regard.

Turning to her right, Adeline saw Grant standing not two yards away from her. He, too, was watching her father and his mother, his whole body tensed into a rigid line of wrath. When he looked at her she could almost feel the effort he was exerting to keep his rage under control.

Moving closer to her, he met her gaze coldly. 'So that's the way of things.'

'And what do you mean by that?'

'Your father and my mother appear to enjoy each other's company. It has not escaped my notice that they spend a good deal of time together.'

'And do you find something wrong with that? They are both adults. If anything were to develop, would you disapprove?'

'It's not for me to approve or disapprove—but there's one thing I do know.'

'And what is that?'

'If my mother wants something really badly, she gets it.'

'Not always. She didn't get Rosehill.'

'No?' Grant looked at her and smiled a wry, conspiratorial smile. 'Not yet, maybe. But it's not too late.'

'We shall see. After tomorrow Father and I will be on our way home—back to reality. You can forget all about us then.'

Grant's eyes swept contemptuously over her. 'I intend to. When you leave in the morning we will not see each other again,' he said scathingly. 'This unfortunate business is over. Done with. It should never have happened. The proposal was an insane idea, and I regret and curse ever having made it.'

'Not nearly as much as I do.'

'You have caused too much disruption to my life, and when you leave I don't give a damn where you go or whose bed you occupy. You, Miss Osborne, have a highly refined sense of survival, and you'll land on your feet wherever you go.'

Adeline felt as if he'd slapped her, but her wounded pride forced her chin up. 'Yes, I will,' she said with quiet dignity. 'That is what I intend.'

Without bothering to excuse herself, turning from him, Adeline went up the stairs. Oh, damn you, Grant Leighton, she thought in helpless rage. I never want to see or think of you again. But she knew she would not be able to stop thinking of him. She had no power over her thoughts. She was trapped by her own nature. Tears gathered on her thick lashes and trembled without falling.

The following morning, when they were leaving and everyone was saying their farewells, displaying a calm she didn't feel, Adeline searched Grant's hard, sardonic face for some sign that he felt something, anything for her—that he might regret her leaving. But there was nothing. The awful feeling that there was nothing she could do beat her down into a misery too hopeless for tears.

Adeline had been back at Rosehill three weeks when a letter arrived from Lettie, informing her that she was in London, staying with Lord and Lady Stanfield at Stanfield House in Upper Belgrave Street, and that they had invited Adeline to come and stay with them. Adeline was delighted— it was just what she needed at this time, when she seemed to be at an impasse in her life.

Her father was none too pleased at the prospect of her gallivanting off to London. He had always demanded respect and subservience from her as his right as her father, but now, since leaving Oaklands, although there was still respect there was no subservience. Of course she was still piqued at discovering Paul had been carrying on with Lady Waverley. It was natural, he supposed, and therefore he must make allowances, but her own behaviour hadn't been much better.

When he saw how determined she was to go to London he capitulated. Their relationship had been strained since their return to Rosehill, so perhaps it was for the best. However, he insisted that she stay at their own London home in Eaton Place, where Mrs Kelsall, the housekeeper, would be able to keep an eye on her. Horace spent a great deal of his time in London, so the house was always kept in a state of readiness.

He was acquainted with Lady Stanfield—a strong woman,

who followed an exacting campaign of work for the Women's Movement—and he was concerned that Adeline, with her new-found confidence, drive and determination, might become drawn in. He was worried that she might be led even more astray…

Determined to enjoy her new freedom, accompanied by Emma, Adeline boarded the train for London. She was looking forward to seeing Lettie. To Adeline's experience, Lettie was the most stimulating woman imaginable, and she felt a mixture of excitement and insecurity at the thought of being with her—certainly life would never be dull.

Chapter Six

The capital was enjoying the last days of summer, while leaves still clung to the trees in the parks and guardsmen sweated in their uniforms along The Mall. Lettie was delighted to see Adeline, although she was disappointed that she wasn't to stay with her—but since there was no great distance between Eaton Place and Upper Belgrave Street it wouldn't matter all that much.

As soon as Adeline entered Stanfield House she was greeted with unaffected warmth. She felt this was a house where courtesy and mutual affection ruled in perfect harmony. Lady Stanfield was happily married. She had one daughter, Marjorie, and a bright twenty-year-old son, Anthony, who had recently joined the Foreign Office. He was a keen fencer, and was looking forward to testing his skill against Adeline's.

Marjorie Stanfield was a small, rather plump twenty-two-year-old brunette, with bright blue eyes and rosy cheeks, whose quiet, unhurried ways were in agreeable contrast to the forceful whirlwind of Lettie. She was not the type to go out looking for experience, but just waited for it to happen. She was deeply in love with a young man called Nicholas Henderson, the eldest son of Lord and Lady Henderson of Woking in Surrey, and there was much excitement in the house over their forthcoming engagement party, which was to take place a month hence.

Determined that the first thing to be done was to get Adeline out of her dull, dark clothes and turn her into an elegant, fashionable young woman, Lettie adopted an air of critical superiority that neither surprised nor annoyed Adeline. She was prepared to accept Lettie as more adult and proficient in worldly matters than herself, and so Lettie and Marjorie whisked her off to the shops. The three of them could be seen almost every afternoon in and out of the fashionable shops along Regent Street, and when Lettie was too busy Adeline went with Emma.

Her father had always given her a generous allowance to spend as she wished, but, having had no interest in self-adornment until now, she had left most of the money gathering interest in the bank. Suddenly shopping became a whole new and exciting experience, and for the first time in her life— urged on by Lettie and Marjorie—she bought hats, gloves and evening purses, and had fittings for riding habits and dresses that were the very height of fashion, colourful and feminine, frivolous and completely impractical.

When she looked at herself in the mirror, adorned in one such gorgeous concoction and with her glossy hair arranged in an elegant chignon, Adeline no longer saw the plain young woman who wore reading spectacles and faded into the background.

'You look so beautiful,' Marjorie enthused breathlessly. Her eyes, dreamy and full of admiration, suddenly became rueful. 'And so tall. How I wish I were as tall and as slender as you, Adeline.'

Adeline could not believe that silks and satins in pastel shades adorned with ribbons and frothing lace could bring about such a change. Yes, she thought, with her colouring, her high cheekbones and her green eyes, she really did look quite wonderful.

Stanfield House was a veritable hive of activity, with people coming and going all the time. It was an exciting time for Adeline. She had been to London often, but now she saw it with different eyes. Suddenly it offered an active social life without the restrictions laid down by her father. The intensity of her enjoyment was no doubt due to the feeling of release which had come with her sudden emancipation from the frustrations of her life before her break-up with Paul. It was as though she had been born anew as a result of some new process of gestation.

She went to the opera or the theatre twice a week, walked in the pleasure gardens during the day, fed the pigeons in Trafalgar Square, rode side-saddle in a high silk hat between the elms along Rotten Row, and journeyed across the river to a concert at the Crystal Palace in Sydenham.

She attended parties at the homes of several people who were prominent in the Women's Movement, and even went to one of the Suffragist meetings, which she found interesting, listening to both Emily Davis and Millicent Garrett Fawcett—two extremely important women who made a deep impression on her.

She met writers, political and religious figures, and people she had read about in the society columns. They all came to drink tea in Lady Stanfield's elegant high-ceilinged drawing room with its watered silk walls. There they had the freedom to speak as openly as they wished on whatever subject they wished—from higher education for women, better employment opportunities for women, right down to the sexual persecution of women—unencumbered by most of the prevailing notions of female propriety.

Much as Adeline liked and respected the women she met, and the work they did, she had decided from the beginning not to become one of them—at least not for the time being.

It was at one such party that Lettie, sipping champagne, told her how the social world gave her pleasure.

'Indeed, I often feel guilty at my willingness to leave my work in order to enjoy dissipation,' she joked.

The remark caused Adeline to give her a frowning, suspicious look. Lettie often went out alone at night. She gave no indication of where she went, and she rarely returned until the following morning, so Marjorie had confided to her. In fact, Lettie had begun behaving rather oddly of late, she'd said, and she was often very pale.

It was clear that Marjorie was worried about her, but Adeline, not wishing to pry into her friend's private life—and presuming her outings were connected to her work—did not raise the subject. However, she sensed all was not as it should be with her friend, and that she assumed a cheerfulness she did not feel.

It wasn't until Marjorie told her that Lettie always implied to her mother that she was spending the night at Eaton Place with Adeline that Adeline, beginning to think there was more to Lettie's nocturnal activities than her work, and that the man she had told her about at Oaklands might have something to do with it, thought it was time she spoke to her.

'When are you going to introduce me to your young man, Lettie?' she asked outright.

Lettie suddenly became tense, and glanced at her sharply. 'Do you want to meet him?'

'Of course. I'm curious. You never talk about him.'

'That's because he—he's not the type of man that you're used to.'

Adeline laughed lightly in an attempt to lighten the conversation. 'Why? Has he got two heads or something?'

Lettie smiled. 'Silly—of course he hasn't. He—he…'

'He?' Adeline prompted, sensing Lettie's reluctance to discuss him but determined to find out more. 'Does he have a name?'

'Jack. His name is Jack Cunningham. He's respectable, of

course,' she uttered rather forcefully—more to convince herself than Adeline, Adeline thought.

'What does he do?'

'He—he owns a nightclub in the West End.'

Adeline was surprised. It wasn't what she'd expected to hear, and she felt an uncomfortable stirring of unease. 'Oh, I see. How interesting. How did you come to meet him?'

'Diana Waverley introduced us at the Drury Lane Theatre. She was there with a large party, celebrating something or other. Jack was among them. As soon as I saw him I was attracted to him.' Lettie sighed. 'I can see you're shocked, Adeline. Mother wouldn't approve—there's nothing more certain—and Grant would definitely have a great deal to say about it. But Jack really cares for me. I know he does.'

The way Lettie emphasised those last four words made Adeline think she was trying to make herself believe this.

'I'd introduce you to him if I could,' Lettie said quickly, 'but it's rather difficult, you see. He—he's so busy. And besides, I couldn't possibly take you to a place like that.'

Adeline looked at her steadily. 'What? A nightclub?' Lettie nodded. 'But you go, don't you, Lettie?'

She shook her head. 'I've been on one occasion, that's all. Jack doesn't like me to go there. He has a house in Chelsea.'

'And you stay all night?'

Sensing Adeline's disapproval, Lettie stared right back at her, and there was defiance in the sudden lift to her chin. 'Yes. It's the only time Jack and I can be together. Adeline— I am an adult. I know perfectly well what I am doing.'

Lettie's words had shocked Adeline, but the sharpness with which they were spoken shocked her more. 'I'm sure you do, Lettie, and I'm not going to be judgemental, I promise. But— well—you do seem to be behaving out of character. I think I know you well enough by now to know it's not like you to carry on a clandestine affair.'

Lettie's eyes clouded over and she sighed. 'I suppose it must look like that to you. Love—or whatever you like to call it—physical attraction—does strange things to people. All I know is that when I'm with Jack I don't want to leave him. He makes me come alive. I feel excitement, danger and passion all wrapped into one. You must know how that feels, Adeline. Didn't you feel that way when you and Grant…?'

Adeline stiffened. She wasn't enjoying the conversation, or the turn it had taken, which threatened to resurrect all the feelings and emotions concerning Grant Leighton she had carefully locked away in her mind. 'Stop it, Lettie. Whatever happened between Grant and me is over, so there's no sense in talking about it.'

'I'm sorry. I didn't mean to upset you. Did I tell you that Grant is in London? He's on his way to France, but he has some business here to attend to first—something about some land he's interested in buying that's to be developed across the river. He's staying at the Charing Cross Hotel.'

'No, you didn't, Lettie—and in any case your brother's activities are nothing to do with me,' Adeline replied, doing her best to ignore the sudden lurch her heart gave at the mere thought of Grant being so close. Quickly she dismissed Lettie's attempt to steer the conversation away from her and Jack Cunningham. 'I—I just wish you hadn't told Lady Stanfield you were staying here with me. I don't like untruths, Lettie. They have an unpleasant habit of being found out.'

'I know, and I'm sorry about that,' she said, sounding contrite. 'I didn't want to involve you. But it's the only way I can see Jack.'

'Can I meet him?' The need to see what Jack Cunningham looked like was driving all caution from Adeline's mind.

Lettie shifted awkwardly and her expression became guarded. 'I don't know. I've told you—he's always working.'

'You can't get out of it that easily. He doesn't work all the time, surely? We can go to his club. If he's busy then we'll either wait until he's finished or go back another time.'

Lettie, knowing that Adeline wasn't going to be put off, reluctantly relented. 'I'll see what I can do.'

The following afternoon they took a cab to the heart of the West End, made up of dance halls, glittering restaurants, rough and tumble hostelries, brothels and dubious hotels of every kind. Leaving the main thoroughfare, they went down a narrow passage towards a projecting porch that threw the door into deep shadow, for it was two-thirds below ground level. A sign above advertised the Phoenix Club. They went down a flight of steps and came to a room below street level. A row of pegs and a short counter—a pay desk, Adeline assumed—were facing them. A couple of lighted gas-brackets hissed on the wall.

Pushing her way through a double swing door, Lettie urged Adeline to follow her, telling her that Jack was usually in his office at this time. Adeline stared around her in amazement. They were in a long vaulted room brightly lit by flaring gas, its floor of polished boards. There were alcoves, each with its own curtain—looped back for now—which could be released from its restraining cords to offer the inhabitants more privacy. Mirrors and pictures adorned the walls, and spittoons were plentiful. The décor was rich and subdued, the chairs plush. At the far end of the room was a raised dais with music stands and chairs, and to the side of this was a spiral staircase, rising into the dark.

A woman, unaware that she was being observed, was almost at the top, and only the lower half of her body could be seen. The train of her gown—a bold saffron-coloured silk with crimson trim—trailed behind her. Adeline watched until she'd disappeared, aware of the cloying fragrance of musk in the air—a fragrance not unfamiliar to her, which brought Diana Waverley to mind. But the woman could have been anyone. The scent was not unusual, and was favoured by many women of her acquaintance.

For the moment the Phoenix Club, flagship of Jack Cunningham's empire, remained dark and silent and private. But during its hours of activity Adeline could imagine how it would look. The cleaners had done their job, clearing away the previous night's debris, but the air was still thick with the odours of stale cigar smoke and liquor.

Suddenly a man appeared from a side room, smoking a cheroot, a glass of brandy in his hand. About thirty-five, he was swarthy, tall and well built, with tight curling black hair, side whiskers and a neatly trimmed moustache. An arrogant, smiling mouth dominated a square jaw.

On seeing Lettie, Adeline observed how his pale blue eyes had narrowed—with annoyance, she thought—but it was quickly gone, and his mouth stretched into a wide, unconvincing smile.

'Hello, Princess. This is a surprise—you know how I dislike you coming here,' he remarked, placing his glass on a table. Taking Lettie in his arms, he planted a firm kiss on her lips. Over Lettie's head his eyes slid to Adeline, standing a few steps behind, watching her gaze about with evident uncertainty. 'I didn't realise we had a visitor.'

Adeline met his eyes, and he looked back at her mockingly. She noticed how he worked his way from her face to the outline of her breasts. Unappreciative of his somewhat brazen interest, she stepped back. A hungry look came into his eyes and she shuddered—violently.

'And a lovely one at that.'

'I—I hope you don't mind, Jack. I know how busy you are, but we were shopping close by and I didn't think you'd mind if I brought Adeline in to see the club—and to meet you, of course.'

'I'm delighted you did. I'm never too busy to see you, Princess, you know that. I've heard all about you from Lettie,

Adeline.' His smile was open and beguiling as he held out his hand and his voice came over to Adeline silken-smooth.

She extended her hand in a businesslike manner and quickly withdrew it after a slight shake, glad she was wearing gloves. Leaning against him, Lettie looked relaxed and happy, with Jack smiling down into her eyes, plainly trying to make a good impression on Adeline. But Adeline could see below the surface.

The moment Adeline had set eyes on Jack Cunningham she'd known she didn't like him, and she'd withdrawn, backing away from his company. It was a mental trick of hers, seldom used, and only when her mind was troubled. When she looked at him she was aware of her own mixed feelings—and something else that she felt. Something not quite nice. The man exuded cockiness. His expression had a certain arrogance that repelled her completely.

No doubt women found him attractive—Lettie certainly did. His demeanour was correct. He moved and spoke carefully. Yet for all his gentility Jack had an untamed air about him. Adeline was afraid. She didn't like the feeling. What did he want with Lettie? When he looked at her the look was intimate, triumphant—one of ownership—the look of a man incapable of love.

'Now you've braved the doors of the Phoenix,' Jack said, his eyes fixed intently of Adeline, 'you can't leave without taking refreshment. You must join me in a drink.'

'Yes,' Lettie said, somewhat breathlessly. 'We'd love to, Jack.'

'Good—something suited to a lady's taste. A glass of champagne, I think.'

'Thank you,' Adeline said composedly, 'but I don't drink anything stronger than tea in the afternoon.'

Jack lifted his glass in a wry salute. 'Very wise. And are you a member of Lettie's ladies' movement—emancipation and equality and all that nonsense?'

'No. Up to now I have not been drawn in.'

'You have different opinions?'

'Not at all. I agree with everything I hear. I admire the work they do enormously, and all they strive to achieve.'

'You're not one of those damned temperance fanatics, I hope, who won't be happy until they've closed down every club and tavern in London?'

'No, I'm not one of those, either.'

The atmosphere was uncomfortable. Lettie was aware of it, and also of the tension inside Adeline. She gave a nervous laugh. 'Look, Jack, do you mind if we forgo the drink? We have heaps to do, and the shops don't remain open all day. I'll probably see you later.'

He shrugged. 'That's a shame. You must arrange to bring Adeline out to Chelsea some time, Lettie—then we can become better acquainted.'

Adeline met his direct gaze without blinking. 'Thank you. I would like that,' she lied. 'Goodbye, Mr Cunningham.'

'The pleasure's entirely mine.'

When they emerged from the club the narrow, dimly lit passage seemed a mite chillier, and the thought of seeing Jack Cunningham again even less appealing. Suddenly a woman stepped out of the shadows, barring their way. In the gloom her age could have been anything from twenty-five to forty. A shawl that had seen better days was wrapped protectively about her thin body.

'Are you Miss Leighton?' she said, her voice low as she addressed Lettie.

Adeline could tell by the way her eyes kept darting to the doorway of the Phoenix Club that she was nervous.

'I am,' Lettie replied.

'I want a word with you—it's about Jack.' She glanced at Adeline. 'Private, like.'

Lettie turned to her friend. 'Would you mind, Adeline? I'll only be a moment.'

'Of course not. I'll wait for you at the end of the passage.'

Looking back, Adeline saw the woman had drawn Lettie back into the shadows and that she was speaking animatedly. After five minutes Lettie joined her, her expression grave.

'What did she want? And how did she know who you were?'

'She—she's seen me with Jack,' Lettie told her with a sudden wariness. 'She knows the work I'm involved with, and has come to me for help. She—she's ill—probably bronchitis—I can't be sure—and she can't afford to pay a doctor. I gave her the address of a charity clinic I know of run by volunteers, where street women who are ill or injured can go. They'll help her.'

'I see. And that's all she wanted?'

'Of course.'

When Lettie moved away to look for a cab, Adeline turned over what she had said, her sixth sense telling her that Lettie was not revealing the whole of it, and for some reason was unwilling to say more.

'You don't like Jack, do you?' Lettie remarked when they were in the cab taking them back to Eaton Place, the woman forgotten for the moment. 'Don't deny it, Adeline. It won't be any use, because I know you don't.' She didn't speak aggressively. She sounded calm and unemotional.

'No,' Adeline replied. 'Since you ask me so directly, I don't especially.'

'I knew you wouldn't.'

'He's not the sort of person who appeals to me—but I'm not the one he's seeing. I don't know him, of course—you obviously know him very well.'

'I'm not sure that I do,' Lettie murmured, averting her eyes.

'Then you should. You should know the man you're—'

Lettie turned and fixed her eyes on her candidly. 'What? Sleeping with?'

'I was going to say having a relationship with, but I suppose sleeping with is the same thing.'

'Do you think I'm wicked?'

'No, of course I don't, Lettie. Please don't think that. To me you are a dear friend, and the kindest, nicest person I have ever known, but I cannot like Jack Cunningham. If you must know, I thought he was absolutely dreadful. He has an air of danger about him—something that's not quite nice—sinister, even—and I do urge you to be careful. Do you intend to go on seeing him?'

Lettie nodded and looked away. 'Yes. I must. I like him. He's fun to be with and he excites me—at least for now.'

'You are of age—I can't stop you doing this foolish thing.' For the first time Adeline saw a mutinous twist in the set of Lettie's lips.

'No, no one can.' After a moment's silence she looked back at Adeline and took her hand firmly in her own. 'Please don't tell Lady Stanfield, will you, Adeline? Promise me you won't.'

'But you must see this is wrong, Lettie,' Adeline said, as calmly as she could.

'Promise me,' Lettie demanded, a fierce, hard light in her eyes. 'This is no one's business but mine, Adeline, and I shall resent interference from anyone. Do you understand?'

Adeline nodded. 'Very well. I promise not to mention it to Lady Stanfield.'

That night Adeline lay awake most of the night, worrying miserably and imagining problems each more fantastic than the last. Her mind was in too much of a turmoil to work coherently. The serious implications of what Lettie was doing gave her no rest. She pictured Lettie—quick, clever and vivacious Lettie—brought low at the hands of Jack Cunningham. He was dangerous, and Adeline was afraid he would love Lettie lightly and discard her—his depth of commitment shallow. What would that do to her?

One thing she knew was that she could not remain

detached. But she was out of her depth. She wasn't the kind
of person to fall apart in a crisis, but this was something she
had never had to cope with. Oh, dear God, what to do for the
best? She couldn't go to Lady Stanfield because she had
promised Lettie she wouldn't. But who else was there?

Grant! Lettie had told her that he was here in London,
staying at the Charing Cross Hotel. Immediately she sat upright
in bed. The idea that had just occurred to her was so simple
she wondered why she hadn't thought of it before—but she *did*
know why. It was because Grant had told her he never wanted
to set eyes on her again. But this matter was too important for
her to be deterred by the furious rantings of a spurned suitor.

Grant would know what to do. Grant would make Lettie stop
seeing Jack Cunningham. Oh, brilliant, wonderful hope. He
would put it right. Yes, she thought, Grant. There was no one else.

Her mind made up, suddenly she felt as if a weight had
been lifted from her shoulders, and her relief was so great she
felt weak. The thought did occur to her that Grant might not
want to see her but when he knew how important it was, and
that it concerned Lettie, he would have to.

And so the following morning found her ordering the
brougham to take her to the Charing Cross Hotel.

The hotel was every bit as grand and opulent as Adeline
had expected, with deep carpets and a plethora of flowers. As
she passed through the foyer she couldn't stop herself from
indulging in a tormentingly sweet fantasy—a frail hope that
made her heart accelerate—that when Grant saw her he would
be glad to see her. She looked at the well-to-do people milling
about. Her face was flushed as she realised she had never felt
so unsure of herself in her life. The qualms she had kept
firmly at bay rushed at her. Until now the need for haste and
a determination not to anticipate trouble had sustained her, but
she felt far from heroic, alone and clutching her reticule.

To her relief she saw Grant almost at once. He was immaculately dressed in a dark frock coat and narrow pin-striped trousers. His chiselled features, his glossy dark hair and his wide shoulders were emblazoned on her brain. He was standing by the main desk, talking to the concierge.

As if sensing her gaze, he turned and looked at her directly—and she saw his face, ruthless and dominating, that rebellious lock of hair dipping over his forehead. Their eyes locked—and those hard silver-grey eyes struck her to her heart—eyes that had not so long ago melted her. She clutched at her memories as recognition flashed between them at the speed of light. Without taking his eyes off her, he strode across the distance that separated them.

Grant stared at her. 'My God!' The words came out unbidden. 'My God, Adeline…' Was this really her? Plain, rather serious Adeline? This tall, stylish goddess of a creature, as rakishly elegant as a fashion picture, with her gleaming dark red hair swept back and up in a perfect chignon beneath an adorable little hat. The arched wings of her eyebrows and the thick rows of dark lashes emphasised her brilliant green almond-shaped eyes. This was a different Adeline Osborne from the one he had known before. He hardly recognised her. She looked stunning.

Then he recollected himself. The mere thought of Adeline Osborne, the reminder of his stupid gullibility where she was concerned, made him want to drown himself in liquor—which was ironic, really, when he remembered it was liquor that had brought them together in the first place. When she had left Oaklands he had told himself that it was over and done with. But it was not as simple as that. She might have disappeared from his sight after flinging his proposal of marriage into his face, but he had been unable to banish her from his heart and mind, and he resented her for having the power and the ability to do that. And seeing her now, looking as she did, was crucifying him, since he had told himself—and believed—that she was nothing to him.

His expression changed, and Adeline actually flinched at the coldness that entered his narrowed eyes—like slits of frosted glass. Her indulgent fantasy that he would be pleased to see her died an immediate death and withered into nothing. It was incredible to her that those firm lips had kissed her, that those hands had caressed and fondled her naked flesh and given her such delight.

'Hello, Grant. How are you?' she said, amazed that her voice sounded calm when she was trembling inside. His grim expression as he met her gaze boded ill.

'I was doing nicely until a moment ago,' he replied curtly. One brow lifted in arrogant enquiry. 'What the hell are you doing here?'

Adeline's heart sank at his uncompromising antagonism. 'I have not come here to aggravate you, if that's what you think. I know you do not want to be involved with anything that has to do with me—'

'Right. At least we agree on that.' His face tightened, but his voice was ominously soft. 'How did you know where to find me?'

'Lettie told me you were staying here. I had to come—though I nearly didn't.' Somewhere in her whirling thoughts Adeline registered that Grant was treating this meeting with a cold nonchalance that was not at all appropriate. 'Do you think we could go somewhere more private?'

'I was on my way out,' he pointed out evasively.

'This really can't wait. I would like to speak to you on a rather serious matter. A few minutes of your time is all I need.'

With an impatient sigh and a brief look at his watch, he said, 'Then since you're determined to enact a Cheltenham tragedy I suppose I'd better listen to what you have to say.'

Momentary shock gave way to a sudden, almost uncontrollable burst of wrath. 'If you think for one minute I *wanted* to come here and see you again, then nothing could be further from the truth,' Adeline retorted frostily. 'I find your company both offensive and repugnant, and I cannot wait to be out of here. You seem to enjoy humiliating me, and you will continue trying to humiliate me as long as we stand here. Are you going to listen to what I have to say or not?'

Grant's jaw tightened, and a muscle began to twitch dangerously in the side of his neck, but he nodded. 'My room. It's on the third floor, so we'll take the lift.'

'Thank you. It won't take long.'

'Fine,' he snapped.

Neither of them spoke until they entered Grant's richly ornamented, opulent suite of rooms. Through an open door Adeline could see a huge, comfortable bed which she did her best not to look at.

'Would you like to sit down?' he asked, casually gesturing towards a velvet chair by the window.

'No, thank you. I'll come straight to the point. What I have to say is that I am deeply concerned about Lettie—and so is Marjorie.'

'You are?' Grant repeated with insolent amusement, perching his hip on the edge of a table and crossing his arms over his chest. The startling silver-grey eyes rested on her ironically. 'I can't think why. Lettie is old enough, and quite capable of standing on her own feet. She has done very much as she pleases for a long time. Mother has accepted the work she does that keeps her away from home and so have I.'

'It has nothing to do with her work. I wish it had. But it's more serious than that. She—she's seeing someone…'

Grant shook his head in baffled disbelief. 'Lettie— seeing someone? What's so very wrong with that? I'm happy to know my sister has the same urges and emotions as every one else. She's been so wrapped up in that damned Women's Movement I was beginning to doubt it.'

Adeline stared at him and began to wonder what had induced her to seek out this cold and uncaring man. Spinning on her heel, she turned to the door. 'Even for a man who believes he has justification for being hostile towards me, that was a nasty remark to make about Lettie. I can see this was a mistake,' she uttered acidly. 'If you cannot bring yourself to listen to why I am so concerned about your sister, then I'll go. I'm sorry to have taken up so much of your time and inconvenienced myself. Please excuse me.'

In six long strides Grant was at the door as she opened it, shoving it closed with a force that sent it crashing into its frame.

'Since you are here, and I'm already late for my appointment, you'd better say what you have to say.'

Adeline spun round and faced him. His black brows were up and his eyes gleamed. Anger leaped in her breast so sharply that it stabbed at her heart like a knife-thrust. 'You really are the most appallingly rude man I have ever met. Do you *really* think I would be here if it weren't important? I am extremely concerned about Lettie—and so will you be if you would have the courtesy to listen.'

Shoving his hands into his trouser pockets, he nodded. Deep inside him he knew it must be a matter of some considerable importance to have brought Adeline to see him, feeling as she did about him. Despite everything he knew her to be, when he looked at her he saw spirit and youthful courage—and also fear in her eyes. Fear for Lettie?

Going to the window, he stood looking out, his shoulders tense. 'Tell me.'

Steeling herself against his reaction, drawing a deep breath, Adeline quickly gave Grant the facts. White and stony-faced, he listened to her, appalled by her disclosure. Scarcely able to grasp the reality of it, he turned and stood looking at her, his composure held tightly to him, his drawn face as blank as still water. Adeline had seen him angry, and she had seen him irritable, but now he was white with a quiet, controlled fury.

'You are telling me that my sister is involved with a night-club owner?' He began pacing the floor in restless fury.

'Yes.'

Fire sprang to his eyes. 'Dear God in heaven! Is that what she's doing when she's not putting the world to rights? Has she taken leave of her senses? What's he like—this Jack Cunningham?'

'Quite the gentleman—but no more than that. I did not like him at all. There's an air of danger about him. He's a taker, a man of terrible force. Lettie will be like putty in his hands.'

'How did you meet him?'

'I was curious about him. I asked Lettie to introduce us.'

Grant's eyes flashed unexpectedly. 'A brave action, and not to be commended. I know about men like Jack Cunningham. You are right to think he's dangerous. Is Lettie determined to carry on seeing him?'

'Yes. She is strongly attracted to him. She resented me warning her against him, and she is annoyed at what she considers to be my interference.'

Grant considered this for a moment. 'Annoyed, is she?' he muttered slowly. 'It seems a poor return for all your kindness and consideration.'

'I suspect she sees more of him secretly than she admits to. She is answerable only to herself.'

'She might think she is—for now. Lettie has always been a bit wild, and appears perfectly independent and careless of her own welfare. Mother and I have let her be too free. We shouldn't have allowed it all this time.'

'Lettie is the victim of a casual affair, and I fear that any day she will be cast aside and hurt by it—deeply so. You have to speak to her. For without your intervention she is doomed.'

'I intend to.' Becoming thoughtful, all at once he ceased his restless pacing. He turned then, and looked at her for a long time, his face quite expressionless, his eyes hidden by the shadows of his brows. The respite had given him back his outward composure, but his face was still marked with anger. Knowing his sister as he did, he felt dread, persistent as a thorn in his foot. 'What's the name of Cunningham's nightclub?'

'The Phoenix Club. Will you go there?'

Grant studied her for a moment, eyes narrowed, and then shook his head. 'No, not immediately. I'll speak to Lettie first. If she agrees to stop seeing him then the affair will die a natural death. But, just in case I intend to find out all I can about Jack Cunningham.'

Adeline bent her head and lowered her eyes for a moment, to shut out the sight of the man who stood before her. He was so stern and oppressive, and yet so very attractive. He took her breath away. Why was she so strongly attracted to him? He had treated her with little more than grudging tolerance since he had known her. His eyes were filled with concern now—but not for her; she knew that. But for Lettie.

'You cannot imagine how difficult it was for me to come here. I feel like a traitor, yet I know that Lettie is prey to her emotions and needs someone to speak some sound common sense to her. I have tried, but she won't listen. She made me promise not to disclose any of this to Lady Stanfield, which is why I have come to you. Have I done the right thing—telling you? Have I helped her or merely betrayed a confidence?'

'You did right to come to me. Anything that concerns Lettie concerns me. It is not for me to admit or deny her right to independence, but anything she does that will hurt my mother or our good name I will not tolerate. You have done all that could be reasonably expected of you, and I am sorry you have been burdened with this.'

'It's no burden. Lettie is my friend.'

'Nevertheless, I suspect it is the most difficult thing you have ever done—and the bravest. You obviously care about Lettie.'

Adeline felt warmth begin to seep through her entire body at his stirring words, and she took heart as his sternly carved features softened. 'Yes, I do.'

'Are you staying with Lady Stanfield?'

'No—at our London house in Eaton Place. I became concerned when Marjorie told me Lettie was staying out all night and implying to Lady Stanfield that she was at Eaton Place with me.'

'And she wasn't?'

'No.'

'Then Lettie ought to have thought more of your having to account for her absence. I am sorry.'

'There's no need to be. Lettie spends a great deal of her time organising committees, or doing the detailed work that goes into mounting campaigns, but according to Marjorie she has lately continually failed to turn up for some of her usual meetings, and is often missing from the house. It's only a matter of time before Lady Stanfield takes note and starts asking awkward questions.'

'Then I must speak to Lettie soon. I apologise for my callousness earlier. I appreciate what you are doing for Lettie.'

'I can only hope she does—but somehow I don't think so. She will take exception to me coming here, so I beg of you not to tell her.'

For a moment Grant looked at her in silence. His well-tailored coat emphasised the breadth of his shoulders. There was a warm glint in his eyes. 'I won't tell her you came to see me. I promise.'

'Thank you.'

A flicker of amusement lit his grey eyes. 'Don't thank me yet. This could get worse. When I tell Lettie to stop seeing Jack Cunningham she'll be like a pit bull with a headache. It could even result in war.'

Adeline laughed. 'Then I shall be completely neutral, and let the two of you get on with it.'

'I may have thought you to be many things, Miss Osborne,' Grant teased lightly, 'but cowardly is not one of them.'

'Oh, I can be the world's biggest coward when it comes to violence.'

'Then we must see that it doesn't. Tell me, has my sister managed to lure you into the Women's Movement yet?'

'I find the work that she does interesting—although she isn't nearly as fiercely fanatical about it as some of the women she's introduced me to—but I prefer not to become involved at this time.'

'But you might?'

'I don't know.'

'Why? Because you think your destiny in life is to marry, make a home and have children?'

'I do want that—eventually—and I shall expect love, consideration and respect. But I will not marry a man who will expect me to be subordinate to my husband, who will wrap me in luxury and see that my every desire is satisfied except for independence and a will of my own.'

'Now you're beginning to sound like Lettie.'

'Perhaps that's because we've spent a lot of time together since I came to London. But we do also seem to spend a great deal of time shopping. As soon as I appeared in town she insisted on changing my appearance, and has almost drained my allowance dry.'

An amused quirk appeared at the corner of Grant's mouth as he regarded her attire, cut with ostentatious flattery. 'I've noticed. What you are wearing is certainly of a more eye-catching colour than I suspect is your natural choice. However, the change flatters you. But I am surprised.'

'You are?'

He looked at her from beneath raised brows. 'I would have

thought it uncharacteristic of you to conform—to wear clothes to please society and to be noticed.'

'You are wrong. I now wear fashionable clothes like this to please myself, not society, and I am grateful to Lettie for showing me how to. Do you find something wrong with that?'

'Nothing at all. It's just that I thought the prim and proper Miss Adeline Osborne was immune to the magic of pretty clothes.'

She smiled slightly. 'Then you were wrong about that, too, for it would seem I am just as weak as all the rest.'

'So it would. You look—extremely elegant—and very lovely,' he murmured, thinking that she also looked so young—in fact he had never seen her looking so young. It was as if in discarding her plain clothes and unflattering hairstyle she had thrown off surplus years with them. When he'd first seen her he had imagined her to be anything up to twenty-five. Now she looked a vulnerable girl of eighteen or nineteen.

His compliment brought an attractive flush to Adeline's cheeks. There was something in what he'd said, or perhaps in the slight tremor she'd heard in his voice as he'd said it, that made her want to believe he meant more by it than he really did. But she did not delude herself to think so. Grant Leighton really was the most unpredictable man. One minute he was making love to her, the next asking her to marry him and then rejecting her completely. He'd told her he never wanted to set eyes on her again, and yet now he was telling her she looked elegant and very lovely. What was she to think?

'Flattery indeed, coming from you.'

'I never flatter anyone, Adeline. My opinions are always given honestly.' His eyes did a leisurely sweep of her fashionable high-necked, svelte-waisted cobalt blue jacket. Her straight-fronted skirt was making him think of the long, glorious legs beneath. A scent of warm violets filled his nostrils and made him want to lower his lips to the curve of her neck. It was all he could do to keep his hands from sliding around her waist and pulling her into his arms. 'A woman can be as beautiful as she feels herself to be.'

'I must confess to never having thought about it.' Adeline looked at him almost candidly, almost shyly. 'Do you mind if I ask you something—and will you promise not to be angry?'

'Ask away. I am all ears.'

'That night—when we were together—when you awoke—did you really think I was the kind of girl who would give herself to anyone?' She looked up into his eyes, trying to read his expression.

There was a moment's silence. Grant watched her face with a slightly cynical lift of his brows, then he shrugged slightly and turned away.

'I must confess to never having thought about it. I thought you were beautiful—but then when a man wakes and finds a naked woman in his arms he thinks all kinds of things—a woman's face can be deceptive.'

Adeline gave a hard, contemptuous laugh. 'I see—and you must have thought it had been so easy to get me into bed.'

Grant swung round and came to her. Adeline could discern in his features no trace of his earlier anger. He was grave, but calm.

'When I awoke I was in so much agony I was convinced a full orchestra was tuning up inside my head. When I saw you lying there I didn't know what the hell to think. I have never been so confused in my life. And when I realised what I'd done I was shocked, appalled and disgusted with myself.'

Despite herself Adeline smiled almost shyly. 'Me, too—at myself, I mean.'

Looking down at her, Grant felt his conscience choose that moment to reassert itself for the first time in weeks, by reminding him that he hadn't been able to keep his hands off her that night at Westwood Hall. How it had come about no longer mattered. He'd subjected her to public embarrassment and censure. Compounding all of that by robbing her of her virginity was inexcusable, but the weak protest of his conscience hadn't been enough to deter him.

Looking at her now—different in her new finery and elegantly styled hair, yet still the same Adeline Osborne underneath it all, despite everything—he thought she was the most alluring woman he had ever met.

'You—will help Lettie, won't you?'

Grant looked down into those beseeching green eyes. Slowly he nodded. Adeline smiled at him. His brain captured the moment in a flash. He wanted her, and neither his conscience nor anything else was going to deprive him of having her again. Only the next time he would make sure he was in full control of all his faculties.

Drawn by the depths of her eyes looking into his, by the soft fullness of the lips slightly parted to reveal moist, shining teeth, and unaware of the passage of time, he made a move towards her. But Adeline turned away from the threatened kiss. The spell was broken.

'I fear I have kept you from your appointment for far too long. I think I'd better go.'

'Yes, I think you better had. I'll come down with you.'

'No, you needn't. I can find my own way.'

'I insist. Besides, I have an appointment to keep.'

'You'll be late. I'm sorry.'

'Better late than never.'

They had just stepped out of the lift when Adeline's attention was drawn by a slight disturbance in the foyer. A woman had entered. In a shimmering gown of saffron-coloured silk with crimson trim, her dark hair pinned and curled beneath a fashionable, elaborately feathered headdress, she was stunning. Like everyone else, Adeline could not tear her eyes off her. When the woman's gaze searched the crowd and came to rest on Grant, Adeline frowned, disquieted.

It was Diana Waverley—the woman she was now certain had been at the Phoenix Club.

Chapter Seven

Pinning a brilliant smile on her face, Diana crossed towards them.

When Grant saw her he stiffened and stood absolutely still, aware and wary. His face was blank, all emotion withheld by an iron control, and then, conscious that Adeline was by his side, watching him, with a lazy, sardonic smile he stepped forward and lifted Diana's hand to his lips for a brief kiss.

Diana looked up at him with a questioning frown. 'Why, Grant. I did not think I would have to come looking for you. You cannot have forgotten our appointment.'

'Diana! I apologise. No, I did not forget. I had an unexpected matter of considerable importance to take care of.'

Diana gave Adeline no more than a brief glance—as if she were of no consequence—before settling her gaze once more on Grant. 'Yes, so I see.' Immediately her attention flew back to Adeline and she gasped. 'Why—goodness me! If it isn't Miss Adeline Osborne! How nice to see you again,' she said, the tone of her voice and the cold look in her eyes belying her words. 'I do apologise. I hardly recognised you. How changed you look.' She was angry. This was not what she had planned.

Not at all. Expelling her breath in a rush of frustrated impatience, she looked up at Grant with a questioning frown.

'Your apology is unnecessary,' Adeline said. 'In fact it is I who should apologise to you for keeping Grant so long.'

'Really?' Diana smiled as her gaze passed over Adeline. It was not a pleasant smile, it was a malicious smile, and instinctively, with the feminine intuition that recognises what is in another woman's mind, Adeline knew that Diana considered Grant her property, and was telling Adeline to keep off.

'Grant and I were—'

'Stop it, Adeline,' Grant was quick to retort. 'There's absolutely no need to explain to Diana.'

'Well, since I have just observed the two of you coming out of the lift, I can only assume that Grant has been entertaining you in his room.' When she looked at Adeline her feelings were transparent—the emotions of jealousy and dislike were hard to mask when they lay so near the surface. 'I am sure it is none of my business, but perhaps it's not something you should choose to bandy about in public.'

Adeline took exception to the slur. Diana's tone, lightly contemptuous and at the same time more than a little suspicious, made Adeline's hackles rise. However, although she was still seething inside from Diana's machinations at Westwood Hall, she faced her with well-feigned assurance.

'You're right, Diana, it is none of your affair. So kindly watch your tongue,' Grant admonished sharply. 'Now you are here we will have luncheon. Adeline is just leaving. I will see her out to her carriage and then I'll be with you.'

At that moment the concierge approached Grant and drew him aside to speak to him on a trivial matter, but it meant he left Adeline alone with Diana.

'Well, I certainly didn't expect to see *you* at the Charing Cross Hotel, Adeline.'

Absently Adeline noted that rubies like droplets of blood

dripped from Diana's ears and neck. Adeline's flesh turned to ice when she met her stare. That Diana Waverley hated her was plain.

'I came to see Grant on a family matter. Make of that what you will, Diana. I have apologised for keeping him from his appointment with you, but it really was important and could not wait.'

'So was his appointment with me. Still, it's not too late. We can take care of our business just as well here as at my house. Unlike you, I ceased to consider my reputation a long time ago. I have known Grant for a long time, and I know him about as well as any woman can.'

Adeline met her eyes. 'Then we are not so very different. I may not have known him as long as you have, but I have known him just as well.' Her smile was meaningful, and they both knew she was referring to the night Diana had tied the scarlet ribbon to her door.

White-lipped, Diana glared at her, knowing she had been caught out. She was reminded that instead of acting like the prim and proper miss she had assumed Adeline Osborne to be, and alerting the whole household to the embarrassing fact that Grant had entered her bedchamber uninvited, she had quietly taken full advantage of the situation—and enjoyed every minute of it, too, no doubt.

Adeline added coolly. 'How is Paul, by the way? I believe you know *him* just about as well as any woman can, too. You know, Diana, I have much to be grateful to you for. I am well rid of him. You may have missed your chance for snaring Grant, but I am sure you will find Paul amenable. I wish you well of each other. Good day. Please tell Grant I can find my own way out.'

Diana felt her cheeks grow hot with the sting of defeat. The reality of what Adeline had said hit her with all the force of a hammer-blow. Her dream of Grant asking her to be his wife had faded to leave a bitter taste in her mouth. She watched Adeline's trim figure leave the hotel. How that little bitch must be laughing at her fate.

After Adeline had left Diana with Grant at the hotel her imagination ran riot. Her emotions were so confused that she felt they were choking her—protests, recriminations, accusations, all were tumbling about in her mind. They were to have luncheon, Grant had said—where, she wondered? In the hotel restaurant or in Grant's room? An image of the bed she had seen—big and comfortable, a veritable erotic pleasure ground for lovers—entered her mind. Thinking of them in it, and what they would do, made her blood run cold. The shock of it all triggered off some sleeping thing inside her, bringing to life and revealing to her the true state of her heart.

So much for Grant's declaration that he never gave second chances, and that what there had been between him and Diana was over, for it was as plain as the nose on her face that he was undoubtedly sharing the favours of that woman with Paul. Perhaps Grant found such a situation entertaining—a bit of fun with no hearts broken—but what he was doing was highly immoral in her opinion. He was just like everyone else—enjoying his little dalliances and flirtations—but she would not be one of them.

However, because she had approached him about Lettie it was inevitable they would meet again. Whatever happened, she vowed she would never again lose her composure as she had in the past, when he had confused her to such a degree that she scarcely knew right from wrong. From this moment on things would be different. She would be completely imperturbable and polite. She was no longer the innocent young girl he could hurt and seduce for his own amusement.

* * *

Adeline spent the rest of the day at home, glad to have some time to herself. The London house was large and imposing, and reflected her father's taste to as great a degree as Rosehill did.

The following morning she was debating on whether to go to Stanfield House, in the hope of seeing Lettie, or take a quiet stroll in the park, when Anthony Stanfield arrived to take her up on her offer of a fencing bout. At first Adeline stared at him in confusion, and then recalled she had indeed invited him over.

'I'll go away if it's inconvenient, or you're not up to it,' Anthony offered, his expression telling her that he hoped she was.

Adeline laughed and led him to the salon, glad of any respite from the quiet atmosphere of the house. 'I wouldn't dream of it. Fencing is just what I need right now, to draw me out of the doldrums. I'll show you where the rapiers are kept and then I'll go and change.'

Shortly before eleven o'clock, Grant arrived at the house to see Adeline. When Mrs Kelsall opened the door and he asked to see Miss Osborne, the housekeeper raised her brows in astonishment. Few visitors came to Eaton Place when Mr Leighton was not in town, and suddenly two gentlemen had turned up within the same hour to see Miss Adeline. She didn't approve of young gentlemen calling uninvited when she was alone, but since Miss Adeline had come to London there had been a change in her, an open confidence and self-assurance Mrs Kelsall had never seen before.

'Is Miss Osborne at home?' Grant enquired.

'She is, sir, in the salon—fencing.' Though Mrs Kelsall was fond of Miss Adeline, she never ceased to voice her disapproval of young ladies indulging in gentlemanly activities, and for them to wear trousers—which Miss Adeline insisted on doing—was quite shocking and unthinkable.

'Then if you will be so kind as to direct me, I will introduce myself.'

Grant opened the door to the salon, where the carpet had been rolled back. He entered quietly, unnoticed by the pair of duellists, their identities hidden by facial masks. One was evidently female. Her lithesome figure was clad in revealing dove-grey trousers and a white silk shirt, and she was fighting with the skill and address of an experienced duellist, moving with an extraordinary grace, as if movement were a pleasure to her. The other, a young gentleman, was not so skilled.

Propping his shoulder against the wall, Grant watched with interest as they parried and thrust, moving ceaselessly about the highly polished parquet floor.

After Adeline had left the hotel yesterday, Grant had sat through luncheon paying no more attention to Diana across from him than he had to the business proposition she had put to him. This had been completely out of character, for he always gave matters of business his whole attention, considering them with unfailing instinct and dispassionate logic and calculating the odds for success before he acted. The only rash act he'd performed in recent years was his behaviour with Adeline at Westwood Hall, and when she'd left the hotel he had set his mind to seeing her again just as soon as he could manage it.

Folding his arms, with a slight smile on his lips, his unswerving gaze now watched her every move, feasting on the graceful lines of her slim hips and incredibly long legs, her whole form outlined with anatomical precision. Adeline was, Grant realised, a brilliant swordswoman, with faultless timing and stunningly executed moves. There was an aura of confidence and daring about her that drew all his attention.

Still unaware of his presence, Adeline suddenly cried enough and whipped off her mask to reveal her laughing, shining face. 'Very good, Anthony. You're improving tremendously. We'll fence some more tomorrow, if you like.'

She was breathless and her cheeks were flushed, her eyes a brilliant dancing green. Her abundance of hair was tied loosely on top of her head, with riotous locks tumbling about all over the place. To Grant at that moment she looked like a bandit princess, vibrant with health and life. His eyes soaked up the sight of her, for which he was more thirsty than water by far.

Anthony was the first to become aware of Grant's presence. His face broke into a welcoming smile as he recognised Lettie's brother. Taking off his breastplate and wiping his damp forehead with his sleeve, he crossed the room towards him and shook his hand. 'Mr Leighton. I didn't realise we had company. It's good to see you.'

'I was enjoying watching you. I didn't want to interrupt such fine swordplay.'

'As you will have seen,' he said, turning towards his attractive partner, his adoring gaze and unselfconscious absorption not going unnoticed by Grant, 'Adeline is more than a match. She has much to teach me.'

Across the room, on hearing Grant's voice, Adeline spun round, her heart giving a sudden lurch. 'I'm sorry. I didn't know you were there.'

He smiled. 'I'm glad. You are an excellent swordswoman, Adeline. Had you been aware of my presence you would perhaps not have performed so well.'

Her sudden smile had a warmth to contend with the glowing sun slanting through the windows. 'You are mistaken. I fence the same regardless of whether I have an audience or not. What has brought you to Eaton Place?'

'I have a matter of some importance to discuss with you. I didn't think you'd mind me arriving uninvited.'

'I'll leave you, Adeline,' Anthony said, shrugging himself into his jacket. 'I have to get back.'

'That's all right, Anthony. I'm glad you came for a practice bout. If Lettie's at home, tell her I'll be along later.'

When she was alone with Grant, she looked at him askance. 'Why do you smile?'

'That young man's in love with you—or if he isn't now he very soon will be.'

Adeline gasped and laughed awkwardly, embarrassed that such a thing could happen. 'Really, Grant, your imagination runs away with you. Anthony and I are friends—good friends—and nothing more, so please don't read more into our fencing bouts than there is.'

His eyes crinkled with amusement. 'There is none so blind as will not see, Adeline. Time will tell.'

'You are being ridiculous. He's only a young man.'

'Exactly! He's a man—and you, Miss Osborne, are an attractive young woman. He couldn't keep his eyes off you.'

Adeline suddenly became embarrassingly self-conscious of the way she was dressed. 'If you don't mind I'll just go and change. I'll have Mrs Kelsall prepare refreshments and then we can talk.'

'Not so fast.' Grant quickly divested himself of his coat and waistcoat, rolling back his shirtsleeves over powerful forearms. Removing his cravat and shirt stud to allow more freedom, he began fastening himself into the breastplate discarded by Anthony. 'I have a desire to test your fencing skills for myself. That's if you're up to it?'

'I'm tougher than I look.'

'So am I.'

He was looking at her with just a gleam of mischief at the back of his impassive handsome face. 'So you court danger, do you, Mr Leighton?'

'All the time, Miss Osborne.'

'Do you fence often?' she asked, curious as to how skilled an adversary he would make.

Grant was already crossing the room to help himself to one of the many fine weapons on display in a glass-fronted cabinet. 'Not as often as I would like.'

'In which case I imagine you'll be a bit rusty,' she taunted, with an innocent smile curving her lips.

His grin was roguish and the gleam in his eyes more so as his hand closed over the hilt of a weapon with a strong, slender blade. 'Imagine anything you like, Miss Osborne,' he retorted, flexing the supple blade between his hands before swishing the air in a practised arc, 'but my infrequency at practice does not mean that I shall be complacent or clumsy, or in need of lessons in self-defence.'

'Maybe not, but I don't think this will take long.'

'Planning to thrash me, are you?' he drawled, one brow arrogantly raised.

'Soundly,' Adeline told him.

Donning a face mask, he advanced towards her. 'As a matter of interest can you see properly? Without your spectacles, I mean,' he goaded.

'My vision is only impaired when I try to read. Otherwise I can see perfectly well.'

'I'm glad to hear it. But don't ever complain that I didn't warn you,' he said with tolerant amusement. 'Replace your mask and prepare to defend yourself, Miss Osborne, or I swear I'll pin you to the wall.'

The challenge to participate in a sport that was as enjoyable to her as riding a horse was much too tempting for Adeline to resist. With a vivacious laugh she replaced her mask and picked up her rapier. In one swift movement she was in the centre of the room, and Grant found himself engaged. Hidden from his view, a feverish flush was on her cheeks and a wild, determined light in her eyes. She moved skilfully, confident she could best him, but careful not to underestimate his ability.

Grant was an excellent sportsman, and accounted an excellent blade, but he soon realised he had his work cut out as his slender, darting opponent left no opening in her unwavering guard. The bright blade seemed to be everywhere at once, multiplied a hundred times by Adeline's supple wrists.

After the initial thrusts Adeline accepted that beating Grant was not going to be easy. He fought with skill, continually circling his opponent, changing his guard a dozen times, but Adeline never failed to parry adroitly in her own defence.

Grant could imagine the face behind the mask—the excitement of the fight would have put colour into her cheeks, a gleam in her eyes and a rosiness on her full lips. The image sent desire surging through him as foils rang together, meeting faster and faster as he forced her to a killing pace. Sweat now soaked her fine silk shirt so that it clung alluringly to her body, outlining the tender swell of her breasts.

Adeline was beginning to weaken, finding herself held at bay by a superior strength. Grant knew this, and with a low chuckle doubled his agility. With a triumphant cry and a snake-like movement he slipped under her blade and decisively thrust home.

Accepting that she was beaten, fair and square, Adeline whipped her mask from her laughing face. 'So, Mr Leighton, you have made good your threat. No doubt you regret wasting your time on such a weak opponent?'

'Nonsense. You were already considerably weakened by your earlier bout with Anthony,' Grant remarked, removing his mask, thinking how truly adorable she looked in complete disarray.

'You are too kind. There are no excuses for my defeat. I was beaten by a superior strength. I accept that.'

'A master?' he pressed, with a broad, arrogant smile.

'You conceited beast. I refuse to flatter your vanity further.'

Grant's grin was wicked. 'And you are magnanimous in defeat. I look forward to repeating the exercise.'

'Next time you won't be so lucky,' she quipped, with a jaunty impudence Grant found utterly exhilarating.

'I'm looking forward to it already. Who taught you to fence?'

'Uncle Max—my mother's brother. He was a military man and fought in the Crimean War. Sadly he died last year.' She placed the rapiers in the cabinet and turned back to him, feeling extremely self-conscious in her trousers. 'I must look a sight. I'll go and change.'

Lifting his gaze from the feminine curves of her breasts, slowly Grant let his eyes seek hers, and Adeline basked in the unconcealed admiration lighting his face. His amusement had vanished. An aura of anticipation surrounded them. It was blatantly sensual and keenly felt by Adeline. It widened her eyes and lingered in the curve of her lips.

Grant's own firm mouth curved in a sensuous smile. 'Believe me, there's nothing wrong with the way you look, Adeline,' he murmured.

Her senses heightened by his closeness, Adeline flushed and smiled tremulously, thinking how incredibly handsome he looked with his hair dipping over his forehead. 'Not to you, maybe, but I cannot possibly sit down to lunch like this. Mrs Kelsall has objections enough to what she considers to be my unladylike attire, and will refuse to feed us unless I change.'

He cocked a sleek black brow. 'Us? Are you inviting me to luncheon, Adeline?'

With an effort, Adeline tore her gaze from Grant's amused grey eyes and looked in the direction of the door. 'Yes—that is, if you like. It's almost lunchtime anyway, and I'm sure you must be hungry after your exertions.'

After showing him to the drawing room, Adeline escaped to her room to swill her burning face in cold water.

Mrs Kelsall had laid a light lunch for them in the dining room. They took their seats opposite each other.

'Please help yourself,' Adeline said, indicating the various cold dishes. 'I must try not to over-indulge, since I am going on a picnic this afternoon.'

'A picnic?'

'Yes.' She laughed. 'I enjoy idling away my days in frivolous pursuits. It's such a lovely day I thought Emma and I would go for a drive along the Embankment and go on to the gardens at Chelsea.'

They applied themselves to the food with unfeigned appreciation, and after commenting on the culinary delights they conversed little until the end of the meal.

Adeline, used to dining in silence with her father, did not babble on, as other women were wont to do, and Grant found this a pleasurable change. There was nothing awkward about the silence, which was comfortable and agreeable. However, he was of the opinion that while women prattled on, they weren't thinking, and when he glanced across at Adeline's serene countenance he was curious as to her thoughts.

Wearing a gown of ruby-coloured taffeta, unadorned and simple, with a well-fitted bodice, she had drawn her hair back from her face. Her almond-shaped eyes and high cheekbones gave her a rich, vivid and almost oriental beauty.

When they had finished eating they retired to the drawing room, sitting across from each other in two large wing-backed chairs. Grant stared at Adeline's profile as she turned her head slightly, tracing with his gaze the lines of her face, the brush of her thick eyelashes, the delicate hollow at the nape of her neck, where a stray strand of hair had come to rest, nestling against her pale skin like a dark red spiral.

'Have you spoken to Lettie?' Adeline asked, looking to where Grant was sitting silently watching her, holding her with his gaze.

He shook his head. 'Unfortunately I haven't had the opportunity. I called on Lord and Lady Stanfield before coming here, but Lettie was out at one of her meetings, somewhere in Kensington. And you?'

'No. Maybe later. What is it you wanted to see me about?'

'I've made enquiries about Jack Cunningham.'

'Oh? Have you found out much about him?'

Grant nodded slowly, his expression grave. 'It wasn't difficult. He's extremely well known, is Mr Cunningham—notorious, in fact—and steeped in vice. One thing I've learned is that he isn't working for good causes—and you are right, he's a dangerous individual. Apparently he isn't one to meddle with, and no one crosses him twice.' A grim smile twisted his lips. 'I suppose if he is to succeed in the hard and dangerous trade he's chosen then he needs to appear a man no one would dare cross.'

'Where is he from?'

'He was born in Whitechapel—one of nine children, father worked on the docks. He's self-made, shrewd, aggressive, determined and unscrupulous, and he has power over a lot of people. He has friends—of a sort. Mostly there are those who hate him and those who are frightened of him—and those who are both. Women seem to like him, but he treats them badly. I suspect he wants Lettie because she stands for something he's never had.'

'And what is that?'

'Class. He's a powerful figure in the underworld, where he reigns over an empire of corruption and debauchery. Nothing is too scandalous to be tolerated. The Phoenix is a gambling and drinking den, and a house of assignation—prostitution. He derives handsome profits from its exploitation. In fact he's made a lot of money out of his seedy nightclubs and brothels scattered all over the West End.'

There was a good deal more that Grant could have told Adeline about Jack Cunningham—his involvement in the sex-trafficking of both women and children he purchased through a network of agents to install in his brothels. Grant considered this widespread victimisation of children an abomination, but he would not embarrass or distress Adeline by divulging this part of Cunningham's sordid empire.

'After visiting the place, somehow it doesn't surprise me to hear that.' Adeline shuddered at the memory.

'Cunningham never soils his own hands with violence. Others do it for him—he has plenty of henchmen. He carries people in his head and moves them about like chess pieces. He also lends money at high interest rates—expending very little risk since for his investment he is careful to command property of a much higher value or favours as security. He's used to getting what he wants, and if anyone opposes him he shows no mercy.'

Adeline paled visibly, appalled by what she was hearing. 'I can't believe Lettie has got involved with somebody like that.'

Grant looked at her sharply. 'How did she meet him? Do you know?'

'Yes. It was at the Drury Lane Theatre—Diana Waverly introduced them.'

Grant stared at her, dumbfounded. For some reason this bothered him. 'Diana knows Cunningham?'

'Yes. As a matter of fact I believe she was at the Phoenix Club at the same time that I was there with Lettie. I saw a woman disappearing up a spiral staircase. I was too late to see her face, but she was wearing the same dress yesterday at the hotel.' Adeline was looking at Grant steadily, trying to measure the emotion lying behind the façade. 'You—didn't know Diana was associated with Cunningham?'

'No.' Grant felt oddly betrayed that Diana had never spoken to him of Cunningham—but then she had no reason to. Until Adeline had brought him to his attention he had never heard of him.

'Well, if she is that is her affair. But he sounds a thoroughly bad lot.'

'He is, Adeline, believe me. Lettie may be independent and twenty-three, but she is still innocent, trusting and unworldly to a man of his calibre. I intend to do everything in my power to put an end to his association with my sister—preferably without coming into contact with Jack Cunningham.'

'That's sensible. If he's as obnoxious as you say he is then it could only lead to trouble. Best to let Lettie finish it quietly—although I hope she doesn't love him so much she will stand against you in defence of him. Is Lettie anything like your other sister who lives in Ireland?' Adeline asked, suddenly curious about Grant's other siblings.

'Anna?' His expression lightened and his lips curved in a smile. 'No. Not at all. Anna is mild-mannered, unselfish, genuinely kind-hearted and willing to take on everyone's troubles. Mother hasn't seen Anna and her family for eighteen months—since she went over for a visit—and naturally she's excited about them coming for Christmas and an extended stay.'

'I'm sure she is. I seem to recall her saying that your brother is also coming home for Christmas?'

'That's right. He's coming home on leave for a few weeks. All his life Roland has wanted to be a soldier. He loves India, and no doubt he will go back there to his regiment when his leave is up.' Grant stood up. 'I've kept you long enough. You'll be wanting to go on your picnic. I'll call at Upper Belgrave Street and see if Lettie has returned.'

Adeline went out into the hall with him, where they paused. 'I do wish you every success with Lettie. Truly. I wish no harm to come to her at the hands of Jack Cunningham.'

Grant looked at her earnest, upturned face. He felt humbled by her generosity of spirit and her compassion for Lettie. Her full mouth was soft and provocative, her shining eyes mesmerising in their lack of guile, and her smooth cheekbones were flushed a becoming pink. Courageous, unpretentious and unaffected, she sparkled from within and shone on the surface. She was, he decided, the most interesting female he had ever met. She was also becoming embarrassed by his scrutiny. Her long ebony lashes had flickered down to hide her eyes.

Grant smiled, his grey eyes glinting with admiration. 'Nor do I.'

'I—enjoyed fencing with you,' Adeline said, suddenly nervous, self-conscious, trying desperately to sound normal. 'The exercise was good, and I can't tell you how good it was to fence with such an expert as yourself. I rarely get the opportunity. I—don't know how to thank you.'

His heavy-lidded gaze fixed meaningfully on her lips. 'We'll have to think of a way,' he murmured softly.

At that moment Mrs Kelsall bustled into the hall, her face in subdued lines. 'What is it, Mrs Kelsall? Has something happened?'

'No, Miss Adeline. Your picnic basket is all prepared, but Emma isn't feeling too well and doesn't think she's up to going out.'

'Oh, I'm sorry to hear that. She was complaining of a headache earlier. I'll go to her.' Adeline was clearly concerned about her maid. She turned to Grant and smiled weakly. 'It looks as though my picnic will have to keep for another day.'

A sudden gleam entered his eyes. 'It needn't. Perhaps you would allow me to accompany you?'

Silver-grey eyes met hers, and she felt her cheeks warm. 'Oh—I couldn't possibly. I couldn't impose on your time.'

His smile broadened into a grin. 'It's no imposition. I have a totally free day.'

'But you don't enjoy picnics.'

He arched one dark brow. 'I don't?'

'Well—I wouldn't have thought you were the type that did.'

'I happen to love picnics.'

'You do?'

'Absolutely. Just make sure there's a bottle of wine in the basket.'

'I'll go and put one in this minute.' Mrs Kelsall was quick to oblige, happy that all the work she'd put into the basket wouldn't be wasted after all.

'You really don't have to do this,' Adeline said to Grant, protesting even while unable to quell the stirring of pleasure his offer aroused.

'I want to. I promise I shall be a capable and attentive escort—and besides…'

'Besides, what?'

'It would be a shame to waste the food.'

'But I thought you were going to see Lettie?'

'I shall call on her later—there will be more chance of catching her then.'

Adeline searched his bold, swarthy visage, unsurprised by his nerve. 'Your persistence amazes me. I shouldn't be going anywhere with you on my own.'

He chuckled, smiling a wicked smile. 'Why not? We might both enjoy the outing. I favour your company, Adeline, and I shall endeavour to be on my best behaviour and as charming as my nature will allow.'

Adeline looked at him with doubt. 'We shall see. It should prove to be an interesting afternoon.'

'It will be what we make it. Now, go and get ready.'

Seated across from Grant in the Osborne landau, with its grey upholstery and the hood down, Adeline experienced a strange exhilaration. She felt wonderfully, gloriously alive for the first time in years as she instructed the driver to take them to the Embankment. There was something undeniably engaging about her handsome escort. He made her feel alert and curiously stimulated.

'You look exceptional, Adeline,' he told her. 'Radiant, in fact. I am honoured by this privilege.'

Adeline smoothed her dark green woollen skirt, knowing it became her extraordinarily well. She wore a fitted three-quarter-length matching coat and hat, which was adorned with small brown feathers. The ensemble combined rich, stylish flair and good taste.

'I am often in London, and I really can't name a sight that I haven't seen. Is there anywhere else you would rather go than the Embankment?' she asked Grant.

'I am at your disposal entirely. The Embankment suits me perfectly well.'

On reaching the Embankment they left the landau, and with a slight breeze in their faces strolled along. The early autumn day was overcast, but it was warm. People strolled along, like themselves, and open carriages passed by, with women showing off the latest fashions. Street peddlers were selling various kinds of food, from drinks and pies to sweets, and further along a brass band competed with a hurdy-gurdy playing a popular dance tune.

The dancing silvered river was busy with shipping of every kind—ferries, lighter men and a string of barges— making their way steadily upstream, the movement keeping the waters constantly on the swell. There were sounds of laughter from the pleasure boats crowded with people enjoying themselves. A woman's hat blew off into the river, causing much hilarity. Some waved to the people watching from the Embankment, and with laughter on her lips Adeline waved back.

Grant looked at her, thinking how adorable she was with her pink cheeks and shining eyes. She put him in mind of a child opening its presents at Christmas. 'Enjoying yourself?'

'I am. I love the Embankment, and today is just like London should be.' She turned towards the river. 'Can you smell it?'

'Smell what?'

'The salt on the incoming tide.'

Breathing deep, Grant could detect a tang in the air—the smell of salt and what he thought might be tar.

For a while they were both engrossed with the scene before them, then they walked back to the landau to continue on their way to Chelsea. Reaching their destination, they told the driver to return to Eaton Place. They would take a cab when it was time to return.

Carrying the picnic basket, and a rug over one arm, Grant gallantly presented his other arm to Adeline, at the same time catching her hand and pulling it through the crook of his elbow, not giving her a chance to deny him. Adeline was tempted to withdraw from his contact, but a small, naughty part of her knew she liked touching him. Very much.

The gardens overlooking the river were mostly for summer strolls and musical entertainments, and the quietness of the autumn day could not be denied. The wind was fresh, but reasonably warm, rustling the dying leaves in the trees and dappling the shade, and Adeline was content to let her escort lead her along the tree-lined lanes and past beds of the last of the summer's flowers. As promised, Grant lent himself to a most gentlemanly comportment and treated her with polite consideration, making her feel as if she were the only woman in the world.

Finding a secluded spot beneath the giant trees, Adeline spread out the rug while Grant removed his jacket, opened the basket and poured the wine. Totally relaxed, they talked about little things—oddities of fact that made simple things interesting. They told stories and joked and laughed at each other, and all the while Adeline was aware of Grant's appreciative gaze on her animated face. In all it proved to be a most enchanting afternoon, and Adeline experienced a twinge of regret that it would have to end.

Stretching out on his side, Grant leaned on a forearm and studied her profile from beneath hooded lids, wondering for the hundredth time what went on behind her placid exterior. 'You are a strange young woman, Adeline,' he murmured, focusing his eyes on a wisp of hair against her cheek.

Without thinking, he reached out and tucked it behind her ear, feeling the velvety softness of her skin against his fingers. She sat still as he ran the tip of his finger down the column of her throat, along the line of her chin to her collar and the cameo brooch at her throat.

'Suddenly I find myself wanting to know everything there is to know about you—what you are thinking, what you are feeling. You are still a mystery to me.'

'In the short time we have known each other, haven't you learned anything about me?'

'I have learned some things. I have learned that you are not the prim and proper miss you purport to be, and that you like making love to inebriated gentlemen when you are the one who can dictate the action, and that—'

'Grant, please!' Resting back on her heels, Adeline was aghast. 'Stop it now,' she retorted, her face heating. 'It wasn't like that, and you know it.'

'No? Are you saying that you *didn't* enjoy making love to me?' He reached into the basket for a sandwich and slowly began to eat.

'No—yes… Oh, behave yourself. You promised me you would.'

Grant was by no means done with her yet. 'Have you done anything like that with anyone else?'

Adeline's cheeks flamed with indignation. 'No—and I have told you so.'

He grinned. 'You have? Forgive me if I don't recall.'

'Will you please stop tormenting me about my—slip of propriety?'

His grin widened at her embarrassment, and then he gave a shout of laughter. 'I like reminding you. I like seeing you get all flushed and flustered and hot under the collar.'

She glowered down at him. 'Now you're making fun of me.'

'I know.'

Unable to stay cross with him—knowing he was teasing anyway—Adeline laughed.

Grant lay back beside her, linking his hands behind his head and staring up at the trees. 'You should laugh more often. You have a beautiful laugh.'

Hearing the sensuous huskiness that deepened his voice, Adeline shivered inwardly. 'Thank you—but you are only saying that to placate me.'

'Do you need placating?'

She sighed, tucking her legs beneath her. 'No. I'm having too nice a time to be cross.'

'Good.'

When he closed his eyes, Adeline let her gaze wander over the smooth, thick lock of hair that dipped over his brow, and the authority and arrogance of every line of his darkly handsome face. She let her gaze travel down the full length of the superbly fit, muscled body stretched out beside her. How well she remembered him lying beside her like this once before when, even sleeping, he had exuded a raw, potent virility that had held her in thrall.

As if he could feel her eyes studying him, without opening his eyes, he quirked the mobile line of his mouth in a half-smile. 'I hope you like what you see.' He sighed. 'You can kiss me if you want to, Adeline.'

Adeline's eyes opened wide in astonishment, and then she laughed. Why, the sheer arrogance of the man. 'I most certainly will not,' she objected, slapping him playfully on the chest with her napkin.

Like lightning, he reared up. His hands shot out and

gripped her upper arms, and he pulled her down onto her back, leaning over her. 'If you won't kiss me, do you mind if I kiss you?' His voice was low-pitched and sensual. 'Are you not curious to find out if it will be as good as when I kissed you at Oaklands? When I found you wandering about my house like a beautiful ghost in your nightdress.' A slight smile touched his mouth, but his heavy-lidded gaze dropped to the inviting fullness of her lips, lingering there.

Hypnotised by that velvet voice and those mesmerising silver eyes, Adeline gazed up at him with a combination of fear and excitement. She tried to relax, but in the charged silence between them it was impossible. And then, as quick as he had been to pull her down onto the rug, so she rolled away from him and got to her knees.

Startled, Grant stared at her, annoyed that he was to be deprived of his kiss. 'Now what?'

'I think it's time to go.'

'If there's anything I can't abide it's an obstinate woman.'

'I'm sure you have most women jumping up to do your bidding.'

'As a matter of fact, some of them do. My fatal charm doesn't seem to work with you. I've no idea why.'

'I'm immune.'

His eyes narrowed. 'No, you're not. Do you really think you will escape me so easily?'

'Escape? What a strange term to use, Mr Leighton. Am I your prisoner?'

'No,' he said. 'It is I who am yours.'

She laughed, beginning to put things into the basket. 'How I wish.'

'You are a cruel woman, Miss Osborne,' Grant accused, getting to his feet and brushing down his trousers.

'I am beginning to understand you and your motives.'

'Which are?'

'You are wasting your time if you are looking for an easy conquest. There must be any number of easier prospects.'

'There must?'

'Mmm. I can think of one in particular who is always most willing. Diana Waverley has a habit of collecting men like other people might collect butterflies.'

'She does?'

'You must have noticed. You seem to spend a great deal of time together.'

'I'm sorry if I gave you that impression. We don't. I think you misunderstand me.'

'Oh, no.' She laughed. 'I understand you very well. I have enjoyed our picnic, but I don't attach any significance to it.'

Grant sighed with mock gravity. 'I can see how difficult it will be to convince you that I am attracted to you.'

'Not difficult at all. I told you—I understand perfectly. Now, fold up that rug and we'll get back before it comes on to rain.'

'We can always wait it out under this tree.'

'No.'

He shrugged, reaching for the rug. 'You win.'

'I always do.'

He slanted her a dubious glance. 'This time.'

When they reached Eaton Place, Grant got out of the cab to carry the picnic basket up the steps. He was about to take his leave when a sudden thought occurred to him. 'Do you ride when you're in town?'

'Yes. Often.'

'Early in the morning?'

'It's the best time.'

'I couldn't agree more. I shall be in Hyde Park at six.' Raising a superior brow he met her gaze. 'Will you meet me?'

Despite knowing there would be whispers and raised brows aplenty if she were seen riding alone with him at such an early hour, she nodded, her gaze open and direct. 'Where?'

'At the corner of Park Lane.' He grinned. 'I'll look forward to it.'

When he'd gone Adeline was so confused by what was happening to her that she scarcely noticed she was going into the drawing room. The whole day had been one of shared pleasures—but she told herself that her attraction to Grant Leighton was dangerous, that because of all that had happened between them, and his close association with Diana Waverley, nothing could come of it. It would have to stop. But when she thought of the way he had looked at her with his mesmerising silver-grey eyes, and her traitorous heart reminded her of how it had felt when he had made love to her, she forgot the danger. She told herself it was nothing—that they had been brought together by their mutual concern over Lettie's liaison with Jack Cunningham, and that he probably didn't realise what he was doing.

Chapter Eight

Grant knew exactly what he was doing—and he was already thinking of doing much more. In fact if Jack Cunningham weren't such a swine, he would bless Lettie's liaison with him, since it provided him with an excuse to see Adeline.

After reaching Stanfield House and being informed that Lettie wasn't expected back until much later, he returned to the hotel to change, then went to Boodles to meet with friends and relax and converse over drinks. Two hours later he got up to leave. In the foyer one of the stewards stepped forward with his topper, brushing its brim before handing it to him.

'Thank you, George.'

'You're leaving early tonight, Mr Leighton.'

'I have an appointment.' Grant intended calling at Stanfield House once more, in the hope that Lettie was home.

A man who had just entered paused and looked at him. He had recognised the name immediately. 'Leighton?'

Grant looked at him coolly. 'That's correct. And you are?'

'Cunningham. Jack Cunningham,' he said, puffing on an expensive cigar and sending smoke swirling into the air. 'We have a mutual acquaintance, I believe. Lady Diana Waverley.'

'Yes,' Grant replied without feeling, as if he were addressing a much lesser man. Taller than the other man, Grant neither smiled nor offered his hand. 'Lady Waverley and I are acquainted. I believe you are also acquainted with my sister, Lettie?'

'I do have that pleasure. Lettie and I have become—close.'

Grant's face hardened into an expressionless mask. 'So I gather.'

'Look, I don't know how much Lettie's told you,' Jack said with amazing calm, 'but my intentions towards her are perfectly honourable.'

'I'd like to believe that.' His tone expressed doubt.

The eyes Grant Leighton fixed on Jack with barely concealed dislike were steady, clever, unreflecting, stirring Jack's resentment and an acute discomfort. Holding his cigar in the corner of his mouth, he tapped his cane against the palm of his hand.

His eyes flicked over Lettie's brother. Attired in princely manner—claret tail coat with velvet collar, crisp white shirt, stock and dove-grey trousers—his was an elegance that could neither be bought nor cut into shape by a tailor. Grant Leighton was one of those individuals whose breeding was so obvious it would show itself even if he were clothed in rags.

Jack was overpoweringly aware of the difference between them. He lived by his wits and, in the eyes of the law, on immoral earnings. Whereas Leighton owned land and property on a massive scale, fine carriages, and a house in the country where he would have servants and ride on his land on one of the splendid mounts from the Leighton stable. In fact he had as certain a future as was possible in life.

'In case you have not heard, we are to be neighbours,' Jack said, undaunted by the other man's reserved manner and slightly veiled contempt.

Grant raised an uninterested brow. 'We are?'

'Yes. I am in the process of buying a house very close to Oaklands—Westwood Hall.'

Now Grant was all attention, but he remained guarded. 'Diana is selling Westwood Hall?'

Cunningham nodded, unable to conceal the triumphant gleam from his eyes behind half-lowered lids. When Diana had approached him for a loan he had seen the extent of her debts, and that she would be unable to pay back the money. With Westwood Hall within his sights he had generously given her what she asked for, intending to turn that generosity to his advantage. It was time to call in the debt.

Ever since he had dragged himself out of the East End he had hungered for great wealth and prestige, and he was determined to achieve them by whatever means necessary. A large country house was part of his agenda, along with a compatible lifestyle, and with Lettie—a refined and respected young woman—as his wife, and however many children came their way, his position in society would be established.

'Between you and me, Leighton, Diana's affairs have reached the point of crisis. The bank has foreclosed on her loans—along with an army of money-lenders. With no means of clearing her debts she has no choice but to let the house go. I'm looking forward to living in the country. When I am in residence you must visit.'

'It's finalised?'

'Not quite—but almost. The necessary papers are drawn up. She will sign in the next few days.'

'I see. If you will excuse me, I have an appointment—but there is just one thing you must understand, Cunningham,' Grant said, meeting his gaze directly. 'Your association with my sister is over. You will not attempt to see her again.'

'Or?'

'You will regret it.'

'Me? Oh, no, Leighton. It is you who will regret interfering.' He smiled ruefully. 'Anyone who crosses me is either very brave or very stupid.'

'I have friends in high places and a great deal of power—enough not to be afraid of anything you can do to me.' There was a rough, dangerous edge to Grant's voice, and his eyes were cold.

'Really? I know a great deal more about you than you know about me,' Jack said, smiling with a touch of arrogance.

Grant smiled back, his look hard, as if he also had secret knowledge that amused him.

Jack saw something, and there was a subtle change in his eyes. Leighton was staring at him, and his eyes read far too much. Suddenly he was uncertain. 'I'm curious. *What* do you know about me?'

'Enough. Your association with Lettie has prompted me to find out all about you, and I don't like who you are or what you are. As to your intentions—or should I say pretensions—if it is your intention to offer marriage to my sister, forget it. It won't happen.'

On those words Grant left the club. He was deeply troubled. He'd disliked Jack Cunningham on sight—the man was as appalling as he'd imagined he would be—and the sooner he saw Lettie and told her to end the affair the better he would feel. But first he must see Diana, and find out what the hell she was playing at.

'I want your advice about something,' Lettie said, when she called on Adeline that same evening.

When Adeline had met Lettie in the hall she'd seemed agitated and troubled in spirit, and this was confirmed now Adeline saw her in the gaslight of the drawing room. She looked wan and tired, and all manner of forebodings began to trouble Adeline. Perhaps Lettie needed someone to talk to? The thought expelled her practicality and provoked her at once to force the issue.

'Lettie,' she said, drawing her down beside her on the sofa and facing her, 'you want more than advice. You want help.

Please tell me what I can do. Anything. I cannot bear to see you like this.'

Lettie was distraught as well as feeling wretched. She was also annoyed with herself that her feelings were so clear, and yet she wanted to share them with Adeline. There was a need in her not to be alone in her distress. When she spoke her voice was low, but steady. 'I want to tell you something that I know will shock you. Something has happened, Adeline, and I need your particular brand of common sense to tell me what to do. Even if it's to throw myself into the River Thames.'

'That's unlikely to solve anything, Lettie,' Adeline said, trying to keep her manner calm and casual. 'Tell me what it is.'

Lettie swallowed hard, and was obviously close to tears. 'It's quite dreadful. I warn you it may be the last time you will ever want to speak to me.'

Adeline knew, even before Lettie told her, that it had something to do with Jack Cunningham. Lines of dread creased her forehead and she felt wretched. 'Don't be silly, Lettie. You do exaggerate. Of course I will. Please tell me what is the matter and let me help you.'

White-lipped, Lettie reached out and gripped Adeline's hands tight. 'Oh, Adeline,' she whispered. 'I—I am pregnant. I am going to have Jack's baby.'

Adeline stared at her in blank astonishment. Continuing to hold Lettie's hands, she sat for a moment, trying to bring order out of the chaos of speculation and shock that choked her mind. She thought for a hysterical instant that she was making some silly joke. Then she saw the truth in her eyes and knew that she meant it.

'Oh, I see.' Realising that she must handle this terrible situation with the greatest delicacy, she said, 'How long have you known?'

'I—I've suspected I might be for several weeks,' Lettie

whispered, the expression of anguish on her face beginning to fade a little now it was out in the open.

'And you are certain of this?'

She nodded. Tears like fat raindrops began to slide down her cheeks. 'A—a doctor has confirmed it—this morning. I had to come to you, Adeline. There is no one else I can talk to about this—no one but you.'

Adeline's heart melted with pity at the sight of Lettie's desolation. 'Oh, Lettie, thank goodness you did come to me. But why have you kept this to yourself? If you have known about your condition for some time, then you must have known when we went to the Phoenix.'

'I did—but things have changed since then.'

'How?'

'I can't tell you that—not now, Adeline.'

'What—what about Jack? Have you told him?'

Lettie nodded. 'He—he's delighted.'

These words were spoken with so much bitterness it bemused Adeline. 'What man wouldn't be on being told he's to become a father? But there's more to this, isn't there, Lettie? If there weren't you wouldn't be so upset. Has—has Jack hurt you in some way—said something? Has—has he not asked you to marry him?'

Lettie glared at her fiercely. 'Marry him? Of course he wants to marry me—the bastard,' she hissed. 'I wouldn't marry him, Adeline—not ever. Oh, at first what we had was fun—but I didn't know him then, what he was really like. Now I do know—I know everything—and I want nothing more to do with him. Now he wants to control me, to bend me to his will—to own me.'

'But what on earth has he done that has brought about this change in you?'

Lettie gulped on her tears. 'Enough. His crimes—his appetite for money and his methods of achieving it—I can't be part of that. But there's more—much more—and it's got nothing to do with any of that. It's far more horrible.'

Suddenly a suspicion occurred to Adeline. 'Has it anything to do with that woman you spoke to outside the Phoenix Club?'

She nodded. 'Yes,' she whispered, her voice barely audible. 'That woman was Jack's sister. I've seen her again since. She—she's told me things—things I can't bring myself to speak about. It's—it's too awful—brutal and cruel. I want no part of him. I don't want Jack Cunningham's baby.' She put her hands to her face. Any reserve she had left disappeared, and she began to cry dementedly. 'Oh, Adeline, I must get rid of it—I have to. I can't bear the thought of bringing a child of his into the world. I will kill myself first.'

Adeline stared at her in appalled silence. What Lettie said was more shocking than her sheltered mind could imagine. Fiercely she took the wretched woman's shivering body in her arms and held her until she was all cried out.

Pulling herself away from Adeline, as though she must finish her tale of horror, Lettie put her face into her hands with shame. 'I—I know someone who knows a doctor who will do it. He—he's fully qualified—in open practice—so it will be quite safe. I have been assured it will be no brutal kitchen surgery of a back street abortionist.'

What Lettie was saying was impossible—too hideous for Adeline's mind to grasp. Absolutely horrified, she reached out and gripped Lettie's arms, forcing her to look at her, unaware that her own cheeks were wet with tears of pity and compassion for her friend. 'Lettie. Lettie, my dear, dear friend, listen to me.' Lettie looked at her, and the pain in her eyes was frightening. 'You must promise me that you will not do that. It is wrong—so very, very wrong—and you could die. I will help you, I swear I will, but you must not abort your child. Oh, dear God, Lettie, I cannot bear the thought of it.'

'But I am desperate, Adeline—and in these matters I find

myself as ignorant as the most wretched servant girl. The option of an abortion is more acceptable than an unwanted pregnancy—than bearing his child.'

Adeline regarded everything that Lettie said with particular horror. 'Lettie, this is a baby you are talking about. A *baby*.'

'It isn't,' she said fiercely. 'I can't think of it as that. It's a monster, and I want to tear it out of me with my bare hands.' In desperation she looked around the room. She made a vague gesture. 'If only there was some medicine—quinine, or mercury, or some such thing—something I could take.'

'No, Lettie. There isn't—and anyway I won't let you.'

Lettie bowed her head. 'How can I tell my mother? Have you any idea what this will do to her? Can you tell me that—and Grant? He'll kill me. I'm not proud of myself. I—could kill myself,' she said quietly to herself.

'Lettie Leighton! Don't you dare talk like that. Please. You terrify me. You will find a way to get through this. I'll help you. Now it's happened you must brave it out.'

'I don't know how I can do that.'

'You will, Lettie. Don't be afraid. Now,' she said, standing up, 'I think the sensible thing for you to do is to stay here tonight. I'll have Mrs Kelsall prepare a room, and I'll send word to Lady Stanfield so that she doesn't worry.'

Lettie stood up quickly. 'No, I must go back. The carriage is outside.' She gave Adeline a wobbly smile. 'Don't worry about me. Now that I've told you I do feel a bit better. I'll plead a headache and have an early night.' Lettie looked into Adeline's eyes and wondered for a moment how they could be so warm and loving after she had listened to the shocking and unbelievable things she had just heard. 'I'm sorry to burden you with this. Do you hate me, Adeline?'

'Hate you?' Adeline placed a comforting hand against Lettie's tear-drenched cheek. 'You must never think that, Lettie. Ever. Our friendship is as steadfast now as it has ever been—undiminished by the knowledge of what Jack Cunningham has done to you. We have to work out what is to be done—and we will do that together.'

Taking Lettie's hand, Adeline accompanied her out into the empty hall, where she put her arms about her and hugged her, then kissed her on the cheek. 'Come and see me in the morning, Lettie—and promise me you won't do anything rash.'

'I promise,' she said huskily. 'I know I can trust you not to speak of this to anyone, Adeline.'

Adeline opened the door to find a light mist had settled over the street. It smelled of soot. Streetlights along the pavement made small pools of ragged light. She watched Lettie walk steadily towards the carriage, her back straight, her head held high, and was suddenly struck by the clamped expression of determination on her face. She looked as though walking across the pavement to the carriage was a goal of such enormity and distance it would take all her strength to reach it.

As Adeline brooded over Lettie's sickening plight—for sickening it was to anyone who knew Lettie—she felt more and more depressed, and so concerned for her friend that she was unable to sleep or concentrate on anything else. It had been bad enough when Lettie had told her she was seeing Jack Cunningham, but this was a situation of such magnitude she didn't know how to deal with it.

Lettie had come to her in an act of trust, so one thing she did decide on was not to confide in Grant. She would support and help Lettie in any way she could, but it was up to Lettie to tell her family, when she felt ready and strong enough to do that. But what on earth could have happened to turn Lettie against Jack Cunningham in the space of forty-eight hours?

She remembered she had promised Grant she would ride with him at six in the morning, and as much as she wanted to see him she wished she hadn't. It would be awkward being in his company, knowing what she did about Lettie.

* * *

Daylight had broken when Adeline trotted towards Hyde Park. The sky was dull and overcast, threatening rain later, but it didn't dampen her spirits for the ride. On reaching the corner of Park Lane she felt a thrill of delight to find Grant already waiting for her, mounted on a tall bay gelding, his muscular thighs clamped to the horse's sides.

She was attired in a green velvet riding habit the same colour as her eyes, which fitted her slender form like a glove, with the heavy mass of her hair anchored beneath a jaunty matching hat. Grant watched her ride towards him, feeling a familiar quickening in his veins. He wasn't surprised to see she was riding side-saddle, with no sign of breeches beneath her habit. No doubt when she was in town she felt she had to bow to protocol rather than risk a scandal by riding astride and wearing men's breeches. The bay shifted restlessly and he tightened his hands on the reins.

Telling her accompanying groom to wait for her, Adeline joined Grant. He was hatless, and wearing a conventional frock coat, light trousers and tan riding boots. His gaze was unnervingly acute.

'Good morning,' he greeted her. Noting how pale and strained her face was, and the purple smudges beneath her eyes, he frowned. Narrowing his eyes, he locked them on hers. 'Is everything all right?'

'Yes, everything's fine,' she replied, forcing a smile to her lips and looking away to avoid his searching gaze. 'I'm just a bit tired, that's all. I didn't sleep very well.'

'Then perhaps a ride to clear your head is just what you need.'

'I hope so.' In no mood for conversation, she gestured towards the park, eager to get on. 'Shall we go?'

'We'll head for the Row. The track will have been prepared for galloping.'

The park was deserted as they rode over the soft green turf.

'Does your father ride when he's in town,' Grant asked, for something to say to break the silence between them.

'No. Riding is not one of his interests.'

'Unlike his daughter. I'm surprised he's allowing you to spend so much time in town alone.'

'So am I. He's not usually so amiable. When Lettie wrote asking me to come to London I was amazed at how easy it was for me to persuade him.'

'Maybe it was because he has invited my mother to spend a few days at Rosehill.'

Adeline looked at him in amazement. 'He has?'

Grant nodded.

'When?'

'About now.'

'Goodness! I had no idea. And I do find it rather odd. Whenever he's expecting guests he always needs me to take care of everything.'

'I'm sure you have a perfectly capable housekeeper to do that. And besides, maybe he wanted to have my mother to himself.'

Adeline looked at him sharply. 'And are you happy with that? At Oaklands you gave me the impression that you did not approve of them becoming *too* friendly.'

'I've changed my mind. If my mother is happy, then I shall be happy for her.'

Having reached the track, both horses tossed their heads, tugging at the reins, eager for a run. They let them go. With the heavy pounding of horses' hooves beneath them they rode neck and neck, flying past St George's hospital and the statue of the Duke of Wellington behind the trees. The sky was peppered with waking birds, but the two riders were too preoccupied with their ride even to notice them. Adeline was exhilarated. The blood flowed fast in her veins, her heart pounded and her skin tingled, and for a while the burden of Lettie's situation was lifted. Grant was right. The ride was just what she needed.

Grant gave his horse a flick with his crop, urging him to a faster pace and pulling away from Adeline by a couple of lengths. Looking back, his hair dishevelled, his coat flapping behind him and his bent arms moving up and down like birds' wings, he grinned back at her and she laughed at him, her teeth gleaming white in her rosy face.

'I'll catch you,' she shouted. 'I swear I will.'

'How much would you like to bet? A kiss?'

The redness in her cheeks deepened, but, goaded by the mocking amusement in his voice, she snatched up the gauntlet of the challenge. 'Done.'

But it was no good. With the promise of a kiss at the end of the race, Grant showed no sign of slowing down—not until they neared the end of the track and he eased his horse to a canter, beating Adeline by a length. Knowing she was beaten, and would have to suffer the consequences, Adeline dropped her horse to a walk and went towards where he was waiting.

Waiting in anticipation for her to offer him her lips, Grant couldn't take his eyes off her. The ride had tinted her face a delicate pink, and he knew that when he touched her mouth he would feel the warmth of her blood coursing beneath her flesh.

'I won,' he declared.

'That's hardly fair. You were already well ahead when you issued the challenge.'

'And that's a feeble excuse if ever I heard one, Miss Osborne. Are you reneging on our wager?'

'No,' she replied, eyeing him warily.

'I'm glad to hear it.' Turning his head, he looked towards a group of trees, smiled wickedly, and then looked back at her with narrowed eyes.

'Prepare to pay your forfeit, Miss Osborne. Pray follow me. When I claim my reward I have no wish to have the whole of London gawping at me.'

On reaching the seclusion of the trees, knowing there was

no escape, with a pounding heart Adeline nudged her horse close to his, intending to give him nothing more than a peck on the cheek. But she should have known that Grant Leighton would be satisfied with nothing less than a full-blown kiss.

He leaned across to her, and instead of drawing away she shyly met him halfway. With his face just two inches from hers, for a moment his eyes held hers, and then, taking her chin gently in his fingers, he let his gaze drop to her lips. Gradually his head moved closer and his lips brushed hers, undemanding, caressing tenderly, as if testing her resilience. Then with the confidence of a sure welcome they settled over hers, becoming firm as he turned his considerable talents to savouring their luscious softness.

The contact was like an exquisite explosion somewhere deep inside Adeline. The kiss deepened, and her lips were moulded and sensually shaped to his. She felt that kiss in every inch of her body. In response, warm heat ignited and radiated through her flesh. Jolt after jolt of wild, familiar sensation pulsated through her. He parted her lips, his tongue teasing and tormenting, sinking into the haven of sweetness and claiming it for his own.

The kiss ended when Grant's horse shifted slightly and they were forced to draw apart. Adeline gazed at his face, at the harsh set lines, seeing the evidence of desire ruthlessly controlled. She wasn't ignorant of his state—had she not seen it once before? Almost kissed into insensibility, she watched his smouldering gaze lift from her lips to her eyes, and then his firm lips curved in a smile and he drew back.

'If we don't stop now I swear I will dismount, drag you from your horse and into those bushes and make love to you—which I have wanted to do ever since our first encounter—to discover what I missed, you understand. So, while I would like to experience more, I will press you no further. The time is not right. Others will soon be arriving in the park and I fear we will be caught out. I live in hope that there will be other times when I will hold you closer and for much longer, Adeline. But now we'll ride at a leisurely pace back down the track, and I shall hand you over to your groom.'

'When will you see Lettie?' Adeline dared to ask, not looking at him lest he saw the guilty secret in her eyes.

'I shall return to the hotel and have breakfast, and then I intend calling on her before she disappears to one of her meetings.'

Not until she had left him and was riding back to Eaton Place did what he had said hit Adeline—he intended further intimacies in the future to satiate his desire. Her face burned. How could she have forgotten that only the day before last she had vowed not to become one of his flirtations? How could she have forgotten how utterly amoral he was, and how supremely conceited?

But his kiss, the feel of his lips on hers, the way her body had reacted, the sensations she had felt, made her want, yearn, for what she knew he could give her.

When Lettie didn't call at Eaton Place that same morning, Adeline, deeply concerned about her, and wondering how her meeting had gone with Grant, went to Upper Belgrave Street—only to be told by Lady Stanfield that Lettie was visiting a sick friend and wasn't expected back until evening. When Adeline asked if Grant had called to see his sister earlier in the day, she was disappointed and angry to be told he hadn't.

After spending some time with Marjorie, talking about her impending engagement party, for which preparations were going on in earnest, still feeling tense and upset because she hadn't seen Lettie, Adeline returned home. She felt as though she were sitting on a volcano, and in awful suspense as she waited for something to happen.

It was shortly after nine o'clock when a cab arrived at the

house with Lettie. Mrs Kelsall opened the door to her, and Adeline met her in the hall.

Lettie just stood and stared at Adeline. She looked ghastly—like death. Her face was as white as parchment, her eyes leaden and as colourless as the sea on a dull day. After a moment, as if she couldn't bear to look at Adeline any longer, she hung her head as though in the deepest shame.

That was the moment Adeline knew what she had done. Something inside her lurched in terror. Why, she didn't know, for surely the worst had happened? Nausea rose in her throat. Oh, dear, sweet Jesus, her mind whispered, what had they done to her? Concern for her friend came to the fore and propelled her across the floor.

'Lettie,' she whispered, taking her cold, trembling hand and placing her arm about her shoulders.

Mrs Kelsall hovered and stared, not knowing what to do. Adeline looked at her. 'As you can see, Mrs Kelsall, Miss Leighton isn't well. Prepare a room for her, will you? And have someone go to Lady Stanfield and inform her that she is staying here with me tonight. Tell her she is not to worry. Some tea would be welcome. We'll be in the drawing room.' She turned her attention to Lettie. 'Come, Lettie. Come and sit by the fire, and when Mrs Kelsall has prepared a room I'll take you upstairs.'

Lettie's movements were wooden as she let Adeline lead her into the drawing room and sit her in a chair close to the fire, where she began to tremble uncontrollably. One of the maids brought in a tray of tea things. Adeline poured, and held a cup to Lettie's frozen lips. But she shook her head and turned it away. Kneeling beside her, Adeline took her hand where it lay in her lap.

'Lettie, please speak to me. I know what you've done— and, oh, my dear, I am not angry, but I *am* concerned. Are you in pain?'

Swallowing hard, Lettie nodded, her eyes swimming with tears. Her lips moved in reply, but Adeline could not catch what she said.

'What is it, Lettie?' she asked, leaning closer. 'What did you say?'

This time she did hear the words.

'The baby…' Lettie's throat was so tight the words were forced out.

Trying to keep her voice from shattering with the sorrow she felt, Adeline drew a long breath and said, 'I'm really sorry you had to resort to this, Lettie. I really am.' Her eyes, too, filled with tears, and all she could do was hold Lettie's hand tighter.

'Please forgive me, Adeline,' she whispered.

'It is not for me to forgive,' Adeline answered quietly. 'Everything's going to be all right. Don't worry any more. But you look most ill, Lettie. I must send for a doctor to take a look at you.'

Lettie's look was frantic, and she gripped Adeline's hand with remarkable strength. 'No—please—please no,' she whispered raggedly. 'It's a doctor who did this to me. No more, Adeline. No more. I can't take it. It's done—over—and I thank God for the release.'

The door opened and Mrs Kelsall appeared. 'The room is ready, Miss Adeline. The fire is lit.'

'Thank you, Mrs Kelsall. I'll take Lettie up.'

'Can I—be of help?'

'Thank you, but I think we can manage.'

Somehow Adeline managed to get Lettie up the stairs and into the bedroom where, like a child, she let Adeline and Emma undress her and put her in one of Adeline's nightgowns of fine embroidered cambric. After unpinning Lettie's hair and sponging her face, Adeline laid her in the bed. Immediately Lettie lay on her side, with her back to Adeline. Closing her eyes, she drew her knees up to her chest and began to whimper.

Telling Emma she could manage, and sending her to bed, Adeline sat beside the bed and began a silent vigil, hoping and praying that Lettie was going to be all right. She was breathing heavily, and sweat stood out on her skin.

The pain got worse during the night, and she began complaining of the heat and throwing off the covers. Becoming more and more concerned, Adeline touched Lettie's head, then wrung out a cloth in a dish of water and placed it on her brow. After another couple of hours Lettie began shivering and moaning, almost senseless, tossing her head from side to side, her fingers plucking at the bedcovers.

That was when Adeline, in desperation, wrote a note to Grant. She sent one of the servants with it in the carriage, to the Charing Cross Hotel, asking him to come immediately and—even though she knew Lettie would reproach her for it—to bring a doctor.

Accompanied by another man carrying a leather bag, Grant came quickly, and saw the anguish full on the white oval of Adeline's face. She stared at him. Tension weighed heavily on his spirit.

'Adeline,' Grant said when the drawing room door had closed. 'Are you all right?' Placing a gentle finger under her chin, he compelled her to meet his gaze, having to restrain himself from taking her in his arms. Her lovely colour had gone and her eyes were haunted. 'What is it? Tell me.'

'Oh, Grant—it's Lettie.'

There was no way to tell him except with the simple truth. And in the next few minutes she told him what Lettie had done. The one thing she failed to tell him was that the decision to abort her child had been Lettie's alone.

In disbelief Grant listened in stunned silence to every word she uttered. In all his life he had never been immobilised by any emotion or any event. The worse the pressure the more energised he became. Now, however, he stared at Adeline as if unable to absorb what she had told him. His lips tightened to a thin line, then he grimaced with suppressed anger.

When she had finished speaking, drawing a long, steadying breath, Adeline looked at him and waited for him to speak.

Pain and anger blazed through Grant's brain like hot brands as he envisaged Lettie facing her ordeal alone. 'Ever since you told me Lettie was seeing Cunningham I thought that with one word from me she would stop. I never imagined I would have to deal with anything like this.' He turned to the man hovering behind him—a middle-aged man, his face creased in lines of grave concern.

'Adeline, this is a friend of mine—Howard Lennox. He is a doctor and will examine Lettie. I know we can be assured of his absolute discretion.'

Howard stepped forward. 'As you know, Grant,' he said in a brusque, businesslike manner, 'I am reluctant to make common gossip of my patients' private health matters. Not even among friends. Miss Osborne, I am happy to be of assistance in any way I can. Will you take me to Miss Leighton? In cases such as this I doubt there is much I can do, but we shall see.' He looked at Grant. 'Wait here, Grant, until I've examined her.'

Left alone, Grant stood for a second to try and calm himself—for the thought of Lettie at the hands of Jack Cunningham and the doctor he had employed to perform an illegal, life-threatening abortion on her was almost more than he could bear. He was certain that Lettie would never have done anything like this without being forced into it. Unable to control all his confused emotions—anger, hatred, bitterness, love for Lettie and the soul-destroying feeling that he had failed her— he knew his rage was so red he wanted to shout, to snarl, to hit someone, to kill someone. Peferably Jack Cunningham. But he must pull himself together before he saw Lettie.

Having woken Emma and left her to sit with Lettie, who

was now quiet and seemed to be sleeping, Adeline returned to the drawing room with Dr Lennox and poured both men a good measure of much-needed brandy.

'How is she?' Grant asked, feeling he was holding onto reality by the merest thread.

Howard shook his head, then tipped his glass and swallowed the brandy in one gulp, shaking his head when Adeline offered him another. 'I have to say she is very ill.'

'She must not die,' Adeline whispered.

'Do not upset yourself, Miss Osborne. While there's life there is hope.' He looked at Grant. 'Some infection has set in, and her temperature is high. She is also in deep shock. But she is your sister, Grant. She's strong, and I believe she will pull through this.'

'Dear God, let us pray that she does.' His set features relaxed, his relief evident.

'I've examined her as best I can. There is some comfort in the fact that the operation was performed by a doctor,' Howard said. 'Some doctors can be found who *will* perform abortions—although they extract a high price.'

'That wouldn't be a problem for Cunningham,' Grant growled. 'But I am of the opinion that the doctor who did this to Lettie owed Cunningham. This doctor would have had no option but to submit to illegal practice.'

'That is a matter of opinion, Grant. Abortion is legal if performed by a doctor. You have made enquiries into Cunningham's background?'

Grant nodded. 'Cunningham controls a hierarchy of individuals who owe him—ranging from beggars at the bottom to specialised lawyers at the top. A quiet word and almost anything can be accomplished. What do you advise we do with Lettie?'

'Well, for the time being she shouldn't be moved.'

'That's not a problem,' Adeline was quick to say, dismayed

that Grant had jumped to the wrong conclusion and was blaming Jack Cunningham for Lettie's condition. But she would wait until Dr Lennox had left before she told him he was mistaken. 'She can stay here for as long as necessary. I'll look after her.'

Grant looked at her gratefully. 'Thank you, Adeline. Hopefully it won't be for too long.'

'Lettie must have been desperate—she must have seen her future as precarious to have done what she did,' Howard remarked. 'Her recovery will take time, and she will require patience and understanding as she comes to terms with what she has done and tries to rebuild her life.' Carrying his bag, he crossed to the door, where he turned and looked back at Grant. 'I understand you're leaving London for the continent shortly, Grant?'

'I am—in a few days, as a matter of fact.'

'Business?'

He shrugged somewhat wearily. 'What else? I expect to be away for several weeks.'

'I'll return in the morning to take another look at Lettie. But if you need me in the meantime you know where to find me.'

Chapter Nine

When Dr Lennox had taken his leave of them Adeline moved to stand close to Grant. His dark head was slightly bent as he contemplated the glowing embers in the hearth, his foot upon the fender. Beneath his coat his muscles flexed as he withdrew his right hand from his pocket and shoved his fingers through his hair—which, as Adeline had discovered, had an inclination to curl when he combed his fingers through its brushed smoothness.

'Would you like to go up and see Lettie now?' she asked softly.

Grant turned and looked at her, fear tightening his eyes. He nodded. 'Yes, I would.'

When Adeline opened the door to Lettie's room Emma rose from her seat beside the bed and quietly went out. Along with every other servant in the house she knew something dreadful had happened to Miss Adeline's friend—how could she not when her arrival, followed so quickly by her brother with a doctor, had caused such a commotion? They were all agog with curiosity, although so far Miss Adeline was saying nothing. But Emma, more worldly than her mistress, was no fool, and, having undressed Miss Leighton and seen the state she was in, had already reached her own conclusions.

Grant moved towards the bed. The tightly huddled woman, impervious to everything that was going on around her, did not resemble his sister. He would have said so, but the hair draped over the pillow, the familiar curve of her cheek, brought back memories of the vital, laughing face. Her eyes were tightly closed, the lashes forming shadowed crescents on her cheeks. She lay in a stupor partly induced by the heavy draught of laudanum Howard had administered.

Bending over, he gently touched her cheek. 'How did she come to this?' he murmured. 'I blame myself. I should have made more of an effort to see her.'

'It's too late to worry about that now,' Adeline whispered, silently wishing he had. If so this wretched catastrophe might have been averted. 'What's done is done.'

Standing upright, Grant moved away from the bed and turned his gaze to Adeline's face. If he hadn't been so anxious about Lettie he would have smiled as he wondered how Adeline had come by her prim and practical streak. Although there was nothing prim about those full, soft, generous lips and the compassionate, caring look in her green eyes, looking darker than usual in the dimmed gaslight.

'Dr Lennox gave Lettie some laudanum to rest her, and some other medication,' Adeline told him. 'She should sleep for a while. I'll ask Emma to sit with her, and when she goes to bed I'll stay with Lettie. I cannot rest while she is so ill.' She looked at Grant. 'Will you stay?'

'I'd very much like to.'

'Then I'll have a room prepared.'

'That won't be necessary. Sleep is the last thing on my mind right now.'

'Then we'll watch over her together.'

Leaving Emma to sit with Lettie a while longer, they

returned to the drawing room. Without saying a word, with his hands shoved into his trouser pockets and his eyes hardened into slits of concentration, Grant stood staring into the hearth, listening to the sharp tick of the ormolu clock on the mantelpiece and watching the flames of the rejuvenated fire licking and dancing. He wasn't aware of Adeline standing close until he felt the pressure of her hand on his arm. Turning, he saw her eyes were anxious and suffering.

'When Lettie arrived here tonight, did she say much to you?'

'No. She was in no fit state. What will you do?' she asked quietly.

'I am a shrewd man, Adeline. All my business life I have looked men straight in the eye as they tried to convince me that black is white and vice versa. And though Cunningham is a clever and devious black-hearted villain, it will take a better man than him to hurt any of mine.'

'Are you saying you are looking for vengeance?'

'You're damn right I am. If that bastard thinks he can get away with near murder he's damn well mistaken.'

'You can't,' Adeline whispered. 'One thing Lettie did tell me is that what she did was her decision alone. He wanted the baby and I suspect he has no idea what she has done.'

Grant was incredulous. 'Dear God, Adeline—are you saying that Lettie aborted her own child?'

'Yes. I— I don't know what Jack Cunningham has done to Lettie—it must be something quite dreadful to have made her want to do what she did—but all of a sudden she hates him with an intensity I was shocked to see.'

'If he's laid one finger on my sister in violence I swear I'll kill him. I might do that anyway.'

'Don't you see, Grant? Vengeance is a private sin to repair damaged pride. Try not to reduce this to a question of marksmanship. Lettie wouldn't want you to do that. Aside from the fact that the crime has been committed by the doctor who—

who—did what he did, and Jack Cunningham for getting her pregnant, there is only one other person who is responsible for Lettie being in the situation she is.'

. His shoulders tensed, Grant turned his head slowly and looked at her for a long time. 'Who?'

'Lettie herself.' Adeline stopped short, seeing those silver-grey eyes flare. Then she went on firmly. 'She went with Jack Cunningham of her own free will. She found him terribly exciting and fun to be with, and she was attracted to him from the start—she admitted as much to me. It's just one of the realities of human nature, I suppose.'

'You and Lettie must have had some interesting conversations,' Grant retorted, unable to calm his anger.

'We have. Plenty. That particular snare—sexual attraction—has kept the human race alive since time immemorial, so Lettie cannot be condemned for that. She probably loved Jack Cunningham in her own way—misplaced as that love was. She told me he had proposed marriage and she'd refused. The decision to abort her baby was hers.'

Grant's eyes glittered like glass. 'Are you telling me I should simply let that low-down bastard off scot-free?'

Adeline swallowed hard as she courageously faced him, seeing the rage and the steel inside him. 'Yes. I think you should consider long and hard before you tear open issues of which you do not know the nature or the extent.'

'I do not think you appreciate the gravity of the situation, Adeline. This is not some Society parlour game. Lettie's well-being is at stake. Cunningham deserves no such consideration.'

'It doesn't matter. What does matter is that you don't create a scandal over this that will sink Lettie for ever.' The way Grant was looking at her sent a chill of fear through her. But she went on bravely. 'Dr Lennox doesn't think Lettie is going to die, Grant.' She looked up at him. 'It is to her mind and heart that the damage lies. You said it would take a better man than

Jack Cunningham to hurt any of your family. You would be a bigger and better man if you could put this behind you. As far as Lettie is concerned the whole sorry business is over.'

'I will not let it pass. I would not be Lettie's brother if I did that.'

'What you will tell your mother and everyone else is up to you. But for now Lettie is going to need you. She is going to need both of us over the coming days.'

He nodded, accepting the sense of this. 'I shall do nothing at all—at least until we know Lettie is out of danger. The less everyone knows about this unsavoury mess the better. But one thing is certain. Cunningham needn't come looking for her after this.'

'He will. He still thinks she is with child—his child, don't forget—in which case he will think he has some claim on her.'

Grant's eyes narrowed as he looked at her curiously. 'How can you know so much? I thought you said Lettie was in no fit state to—' Grant began, and then the enormity of what she had said sank in. He felt the blood draining from his face, and his eyes, full of accusation, slid towards Adeline, trapping her in their burning gaze. 'You also said the decision to go through with this was hers, so some conversation must have taken place between the two of you when she arrived— a great deal, in fact.'

His gaze raked Adeline's guilt-stricken face, and she watched in agony as his eyes registered first disbelief and then anger— an anger so deep that all the muscles in his face tightened into a mask of fury.

Adeline stared at him and seemed confused, which further heightened his anger. 'Grant, let me explain—'

'You already knew, didn't you?' he demanded. 'You already knew Lettie was pregnant.' Anger began to gather like a hard ball somewhere in the vicinity of Grant's stomach. 'When Lettie recovers I'll find out the truth from her—but that does not excuse you from not telling me.'

'It—it was what Lettie wanted. I thought it was for the best at the time—'

'*You* thought it was for the best? Since when were *you* an authority on what is best for Lettie?' he said, cutting her off, passion making his voice shake. 'You *knew*. You knew when we met this morning. We were together a whole hour and you said nothing. You had no right to keep a matter as important as this from me.'

'I knew, yes—but Lettie had promised me she wouldn't do anything,' Adeline said, coming to her own defence. Forcing herself to keep calm, she spoke in a controlled voice. 'The last forty-eight hours since Lettie told me of her affair with Jack Cunningham haven't been easy. In fact they have been very difficult indeed. Lettie promised me she would do nothing drastic, Grant, and I believed her.'

'But she did mention getting rid of it, didn't she?'

'Yes—but—'

'Adeline, don't you see?' he flared accusingly, his emotions storming inside him, his composure in shreds. 'Had I known about any of this I could have stopped her. She wouldn't be in the state she's in now.'

'I don't believe that. Looking back, I realise that when she came to see me she had already made up her mind to go ahead with it.'

'And you really believe that, do you? Well, I don't. Lettie would never have done this appalling thing had she not been forced into it by what Cunningham did to her.'

Adeline had to summon all her patience to stop herself bursting out in a fury. Grant's inquisitorial, aggressive manner angered her beyond belief. He was playing the part of the injured party a little too well—demanding explanations without the slightest trace of consideration.

'At least she is safe, and Dr Lennox says she should recover. We must be thankful for that.'

'Safe, yes—no thanks to you,' he snapped unfairly.

It was as if he had thrown a bucket of icy water over her. 'That's a dreadful thing to say to me, Grant. It isn't due to me.'

'The facts speak for themselves, Adeline.'

The injustice of his accusation brought an angry flush to her face and she looked as maddened as him. 'When Lettie came to me she wanted to confide in someone she could trust. I broke that trust when I sought you out at your hotel after the first time she came to speak to me in confidence. I wasn't prepared to do that again,' she told him, throwing back her head indignantly. 'I did the best I could to prevent Lettie going ahead with aborting her child, and now you storm at me for not telling you. When I left you after our ride, I truly thought you would go and see her—as you said you would—and that she might tell you herself. Clearly you had other matters to attend to that were more important.'

'That was my intention. But when I returned to the hotel, D—' He stopped himself from mentioning Diana's name, knowing how it never failed to kindle Adeline's ire, but it was too late.

Drawing herself up, Adeline looked at him sharply, knowingly, and nodded. 'But Diana Waverley turned up?' she uttered scornfully. 'Don't bother to explain, Grant. I'm not interested. If your affair with Diana took precedence over Lettie's troubles it has got nothing whatsoever to do with me.'

'God in heaven—there *is* no affair between Diana and me,' he gritted coldly.

'No? You certainly behave as if there is—and anyway, I don't believe you. Still, how you spend your time is up to you. However, that woman has done enough damage to my life, so kindly refrain from speaking of her again in my presence. Perhaps now you will realise how serious I considered Lettie's situation to be. I truly thought you would go out of your way to do something about it. I was relying on you—fool that I was.'

'You still had no right to keep it from me.'

Slowly Adeline moved closer, and her eyes met Grant's proudly, with a look as cutting as steel. 'How dare you? How dare you put me in the wrong? How dare you transfer the blame to me to ease your own conscience? That seems a nice, easy way out of a difficult situation—a coward's way out. I would not have believed it of you, Grant.'

Grant's tone was haughty, his eyes like shards of ice. He seemed bent on regaining the advantage. 'I think you've said enough. Who do you think you are, to meddle in my family's affairs?'

'Lettie's friend,' Adeline stated coldly. 'But since you think I am interfering, then I must admit I am not entertained by your family disputes.'

'In which case I shall have Lettie removed from this house first thing in the morning.'

'You are right,' she flared, her eyes blazing. 'What happens to Lettie concerns you alone. I shall leave you to decide what to do with her. Do whatever you feel must be done, but remember that it will be against Dr Lennox's advice. Meanwhile, while she is in this house, I shall tend her. Do you have any objections to that?'

They faced one another, not speaking, their fury bouncing off each other. Adeline thought bitterly that she had never imagined the night would end like this. Her defiance had struck him to the quick of his being. Now they would simply set about destroying each other as ferociously as mortal enemies. Was it for *this* that she had befriended Lettie when she'd needed her most?

'I would be grateful,' he said curtly.

'Thank you,' Adeline said, with all the dignity she could muster. 'And now, since you can do nothing but insult me, and will clearly have no need of my assistance in nursing Lettie after tomorrow, I think you had better leave,' she said icily. 'If she should wake and find you like this it will only upset her.'

'You are right. I have changed my mind about staying the night. I can see Lettie will be in capable hands.' He crossed to the door, where he turned and looked back at her. There was a deep anger inside him. 'No matter what it costs, I cannot ignore what Cunningham has done. I do not underestimate his intelligence or his will for a moment, but they are irrelevant. It does not make me reconsider anything—only makes me more resolute. Now, if you will excuse me, I shall be at my hotel if I am needed.'

Adeline watched him go. There was no word of affection, just a cold nod as he closed the door. She stood staring at it for a long time, deeply hurt by what had just occurred. The man was a monster. It was not her fault, what had happened to Lettie, but Grant would never be convinced of this, and the tender feelings that had grown between them when they had fenced and ridden together died as a sudden frost withered a young plant.

Perhaps the kiss he had given her, having won the race, had meant nothing at all—had been nothing more than a pleasure satisfied? Anger stirred once more in Adeline—anger at herself for so readily succumbing to the embrace of this hard, cold man who had invited her love after the aggressive nature of their past encounters.

Drawing herself up proudly, she went to relieve Emma. She, too, could be hard and cold. Grant would never know how much he had hurt her. I won't let him treat me like that again, she vowed, staring down at his sleeping sister and settling herself into the chair beside the bed. Adeline the vulnerable fool, ready to give her heart to the first man to hold her in his arms and whisper sweet nonsense, had hopefully learned more sense, she told herself, resolutely ignoring the treacherous small voice at the back of her brain that mourned her passing.

Grant didn't remove Lettie from the house in Eaton Place. When he called the following morning, Adeline sensed that he wanted to get back on the easy footing they had been on before last night, but she was determined not to risk a second rebuff.

Having left Lettie with one of the maids watching over her, tired and not in the best of moods, Adeline had been in the garden, taking a breath of air, when Grant appeared, looking devastatingly handsome in a tweed suit.

Standing on the terrace, he had paused and looked around, searching for her. When he'd seen her, standing against some tall trellising over which pink and white roses clambered in profusion, he strode towards her with that easy, natural elegance already so familiar to her.

Perfectly still, with her hands folded at her waist, she had waited for him to reach her. Ever since she had known this man she had told herself that she was drawn to him because of his compelling good-looks and his powerful masculine magnetism—the strange hold he had over her was merely an ability to awaken those intense sexual hungers within her.

But she realised it was more than that—that was just the tip of an iceberg whose true menace lay in its unfathomable depths. While she had vainly set herself against the carnal forces he inspired in her, something deeper and dangerously enduring was binding them inexorably together. How could she possibly resist him? But resist him she must if she was to have peace of mind.

'At last I've found you,' he said, taking her arm and drawing her down onto a wooden bench, where they sat facing each other. His eyes complimented her warmly on her appearance—for despite the purple smudges beneath her eyes, in her sky blue dress with a high-necked bodice, she looked fresh and immaculate.

Adeline caught the clean, masculine smell of him. The onslaught on her senses was immediate, and she longed to respond to the pressure of his hand on her arm, to feel his mouth on hers, setting her skin tingling and her blood on fire.

But this was the man whom she had decided she would never allow to breach her self-control. The memory of Diana Waverley, with her sly, insolent smile, and the cruel things Grant had said to her last night stood between them.

Her lips curved in a slight smile. 'So you have, Grant. Have you been up to see Lettie?'

He nodded. 'Mrs Kelsall kindly let me go up. She's sleeping, but she does seem a little better.'

'I think so. Dr Lennox should be along soon. If you still wish to remove her from the house then I think you had better wait until he's seen her, don't you?'

'Adeline, if it's in Lettie's best interests that she remains here then I would like her to stay. She couldn't be in better hands. I know that.'

'I told you last night, Grant. Lettie can stay here as long as it is necessary.'

'Thank you. All night I've been cursing myself for a fool. I want to apologise for my boorish behaviour, for which I am ashamed. I was cruel and thoughtless and I deserve to be horse-whipped, for I realise I must have left you feeling deeply hurt. I assure you that wounding your feelings was never my intent. I am here not only to see Lettie, but to make amends.'

'Ashamed, Grant?' Adeline said brightly, giving him no help. 'I am certain there is nothing for *you* to be ashamed of. And isn't it a little late to withdraw anything you may have said to me last night?'

'Adeline, please,' said Grant in a low, rapid tone. 'I spoke hastily, and you have every right to be angry. I was knocked sideways by what Lettie had done—and when I think that I could have prevented it, had I known—'

'If I had betrayed Lettie's confidence and told you? I think that is what you mean, Grant.'

'I don't want to argue about that now, Adeline. Last night, when I received your note asking me to come at once and to bring a doctor, I imagined the worst, and my later anger was caused partly by relief yet also by a feeling of having let Lettie down in some way.'

And part sorrow, guilt and rage for having given his time to Diana when he might have been with Lettie, Adeline could have added. She would not give in to the old attraction that was making her heart race and her legs feel drained of strength.

'I don't suppose Lettie will see it like that,' she said, standing up and walking back towards the house.

Looking at her stiff back, and the proud way she held her head, Grant wanted to go after her and shake her. He knew she was playing a part. He believed that behind that bright expression and glib speech the real warm, passionate Adeline was still to be found—only he had lost the key to her. Temporarily, he hoped. Those ill-considered accusations and insults he had thrown at her when he had vented his fury on her had driven the young woman he had come to feel so deeply for underground, had replaced her with this proper, guarded person who carefully kept him at arm's length.

Getting up and striding after her, he took her arm and jerked her round to face him. 'Adeline, I am truly sorry. I shall not be happy until you tell me you forgive me.' He smiled crookedly at her, willing her to respond as she had in the park.

But there was no answering spark in her eyes as she answered abstractedly, 'Set your mind at rest, Grant,' she said with a brittle laugh. 'For my memory of last night is extremely hazy, and I really cannot recall all that you said to me. There is not the least need to apologise, so please, let us not speak of it again. Now, let us go in and await Dr Lennox.'

It took another twenty-four hours for Lettie's temperature to subside, and then she emerged from her nightmare world.

Dr Lennox visited her twice daily and said she was making swift improvement. Grant visited every day. Lettie was tearful when she saw him, and deeply ashamed that he should know of the terrible thing she had done. She expected him to be furious, to verbally chastise her, but to his credit he issued no recriminations, merely took his sister in his arms and held her, and gave her no word of censure. Adeline was relieved.

Grant called on Lord and Lady Stanfield to explain that Lettie had taken a severe chill and would remain at Eaton Place with Adeline. When asked if they could visit, he politely told them he would let them know when she was feeling up to receiving visitors.

Once the tide had turned, Lettie made rapid strides towards recovery. Luckily she was blessed with a remarkably vigorous constitution. After three days she was able to leave her bed and sit in a chair by the window, and on the fourth day she was able to go downstairs and sit out in the garden. But her face looked drawn and thinner, and there was a haunted look in her eyes. Still she had not spoken of what had turned her against Jack Cunningham, and Adeline had not tried to draw it out of her, believing she would speak of it when she felt ready.

Later she was in the drawing room, her face transparently pale, her shoulders draped in an ermine wrap. Sitting beside her, Adeline took her hand and held it. For the time being they were alone, but they were expecting Lady Stanfield and Marjorie at any minute, and Grant had said he would look in.

'I hope you are feeling up to visitors, Lettie.'

Lettie stared at her, her eyes bleak with the kind of self-knowledge she could neither accept nor pardon. 'Yes, I am looking forward to seeing them. But I do not feel brave enough in my afflicted state to return to Stanfield House and endure the inquisitive glances and questions of the many people I will come into contact with. In a few days' time I have decided to go home to Newhill Lodge—and Mother. I have to get away from London—from Jack.'

'I think that's a good idea, Lettie. I know Grant is to go to France in three days' time, so he will be unable to go with you. But Emma will accompany you.'

Lettie looked at her with eyes that were opaque, awash with tears. Her suffering was real, and a familiar look of distress crossed her face. 'That's very kind of you, Adeline. If you can spare her I would be most grateful. Besides, she knows what I've done, and she has not judged me as others would.'

'Emma can be trusted, Lettie. You can rely on her discretion.'

'You've been so good to me. I don't deserve it. I—I think I will tell my mother what I have done. I don't know how, but I will. I cannot keep such a secret from her. I just hope she will understand. It is my vanity, my wilfulness and my immorality that has brought about this mess. I'm not proud of myself, Adeline,' she whispered. 'What I did was wrong— some may call it wicked. I thought I was doing the right thing—but I feel mutilated.'

'And Jack Cunningham?'

Lettie's eyes clouded with pain and she looked away. 'I never want to see him again. I hate him, Adeline. People say time heals all wounds. I can only hope they're right.'

Grant was the first to arrive. He strode in and gave his sister an affectionate hug before turning his attention to Adeline, who greeted him with a cool nod. He frowned. There was a quietness in her now, a restraint when they were together, and he was acutely aware of it. Adeline Osborne had become in his sight a woman as alluring and desirable as any he had ever known, and even though she rebuffed him at every turn he wanted her. She had become a challenge—a beautiful, vibrant, adorable challenge—a passion.

Lady Stanfield and Marjorie entered the house like a summer breeze, their presence creating an atmosphere of freshness and vitality that was badly needed. They were concerned that Lettie had been so ill, and glad she was beginning to feel better.

Marjorie, full of excitement over her engagement party two days hence, was disappointed when Lettie told her she did not feel well enough to attend. The truth was that she couldn't face it and, knowing this, Adeline did not join Marjorie in trying to persuade her.

Defeated, Marjorie sighed and looked at Adeline. 'You'll still come, won't you, Adeline? You have to. I must have at least *one* of my friends there.'

'Of course Adeline will come,' Lettie was quick to reassure her. 'I don't see why she should forgo your party because of me.'

Suddenly a scheming gleam entered her eyes, making her look more like her old self as her gaze slid to her brother, leaning idly against the window with his arms crossed over his chest. She smiled inwardly, not having forgotten her intention to try and bring Grant and Adeline together.

'In fact, I think Grant should escort her. After all, it's important that at least one member of the Leighton family be there to represent us— and as you know, Mother is unable to get to town just now, so that leaves Grant.' Her look became one of pure, unadulterated innocence as she fixed her eyes on her brother. 'You have no other engagement that night, have you, Grant?'

Her suggestion brought startled glances from both Adeline and Grant. Adeline was not at all in agreement, but one look at Grant and she sensed his absolute and unquestioning co-operation. A lazy smile curved his lips and his eyes gleamed wickedly.

'Nothing that can't be put off, Lettie. I shall be delighted to escort Adeline to the party.'

Grant's ready acceptance brought everyone's instant attention. Adeline stared at him blankly. There was something subtle in the way his smile had changed that made her uneasy. Her mouth opened and closed again.

'Ooh, that would be lovely,' Marjorie enthused happily.

'Absolutely,' Lady Stanfield agreed.

'It's very good of you, Grant, but I don't need an escort,' Adeline remarked, tossing him a vengeful glance.

'Yes, you do,' Grant countered smoothly, enjoying every minute of her discomfort.

'Of course you do,' Lettie agreed.

'And I would so like Grant to be there,' Marjorie said.

Adeline looked from one to the other, unable to believe she had been so easily manoeuvred into a situation she would rather have avoided. Grant was looking at her in tranquil, amused silence, but she noticed there was an infuriating arrogance about the man's smile, and even in the way he was lounging against the wall.

Grant saw her features tighten, and he recognised the ominous glitter in those narrowed green eyes. 'Am I to take your silence for acceptance?' he asked, knowing perfectly well that she couldn't object to him being her escort when everyone else was in favour.

'Don't you think it will raise speculation about us if we arrive together?'

A slow grin came with his answer. 'You seem to forget that the party is being thrown by Lord and Lady Stanfield in a very unconventional household where that sort of thing doesn't count. Besides, I never thought I would see the day when you were conscious of propriety. I think both of us have laid waste to all the usual conventions—especially among certain elements of society where they count for so much.'

Knowing that to argue further would draw everyone's curious attention, she merely glowered at him. He really was the most provoking man she had ever met. She knew what he was about, and that he would go to any lengths to make another conquest, but, as his prey, she was just as determined to make it difficult for him. He intended to seduce her, and nothing was going to deter him from trying.

For her sake, the sooner he was across the Channel in France the better.

It was late afternoon when the door bell rang. Mrs Kelsall answered it, and a moment later came upstairs to tell Adeline that a Mr Cunningham wished to speak to Miss Leighton.

Adeline rose from her dressing table, straightened her skirt, reached up automatically to make sure her hair was tidy, and walked towards Mrs Kelsall.

'Show him into the drawing room, Mrs Kelsall. I'll see what he wants. Please don't tell Miss Leighton he's here.'

Jack Cunningham was standing in the middle of the drawing room, looking totally at ease. Immaculately dressed, he had the sleek, polished patina of great affluence—every inch the gentleman, in fact. But gentleman he was not. Keeping her distance, Adeline felt a rush of distaste. Resenting his intrusion into her home, and hoping his visit would be of short duration, she didn't do him the courtesy of asking him to sit down.

Looking at him with a cool composure she was far from feeling, she said, 'Mr Cunningham! What brings you to Eaton Place?'

'Thank you for seeing me. I am here to see Lettie. I know she is staying with you and I would like to speak to her.'

'I'm afraid Lettie doesn't want to speak to you, Mr Cunningham. I find your presence in my home offensive and I would like you to leave.'

He looked surprised by her coolness, and wondered at the reason for it. His features tightened. 'Leave? Not until I have seen Lettie. Please don't fear me.'

'I don't.'

'Good. I rarely harm anyone—unless provoked.'

'Mr Cunningham, I think you had better leave,' Adeline repeated coldly.

'Really, Miss Osborne, I did not expect to be received with so much hostility, and I cannot imagine why. You speak as if I have done Lettie harm—which is not the case, I can assure you.'

'No? As a result of her association with you Lettie has been—poorly,' she told him. It was not for her to tell him what Lettie had done. She must do that herself. All she wanted was for him to be gone from her home. 'I would like you to leave at once,' she insisted, her utter contempt for him manifested in her narrowed eyes and the disdain that curled her lip. 'You are not welcome in this house.'

Jack's eyes narrowed curiously. 'Lettie has been ill?' he prevaricated. 'Why was I not informed?'

'Why should you be, Mr Cunningham?'

'I am sure you know by now that Lettie is carrying my child. I have every right to be informed if she is not well. I insist on seeing her,' he demanded impatiently. 'I will not leave this house until I have done so. Kindly go and fetch her.'

'You have no rights.' A deep voice spoke from the doorway, causing Jack to spin round and face Grant Leighton, who was striding towards him. 'You crawling bastard,' Grant hissed, his fists clenched at his sides. 'Do you think that by coming into Miss Osborne's house and raising your voice you can terror- ise her into submission? You will not see my sister. I will not allow it.' His voice was implacable, his manner implying that it would give him a great deal of pleasure to throw him out.

Jack appeared not to mind. He smiled smugly. 'I am here on perfectly legitimate business, and I would be pleased if someone could tell Lettie I am here,' he persisted.

'By God, Cunningham, I'll see you dead and in hell before I let you get your filthy hands on her again.'

'Even if I say that I will do the decent thing by her?'

'Decent!' Grant's voice was pure venom. 'You are even more of a lecherous swine than I thought you were—not to mention liable to legal sanctions for all your corrupt dealings. But no matter. Decency requires sufficient imagination to see beyond one's acts to their consequences.'

'What the hell are you talking about, Leighton?'

'Please stop it, Grant. I fight my own battles.'

The quiet voice cut off Grant's angry tirade. They all turned as one to see Lettie standing in the doorway. At once Jack Cunningham was the smooth charmer, bowing his head and smiling a slow, charismatic smile which was meant to tell everyone present that he wouldn't harm a fly.

Lettie was dressed with her usual elegance in a soft lemon-coloured gown, her hair brushed back smoothly into a meshed net. As she moved farther into the room she looked at Cunningham directly. Her face was white and so were her lips, and her glittering eyes were ice-cold.

'How dare you come here? You had no right. How did you know where to find me?'

'It wasn't difficult. Do I need an invitation to see you, Lettie? Will you not spare me a few minutes so that we can talk in private?'

'She's going nowhere with you, Cunningham,' Grant growled. 'You have violated my sister, and you expect her to continue being your whore.'

Adeline flinched at Grant's choice of word, which she knew would hurt Lettie. But he could be as hard and exacting as any man, and Jack Cunningham's offensive intrusion was making him increasingly furious.

Lettie drew herself up, her face set, her eyes flashing. 'My brother is right. We have nothing to say to each other, Jack. Please go.'

'Lettie,' he wheedled, holding out his hands to her. 'Come back to me. What we have is good—'

'No, Jack. It's over. I never want to see you again. Ever.'

'Come now, Lettie. My intentions are entirely honourable. I want you to marry me—to be my wife.'

'Wife!' Lettie's indignation and fury rose, choking and hot. 'You have a warped sense of honour, Jack. What do you intend doing with the wife you already have?'

Adeline and Grant stood there, looking at Lettie for the one awful, drawn-out moment it took them to recover from her shocking revelation. It was enough time for Lettie to draw enough breath back into her lungs, to look at Jack and say with appalled breathlessness, 'Or don't you remember, Jack?'

Caught off-guard, Jack looked at her a long time without bothering to open his mouth. Lettie saw the truth in his eyes. His face changed. His smooth, masculine good-looks departed as everything in his countenance pinched and tightened, and for the first time she realised how mean he looked, how hard.

'Yes, he has a wife. Her name is Molly,' Lettie heatedly told Grant and Adeline. 'She is in the asylum, where she has been incarcerated for the past ten years, after being delivered of a stillborn child—her third, I believe. Unable to forgive her inability to give you a living child, you put her there—didn't you, Jack?—letting everyone believe she was dead. The loss of her children and her freedom drove her insane. Do you dare to deny it?'

Jack looked at Lettie and his face was like stone, as were his eyes. A blue vein twitched on his temple, and a creeping chill slithered down his spine when he thought of his wife. 'How did you find out?'

'I have ears, Jack. I listen. I went to see her—in a place that must surely be as close to hell on earth as is possible to get. In the course of my work I have seen all kinds of things, but this is different—the terror, the inescapable certainty of death, helpless and without dignity. How could you do that to your *wife*?'

The eyes Jack fixed on his accuser were filled with loathing for the woman he had locked away from the world. 'No, not a wife—a madwoman who should have died when she bore another dead child and rid me of her burden. She ceased to be my wife when the asylum door closed on her. As far as I am concerned she is as dead as her stillborn children.'

'You have a wife—a living wife—which the law recognises even if you do not,' Lettie whispered, truly appalled. 'You are despicable. And you would have entered into a bigamous marriage with me—knowing your wife still lives. How could you, Jack? How could you? Have you no compassion for her at all? She is *ill*.' Lettie was unable to believe how uncaring this man could be.

'Aye—an illness that grew into insanity and violence with each day.'

'If she became insane then you drove her to it—you and that place you put her in.'

Grant saw an instant of pity in Lettie's eyes when she looked at her lover. Because she recognised his horror of the disease that had consumed his wife. He also saw that Cunningham had lost Lettie not solely by his deceit, but in her contempt—that awakening of disgust which was the end of love between a man and a woman.

'I find your obsession with having a child strange,' Lettie remarked coldly, 'when I think of the small victims who pass through your hands to satisfy the appetites of the customers in your brothels. You disgust me.'

'Enough,' Jack hissed, his eyes blazing. 'Shut your mouth.' Her unflinching stare seemed to increase his fury two-fold.

Grant stepped forward. 'Why should she, Cunningham? Lettie has every right to speak freely in this house—although I had no idea she was as aware of the extent of your sordid dealings as myself. The very nature of your *other* business, which brings about its own secrecy, makes you unfit to associate with decent, respectable society.'

Suddenly chilled by what she was hearing, and the realisation of what it implied, Adeline felt twin sensations of horror and disgust rise like bile in her throat, forming a painful obstruction as she stared at this evil that had entered her home. Too stunned to act, too sickened even to comment upon what she was hearing, she remained motionless.

'How I choose to make my money is my affair, Leighton— and so is Lettie and the child she is carrying. It is mine, and as its father I have rights.'

'There no longer is a child, Jack. So you can forget any claim you might have had,' Lettie threw at him, almost triumphantly. 'I didn't want it. I don't want anything of yours.'

He frowned. 'No child?' Suddenly comprehension dawned. It hurt him, and he could not conceal it. His body went rigid, his right hand flexed and unflexed, and the muscles of his jaw twitched in reaction. 'I understand you have been ill. Have you miscarried?'

'No, Jack. When I found out just how vile you are, I realised I could not bear the child of a monster.'

Shock and grief registered in Jack's eyes, and for the first time there was an emotion in him quite different from anger. But it lasted only an instant. 'Good God! You got rid of it.'

There was utter silence for a second, then Jack's face went white as he truly understood what he had heard. 'To satisfy your own whim, you deliberately killed our child.'

Lettie wrapped her arms around her waist and nodded. 'Yes—yes, I did. I'm not proud—but, yes. I made a choice— the right choice for me. I couldn't bear the thought of giving birth to a child of yours.'

'You bitch.'

Lettie's face was tense, and pale also. She raised her brows very slightly. 'Really?' She shrugged. 'Think what you like. Now, please go—get out. You sicken me. I don't want to see you again, and that is my final word.'

Jack looked frightening. His lips were drawn back from his teeth in a snarl, but his body was trembling. There was hate in his eyes. He glared at Grant. 'I congratulate you, Leighton. Your digging into my private life has given you what you wanted. But if you imagine you can do that and get away with it you are mistaken.'

When it looked as if he would argue further, Grant strode towards the door and opened it. 'You heard what my sister said. Get out. If I have the least suspicion of you attempting to see Lettie, even indirectly, I shall know how to set the story of your squalid affairs circulating round town which will bring the full investigation of the law down upon you. Since both moralists and police alike have been clamouring for a London clean-up since the beginning of the decade that's bound to happen sooner rather than later anyway. I'm only surprised you've got away with it for so long, and that your establishments have remained free from searches by the police.'

'Not every policeman is honest, Leighton.'

'It takes more than a nod and a wink, Cunningham. On the whole the police are virtually incorruptible, and proud of the work they do. I know there are those who can be bribed, but I promise you I will do everything I can to bring you down.'

'By God, Leighton,' Jack breathed, his voice intense, 'you'll pay for this.' His gaze flashed to Lettie. 'Both of you.'

Never had Adeline seen such hatred. The pure, naked, terrifying hatred of Grant. And why? Because he had got the better of Jack Cunningham.

'There will be no recriminations if you know what's good for you—if you don't want to spend the rest of your days behind bars. You, Cunningham, are scum.'

He had spoken quietly, too quietly for Cunningham to muster up words to reply. Grant held his eyes with a steady, unflinching stare. There was no pretence between them.

'And one more thing. If marrying Lettie and buying Westwood Hall was your way of insinuating yourself into respectability you can forget it. Diana's luck has turned and she has repaid her debts. Westwood Hall is no longer for you. Now, get out.'

Without saying another word Jack Cunningham left the house.

Grant hoped it would be the last they saw of him, but somehow he didn't think so. Cunningham wasn't the sort of man who would simply walk away without trying to wreak some kind of vengeance. There remained the threat that he might reveal what Lettie had done, and in so doing bring her down with the scandal.

When the door had closed, Grant went to his sister, who looked shaken by the whole unpleasant episode. Adeline rang for tea. She was troubled by everything she had just heard, and Jack Cunningham's shock at the loss of his child had had a ring of sincerity she had not expected.

'Lettie, did you go to the asylum by yourself?' Adeline asked curiously.

'No. Alice was with me.'

'Alice?'

'Jack's sister—the woman you saw outside the Phoenix Club. She's fond of Molly, and does what she can.'

'So—all that talk about a charity clinic wasn't true?'

'No. I'm sorry, Adeline. I couldn't tell you what she wanted then because I didn't know myself—only that it was of a serious, secretive nature. I met her afterwards and she told me how Jack had cast his wife off as he did his family when he began to prosper. To protect her from his wrath, I didn't tell Jack it was Alice who told me. The poor woman has approached him several times for money to make Molly's life easier, but he refuses to support any member of his family.'

'Then he truly is a monster, and you are well rid of him.'

'I know that now. Imagine what it must have been like for Molly—the man she trusted, maybe even loved, threw her aside like so much rubbish when she most needed him. Sadly she remains imprisoned—not only in that place, but in her mind—beyond all human help.'

The situation was so tragic there was nothing Adeline could say. Grant seemed to be preoccupied. She watched him pour himself a large brandy, then look at it a long moment, seeing the light burn through its amber depths.

What was he thinking of? she wondered. Or who? She recalled Frances telling her that Diana was in trouble financially, but she had had no idea she was in so much debt that she was forced to sell Westwood Hall. And Jack Cunningham had been hoping to buy it. Grant must have found out about the transaction and, loath to have Jack Cunningham as his neighbour, bought it himself—which testified in Adeline's mind to the close relationship between Grant and Diana Waverley.

Chapter Ten

When Grant arrived at Eaton Place on the evening of the party, he looked up automatically and saw Adeline coming down the staircase in a gown of gold-spangled satin, which hugged her slender curves and left her arms and shoulders bare. With a rope of white diamonds around her throat, and her hair curled up and secured with diamond and emerald combs which flashed as she turned her head, she looked glamorous and bewitching and captivating—and also lovely, soft, and eternally female.

Grant stared in stunned admiration, an appreciative smile working across his face. 'My God! You are beautiful. You look like a golden goddess.'

Caught up in the anticipation and excitement of Marjorie's engagement party, in the spell of his compelling silver gaze and his proud, smiling black and white elegance, Adeline found herself laughing softly. 'I'm glad you like it. Lettie chose it. I wanted to wear something more subtle, more subdued, but Lettie wouldn't hear of it.'

In fact, for the first time in days Lettie had seemed more like her old self as she had taken a delighted enthusiasm for the event and for making her look glamorous. Grant's arrival had increased Lettie's enthusiasm dramatically—which had aroused Adeline's suspicions. Not for the first time had it entered her mind that Lettie had some romantic notion of bringing her and Grant together.

'I never credited my sister with having such excellent taste,' Grant murmured, his gaze settling on the swelling globes of Adeline's breasts above the scooped bodice. 'The gown is both elegant and daring—and perfect.'

Seeing where his heavy-lidded gaze dwelt, and almost feeling his eyes disrobing her, Adeline flushed scarlet. 'Have you had an edifying look?'

His grin was roguish. 'Not nearly enough—but I have all night to gaze. How is my dear sister, by the way?'

'Well, but resting. Would you like to go up and see her before we leave?'

'If she's resting I won't disturb her.'

Adeline reached for her satin cape, but Grant took it from Mrs Kelsall.

'Allow me,' he offered.

Scarcely breathing, Adeline waited as those strong, lean hands draped the cape over her shoulders.

'Mmm,' he breathed from behind her, his mouth close to her ear. 'You smell nice, too.' He smiled, sublimely confident and pleased. He was going to enjoy tonight.

Adeline turned her head and looked at him. The amusement in his eyes was slowly replaced by a slumbering intensity. 'I think we'd better go, don't you?'

'Your carriage awaits, my lady,' he teased, then with solicitous care escorted her out to the waiting coach.

Once inside, Adeline cast an apprehensive eye at Grant as he settled himself beside her. How handsome he looks, she thought, as she stole a glance at his disciplined, classical profile. Just being with him made her heartbeat quicken. Reminding herself that, desirable and charming as he might be, he was still seeing Diana, and that if she wasn't careful she was in danger of forgetting her vow to keep him at arm's length, she knew it was imperative that she keep her head tonight.

It was only a short distance to Stanfield House, which was ablaze with light. The street was crowded with vehicles, each depositing its resplendent occupants at the front of the house. Adeline could hardly breathe for admiration as they climbed the steps and entered a hallway as large and echoing as a church. A curving staircase swept down from the landing to the marble floor.

They were met by Lord and Lady Stanfield and the engaged couple, their faces wreathed in smiles.

'Adeline, Grant—I'm delighted to see you!' Lord Stanfield said, his florid face between bushy mutton chop whiskers alight with geniality. 'How is dear Lettie? I'm sorry her illness has prevented her attending the party. Allow me to present Lord and Lady Henderson.'

When greetings had been made, and they were moving on, Grant bent his head close to Adeline's.

'The engaged couple look well matched.'

Adeline glanced back at Marjorie and Nicholas and laughed lightly. There was no denying the melting look in their eyes when they looked at each other, and Nicholas had his arm about Marjorie's waist, hugging her to his side as if she were a flower he wished to preserve. 'They are. Perfectly. It's a match made in heaven and Lady Stanfield is very happy about it. But then who wouldn't be? Marjorie is marrying a title, and noble titles are neither to be ignored nor laughed at.'

Not impervious to the stir they were creating—for when they had entered together a whispered murmuring had descended on the guests in the hall, and every eye had turned in their direction—Grant took her hand and, tucking it possessively in the crook of his arm, proudly led her towards the principal reception room. It was a singularly possessive gesture that somehow added to Adeline's well-being.

'This has all the makings of being an enjoyable evening,' Grant commented, nodding pleasantly to those he knew.

Gliding beside him, Adeline gave him a sudden enchanting smile, determined to be friendliness personified where he was concerned for this one night. To be otherwise would spoil the party, and she did so want to have a good time. She could only hope that his restraint would continue and her resistance would not be tested. Just the memory of his kiss could sap the strength from her.

'I do hope so. I can't help thinking of my own engagement party when I thought I would marry Paul. It was nothing like this.' Her eyes sparkled with excitement and delight. 'Since coming to London I've done many varied and interesting things—but this is my first party, and I am wearing my first party gown, and I am determined to enjoy myself.'

Grant laughed, a throaty, contagious laugh, and his eyes suddenly seemed to regard her with a bold, speculative gleam. 'Then we must make it a night to remember.'

Entering the large salon, they saw that it had been converted into a ballroom for the evening. Crystal chandeliers were suspended from an ornate ceiling, and gilt-framed mirrors reflected the dazzling kaleidoscope of jewellery and gowns. The older women were attired in rich colours, the younger ones in whites and creams and palest pinks. Everywhere there was the clink of glasses, the hum of conversation and the trill of laughter, and music rose and fell. It was an interesting gathering of society people, and others involved with Lady Stanfield's work. Large doors opened out onto a spacious terrace hung with fairy lights, and in a room next door a buffet table groaned under the weight of delicious food.

Every gaze seemed to swivel their way, and Adeline had

the disconcerting feeling that every person in that room was either looking at them or talking about them.

'Is it my imagination, or is everyone staring at us?' she whispered to her escort.

'It isn't your imagination.' Turning slightly away from her, his expression pleased and confident, Grant scanned the crowded room. 'Do you know anyone here?'

'Yes, several. And you?'

'A few.'

'Then let's circulate and relieve their curiosity.' Taking a couple of glasses of sparkling champagne from a salver being carried by a passing footman, he handed one to her.

Taking a sip of the wine, and fortified by its potency, Adeline looked at him as he escorted her to the nearest group, feeling a glow of warmth infuse her whole being. He really did look breathtakingly handsome in his elegant black evening attire. It fitted his broad-shouldered figure to perfection. Women seemed to gravitate towards him—and little wonder, Adeline thought, seeing many women cast flirtatious glances his way. She sensed a jealous malevolence in their attitude to her. Seeing him like this, among the glittering members of society, admired and courted for his friendship and business acumen, she could hardly believe that this was the same man who had made love to her at Westwood Hall, and had played havoc with her senses and emotions ever since.

After exchanging greetings with those they knew, being introduced to others of note and drinking two more glasses of champagne, they found themselves alone.

Adeline sighed. 'I'm sorry Lettie didn't come. I know she was so looking forward to it before…well, before. I feel rather guilty being here enjoying myself, while Lettie is feeling so distressed.'

'You may relax. Lettie wanted you to come, and she will hardly protest if you enjoy yourself, so there's no reason to feel guilty. And the music is most entrancing.' Seeing Anthony Stanfield and two other young gentlemen bearing down on them, with the obvious intention of asking Adeline to dance, Grant looked down at her. His gaze was slow and pointedly bold as he perused her soft and exquisite radiance. 'Dance with me, Adeline,' he said, taking her hand.

Her piquant denial was prepared, but the flowing, seductive strains of the music made Adeline want to move to its rhythm. For a breathless moment she envisaged herself in his arms, dancing with him. A thrill went through her, bringing a flush of colour to her cheeks, and she could no more deny the moment than ignore the hand of this man she held close to her heart.

Placing her hand in his, she smiled up at him. 'I'd love to.'

His mouth tilted upward in a roguish grin, and the warm, glowing light in his eyes made her blood run warm. In fact, as she stepped onto the dance floor and he drew her into his arms, whirling her about in a wide sweep of the floor, she felt positively wicked. She was a woman who felt as if she were reborn, and here she was being envied by everyone here tonight for being with this man.

'You dance divinely,' Grant observed as she moved with that natural, fluid motion of hers. 'You must have had a good instructor.'

She laughed lightly. 'I did. That's one thing my father insisted on. Apparently my mother was a good dancer.'

'I see. And do you look like her?'

'No. She was smaller than me, fair and very beautiful—whereas I am something of a curiosity in the family.'

He gave her a wicked smile. 'I'm somewhat partial to curiosities.'

Adeline's laughter bubbled to the surface like a subtle flowing stream through Grant's mind, and its effect was devastating. The fact that he wanted her was becoming hard-pressing reality.

When the dance ended Lady Stanfield appeared beside them. 'I'm glad to see the two of you enjoying yourselves—but you will dance with Marjorie, won't you, Grant? She's so glad you came, and she would like to talk to you about dear Lettie. Marjorie is going to miss her terribly, but I dare say she'll be back in London before too long.'

'I would think so. Lettie soon tires of the country, and as you know she is never happy unless she's busy. It would be my pleasure to dance with Marjorie. I shall ask her to dance the next with me—another waltz, I believe—before the music starts.' Excusing himself to Adeline, he disappeared into the throng.

Suddenly finding herself alone, Adeline was glad when Anthony appeared by her side. The celebration of his sister's engagement had made him more inebriated than he had ever been in his life, and, emboldened by this, he had turned his eyes on the fair Adeline Osborne, whose outstanding skill with the sword had made him her adoring slave.

'My God!' he exclaimed with unconcealed admiration when he was standing directly in front of her. 'You look ravishing, Adeline—although,' he said, bending close and speaking in a teasing conspiratorial whisper, 'I much prefer to see you in trousers. You have the most incredibly long legs—has anyone ever told you that?'

'I know perfectly well how long my legs are, thank you, Anthony,' she said jokingly. 'I do see them every day, you know.'

Anthony burst out laughing. Taking her hand, he drew her into the buffet room. 'I'm sorry, Adeline. I'm a bit tiddly, I'm afraid. But never mind. Come and meet my friends and have some more champagne, and we'll be tiddly together.'

Adeline's usually level head deserted her as she allowed him to lead her into the heart of a crowd of boisterous young people, all larking about, reclining on velvet-cushioned ottomans and having tremendous fun. Anthony handed her an over-large glass of the sparkling wine, which she drank faster than she ought, and for the next half an hour she joined in their high-spirits, making a spectacle of themselves.

She drank more champagne—far more than she was used to, and she would feel the effects later—laughed a good deal—causing heads to turn and look at her—and when Anthony pulled her onto the dance floor for a waltz it was anything but, because they polkaed about the floor.

When the music ended he danced her onto the terrace, and before Adeline had the faintest conception of what he would do, he had spun her round like a top, sending her reeling, then covered the distance he had opened between them. Catching her round the waist, he pressed his eager mouth passionately to hers.

Adeline was so astonished that for a moment she could not move. She had treated Anthony as a friend and had been having so much fun that she had scarcely noticed the adoring looks he gave her, but this was no boyish peck. It was a full blown man's kiss, hot with desire, and when they finally drew apart he whispered, 'I have wanted to do that from the moment I saw you,' and kissed her again.

Adeline pushed him away, although her sensitivities were not offended. 'Anthony, you must be mad. Please don't do this. Stop it now.'

But she was unable to resist his arms, which seemed to be all over the place, and Anthony pulled her back, uttering a torrent of lover's words against her cheek, his voice squashy with drink.

Again she shoved him away—as a voice spoke behind them. 'Well, here's a pretty spectacle.'

The voice was hard, the eyes, when Adeline turned to look, murderous and as hard as flint.

Grant stood rigid. His eyes were colder than ice and there was a thin white line about his mouth. How dared this youth kiss this lovely girl with her rosy cheeks and stars in her eyes—put his hands on what was…what should be Grant

Leighton's? Did he not think of her day in and day out? Did she not fill his head and his dreams? Did he not know what it was like to hold her in his arms and recognise in Anthony Stanfield what he himself felt? And could he blame him?

Dear Lord, what was wrong with him? How could he let a woman affect him as this one did? He wanted to reach out and punch young Stanfield in the mouth, fling him away from Adeline—which was so out of character. It was with a great effort of will that he managed to keep his emotions in check, his expression one of calm composure as he looked from one to the other.

Anthony, past all caution, and seeing nothing wrong with the situation, laughed—and instinct told Adeline she, too, had to make light of it. However, when she looked at Grant she squinted her eyes, seeing double. He was all a blur. She also felt giddy and rather strange.

'Why, Grant, how stern you look. I can't think why you should. Anthony and I weren't doing anything wrong—in fact, Anthony feels he must kiss all the ladies present? Is that not so, Anthony?' She giggled and hiccupped, and clutched at Anthony's arm for support.

'That's right,' Anthony mumbled, struggling to stand straight and beginning to look a bit green around the gills. His teeth felt as if they were afloat at the back of his mouth…he really must find somewhere to be sick. 'Would you excuse me?' he said, his voice straining with the effort. 'I think I need to go somewhere.'

Adeline and Grant didn't say a word as he weaved himself down the steps of the terrace and disappeared into the darkness of the garden, but Grant watched his departing figure with a mixture of pity, amusement and disgust. Despite the absurdity of it, he felt the first sharp twinge of jealousy in his adult life.

'There goes a young man who will have one hell of a hangover in the morning.'

'Poor Anthony. He really has drunk a lot of champagne— enough to sink a ship.' Adeline looked at Grant and tried desperately to focus on his face. He was a dark, invincible figure, forbidding, intimidating, and yet strangely compelling. 'Why did you come looking for me, Grant? Must you watch me so closely?'

Grant raised one black devil's eyebrow. 'I am your escort. I'm merely safeguarding your honour.'

Adeline giggled. 'It's a bit late in the day to defend my honour, Grant. You of all people should know that.'

'You seem to be enjoying yourself,' he commented, ignoring her statement for the time being.

'I'm having a truly wonderful time. Really, Grant, do you have to look so—pompous, so aloof?'

Her reproof brought a scowl to his face. 'Come inside and have something to eat.'

'I'm not hungry, but I'd love some more champagne.'

'Don't you think you've had enough?'

Adeline looked at his face, which was a hard, angry mask. She frowned her annoyance. 'Grant, there is one thing you should realise. My whole life has been one of compliance. I have never been able to please myself. And suddenly I feel like a bird that has been set free from its gilded cage,' she said laughingly, throwing her arms wide to demonstrate the fact, and doing a rather wobbly twirl. 'I am enjoying myself as I have never enjoyed anything in my life. Please don't spoil it.' She smiled up at him serenely, clutching his arm to maintain her fragile balance. 'Have you come to ask me to dance?'

'I would, if I didn't think you would fall over,' he remarked. The anger he had felt at seeing her kissing young Stanfield was abating, for in her weakened state she really did look both vulnerable and adorable and incredibly lovely—a loveliness not just of face and form, but in her heart and soul. It shone from her, and she was completely unaware of it, and that was what was so special about her.

'Yes, you're right. I do feel a bit wobbly,' she said, relinquishing her hold on his arm and flopping down onto the low terrace wall. 'I'm feeling a trifle dizzy from all that dancing.'

Grant cocked a dubious brow and, propping one shoulder negligently against the trellising, regarded her attractively flushed face and shining eyes with a twisted smile. 'Dancing? Are you sure it's not the effects of the champagne?'

Looking up at him, she smiled, thinking how incredibly handsome he looked in the soft glow of the fairy lights. 'It could be, I suppose.'

'That was quite a show you put on on the dance floor. Do you normally dance a polka to a waltz?' he said quietly, his lips twitching in ill-suppressed amusement.

Adeline blinked up at him. 'Did we?' She scowled, seeing a glint of censure in his eyes despite his smile. 'Grant, are you cross with me?'

'No—although you did make something of a spectacle of yourself. Perhaps you should rest awhile?'

'I'm having too good a time to rest.'

'Adeline, have you eaten anything at all?' he chided.

She chuckled at his dark scowl. 'No, not yet. I don't seem to have had the time.'

'Perhaps if you'd spent less time drinking champagne and kissing Anthony Stanfield you might have found the time.'

'Grant? You cannot be angry at a young man's tipsy kiss— or…' she murmured, tilting her head to one side and looking up at him askance. 'Or is it the green eye of jealousy, perhaps?'

He looked down at her. 'Should I be jealous?'

'Of course you should. Anthony kisses very well.'

'Like hell he does. I marked well how little you resisted— no doubt these kisses are a frequent occurrence when Anthony visits you at Eaton Place on the pretence of fencing lessons.'

Adeline threw him an indignant look. 'Now you are being silly—and you are beginning to sound just like my father. But you were right, you know. I think Anthony *does* have feelings for me—or it might be the champagne, I suppose,' she murmured airily. 'We are both a bit tipsy.'

'Tipsy? That is obvious. Drink makes a window for the truth, Adeline.'

'And you would know all about that, wouldn't you?' she accused, standing up and jabbing a tapered fingernail into his chest. 'The first time we met you were disgustingly drunk.' An unconsciously provocative smile curved her lips and she moved closer to him, her narrowed eyes warm and meaningful on his. 'Pity you can't remember the incident as well as I can.'

He grinned impenitently. 'Care to try it again? You can show me what I missed.' He raised a brow as he waited for her answer— and his eyes clearly expressed his wants.

Adeline felt herself falling under the spell of that rich, deep voice, and the bold stare touched a quickness in her that made her feel as if she were on fire. 'You—you're jesting.'

'No, I'm not. You told me how wonderful it was for you. Wouldn't you like to experience that again?'

'And become your mistress? Do you know that to almost everyone here tonight the general consensus is that I am already your mistress?'

Grant smiled. By escorting her to the party he was making certain everyone thought she was. 'And does that concern you?' he asked, watching her intently.

'Of course it does—because I'm not,' she retorted, in a voice of offended dignity. 'If I was it wouldn't matter. But you'd be quite worn out trying to keep two mistresses happy and content.'

Grant's amused laughter took the sting out of her words. 'When I have expended so much energy on you, Adeline, can you believe I have any interest in another woman? Is it my association with Diana that raises your ire?'

'My ire, as you call it, is justified and you know it. Carrying on with Paul and not even bothering to hide it. Her behaviour was quite disgraceful.' She paused, thoughtfully. 'Although if she hadn't I suppose I'd have had to marry him, so if for nothing else I must be grateful to her for that. You have seen a good deal of Diana of late, so why shouldn't I think the two of you are having an affair?'

'And why should you care if I am seeing Diana?'

Her eyes snapped. 'How conceited you are, Grant Leighton. I don't.'

'Yes, you do.'

Those glowing eyes burned into hers, suffusing her with an aura of warmth. How could she claim uninterest in this man when his presence could so effectively stir her senses?

Grant's gaze dipped and lightly caressed her breasts before moving back to her face. 'I am single-minded in my pursuits, Adeline.'

'Really? What are you saying?'

'That I want you.'

Adeline took a step back, resisting all on the strength of her fear. Grant saw her fear and played on it gently, lest her fear destroy the moment, but it took extreme exercise of will.

Taking her hand he drew her back to him. 'I would like to see what your determination to stand against me can bear, Adeline.'

His nearness sapped Adeline's strength and weakened her will, drawing out her every resolve until she didn't know what to think any more—what to do. She knew with certainty that she would never be free of Grant Leighton, and with each day he grew bolder. She saw the hard flint of passion strike sparks in the silver-grey eyes as they moved upon her face.

Grant realised that beneath her fine clothes she was what every man dreamed of—a vision of incomparable beauty—and he wanted to see for himself, to possess it. His long-starved passion flared. She had got under his skin, into his blood, and her mere touch, the scent of her, sent desire running through his veins. She was sensual, unaffected and yet sophisticated, and as he looked at her his mind drifted back to when he had robbed her of her virtue.

It gave him satisfaction to know he had been the one to take it, and he was impatient for the time when he could repeat the act—only this time he would be the most tender of lovers, and have her moaning with rapture. His eyes revelled in their freedom as they feasted hungrily on her face—her lips.

Adeline felt it, felt devoured by it, and it took an effort of will to remain pliant beneath his probing eyes. 'What—what is it you want?' she asked. Her voice didn't sound her own to her ears.

'You,' he answered.

'Oh, I see.'

'Yes—and I think you want me. Let's get this clear. You don't want to eat. You don't want to dance. So—why are we still here?'

Adeline kept her eyes carefully on his face. 'Where should we be?'

'Somewhere else.'

'Where do you suggest? Your—hotel room, perhaps?' she whispered, her eyes on his lips.

'Yes, but not tonight. Not when your head is clouded with champagne. When you come to my bed—'

'When?' Her eyes snapped. 'You are certain of that, are you? Not if?'

'It's inevitable, Adeline, and only a matter of time—perhaps tomorrow, when we have taken Lettie to the station.' His smile was salacious. 'That will give you something to think about from now until then. When you come to my bed—of your own accord—it will be an intoxication of a different kind that brings us together. We shall both be fully aware of what is happening between us, I promise

you,' he said, on a note of tender finality. 'But I warn you—
you may find something more eternal, more binding than a
simple act of love.'

In her fuddled mind, Adeline had no idea what he meant
by that. Earlier she had made a conscious decision to keep
him at arm's length—now she was about to renege on her
decision. Nervous, she turned her gaze away and gnawed on
her bottom lip.

Grant watched her warily, and her eyes wavered beneath
his direct gaze. Lifting a finger, he slowly traced the soft
fullness of her bottom lip, then murmured, 'You're trembling.'

'Am I?' She watched his gaze turn warm and sensual.

Gently taking her chin between his thumb and forefinger,
he nodded. 'I'll forgive you for kissing that young reprobate
if you kiss me now.'

Adeline's whole body stilled as his finely chiselled lips
began to descend to hers, and she sought to forestall what her
heart told her was the inevitable by saying, 'What if someone
should come out onto the terrace and see us?'

A flame appeared in his eyes and kindled brighter, and his
warm lips trailed a hot path over her cheek to her ear. 'Let
them. It doesn't matter,' he murmured huskily.

His tongue lightly touched the lobe of her ear, delicately
probing the crevices, until Adeline shivered with the waves
of tension shooting through her. The instant he felt her trembling response his arms went round her, drawing her into his
protective embrace. His hand curved around her nape, sensually stroking, and his warm breath caressed her cheek as his
mouth began tracing a path to her lips.

Imprisoned by his embrace, seduced by his mouth and caressing hands, Adeline pressed herself close to his hard body, moving
her hands up his broad chest, her fingers sliding into the soft hair
at his nape, her body arching to his, fitting his powerful frame.
Slowly she slipped into a dark abyss of desire as she fully

received his kiss, first with hesitancy, then with welcome, then with passion, feeling a wild, incredible sweetness.

The tender offering of her mouth wrung a half-laugh, half-groan from Grant, and, tightening his arms, he seized her lips with his in a kiss of scorching demand, crushing down on them, parting them, his tongue driving into her mouth with a hungry urgency. Adeline's world careened dizzily. His mouth was insistent, demanding, relentless, snatching her breath as well as her poise as primitive sensations went jarring through her entire body. The fierceness of his kiss changed to softness, to the velvet touch of intoxication, and the breath that sighed through her lips was the sigh that came when a woman was deep in the pleasures of the flesh.

When Grant finally released her lips an eternity later—which took more effort than he'd expected, leaving him feeling almost bereft—Adeline surfaced gradually from the sensual place where he had sent her, still feeling the thrill of the invasion of his tongue, and all the sensations that had followed. Forcing her eyes open so that she could look at his face—hard with passion, eyes smouldering—with trembling effort she collected herself, and as he looked down at her she drew a deep, ragged breath.

Until now she had tried to convince herself that her memory of the passion that had erupted between them at Westwood Hall was exaggerated, but his kiss had surpassed her imaginings. A breeze riffled through the trellising, teasing the trailing roses and caressing her bare shoulders. His hands stroked soothingly up and down her arms and his eyes held hers. Suddenly the sounds of music and laughter began to penetrate Adeline's drugged senses, and a noisy group of young people burst onto the terrace.

Grant's sensual lips curved in a half-smile and, reaching out, he tucked a stray strand of hair behind her ear. 'It's getting late. Would you like me to take you home?'

'Yes. I promised I'd call in and see Lettie before going to bed. I'm going to miss her when she goes home.'

Grant's grin was tigerish. 'Not immediately, I hope.' As much as he didn't want to send Lettie back to their mother, he was impatient for the short time he would have alone with Adeline before he had to leave for the boat train to the continent. 'I shall try and restrain myself until tomorrow, when we will settle this matter between us—you will be mine before the day is done.'

Adeline stared at him, realising he meant every word he said. Her mind reeled beneath the impact of the last few minutes. Grant meant what he said and she was absolutely certain that she would be unable to withstand his persuasive, unrelenting assault—and now she wasn't at all certain that she wanted to.

The next morning it was a pale and troubled Lettie that Grant and Adeline put on the train for Ashford. Emma was to go with her. Weak as she was, Lettie was going home to Newhill Lodge and her mother. She felt she would stifle if she stayed in London any longer, with her mind going round and round in distressing circles of—what? Sorrow, aching loss, regret, guilt? What she did acknowledge was that the physical pain had diminished, and so had the mental pain, if she would admit it to herself.

Adeline and Grant watched the train until it was out of sight, and then they left the station and returned to where the carriage was waiting. Assuming they could carry on where they'd left off last night, and refusing to relinquish control, acting on his words and intending to have things his way, Grant instantly told the driver to take them to the Charing Cross Hotel.

Seated at his side, Adeline looked at him. Before Marjorie's party she had told herself she would refuse any attempt he made at seduction. Then at the first possible moment she had practically thrown herself at him. Grant turned his head and caught her watching him, and a shock of lightning seemed to shoot from his body straight into hers. Without moving a muscle or saying a word he was emanating an aura of predatory male that was tangible enough to cut with a knife.

Adeline wondered what she was letting herself in for. Last night her head had been so fuddled with champagne that she'd have agreed to anything he suggested—but that had been last night, and now her stomach cramped with nervous uncertainty. But Grant was hardly a stranger, an unknown entity. There was no denying that she was wildly attracted to him. She thought of him a thousand times a day, and every thought was sweeter than the last. And there was no denying that the idea of repeating what she had experienced before made her knees weak.

'What time do you have to leave for your train?' she asked, for something to say—anything to break the silence between them.

'Why?' His brows drew together and a gleam of intent entered his eyes. 'Are you afraid I'll be rushing off?'

'No,' she said, looking away. 'I—I just wondered, that was all.'

Placing his finger beneath her chin, he turned her head back to his. In silence he studied her face, as if he were searching for an answer, then he leant forward and captured her mouth, kissing her long and deep. When he finally lifted his head he gazed down into her eyes, unconsciously memorising the way she looked, all flushed and alluring.

'Four o'clock,' he murmured in answer to her question. 'So that leaves us plenty of time to—' his eyes fastened greedily on her lips once more '—get to know one another.'

Adeline's senses were beginning to reel with the shock of her decision and his closeness, and her treacherous heart began to beat a trifle faster. She suffered what remained of the journey in a state of tension, anticipating what would happen when they reached his rooms.

The hotel was busy with people coming and going. They took the lift to the third floor. On opening the door to his suite of rooms, Adeline was surprised and more than a little embarrassed to see a well-groomed, middle-aged man standing at a desk, carefully putting papers and files into a large leather case. He looked up and smiled.

'Ah, Vickers,' Grant said. 'Allow me to present Miss Osborne. Adeline, this is John Vickers—my secretary, valet. Call him what you like, but I could not do without him.'

'I'm pleased to make your acquaintance, Miss Osborne,' Mr Vickers said courteously, closing the case and carrying it to the door. 'Now, you must excuse me. I have things to do before we leave.' He looked at Grant. 'I'll see you in the foyer at three-thirty, Mr Leighton.'

Grant followed him, giving the stalwart secretary a set of instructions before closing the door on him. 'Vickers is to accompany me to France,' Grant explained, walking back to Adeline. 'He's been with me a long time. He's highly competent, discreet and indispensable.' Suddenly he became aware of Adeline's stillness and he frowned questioningly at the look of apprehension on her face. 'Adeline? Is there something wrong?'

Clutching her reticule with both hands, Adeline looked at him, her faltering courage beginning to collapse. 'I can't do this,' she whispered. She'd spent the time while he was talking to Mr Vickers trying desperately to decide whether her misgivings were based on good judgement or panic.

Wordlessly, Grant took her reticule and placed it on the desk, then he took her gloved hands and drew her towards him. 'What do you mean, you can't?' he demanded gently.

'I can't, Grant. Not now.' Her voice trembled and she looked towards the door in her desperation to escape. 'I—I think I need time.'

Drawing her hands from his grasp, she moved away from him. But the urgency and regret in his deep voice checked her in midstep and made her fear of him absurd. 'I am to leave for the continent at four o'clock, Adeline. Time is the one thing we don't have.'

That there'd be time enough for loneliness when she returned to Rosehill made her realise how foolish she was being to turn down an opportunity that was heaven sent. All her defences began to crumble. She could not deny herself the memories he'd make for her if she stayed.

When she looked at his handsome features an ache swelled in her chest. 'Grant,' she whispered a little shakily, and watched his expression soften at the sound of her voice. 'I'm sorry.' She held out her hand in a gesture of conciliation. 'For a moment I—I panicked.'

Grant saw the yielding softness in her eyes, and somewhere deep inside him he felt the stirrings of an emotion that made him reach out and draw her into his arms. He wanted her so much he couldn't bear to think she would deny him now. When she melted against him, the hot, sweet smell of her whipped up the blood in his veins. Releasing her without a word, and with his eyes holding hers like a magnet, he took her hand and drew her into the bedroom, closing the door firmly behind them.

Taking off his outer garments, he then removed Adeline's hat and with infinite care unpinned her hair. When the last pin was out she gave her head a hard shake, and her hair tumbled down her back in a shining mass. Grant marvelled at its luxuriant, thick, rich texture and colour, running it through his fingers, pausing now and then to kiss her lips, her cheek, her neck.

Her eyes drifted closed and her breath came out in a sigh as she kissed him softly and felt his lips answer, moving on hers, while his arms tightened around her. Breaking the kiss, she half opened her eyes and saw that the silver-grey eyes were beginning to smoulder.

With his lips against hers, Grant murmured, 'Let's go to bed,' his long fingers beginning to unfasten the buttons down the front of her three-quarter-length coat.

Grant obviously had no inhibitions about undressing in front of her, but Adeline was self-conscious enough for them both. When she turned away, Grant realised that she was embarrassed and shy about revealing her naked body. With an understanding smile he went to her and turned her round. Placing his finger beneath her chin, he tilted her head to his.

'Do you forget, Adeline, that I have seen you naked before now? You have a beautiful body—so why the reticence? Come. Since there is no lady's maid to assist, allow me to oblige.'

The sight of Adeline's naked body—a miracle of ripe curves and glowing flesh—made Grant's heart slam against his ribs. Her breasts were perfect, her legs just as long and shapely as he remembered. In fact, she was stunning. Whoever had thought Adeline Osborne plain and uninteresting did not know her—and nor would they, he vowed, swearing that no other man but himself would ever see her like this.

'You take my breath away,' he whispered, drawing her against him.

When she wound her arms around his neck and placed soft, feather-light kisses on his neck, the solid wall of his chest and his sinewed shoulders, his heart constricted with an emotion so intense, so profound, that it made him ache. Her breath was sweet against his throat. Dear God, she was so warm, so womanly, long and slender, but curving against his body, doing what she could to get even closer. His male body rejoiced in it, for it told him he held a warm and willing woman in his arms.

To Adeline, the moment was one of poignant discovery. His skin felt like warm silk over steel as her fingers slid through the short, dark matting of hair on his chest. His jaw was set, his cheekbones angular, his mouth firm yet sensual, his eyes hard and dark with passion—and for now he was hers.

When he pulled her down onto the bed their restraint broke, and together they were caressing, seeking hands and eager mouths. They were both aflame, both burning with the same need. He was kissing her with a raw, urgent hunger, his hands claiming her body, sliding over her breasts, her waist and back to her face, shoving his fingers into her silken hair, holding her a willing prisoner. She moaned with joy as his mouth touched her breasts, and so lost was she in the desire he was so skilfully building inside her that she scarcely noticed when he eased her body beneath his own.

As he entered her she expelled a breath at the exquisite sensation of her body opening to him like a flower. No holding back, she strained towards him with trembling need, each instinctive, demanding thrust pushing her closer to the edge and bringing exquisite pleasure. Grant, unlike Adeline, did hold back, for he wanted her to experience as much as his body would allow before he lost control.

Afterwards, when their passion had finally exploded in a burst of extravagant pleasure, in languid exhaustion and bone-deep satisfaction they lay close together, facing each other, breathless from exertion, clinging to the fading euphoria. Contentment stole over them both, lapping gently. They trembled with the rapture of their union, the passion which Grant had known with no other woman. Sliding his fingers over her spine, he watched her open her eyes. Smiling, she nestled closer. Grant placed a kiss on the top of her head.

'You are exquisite. How do you feel?'

'Wonderful,' she breathed, and she did.

As sanity returned it became obvious to her that the man who had just made love to her was indeed the same man who had made love to her before—but this time his technique had been perfect, unimpaired by alcohol. He had taken her not just sexually, but with a deeper, infinitely more alluring need—something profound.

'What we did was very, very special to me.' She raised her head and gave him a slumberous smile, sated and happy, the smile of a woman fulfilled. 'Thank you.'

He shoved the hair from her smooth cheek, his eyes warm and serious and very tender. 'My pleasure, Miss Osborne. Now I know what I missed, I am impatient to make up for lost time.'

Nestling closer to him, Adeline closed her eyes, letting the warmth deepen inside her, driving out everything else. At length she whispered, 'I'm going to miss you. Will you think of me in France?'

His arm tightened round her. In that moment he realised that leaving her was going to be the hardest thing he had ever had to do. 'All the time. I wish I didn't have to go.'

She sighed against him. 'So do I. Why are you going?'

'Like your father, I am a businessman, Adeline, and a number of speculative ventures have come to my attention. I am interested in investing in several companies in France, and arrangements have been made for me to meet some prominent businessmen over there.'

'But why go there? If the companies are limited why not simply buy shares in them?'

'Because, my darling girl, I wish to know the real position of the companies I am to sink my money into, to be sure in my own mind that they will not fail to meet their liabilities. If they do, and my investments collapse, then I will only have myself to blame.'

Adeline sighed against him. 'You are very astute, Mr Leighton.'

'I have to be.'

'Must you go?'

He nodded his head, and even though his voice was still soft, it was steadier and more resolute. 'Yes. Don't make it harder than it already is.'

Adeline wondered desolately how it could possibly be any

harder, but she swallowed down that futile protest. 'I won't. I suppose if it's business then you have to go.'

'Do you intend staying in London?'

'For a little while. I've never been away from Rosehill for so long—or from my father—and I'm rather enjoying my freedom.'

'I'd like to see the look on his face when his daughter returns as a stylish, independent young woman.'

'He probably won't notice.'

'Yes, he will. You'll see.'

'Will—will you write to me?' she asked hopefully.

'Only if you promise to write back.'

She nodded. 'You know I will.'

They fell silent, each content to hold reality at bay for the time they had left together. After a prolonged moment of silence, Adeline whispered, 'What are you thinking about?'

Grant tipped his chin down, the better to see her, wiping shining strands of hair from her forehead. 'I was thinking how lucky I am to have you here with me now. I knew within minutes of seeing you that you were quite unique.'

'Yet you knew nothing about me, about my character, which is what makes a person.'

'I knew by the way you rode your horse. It was obvious you didn't give a damn what people thought about a woman riding astride—and wearing breeches to boot. I was full of admiration. I also thought you were the most vital, energetic young woman I had ever seen—quite magnificent, in fact. And now I have come to know you I realise I was not mistaken in my opinion.'

Rolling onto her stomach and leaning on her elbows, Adeline looked into his fathomless eyes. 'Truly?'

'Truly.'

'And were you not disappointed when you realised who I was—plain, shortsighted Miss Adeline Osborne from Rosehill? People have always had the most odd reaction to my looks.'

'I can't imagine why,' he said, his mouth quirking in a half-smile as he pulled her down onto his chest. 'I have never considered you plain—interesting, yes, and discerning, certainly not dull, and never plain.'

In Grant's opinion he spoke the truth, because as she sprawled across his chest, her deep mahogany-coloured hair shrouding them both, she looked like a bewitching, beautiful, innocent goddess.

'But I have odd eyes, don't you think?'

'Take it from me, Adeline,' he murmured, his senses alive to every inch of the form so languorously stretched across him, 'there is absolutely nothing wrong with your eyes, or your nose—which is adorable, by the way—and your mouth is perfect and extremely kissable. So you see, along with all your other feminine assets, you have all the requisite features in all the right places.' His gaze settled on her mouth. 'And, speaking of your mouth,' he said, watching her tongue pass over her full bottom lip in a most seductive manner that made him acutely aware that his body was stirring to life with alarming intensity, 'I think it's time you kissed me. We haven't much time left, and I don't want to waste a minute of it.'

Happy to do as he asked, Adeline lowered her head and lightly placed a kiss on the corner of his mouth. Her eyes darkened with a love she wasn't trying to conceal from him any more. 'What is it I have to do to please you?'

Rolling her onto her back, he smiled down at her. 'I'm open to suggestions. Show me.'

Chapter Eleven

Loving Grant from the bottom of her heart, Adeline tried to block out the painful moment when they would have to part. When it was time for him to leave, Adeline accompanied him to the ground floor of the hotel. It wasn't until they reached the foyer that she realised she had left her reticule in his rooms.

'I'll go back and get it,' Grant offered.

'No, I'll go. You go and find a cab. I won't be long.'

Having retrieved her reticule, Adeline stepped out of the lift and looked around her, searching the people milling about for the face she loved. And there he was. She was about to cross to him when she saw him bend his head to the woman who seemed to be clinging to his side. His arm was half about her waist and her hand was placed possessively on his arm.

It was Diana.

It was the expression on Diana's face that caught Adeline's attention and held her momentarily transfixed. Her eyes were direct, intensely earnest, and she was looking at Grant as if she were telling him something profoundly important. Grant, standing with his profile to Adeline, was speaking softly, closer to Diana than was customary for mere friends, and he seemed—at least for the moment—oblivious to anyone else.

Numb with shock, she felt a silence seem to fall around her—a silence in which every sound was muted, a silence in which she seemed embalmed for a moment. And then she spun on her heel and walked out of the hotel. She got inside a cab and told the driver to go to Eaton Place, and to hurry. The man obeyed instantly, snaking his long carriage whip over the horse's back and urging it forward, ignoring delivery carts, drays and other hansoms which swerved out of their way.

Inside the cab, Adeline felt as if she were existing in some kind of remote space, isolated from everything. The only thing she could think of was Grant and the pleasure he had given her—the intense, undreamed of, unimaginable pleasure—and now Diana had appeared once again to spoil everything. She felt desperately wretched and unhappy. How could he? she thought angrily. But anger did not help her. She felt lost and bewildered.

As soon as she entered the house, Mrs Kelsall handed her a letter that had arrived earlier. It was from Rosehill.

When Adeline didn't meet him in the foyer, Grant returned to his room to find she wasn't there either. Puzzled as to where she could be, he waited a while in case she turned up before going to Eaton Place—only to be told by Mrs Kelsall that Adeline had received an urgent message from Rosehill. Her father had been taken ill and she had left for the station almost immediately.

For the second time that day Grant rushed to Victoria Station, in the hope of seeing her. But he was too late. He was to leave himself to catch the boat train shortly, so he was unable to go after her, but he was curious as to why she had left the hotel without saying goodbye. Then the reason why she had gone hit him like a hammer-blow.

Diana! She must have seen him with Diana—and, based on her reaction, she had imagined the worst. She was torturing them both this way because she was angry and hurt. 'You little fool!' he murmured, staring at the empty railtrack. She had done it again, without giving him an opportunity to explain. And now it was too late.

He could imagine the wrenching look on her face when she had seen him with Diana—and the image haunted him. It tore at him, along with his other worries about her. There were so many things he needed desperately to say to her—and he would. He would write to her the moment he reached his hotel in Paris.

All the way to Rosehill, Adeline was filled with a mixture of emotions: in particular, worry about her father, and second to that a growing fury—a furious disbelief—that she had allowed a man to treat her as Grant Leighton had done. She felt rage that he had had the audacity to do so. She had the desire to shout her rage out loud. What sort of a woman did he think she was? How *dared* he? How *dared* he lure her to his hotel room and do what he had when all the time Diana Waverley had been waiting downstairs? No matter how hard he denied they were having an affair, she did not believe him and never would. How could she when she had seen the evidence with her own eyes?

Well, she could do nothing about Grant Leighton just now. Her father was ill and he needed her—but, dear Lord, she'd have something to say to him when the time came.

On reaching Rosehill, Adeline knew her face was set in lines of anxiety.

'How is Father?' were the first words she asked Mrs Pearce, who had been the housekeeper at Rosehill for as long as Adeline could remember.

'Dr Terry's with him now, Miss Adeline.'

'What's wrong with him?' Adeline asked, removing her hat and gloves and handing them to a hovering maid.

'It's his heart, Dr Terry says. He collapsed last night at dinner. We managed to get him to bed. It was fortunate Dr Terry was at home and able to come at once.'

'Is he conscious?'

Mrs Pearce nodded her grey head. 'He's very poorly, but the doctor will tell you more.'

When Dr Terry faced Adeline he was as reassuring as he could be.

'He's had a minor heart attack, which I believe was brought on by stress. I've advised him time and again not to work so hard—but you know what he's like. His condition is stabilised, and I don't believe there is any danger—providing you can get him to take things easy.'

'I'll certainly do my best.'

'I've given him a draught that seems to have relaxed him, and he'll be relieved to see you, my dear. Your presence will hasten his recovery, I am sure.'

Knowing full well that her presence was unlikely to make any difference whatsoever, Adeline let her lips curve in a wry smile. 'Let us hope so, Dr Terry.'

'I've taken the liberty of employing a nurse—a Mrs Newbold—who is extremely competent. She arrived this morning and has already settled in to her duties.'

'Thank you. I do appreciate that.'

'There's nothing more I can do for now. I'll call tomorrow. Just make sure he stays quiet.'

As soon as Dr Terry had left, Adeline went up to her father. He was propped up against the pillows, his face grey and drawn with the hint of tiredness and pain. The signs of fleshiness were beginning to fight against the hardness of it, showing his advancing age, but his intelligent eyes were keen as he watched her approach the bed with quiet assurance.

'Adeline,' he said throatily.

She bent over and lightly kissed his cheek. 'Hello, Father,'

she said, searching his face. He had always seemed so inde-
structible. Nothing had seemed beyond the reach and scope of
his energy and intelligence. 'I came just as soon as I could. How
are you?' she ventured. 'Dr Terry seems pleased with your
progress.' She smiled. 'You always did confound predictions.'

He nodded, his gaze on her face. 'I'm glad you're home,
Adeline. All this fuss.' He glowered at Mrs Newbold, hovering
across the room. 'I can't stand it.'

'It won't be for long. I'm sure you'll soon be up and
about—but you're going to have to take it easy for some time.'

'So everyone keeps telling me—and I fear they're right.'

A sad smile rested briefly on his lips, and when he looked
away Adeline knew his very attitude was an admission of
weakness. He who had always had determination, stamina,
will—who had demanded and been paid the homage of lord
and master for so long—had in the last moments been toppled
from his pedestal, and the recognition of his fall was mutual.

He looked at Adeline and a softening entered Horace's
eyes. 'I've missed you, you know.'

'Have you?' Adeline could say no more in her amazement.
Her father, who had always seemed so remote—uncaring—had
missed her, and he was looking at her in the most extraordinary
way. She marvelled at it, and something inside her softened and
shattered. Her quick, observant eyes saw the varied emotions
flickering in his own. He had changed. Never before allowing
her to come too close, now he seemed to welcome her.

Smiling softly, a warmth in her eyes, and taking his hand,
she sat on the edge of the bed facing him. 'I've missed you,
too. When I left for London there was so much constraint
between us—of my doing entirely. I accept that, and I am so
sorry, Father. I never meant to hurt you. Truly.'

'It doesn't matter now,' he said hoarsely, gently squeezing
her hand. 'I'm just glad to have you back. You look—different, somehow—quite fetching, in fact. Your hair…'

Adeline laughed brightly. 'It's supposed to be the new me, but I'm still the same underneath. I—I saw Grant Leighton in London. I—understand his mother has been a guest at Rosehill whilst I've been away?' Did she imagine it or did a twinkle enter his eyes?

'She has, and most delightful she is, too. We have much in common, Hester and me. In fact I would like you to write to her—tell her what's happened and that she must feel free to visit any time. I—would like to see her.'

'I'll do that.'

'So, you've seen Grant Leighton, have you?'

'Yes, on—on several occasions,' she said, lowering her eyes.

Horace settled into the pillows, observing his daughter with careful scrutiny. He didn't need a crystal ball to tell him that all was not as it should be with her. 'Do you regret not accepting his proposal of marriage, Adeline?'

She shook her head. 'It's in the past, Father. At the time there was so much unpleasantness. I—prefer not to speak of it.'

Horace did not question her on the subject of Grant Leighton any further. There were areas of the heart into which one did not intrude.

Adeline greeted Hester Leighton in the hall, relieved that she had come at last. Her features were as soft and feminine as she remembered, but there were shadows under and around her eyes that had not been present before.

'It's very good of you to come, Mrs Leighton. Father is so looking forward to seeing you.'

'I would have come sooner, but I didn't want to appear intrusive,' Hester said, smiling softly.

'You knew my father was ill?'

Hester raised her brows delicately. 'I had a letter from Grant. He mentioned that he'd seen you in London, and the reason why you had been summoned back to Rosehill.'

'I see.' And Adeline did see. What Mrs Leighton had said told her that Grant must have followed her to Eaton Place when he had found she had left the hotel. Had he been surprised? Had he realised why? 'The hall is chilly. Come into the drawing room. It's warmer and faces on to the garden…' She smiled suddenly. 'But you will know all about that, since Rosehill was your home for many years.'

'I do, and you are right.' Hester accompanied Adeline across the hall and into the warmer, far more agreeable room. 'I always loved it in here. It gets the sun for most of the day, and the garden is as delightful as I remember.' Her eyes misted as she looked out of the long windows. 'I have so many memories wrapped up in this house—happy and sad. When I heard your father might sell it I sent Grant to see him, to try and buy it back. Did you know?'

Adeline nodded. 'Father intended giving it to me as a wedding present when I married Paul —but that's in the past. But what am I thinking of? You must have some refreshment after your journey. Then I'll take you up to see Father.'

'Thank you,' Hester accepted. 'I would like that.'

When they were seated, Hester asked, 'How is Horace?'

'You will be pleased to know he is a little better. The doctor is pleased with his progress and thinks he will make a full recovery.'

Hester's relief was evident. 'I am so glad.' She paused before continuing, as if considering her next words carefully. 'Adeline, I do so hope you don't mind, but on your father's invitation I stayed at Rosehill while you were in London.'

'Mrs Leighton, this is my father's house. I think he is old enough to invite who he wants to stay. I certainly have no objections.'

Hester smiled with relief and sudden genuine pleasure. 'So you don't mind?'

'Not one bit. Between you and me, Father spends far too

much time working—which, in Dr Terry's opinion, may well have something to do with his heart attack. Some female company is what he needs.'

It was after dinner, after Hester had spent some considerable time with Horace, talking and reading to him, when, stirring her coffee, she tilted her head to one side and studied Adeline. She said with a smile, 'You know, you do look different.'

Adeline laughed. 'I know. It's all down to Lettie. She thought I needed taking in hand.' Adeline saw a shadow cross Mrs Leighton's face. She waited. To ask its cause would be an intrusion, but instinctively she knew it concerned Lettie. 'How is Lettie?' she asked, speaking calmly.

Hester sighed. 'She is well, considering all she has been through—although I do worry about her. I wanted her to come to Rosehill with me but—well… I know what happened to her in London,' she said quietly. 'She told me everything, Adeline. I was appalled and extremely shocked—angry, too—to think my darling daughter endured what she did alone. I have you to thank for everything you did for her. Thank you so much for taking care of her.'

Adeline looked at Mrs Leighton and saw her exquisite high-boned face was drawn, her eyes far away, sad and angry. 'I am glad she felt that she could confide in me.'

'Poor Lettie. I feel an intense sadness for her. She had the passion, the intelligence and the courage to dare anything. Now she sits brooding and just looking at nothing for most of the day. I cannot condone her affair with that—that night-club owner, or what she did.'

She looked dejectedly down at her hands, folded in her lap. 'I cannot even bring myself to speak his name. I wish she'd never set eyes on him, and I cannot forgive the hurt he has caused her. Lettie espoused the Women's Movement because she cares about injustice. Where's the justice in what that man has done to her? However, I will not allow my anger to make me forget myself. Yes, Lettie told me many things—things best kept silent, if we are to live in any kind of peace. I am sure if you will consider it you will agree with me.'

Adeline understood that Mrs Leighton was asking her to keep what she knew to herself—not to tell her father. 'I agree with you. Sometimes to forget is the only sane thing to do— otherwise one becomes imprisoned by the past. Console yourself with the fact that the affair is over. Lettie is strong and will put this behind her. She has the support of her family and some stalwart friends.'

'Yes, I know. But there will always be a part of her that is damaged, and when I think of what that man is guilty of— that he has simply walked away unpunished... At least as far as Lettie is concerned.' She shook her head. 'Grant says he is being investigated by the police for crimes which I know very little about—nor do I wish to.'

'I am glad he's under investigation. But if the truth were to come out about Lettie it would bring shame on her, and Lord knows she has already paid a high enough price for her foolishness.'

Reaching out, Hester squeezed Adeline's hand in gratitude. 'That I do know. The injustice of it pains me greatly, but you are right. Lettie must move on—we must all move on and look to our good name. Scandal can be so damaging, so destructive. We mustn't let it.'

'I couldn't agree more.'

Suddenly Hester brightened. 'Adeline, how would you and your father like to spend Christmas with us at Oaklands?' She saw doubt cloud Adeline's eyes, and, afraid that she was about to refuse, went on quickly, 'I will not take no for an answer— and I know I can speak for Grant. I take Christmas very seriously—even when the family isn't complete. I make it an event every year, and savour the ritual. I would so like you to be there.'

* * *

Adeline had grave doubts about returning to Oaklands, but not so her father. He was delighted at the prospect of spending some time with Hester. The time she had visited him at Rosehill, when Adeline had been in London, seemed a long way in the past, and since his heart attack he had been realising more and more every day how he missed her.

He continued to get better, and when the time came for them to leave for Oaklands he was back to his old self.

Adeline's time had been taken up with writing and sending out Christmas cards to friends and family, and buying presents. She had chosen two rather beautiful silk scarves—one for Lettie and one for Mrs Leighton. Because she wasn't sure how many children would be there, she had also bought a selection of novelties and chocolates.

Grant was more difficult. After a great deal of deliberation she had chosen a gold cravat pin—plain, yet tasteful—hoping it would be an appropriate gift for their host and that he would like it. She had tried to keep herself focused on preparing for the visit, but her fragile control had begun to crumble the closer the time came for them to leave for Oaklands.

Grant had promised to write to her and he hadn't. She could only assume that what had happened between them hadn't meant as much to him as it did to her. She tried to imagine their meeting. Would he be angry because his mother had invited them? Would he be glad to see her or want to show her the door?

With firm determination she pulled her mind away from this nonsensical preoccupation and concentrated on what she would take with her. A terrible premonition of Christmas being a disaster quivered through her—and yet she felt she had been serious too long, and should be none the worse for a little light entertainment, which she intended her Christmas at Oaklands to be.

* * *

Since they had left Rosehill the day had become colder, with a knife-edge to it, and the sky was lower and heavy, with more snow in the air. There had been a fall during the night, with slight drifting in places, disrupting both road and rail travel. As the Leighton carriage, which had met them at the station, approached Oaklands, Adeline was as impressed by the house in its colour-bleached surroundings as she had been on her first visit.

Seated across from Adeline and Emma, her father was tucked beneath a thick rug, his chin sunk deep in the collar of his coat, his fur-trimmed hat pulled well down over his ears. Beside him, attentive and concerned for his master's well-being at all times, sat Benjamin, his manservant of many years.

They climbed out just as the door opened, and Hester came to welcome them. Horace strode the couple of paces over to her and took her in his arms. Normally Adeline would have been slightly shocked by this show of familiarity, but at that moment she could think of nothing other than seeing Grant again.

Hester stood back and gave Horace a close look. 'I'm so glad you're feeling better, Horace. Indeed, you do look much improved since I saw you last, thank goodness. Do come inside,' she said, after greeting Adeline warmly and ushering them into the hall. 'We were beginning to think you might not make it with all this snow—and more on the way by the look of the sky. Still, the children are loving it, and it keeps them occupied so we mustn't complain.'

Leaving Emma and Benjamin to follow on with the cases, Adeline entered Oaklands. The hall, which was lavishly decked with holly, mistletoe and red-veined tree ivy, was warm and inviting, with happy-faced servants flitting to and fro, and delicious Christmassy smells drifting on the air from the kitchen.

Removing her bonnet and warm coat and handing them to

a servant while her father was conversing with Hester, she felt Grant's presence. Adeline's gaze was drawn towards him. He stood in the doorway to the drawing room, the daylight shining in from the windows behind him. There was a moment frozen in time when they looked at one another across the days that had gone by since they had parted in London, and then he was striding forward.

Dressed casually, in an open-necked shirt, tweed jacket and cord trousers, he was just as she remembered—his dark hair outlining his darkly handsome face, the same magnetism in his silver-grey eyes, the same firm yet sensual mouth. The hall seemed to jump to life about him as his presence filled it, infusing it with his own energy and vigour.

His eyes having taken their fill of her, Grant let his mouth curl slightly at the corners, suddenly alive with interest as he strode towards her. Adeline could feel the heat of embarrassment creep from her neck up her face. She was conscious of his nearness, of every detail about him once more, and the energy that radiated from him. Unable to drag her eyes away from his, she felt the black wave of apprehension lifting a little.

'Welcome back to Oaklands,' he said, shaking hands with Horace before letting his silver-grey gaze sweep over Adeline's face once more. 'It's good to see you both.'

Adeline could do nothing but stare at him. The rush of familiar excitement had caused her to become tongue-tied, strongly affected by the force of his presence.

Emotions swept over her as she remembered the intense passion they had shared. Sometimes at night she imagined him in her bed, and her heart would beat faster—to both her disgust and her rising passion—her thoughts would be in disarray, desire and reason conflicting. Then she would reproach herself. The presence of Diana Waverley in his arms still haunted her, but the eyes looking at her now dared her to fall into the same dangerous trap in which she had allowed herself to be ensnared in London, causing her to lose her self-respect and her sanity.

Pulling herself together, she chose directness. 'Thank you for inviting us to share the Christmas celebrations with you. We had intended spending it quietly at Rosehill—Father's illness, you understand—but when Mrs Leighton invited us to Oaklands, Father was easily persuaded.'

He raised a questioning brow. 'And you, Adeline? Were you easily persuaded?'

'No,' she answered truthfully. 'But I was outnumbered.'

He nodded slightly, knowing just how difficult it must have been for her to come here with matters unresolved between them. 'I'm glad you were,' he said quietly, and then went on to say, in a more conversational manner, 'You will find a large complement of family staying. As you know, my sister Anna and her husband David have travelled over from Ireland with their children. They have brought David's sister Kathleen and her two children with them. Her husband's a sailor and somewhere on the high seas. And Roland arrived from India just last week, so it promises to be a lively affair.'

'I'm looking forward to meeting them—and I'm longing to see Lottie again. Is—is she well?' she ventured to ask.

'Subdued, but on the whole she is quite well, and looking forward to being reunited with her good friend.'

A woman came to stand behind him. She was fresh-complexioned, and sufficiently like Grant to tell Adeline that this was Anna, his sister. She smiled warmly.

'You must be Adeline,' she remarked. 'I am Anna, and I'm so glad to meet you at last. I've heard so much about you from Lettie that I feel I already know you. You must come and meet David, my husband, and our boisterous brood of three.'

Adeline followed her into the drawing room, where a log fire blazed in the enormous fireplace. Immediately David, a charming, easy-mannered man, handed her a glass of punch.

She was overawed by the large gathering, and seemed to be surrounded by an onslaught of people—not only immediate family, but aunts and uncles, and she was sure she was introduced to a major and a lord whose names she couldn't possibly remember just then. They were all from different parts of the country, and all of them were welcoming, promising a Christmas unlike any other.

Roland's pale blue eyes appraised Adeline. Friendliness and charm he possessed in good measure, and there was a similarity of features between the two brothers. Like Grant, Roland was dark-haired and tall, but he seemed to lack the power and authority of his older brother. As Grant introduced them she warmed to him as he took her hand and kissed it, bowing with an essence of grace and charm.

'I am delighted to make your acquaintance, Miss Osborne.'

'Please—you must call me Adeline.' She gave him the warmest of smiles.

His answering grin was roguish, his even teeth very white against the tan of his skin. 'Thank you. I shall. I'm glad you were able to come, Adeline. Lettie's been singing your praises ever since I arrived—and I can see why. Are you aware that apart from Lettie you are the only unattached female here?'

Laughter crept into Adeline's voice when she replied. 'No, I am not. But I don't think I've ever been made to feel so welcome.'

'The Leightons are famous for their hospitality—is that not so, Grant?' he said, slanting a look at his brother, who returned his sideways glance with an identical one of his own, hiding his irritation behind a mask of genteel imperturbability. He knew his brother was trying to bait him. 'I don't think anyone would blame me if I took it upon myself to get to know you better before you disappear back to Rosehill.'

Adeline was unable to suppress her laughter. She looked at him directly and smiled enchantingly. 'Then I would advise you to be careful. You're liable to turn my head,' she teased—

something the old Adeline would never have dreamt of doing with a complete stranger. 'Are you always so impetuous with the ladies, Roland?'

'As far as I am aware a young lady has yet to catch Roland's eye,' his mother remarked jokingly as she passed them in a rustle of bronze taffeta to sit beside a rather stout Aunt Maud, who was looking decidedly flushed from imbibing too many glasses of punch. 'At least one of my sons is still heart and fancy-free—as the saying goes.' She exchanged a penetrating look with Grant before saying, 'Is that not so, Grant?'

Grant's lips twitched in a smile and he merely nodded.

Mrs Leighton's casual remark went straight to Adeline's heart, and for a moment she was bewildered. What had she meant by it? Who was the woman that held Grant's heart?

While Adeline's attention was diverted elsewhere, Grant moved closer to his brother. 'Roland,' he drawled, in a steely voice that was in vivid contrast to the expression of bland courtesy he was wearing for the sake of his guests, 'while you are at Oaklands, brother mine, feel free to lavish your attentions on any one of the available females from round about, but I am already committed to that particular young lady—as you well know.' The grooves beside his mouth deepened into a full smile that was complacent and smug. 'I have no desire to be free of the obligation. Is that clear?'

'As crystal,' Roland replied with a low chuckle. Giving his brother a conspiratorial wink, he murmured, 'Far be it from me to spoil the surprise you have in store for Miss Adeline Osborne,' before sauntering away.

Trying hard not to look at Grant, Adeline was glad of the distraction when she felt a tug on her dress. She looked down into the shining face of a little boy no more than six, beaming up at her.

'Hello. I'm Gerald.'

'And I'm Mary,' said a little girl with rosy cheeks, huge

blue eyes and black curls, perhaps four years old. 'Would you like to come and see the Christmas tree? I can show you.'

'Not now, darling,' Anna said, scooping the child up into her arms. 'Miss Osborne has only just arrived. There will be plenty of time to show her the tree later.'

'Oh, but I'd love to see it,' Adeline said, smiling at Mary. 'Will you show me, Mary—you, too, Gerald?'

'Yes,' they cried in unison, and Mary wriggled out of her mother's arms and grasped Adeline's hand.

'You'll be sorry,' Anna warned her laughingly. 'They'll never leave you alone now.'

'I hope not. I think they're charming.'

'Off you go, darlings,' Anna said, shooing them away as another boy and girl of similar ages—Kathleen's offspring—joined them. 'Nanny will be down shortly, to whisk you off to the nursery for tea, so be quick.'

'Uncle Grant must come, too,' Gerald enthused, jumping up and down with excitement.

Playfully ruffling his nephew's curls, Grant looked at Adeline and gave her a long-suffering smile. 'Woe betide me if I refuse.'

Altogether, amidst a great deal of chattering and laughter, the children made a wild dash along the passage to the big library—Adeline and Grant following at a more sedate pace. The door stood open to allow all those who passed a glimpse within and an invitation to step inside.

The children piled in. Holding hands, they advanced towards the light until they stood in the very centre of it. It was a glorious moment of realisation. They stood in a line, as still as statues, gazing with something like awe at the sight that confronted them. There was something magical in the air, and the delicious fragrance of singed fir branches permeated the room.

The Christmas tree, an import from Germany and popularised by Prince Albert, was the centrepiece of the decoration. Surrounded by a multitude of gifts, this particular tree was planted in a brightly decorated tub in the corner of the room and towered high above their heads. Secured at its pinnacle was a beautiful fairy with golden hair, a flowing sequin-spangled white dress and a wand. The tree was brilliantly lit by a multitude of little tapers, and everywhere sparkled and glittered with bright objects, reflecting warmly on the leatherbound gold-lettered books which stocked the shelves that lined the walls.

'Why, it's beautiful!' Adeline exclaimed, as awestruck as the children.

'And essentially for the children,' Grant laughed, pointing to a rosy-cheeked doll hiding behind a branch. 'It's also dangerous, and Mother makes sure there is always one of the servants with a wet sponge on tree patrol to guard against fire.' He looked at her. 'No doubt you celebrate the festive season at Rosehill in similar style?'

'Yes, and often several elderly relatives come to stay. Sadly we lack children. We always have a tree—but not nearly as large as this.'

Adeline knelt on the floor with the children in front of a nativity scene that had been set up, gazing with wonder at the wooden image of the baby Jesus in the crib, surrounded by figures of people and animals. She laughed when the children enthusiastically began telling her who the figures were supposed to represent, all talking at once, some louder than others, to make themselves heard.

She was rescued by the sudden appearance of Nanny. Wearing a starched white apron, she came bustling in and ushered her young charges out and up to the nursery for tea.

Left alone with Grant, Adeline moved closer to the tree. To be within close proximity to him was agonisingly difficult, and she couldn't help thinking what a strange situation this was. When she had last seen him she had been furious with him, fully intending to give him a piece of her mind when she saw him again, but here she was, unable to utter a cross word and thoroughly nonplussed by his manner.

Grant perched his hip on the edge of the desk, and a slow, lazy smile swept across his handsome face as his eyes passed over her shapely figure with warm admiration. He watched her tuck a stray wisp of hair behind her ear before reaching forward and lightly touching a decoration on the tree. For a moment the bodice of her gown stretched tight across the slim back.

The firelight and tree lights had turned her glossy reddish-brown hair a darker shade, touched her lips to a deeper red. Her face was in repose—vulnerable, thoughtful, like the children dreaming of Christmas, dreaming of something wonderful to happen. He had missed her. When he had found her gone from the hotel it had been like an arrow to his heart. How well he remembered the enchanting sexuality that she had brought to his bed, the wanton loveliness.

In his experience with women—and his experience could not be truthfully termed lacking—he had been most selective of those he had chosen to sample. Yet it was difficult to call to mind one as delectable as the one he now scrutinised so carefully. Even now, having known her as well as a man could know a woman, there was a graceful naiveté about Adeline Osborne that totally intrigued him.

'What are you thinking about?' he asked quietly.

Adeline turned her head and found him studying her. 'Nothing too profound,' she hedged. 'Just—things in general.'

'Care to tell me about them?'

Trying to avoid both his searching gaze and the entire discussion, she looked away at the Christmas tree. 'They really aren't worth discussing.'

'Why don't you let me decide that?'

She looked back at him, thinking of the short time they had spent together in his hotel rooms, how he had made love to her with that mixture of exquisite tenderness and demanding urgency. Unfortunately, with the passing of time she was finding it more difficult to cling to the illusion that he was her devoted lover. Now she was unhappily aware that the man who had made love to her with such wonderful passion, who had made her feel that she was the only woman he had ever made love to, had also made love to countless others—including Diana Waverley. She had been reduced to the status of an old friend—a passing acquaintance.

Grant had never intended falling in love with her. He had simply needed her then, that was all. She had never loved Paul, so he had never had the power to hurt her. But she did love Grant—with all of her heart—and he did.

'Have you always been so persistent?' she said, in answer to his question.

'Mother always did tell me it was one of my most unattractive qualities.'

Aware that someone had entered the room, Adeline looked beyond him to the doorway. It was Lettie. Adeline's eyes became riveted on the lovely brunette clad in an emerald-green gown. The two of them looked at each other and slow smiles dawned across their faces. Lettie's voice was a whisper filled with pure delight.

'Adeline! I'm so glad you're here at last.'

As Lettie approached with her arms outstretched, Adeline noted the dramatic changes in her and wondered a little apprehensively if the changes went too deep to be put right. But the ties of friendship pulled them together, and suddenly they were flinging their arms around one another in fierce hugs, laughing joyously.

'Oh, Adeline, you look wonderful. I've missed you so much.' Lettie laughingly hugged her again.

'I've missed you, too.'

'How long are you staying?'

'Until the day after Boxing Day.'

'Then I shall do my best to try and persuade you to stay longer. Oh, I'm so glad Grant invited you.'

Adeline stiffened. 'Grant?' She looked to where he had moved, to lounge gracefully against the window. His hands were thrust deep into his trouser pockets, his jacket open and pushed back to reveal the pristine whiteness of his shirt. He was looking at her with that half mocking expression which she knew so well. '*You* invited us?'

'Of course he did.' Lettie was quick to answer for her brother. 'Didn't you, Grant?'

'But I—I thought your mother…'

'Mother asked you on Grant's behalf. Is that not so, Grant?'

He nodded, not in the least embarrassed at being found out. 'I was in France, remember? I wrote to Mother, asking her to invite you and your father.'

'Oh! I—I didn't know.' Suddenly Adeline's heart almost burst with happiness. Grant *did* care for her after all. He had wanted her here.

'While you were in London, as you know, Mother and Horace saw a good deal of each other and became close. When I heard of his sudden illness it got me thinking. I thought that perhaps they would like to spend Christmas together—providing your father had recovered and was fit enough to travel.'

'Oh—I see,' Adeline managed, in a relatively normal voice, her heart sinking. And she did see. And the knowing took away the pleasure she had in seeing him again.

She felt as if he had slapped her. He was treating her as if there had been nothing between them—as if they had never shared the intense passion between a man and a woman. It was incredible to her that those arms had held her, that those hands had caressed her, that those firm lips had kissed her. Feeling absolutely wretched, deeply hurt and disappointed, she hoped she did not show her feelings. She should have guessed, of course. He hadn't been thinking of her at all.

Sensing the distress Adeline was doing her best to conceal, Lettie glowered at her brother, wondering how he could be so insensitive. 'Grant, stop being obnoxious.' Slipping an arm through Adeline's, she smiled at her reassuringly. 'Ignore him, Adeline. He's teasing you. You don't mind if I steal her away, do you, Grant? It's ages since we saw each other, and I'm so looking forward to catching up.'

'Go ahead. Adeline hasn't been shown her room. You can do the honours, Lettie.'

With a blizzard raging outside, dinner was a merry meal. The children were in bed, and everyone was chatting away amicably, with no awkward silences. The topic of conversation varied from the agricultural depression and Captain Webb's swimming of the channel in August, to the state of the nation. The Major—Grant's paternal uncle—sat across from them. He was a tall, elderly man with a shock of iron-grey hair, who had never married and had fought in the Crimea. Always one to appreciate an audience, he regaled them with tales of his travels throughout Europe and beyond, and told them humorous stories about his time in the army.

Seated beside Lettie, who looked relaxed and was more like her old self, Adeline felt a lightening of her spirits—but she was hurt by Grant's seeming uninterest.

She would have been surprised to know that she rarely left his sights as he watched her covertly from beneath his lashes.

For the remainder of the evening Grant was the perfect host. Every time Adeline glanced his way he was conversing with another aunt or uncle, her father or his mother, and all the time her heart cried out for him to look at her, for him to come and speak to her, to see the same look in his eyes as when he had made love to her.

Chapter Twelve

The following morning, which was two days before Christmas Eve, the blizzard had passed, and after breakfast the men, equipped with spades, began shovelling snow from the drive.

Holly bushes, bright with red berries, and trees, their branches heavy with snow, stood sharp against the azure blue sky, and the sun shone on the glittering white unblemished landscape. A fox had made his way across the garden, leaving his paw marks in the snow. The air was sharp and crystal-clear, and everything was still. Beyond the gardens, men, women and children from the village and round about whooped and whirled in exhilaration on skates on the frozen lake.

Wearing colourful scarves and gloves, and hats pulled well down over their ears to combat the elements, adults and children with happy voices dragged toboggans and floundered comically in the deep snow, stepping out of the house into the magical wonderland and making their way to a hill beyond the gardens. Roland and Grant were to supervise the sledging, while Lettie and Adeline, serviceably attired in warm coats, woollen skirts and stout leather boots, preferred to stay closer to the house to build a snowman.

With much hilarity, and enjoying themselves enormously, together they began to roll the bottom half of the body. The larger it got the heavier it was to push and, panting with the effort, they turned round and braced their backs against it, laughing helplessly as they pushed it along. Suddenly Roland appeared, and immediately engaged Lettie in a snowball fight, shrieking and dashing about like children. He playfully shoved some snow down Lettie's neck, and when she was thoroughly wet they disappeared into the house to change.

Grant watched the antics from his vantage point on the hill, never having imagined he would see Adeline doing such a mundane thing as building a snowman and playing in the snow. When he saw Lettie and Roland disappear, unable to resist the temptation to go and help her finish the snowman, he went to join her, leaving Anna and David with the children.

When she saw him a smile appeared, lighting up her whole face, and Grant melted beneath the heat of that smile.

With hands on hips he inspected the ball of snow gravely, looking the picture of vastly amused male superiority. 'It looks like a man's job to me,' he said.

Adeline gasped, her expression one of mock offence. 'Don't you dare let Lettie hear you say that. She'd make you retract every word.'

'I don't doubt that for one second. But I still say you need a man to roll that thing. Permit me.' And without further ado he rolled the ball of snow a bit farther.

Laughing as she watched him flounder beneath the strain, plunking her hands on her hips, Adeline gave him a look of com' disapproval. 'There you are, you see—it's not as easy as you think.'

Determined to roll it a bit farther, tensing his muscles, Grant rolled it until Adeline shouted that it was quite large enough, thank you. Standing back and slapping the snow off his leather gloves with a triumphant grin, he looked admiringly at the huge ball of snow and said, 'There you are. It's much improved, don't you agree?'

When Adeline replied her voice was soft and extremely sweet. 'Yes, Grant, I'm sure you're right,' she said with un-characteristic meekness—and the next thing Grant knew her hands had hit him squarely on the chest, catching him completely by surprise, sending him flying backwards to land spread-eagled in a snowdrift.

'Why, you little hellion,' he cried with a bark of laughter as he struggled to get out of the drift.

'That,' she told him, joining in his laughter, 'was for arro-gantly assuming I am incapable of building my own snowman. Pride comes before a fall, don't forget. Come on, Grant—get up.'

'My pride is in ruins,' he laughed. Getting to his feet and brushing the snow off his caped coat and hair, he knew he wasn't immune to the absolute exhilaration that came from being out of doors surrounded by snow—which he'd always hated before—while Adeline, her hair tucked beneath a mul-ticoloured tam-o'-shanter, cheeks the colour of her bright red scarf, was a breathtaking marvel, with her huge jewel-bright green eyes and wide, laughing mouth.

'It's dangerous to be within my range,' she shouted, moulding a snowball. 'I have an excellent aim.'

'That does it. You'll pay for that,' Grant shouted as the snowball hit him on the side of his head. Reaching down with both hands and scooping up some snow of his own, he squeezed it into a ball, grinning broadly, and with a danger-ous gleam in his eyes purposefully advanced on her.

'Oh, no—no, you don't,' she cried, beginning to back away, choking on her laughter. 'Stop it, Grant—you mustn't. Let's be sensible about this. I don't like snowballs—I'm warning you...'

Suddenly Grant lunged and landed a direct hit on her shoulder. With a shriek, bent on revenge, she made another snowball.

'You devil. You're mad. I'll get you back. I promise to snowball you senseless if you don't stop.' And, so saying, she flung it at him before whirling and making a dash for it.

'And I'll teach you the folly of daring to provoke me,' Grant shouted after her, scooping up more snow and giving chase.

Encumbered by her skirts and the deep snow, when Grant tackled her Adeline pitched forward with a screech, landing face down in the snow with Grant on top of her.

'Help!' she cried. 'Help me up.'

Grant shifted his weight and got up. Rolling onto her back and laughing helplessly as Grant bore down on her once more, wiping the snow from her face, she scrambled to her feet, begging for mercy and holding her hands in front of her to defend herself from the threatening snowball. But he showed no mercy as he began pelting her with more snow, which only made her laugh harder. It was impossible not to respond to this man as his masculine magnetism dominated the scene. A curious sharp thrill ran through her as the force between them seemed to explode.

Determined to get her own back, and not to go down without a fight, her face shining, convulsed with glee and excitement, she impetuously joined in. They became like a couple of children, cavorting about and shattering the quiet with their laughter, until they were thoroughly spent and covered in snow. Reluctant to return to the house and end this pleasant interlude, they turned their attention to the more serious business of finishing the snowman. It was a poor effort, but the lump of snow with its funny hat, Adeline's scarf tied around its neck and a bent carrot for its nose made the children laugh hilariously.

A quiet but happy band of children and adults slowly made their way back to the house to partake of hot mince pies and toasted crumpets deep in hot butter before a log fire roaring in the grate.

Later there was a progressive round of children's games which required a great deal of frolicking, popping in and out of rooms and hiding behind curtains and chairs, then hunting the thimble and Blind Man's Buff, in which both children and young adults participated—the adults leaving off to chastise a child that was becoming too boisterous, or to pick up one that had fallen, becoming tearful and needing comfort. They finished off with something quieter—conjuring tricks, performed by a remarkably talented David.

After breakfast the following morning, Lettie and Adeline, carrying skates and with linked arms, headed for the lake which, unlike the previous day, was deserted. It was surrounded by beech and oak, and the berries on the rowan glowed a deep orange-red. It was still cold, but the temperature had risen significantly overnight and already snow was dripping off the trees. The lake where the Leighton children had spent many a happy hour larking about in boats was large and teeming with fish. It was shallow around the edge, but shelved quickly towards the centre, where there were deep and dangerous undercurrents.

Adeline and Lettie spent a pleasant half-hour skating on the ice—keeping to the edge since they were unsure as to how thick it was in the middle now the thaw had set in. Adeline was not as accomplished a skater as Lettie, who laughed at her nervousness, but it was great fun—even though Adeline spent most of her time either hanging onto Lettie or down on her behind. At such times she was grateful to her wad of petticoats, which lessened the pain but did little for her humiliation.

It was when they stepped off the ice to recover their breath that they were approached by a man. They had been so wrapped up in their fun and frolics they hadn't seen him approach.

'You seem to be enjoying yourself, Lettie.'

Something of the voice penetrated the two young women's

initial fear and turned it to ice-cold horror. The voice was that of Jack Cunningham. Together they spun round to stare into two glacial pale blue eyes. Adeline looked at him and froze, feeling a chill colder than the air that came off the lake.

Lettie was stunned by Jack's sudden appearance, and the way he looked—and, hardened as she felt towards him, she could not repress a gasp of horror. He was barely recognisable. His usual elegance had vanished, and with his shapeless trousers and an overcoat which had seen better days he looked more like a man who had fallen on hard times and sunk to the very edge of the criminal world.

But it was his face that shocked both girls the most and held their attention. His skin was pasty beneath the dark stubble of his chin, his cheeks sunken and his eyes hollow. His sudden harsh laugh made them jump.

'What's the matter, Lettie? Are you having trouble recognising me? I have no difficulty knowing you. You are still the same murdering bitch.'

His mocking tone reawakened all Lettie's anger against him. 'Don't worry, Jack, I recognise you. Though I must confess you are somewhat altered. Who would guess that the rich and arrogant Jack Cunningham would ever be brought so low? The police have you under investigation, I believe, on the grounds that your premises are used for immoral purposes—and not before time.'

'A complaint has been lodged against me, and as you damned well know the complainant was your brother,' he growled.

'And this time the police couldn't be bribed,' Lettie retorted scornfully. 'I know Grant went above their heads and used such powerful influence that the Home Office insisted on a strict investigation. I thought you had been arrested.'

'They couldn't catch me.'

'So you are on the run from the law.'

'Exactly.' As his words came pouring out his features grew

ugly, contorted with anger and a wild hatred. 'You have made a fool of me—you and your brother. I won't go down before I've paid back the bastard who informed on me and the bitch who got rid of my child. I've been here for days, watching and waiting for this moment. I intend to savour every second of it.'

Lettie's voice was cold and disdainful. 'Come to your senses, Jack. You are out of your mind. Have you thought what the consequences of such action might be?'

'What does that matter to me now? I've lost everything else—everything I've worked for has been stripped from me—and it's you—you I blame.'

'And Grant? Are you going to hurt him too?'

Jack's eyes glittered like ice. The minute the police had entered the Phoenix Club he had known with absolute certainty that his comfortable life was at an end, destroyed by the power of Grant Leighton, stripped of everything that was of value. Nothing remained of the prestige and pleasure-seeking that had marked his existence since he had left the ranks of the working classes.

Raw emotion had robbed him of any kind of reason, any kind of judgement. He wanted to make them suffer physically with his own hands, until they were too helpless to ask for mercy. His eyes narrowed and gleamed with a murderous light. 'I'm not going to hurt him. I'm going to kill him. As for you, I could break your neck.'

His eyes were intent on Lettie's, and she could see it was no idle threat.

Adeline felt tension coiling in the air around them, invisible but potent. The shock of Jack's appearance had worn off, and she appraised their situation. They were on the opposite side of the lake from the house, and there was no hope of raising attention. She had to believe that Jack would bluster and threaten and let them go, but the merciless way he was looking at Lettie and his tightly clenched fists told her he intended to harm her.

'Lettie, go—get away,' she urged frantically, with no thought to her own safety. 'Can't you see why he's come here?'

When Jack reached out to grab Lettie's arm she backed away and, spinning round, took to the ice. She began skating for all she was worth in the direction of the house, not thinking he would follow, or that instead of keeping to the outer limits of the lake, hoping to cut her off, he would head straight across the middle, with a roar of furious frustration.

Not having moved, with her heart in her mouth, Adeline watched in horror as the scene began to unfold before her eyes. Seeing Lettie disappear round a curve in the lake, she wasn't aware of the moment when Jack vanished. One minute he was there and then he wasn't. Horrorstruck, she stared at the empty lake stretching out before her, knowing full well what had happened. The ice had broken and Jack had gone through. In desperation she stared around for help. All she saw was a frozen white winter land—no movement, no help.

Alone in the conservatory, Grant stood looking out over the gardens, feeling strangely content and pleased with himself. The sun shone on breathtaking beauty, melting the snowman, which had given him so much pleasure in building it with Adeline. Trees stood sharp against an azure sky, the snow on their branches glittering like scattered diamonds.

Letting his gaze travel beyond the gardens to the lake, with some amusement he had watched Adeline's and Lettie's antics on the ice, which seemed to have involved a great deal of laughter. Although Adeline had had difficulty keeping her balance, they'd been having such fun. He thought of Adeline as she had been yesterday, when they had built the snowman. She had been full of fun and life, incredulous and amazingly natural. She had taken his breath away. Her cheeks had been as red as poppies, her eyes jewel-bright. And as he'd watched

her from a distance, he'd felt the melting of something warm
and sweet run through his veins like warm honey.

She really was quite magnificent, he thought, with a catch
in his heart.

Trees and bends obliterated parts of the lake, and the girls
weren't always visible. When they stepped off the ice he
watched a man approach them. Too far away to see who it
was, he had no reason to be alarmed—but when he saw Lettie
turn and begin skating frantically away, with the man in
pursuit, he looked to where Adeline stood, a forlorn, still
figure against the stark white backdrop. As if he could feel
her distress, he threw open the door and with long strides ran
towards the lake.

On reaching the edge he stopped and looked around. The
man had disappeared. Where had he gone? Then he saw
Adeline. Having removed her skates, she was running towards
him, pointing to the centre of the lake, where there was
nothing but a black hole. Lettie had stopped and was staring
at where Adeline pointed.

Absolutely distraught, Adeline could feel her heart beating
heavily. When she reached Grant she was gulping her words
out while she blinked up into his face. 'The ice—his weight
must have been too much for the thin ice. He—he's gone
through, Grant. He's in the water. What can we do? If we
attempt to get him out there's a danger we'll fall in, too.'

Gathering her in his arms, he drew her close, and all the
while he held her he was aware of her body near his, of her
breath sweet and warm against his throat. 'There now. Don't
distress yourself. Who is it? Do you know?'

'Jack—Jack Cunningham. I believe he wanted to harm
Lettie—you, too, Grant—he was so full of hate. But—oh, this
is all so awful.'

They were joined by Lettie and Roland who, like Grant, had
seen what had happened from the house. Grooms and servants

began to appear—summoned by Roland on his way to the lake—one of them carrying ropes, another planks of wood.

Acting swiftly, Grant thrust Adeline away from him. After removing his jacket, grim faced, he took one of the ropes and fastened it around his upper body.

Cold and shaken, Adeline stared at him in horror and disbelief. 'Grant, what are you doing? You can't go in there. Jack must be dead by now. No one could survive this long in freezing water.'

'I have to do this, Adeline. I have to see if I can find him, otherwise I couldn't live with myself. If he's dead, then so be it. But at least I will have tried.'

'Adeline's right, Grant,' Roland said, concerned by his brother's decision to go under the ice, where the water swirled restlessly. 'It would be impossible to withstand the cold beneath this ice for long.'

'I have to, Roland. Just keep hold of the rope and haul me out if I'm down there too long.' His face was closed when he stared at Adeline for a moment, then he turned and stepped onto the ice, making his way to where Jack had gone through.

When he plunged into the icy water, rooted to the spot Adeline fastened her eyes on the point where he'd disappeared, unaware that she was holding her breath, or that a stricken Lettie had come to stand beside her and had taken her hand in a firm grip. She couldn't bear it, standing there, safe in the sunshine, while Grant was in dreadful danger under the ice. He had been down there a long time. Why didn't he come back up? And then the sight of his dark head surfacing revived her fading hopes.

Shaking the water from his hair and gulping in air, Grant disappeared once more. The longer he remained under water, the more Adeline felt as if she were dying, and she had to fight against the creeping, growing weakness which froze the blood in her veins. Her soul, her very life itself, was concentrated in her eyes, fixed unmoving on the spot where he'd gone under. Tearing her gaze away, she looked at Lettie anxiously.

'He's been down there too long, Lettie. He'll have to come up soon or he'll freeze to death.'

'He will—look…'

Grant had located Jack's body, several yards from the spot where he'd fallen in. Dragging it to the surface, he tied the rope beneath Jack's armpits.

'Pull me out first,' he shouted to the men. 'Before you have two corpses on your hands.'

With great effort, and much slipping and sliding, this they did. A blanket was thrown over Grant's shoulders, and he stood and watched as Jack's body was hauled out before going to where Adeline and Lettie stood huddled together. His face was drawn and ashen, and water dripped from his wet hair. He smiled at them with difficulty, to try and allay their fears.

Adeline's relief was immense, but she could not control her trembling.

Grant touched her cheek, looking at her tenderly. 'I'm all right. Don't worry.'

'What will happen to Jack?' Lettie asked, looking across the ice at Jack's lifeless body.

'The police will take him away. There will be questions asked, which I will deal with. Come, let's go back to the house. We'll leave them to it. There's nothing we can do here, and I must get out of these wet clothes. We have to inform Mother what has happened, but we'll tell everyone else that there has been an accident and that some unfortunate skater has gone through the ice.'

Hester received the terrible news in complete silence, before looking at Lettie who gazed straight ahead, dry-eyed. She stood passively, showing no emotion, her mind seemingly elsewhere. Secretly she was filled with a relief so profound she truly believed she might expire from it. Jack Cunningham was dead. Now she could get on with the rest of her life.

The following day everyone was relieved to find Grant no worse after his ice ordeal.

It was Christmas Eve, and with the dark came the carol singers, lighting their way with lanterns. As all the well-loved carols were sung all those who had known Jack Cunningham were determined not to let his death intrude and spoil the Christmas festivities. Afterwards there was much jollity as mulled wine and hot mince pies were handed round. And then it was time for the children to go to bed, each one excited about the imminent arrival of Santa Claus.

Where there had been chaos now there was calm, as exhausted adults revived their spirits, roasting chestnuts and drinking port wine, and when the church bells rang out the midnight hour Adeline, along with several others, went to celebrate Midnight Mass at the village church—the oldest custom of the Christmas festival.

On Christmas morning it was church again, after which Grant handed out gifts to the staff, and at midday there was the traditional Christmas dinner in the dining room, with the mahogany table extended to its full length. Evergreens adorned the walls and candles guttered in candelabrum along the centre of the table, along with baskets of nuts tied with red and gold ribbons. Turkey was served with all the trimmings, followed by Christmas pudding, brought into the room ablaze.

When everyone was replete, Grant rose to his feet to propose a toast, and Adeline was more than happy to see he was wearing the gift she had given him earlier. As if he'd picked up on her thoughts he fingered it, and his grey eyes locked onto hers in silent warm communication. The ghost of a smile flickered across his features.

After the meal guests retired to their rooms, to loosen tight clothing and take a nap in readiness for later, when neighbours and local dignitaries had been invited to a quiet, cold buffet supper.

Having no desire to rest, Adeline went in search of Lettie, finding her in a small sitting room with her mother and Anna. Conversation ceased and gazes swivelled to her. Adeline frowned, wondering bemusedly why she sometimes caught the three of them looking at her oddly.

'I do hope I'm not intruding. Is anything the matter?'

The three of them exchanged awkward glances.

'The matter? No—no, we were just discussing the party tomorrow night—is that not so, Mother?' Lettie was quick to say.

Looking rather startled, Mrs Leighton looked from Adeline to Lettie and back to Adeline. 'Yes—yes, that's right. Every Boxing Day night there's a traditional ball for the servants. As you will know, Adeline, they all work so hard at Christmas time. They are an integral part of the household—and it's their home, too, one mustn't forget. Since they are unable to be with their families they are given special treatment.'

'It sounds like fun,' Adeline said.

'It will be,' Lettie enthused. 'Grant has to lead the dancing with Cook, and Mother with the house steward. On the whole everyone has a good time. I hope you've brought your best party dress, Adeline.'

'My very best—which you helped me choose in London.'

'What's this about a party dress?'

They all turned as one to Grant, who had just come in.

'We were just telling Adeline about tomorrow, Grant,' Lettie answered.

He looked in alarm from his mother to Lettie. 'Tomorrow? You were?'

'Tomorrow night. You know—*the dance.*'

As Adeline looked at Grant she heard the emphasis Lettie

placed on the words, and she also heard Grant expel his breath in a rush of relief.

Lettie got up and linked her arm through Adeline's. 'Let's take a stroll around the house, Adeline. I ate far too much plum pudding and feel the need to walk it off.'

'Don't feel you have to leave on my account.'

Lettie smiled sweetly at her brother. 'We're not. I just want to talk to Adeline, that's all.'

They sauntered to the conservatory, sitting in wicker chairs and looking out over the snow-covered landscape. Tall, exotic plants reached the glass roof. There was the sound of falling water, and the smell of flowers and damp earth filled the air.

Lettie told Adeline that when Anna and David returned to Ireland she had decided to go with them for a short stay.

'I feel I have to get away for a while, Adeline, to try and rebuild my life into the best I can salvage— without Jack. You know, I feel enormously relieved now he can no longer threaten me. It was rather tragic—the way he died—but when Grant told me the police had found a firearm in his pocket, I realised he did mean to kill me—and Grant. He really hated me.'

'You must put it behind you, Lettie, and try not to feel too bad about what you did.'

'I know— and I will. When I get back I intend to throw myself into my work again. It's a man's world, Adeline, with a woman's part in it defined as very little. My affair with Jack taught me that if nothing else.'

'I'm going to miss you.'

Leaning back in her chair and folding her hands in of front her, Lettie looked at her, a small, secretive smile playing on her lips. 'Oh, I don't know. I think you might have other things on your mind and will have no time to miss me.'

'What on earth are you talking about?'

'You and Grant.'

'What about me and Grant?'

'Well, it's just that you seem to be getting on well.' She smiled knowingly. 'I was watching you the other day.' She raised her brows. 'The snowman?'

Adeline felt her face go red. 'Oh, that. We were enjoying ourselves.'

'Very much, by the look of things. Are you still in love with him?'

The direct question took Adeline by surprise. 'I—like him, of course.'

'I think it's more than that,' Lettie said quietly.

'Lettie, apart from our antics in the snow, he's hardly spoken two words to me,' Adeline retorted, unable to conceal the frustration she felt at Grant's indifference. 'He treats me just like all his other guests. I don't think he sees me half the time.'

'Grant is as aware of you as you are of him. He can't tear his eyes off you when he thinks you aren't looking.'

Adeline's heart soared precariously. 'He can't?'

'He certainly knows you're here,' Lettie said, laughing. 'He's got something very special as a Christmas present for you,' she went on. 'I know you'll like it.'

'He has?' Her interest and her heart quickened. 'What is it?'

Lettie's eyes twinkled mischievously. 'Ah, that would be telling—and it's for Grant to reveal it. I hope you'll be pleased.'

Adeline was becoming more intrigued by the minute. Everyone was behaving most strangely.

Adeline stood in the hall as the evening's guests began to arrive. She was watching the door when Diana Waverley, wrapped in sables and with exquisitely coiffed hair, swept in, her manner one of haughty arrogance. The sight of her here at Oaklands momentarily scattered Adeline's defences, and she felt her heart sink in dismay. As she handed her furs to the house steward, Diana looked striking in a sweeping plum-coloured gown of costly good taste, the low-cut rounded neckline of her bodice exposing a generous glimpse of full, creamy breasts.

Adeline wholly understood Grant's infatuation, and it hurt her more than she had imagined anything could—more so as she watched Grant receive her and introduce her to his mother. Why hadn't he told her he'd invited Diana? If so she could have prepared herself. And why had he invited her anyway?

Diana's gaze passed idly over those present. When she saw Adeline surprise registered briefly in her eyes, and then with a smug, superior curve to her lips she turned her full attention on Grant.

A while later, as Adeline surreptitiously watched Grant's tall figure moving among his guests, she saw him accosted by Diana once more. He bent his head low as he listened attentively to what she had to say, smiling at him all the while. He laughed, and Adeline flushed as she recalled the way he had laughed and frolicked with *her* in the snow. Without warning he turned, and Adeline was caught in the act of staring at him. His gaze captured hers, and a strange, unfathomable smile tugged at the corner of his mouth. Slowly he inclined his head towards her.

Stiffening her neck, she turned away from him to speak to Lettie. She couldn't trust herself to look at him again.

'What is that woman doing here?' Lettie whispered, her irate eyes shooting darts at Diana's back.

'I suppose, like everyone else, she must have been invited,' Adeline replied tightly.

'I don't think so. Grant wouldn't be so cruel as to do that to you, Adeline. Diana's been stalking him ever since her husband died.'

'He certainly looks interested enough. He's hardly left her side since she arrived.'

'If you watch carefully you will see it's Diana who is monopolising Grant. If he was interested he'd have offered for her years ago. I can't imagine how she has the effrontery to come here. I am certain she wasn't asked—but then she's brazen enough for anything.'

Adeline agreed, but her disappointment and frustration stayed with her. Having spent some time conversing with Anna, she was about to join Lettie once more when she was suddenly confronted by Diana herself.

Diana hadn't expected to see Adeline at Oaklands, and she strongly resented her presence. Suddenly she felt her hopes of reviving an affair with Grant shrivel, and a flare of jealousy reared its miserable head.

'I didn't expect to see you here at Oaklands, Adeline. I'm surprised.'

'Really?' Adeline exclaimed, trying hard to hold onto her composure. 'My father and Mrs Leighton are close friends. Following his recent illness she thought it would be nice for them to spend Christmas together.'

'I see. Then that explains it.'

'Explains what?'

'Why you are here.'

'And I had no idea *you* had been invited.'

'No? How very remiss of Grant not to tell you. When I last saw him he was very insistent on my knowing he was to spend Christmas at Oaklands, and that there would be the traditional supper party tonight. So I knew what he meant, and that he was expecting me. I came with Sir John and Lady Pilkington—they live between Oaklands and Westwood Hall.'

Taking a glass of wine from the table Diana looked around the company milling about, eating and drinking and conversing with friends. 'Well, isn't this cosy? And such congenial company. Of course I know most of them—neighbours, you understand.' Her eyes came to rest on Grant, and she smiled. 'And Grant is the perfect host—don't you agree?'

'Absolutely.' And how handsome he looks, Adeline thought

as she stole a glance at Grant's disciplined, classical profile as he circulated among his guests.

After a moment, and seeming reluctant to move on, observing Lettie laughing delightedly at something her male companion was saying, Diana said, 'Lettie seems to be in good spirits—considering.'

Alarmed by her comment, Adeline looked at her sharply. 'I'm sorry? Considering what?'

Diana's eyes were hard as they met Adeline's. 'Jack Cunningham was an acquaintance of mine, too, don't forget.'

Adeline's expression remained unchanged. Clearly Diana didn't know that Jack was dead, and she had no intention of informing her. No doubt Grant would tell her.

'Fancy asking Lettie to marry him with a wife still living— a lunatic,' Diana went on with incredulity. 'Well, who would have thought it? And when Lettie found herself to be in a— certain condition, it didn't go unmentioned by Jack.'

'If you feel any gratitude at all to Grant for coming to your aid when you found yourself to be financially embarrassed,' Adeline said harshly, having no real proof that he had, but chancing it anyway, 'I must ask for your complete discretion. Apart from Mrs Leighton no one in the family has any idea what happened, and that is what Lettie clings to.'

Diana's chin tilted upward and her eyes directed towards Adeline, their slanted gaze cold and without merriment. Her voice quivering with anger, she demanded, 'How do *you* know about my business arrangement with Grant? Has he said anything?'

Their gazes held, each reading the other's expression. 'No—he wouldn't. But I have ears, Diana, and I'm not stupid. However, that's not my concern. Lettie is. Despite her outward appearance she is still extremely fragile. I think any kind of confrontation would be a grave mistake. Please respect my wishes on this.'

Diana's eyes narrowed. 'I may be many things, Adeline, but I am no tittle-tattle. I've had dealings of my own with Jack Cunningham, so I know exactly what he is capable of. I can assure you that should Lettie's sordid little secret surface, I will not be the one responsible.'

'Thank you.'

'Please excuse me.'

Adeline was glad to.

The evening was drawing to a close when she saw Grant approach Diana and take her arm. The two left the room together. It was as if a dagger had been thrust into her heart. Christmas had changed. Diana had spoilt it.

She got through the next hour as best she could, but it was hard to keep smiling. Deeply wounded, she thought she would never believe her own instincts again. She had been so sure that Grant was beginning to love her.

Following her angry confrontation with Grant, after he had taken her to his study to speak to her, Diana left, realising she had underestimated Adeline Osborne. She had resolved herself to the fact that there was no hope for anything where Grant was concerned.

Feeling the need to get out of the house, to be by herself, Adeline went to her room to don coat and boots and slipped out of the front door, unaware that Grant was watching her. The night was bitterly cold. It penetrated her clothes. Yet she was thankful for its sharpness, for it cleared her mind of the fog caused by the day's over-indulgence.

Wistfully she gazed towards the sickle moon and starlit sky as quietness invaded her mood. Pulling the collar of her coat over her ears, and leaving the house behind, she walked to a wooded area beyond the gardens. She took the opposite direction to the lake, since she did not want to be reminded of the tragic events. Unafraid of the silence and the eerie trunks of oak, beech and lime, she was glad to be alone.

Somewhere an owl screeched, but apart from that silence gathered around her in that white winter world. She allowed her captivated senses to propel her further into the trees. Suddenly, seeing a slight movement ahead, she paused, her senses alert. Her eyes widened with surprise and pleasure on seeing a vixen, lithe and velvet footed, totally unaware of her presence. Her lips parted in a smile of delight on seeing two cubs rolling around close to their mother, yelping and snapping in play. Not wishing to frighten them away, without moving she watched, entranced. The sight held her enthralled, and she was bound in the spell of the moment.

A moment later instinct told her that she was not alone. Someone had come to stand behind her. Her heart began to race, urging her to run away, but she couldn't move. That was when the subtle scent of sandalwood assailed her nostrils and a powerful pair of arms slipped around her waist, drawing her back against a tall, long-limbed individual.

Lowering his head, he whispered, 'Be still. Do not make a sound unless you wish to frighten them away.'

Adeline froze for an instant of time as the familiar voice scattered her thoughts. She had no need to see the man's face to know who stood behind her. In that moment, when all her senses seemed to be heightened nearly beyond all endurance, she felt a frisson of recognition as deep and primeval as life itself. Hot breath smelling of brandy touched her skin as the warning was whispered against her ear, and she could feel a powerful heartbeat behind the hard muscle. Unable to struggle, unable to utter even the smallest sound, she was unaware that she was holding her breath. Her eyes were still locked on the fox and its cubs when the voice came again.

'A rare, enchanting sight, is it not?'

'It is indeed,' she whispered.

Adeline found herself wanting to turn and look at him, to surrender to the masculine strength of him and the hypnotic sound of his voice. The feel of his arms was electric. It flashed along her nerves like a powerful current. Her skin tingled and grew warm, and some dark and secret thing stirred inside her. It was as if the very essence of herself had been altered in the space of a heartbeat. Unable to struggle, unable to utter the smallest sound, all she could do was remain pressed against that powerful body.

The anxious vixen watched her cubs, nudging them with her nose, and to the cubs her protection was pleasing. Then her instincts came to the fore. She stiffened and looked in their direction with bristling hair, her face distorted and malignant with menace. Sensing the threat of humans, her lips writhed back and her little fangs were bared. Passing her unease to the cubs, she drew them back, discomfited, and slid into the shadows.

For all its intensity the moment had been brief. Grant released her and took a step back. Feeling weak, as if all the strength had been sucked from her body, Adeline turned slowly and faced him, her breasts measuring the steady rise and fall of her chest as she breathed. The moon was behind him so that its pale light fell upon her face, leaving his in dark silhouette.

'Why have you followed me?'

'Because I wanted to. Do you mind?'

She shook her head. 'No.'

'I hope you are enjoying Christmas.'

'Very much—although the events at the lake have cast a cloud over the festivities. What did you tell the police?'

'The truth—that Cunningham came here to kill me because I had informed on him. Naturally I made no mention of Lettie. They will liaise with the police in London, which will confirm what I told them.' His expression softened. 'I'm glad you came, Adeline.'

'And I'm happy to have been asked. I am grateful that you

have welcomed us so generously at what was intended as a family reunion. It has gone so quickly.'

'It isn't over yet.'

'Almost,' she said.

'No, it isn't. You have Boxing Day to get through.'

Was she imagining it or was there a hidden meaning to his words? Moving away from him, Adeline looked back to where she had seen the vixen, wishing she could see it once more. But she knew it would not return. With a rueful sigh she lowered her head. 'It's cold. We should go back.'

Placing his hands on her arms, Grant turned her to face him. 'Adeline, wait. There is something I must ask you. You have been here for days, and yet we have had little chance to speak privately. Why did you run away from me in London?'

She took a deep breath. At last he had raised the subject that had been on their minds since she had come to Oaklands. 'Why didn't you write?'

'Because what I had to say to you I wanted to say in person. So, why did you leave without saying goodbye?'

'You know why, Grant.'

'You deserted me.'

'I didn't.'

'That's how it felt to me. Why did you let me make love to you?'

'I suppose when emotions are running high people do mad things.'

'And are your emotions running high now?'

'When I'm with you my emotions are always running high—in fact they're all over the place, even though I firmly try to suppress them. You ask why I let you make love to me.' Her lips curved in a slow smile. 'I ignored all my instincts. I went with you to your hotel without reservation. And then I saw you with Diana. It almost destroyed me. I'm not going to put myself through anything like that again.'

'But you want me. You can't deny that.'

Even in the gloom Adeline could see his eyes sparkle. 'I'm human. You've proved that. Why didn't you tell me Diana was coming tonight?'

'It was a surprise to me. She was not invited, Adeline. I would not be so insensitive as to do that to you. After the initial shock of seeing her I tried to play the perfect host. She clearly misunderstood something I said when I saw her briefly in London on my return from France—I had to see her to discuss the Waverley estate, and she interpreted it as an invitation.' He grinned. 'Mother was none too pleased to see her, but she coped wonderfully. Nothing ruffles her.'

Adeline understood then just how madly possessive Diana was over Grant, and that he did not love her in return. 'Did you tell her about Jack?'

He nodded. 'I saw no reason not to. She would have found out some time.' For a long moment Grant's gaze lingered on the elegant perfection of Adeline's glowing face, then settled on her entrancing dark eyes. As he had watched her earlier, mingling with his guests, he had wanted more than anything to thrust everyone out through the front door and snatch her into his arms to kiss that full, soft mouth until she was clinging to him, melting with desire.

'Adeline, there is no Diana and me. There hasn't been for over two years. She wanted commitment. I didn't. Six years ago I might have married her, but she chose to marry a title instead.'

'But both times I was at your hotel she was there. You were—familiar together. What was I to think?' She saw the twinkle in his eye, the twist of humour about his mouth.

'I think you suffer from an over-active imagination, and because of it you have suffered a lot of unnecessary heartache. The first time you saw her she had arranged the meeting to ask me for a loan. I refused. The second time she came to thank me for digging her out of her financial hole—and I only agreed to do so because of Jack Cunningham.'

'You bought Westwood Hall, didn't you?'

He nodded.

'I thought so. What will you do with it?'

'When Diana has officially moved out I'll put the estate on the market. Cunningham gave Diana a hard time when he realised what she'd done—turning her back on his offer and selling to me instead. She's now decided to marry Paul.'

Adeline was astounded. 'She has? But earlier I thought she hoped…'

'That I would marry her? Never. I had a private word with her before she left and made her realise there can never be anything between us. She put off giving Paul his answer until she knew there was no hope for us.'

'Paul's a wealthy man, so she will not be disappointed in that, but I doubt they will be happy together.'

'So do I.' Lifting his hands and pulling her collar up over her ears, Grant looked down into her face. 'Not as happy as you and me. I love you, Adeline Osborne, and I am going to marry you. I have loved you from the morning I awoke and found you next to me. You were naked and beautiful, and your hair was spread about us both. We have been lovers ever since—we must look on that night as a gift from fate. When you left me so suddenly in London it tortured me. When I was in France I thought of you all the time. I couldn't work. I couldn't sleep. My mind was so full of you and you were so deep in my heart it hurt. I'd like this to be our new beginning. You *will* marry me?'

He spoke in that low, husky voice that was half-whisper, half-seductive caress. Adeline remained silent, too afraid to speak at first. She could scarcely believe this was happening. Tilting her head, she looked deep into those sober silver-grey eyes, so gentle, so full of love. His expression was serious.

She could feel the power he exuded, but she sensed his ruth-lessness, too—a man would have to be ruthless to achieve what he had achieved through life.

'Yes,' she whispered. 'Oh, yes, Grant. I will marry you. I shall be proud to marry you.'

'Thank God for that. I didn't want a repeat of my first proposal of marriage, when you gave a definite no. And thank you for your gift,' he murmured. 'It's perfect. I have a gift for you—a surprise, which I shall give you tomorrow. But for now...' He took something out of his pocket.

'What is it?'

'Mistletoe.' His lips curved in a provocative smile. 'You know what that means.'

'I have a very good idea.' She glanced at the sprig he was holding just above her head and smiled teasingly. 'I see there are plenty of berries on it.'

'Naturally. When I came after you I had an ulterior motive, so I made quite sure of that. Mistletoe is a licence for intimacy—and in pagan times it was connected to fertility.'

'Really?' she whispered, arching her brows, pretending ignorance.

He nodded. 'And did you know that each mistletoe berry represents a kiss?'

'It does?' She saw a purposeful gleam in those heavy-lidded eyes.

'Every time a visitor to the house is kissed, one of the white berries should be removed. When all the berries have gone, the kissing has to stop—which is why I chose a sprig with plenty of berries on it.'

'Well, it looks as though we've a lot of kissing to get through. So we'd best get on with it before we both freeze to death.'

'My thoughts exactly.'

Before taking her in his arms, Grant pushed the stem of mistletoe into her thick hair. Despite the cold his lips were warm when they covered hers, touching her mouth with an exquisite gentleness that stunned her into stillness. They caressed, lazily coaxing, hungry and searching, fitting her lips to his own, and then his kiss deepened and he kissed her endlessly, as if he had all the time in the world.

Of their own volition Adeline's fingers curved around his neck, sliding into the soft, thick hair at his nape, feeling a pleasure and an astonished joy that was almost past bearing. She pressed herself against him, answering his passion with the same wild, exquisitely provocative ardour that had haunted her dreams since she had left him in London. The arms around her tightened, moulding her body to his, and she clung to him as ivy clings to a tree, and the strength in that hard, lean body gave her strength, gave promise of more pleasure.

Dragging his lips from hers, Grant looked at her upturned face. His eyes glowed. 'Well, I suppose that's one berry gone.'

'No—leave it. I don't want the kissing to stop. Not ever.'

Touching her cheek with his fingertips, and then wrapping his long fingers around her chin, he tilted her head back, his eyes smiling into hers. 'Anything to oblige.'

Again his mouth covered hers. And so it went on. And the sprig of mistletoe kept its berries.

Chapter Thirteen

The following morning at eight o'clock they met at the stables, as arranged the night before. The weather had turned warmer overnight. A thaw had set in and the snow was melting fast.

Grant watched Adeline walk towards him, a look of unconcealed appreciation on his handsome face as he surveyed her, warmly clad in a dark green velvet habit.

'How can anyone look so lovely at this time in a morning?' he commented warmly.

With grooms going about their chores, Adeline suppressed the urge to fling herself into the arms of her handsome lover and gave him a brilliant smile instead. But she slanted a scowl of disapproval at the horse she was to ride when she saw the groom about to place a side-saddle on its back. 'Oh, no. Not that.'

Grant quirked a brow. 'No?'

'No.' The reason was plain enough when she raised her skirt to reveal her breeches.

Grant gave a shout of laughter. 'Adeline Osborne, you are outrageous.'

Tossing her head, she gave him an impish smile. 'I like being outrageous. In which direction shall we ride?' she asked when they were mounted, having got her way with the saddle.

'Through the park in the direction of the village, I think.'
Curious, she asked, 'Why the village?'

For some reason that question seemed to amuse him as he gathered his reins and they rode out of the stableyard. Seeing her worried look, he said casually, 'I have an appointment with the vicar at nine o'clock. Our meeting won't take long. It will give the horses a chance to rest awhile before riding back.'

Urging their horses into a lunging gallop, they crouched low over their necks, thundering over the snow-covered turf with ground-devouring strides. They rode at full speed, side by side, effortlessly leaping hedges in graceful unison. Approaching the village, they slowed their horses to a canter and rode in the direction of the church.

Adeline was surprised to see several people standing in the porch. The closer they got, the more she recognised them all—her father and Mrs Leighton, Lettie and Roland. Drawing her delicate brows together, she cast Grant a bemused look.

'How strange. What are they doing here? Who are they waiting for?'

'Us.'

Stopping outside the gate, Grant dismounted and asked her to do the same. Sliding from the saddle and into his arms, she looked at him.

'Us? Is there something going on that I don't know about, Grant?' Her heart was beginning to beat with nervous anticipation. She looked towards the small group of people, all waiting expectantly—for what?

'I promised you a surprise and this is it. Last night I asked you to be my wife. You said yes, so I thought there was no time like the present to get married.'

'Oh!' The gasp escaped her lips as she was roused from her shock. Her eyes flew to Grant, who could only smile lamely as he stared at her. 'But how could you…? I mean—there hasn't been time…'

'I arranged it as soon as I got back to Oaklands.'

She was incredulous. 'But—that was ages ago.'

'Three weeks, to be exact.'

'You were so certain I would say yes? You assume too much, Grant!' she declared, but softened and brushed a kiss on his lips as a thrill of excitement sped through her veins.

A smile twisted his lips. 'One way or another I was determined you would be my wife.'

'Weren't you afraid that I would leave?'

'I would have followed you. You have my heart, Adeline. I love you more than I can ever love anyone again.'

She placed her gloved hand tenderly against his cheek, and her look was one of adoration. 'And I love you, Grant Leighton. More than you will ever know. But I cannot believe you have done this. And your mother—and Lettie—were they in on the deception, too?'

'I'm afraid so.'

'And Father?'

'Was let in on the secret when he arrived. He has no objections—have you?'

'What possible objections could I have? Although I am surprised Father didn't tell me. He doesn't normally tolerate deceit in anyone.'

Grant was standing close, looking at her with grave eyes, his cheekbones taut, his firm lips parted. 'Will you marry me now, Adeline—here, in this church? The vicar is waiting inside.'

Something caught at Adeline's heart—a warming hope that all would be well between them and they would enjoy each other without restrictions. Tilting her head to one side, she slanted him an adoring look. 'Well—I have nothing better to do today, so we might as well.'

'In your riding habit?'

'I would marry you in rags, Grant Leighton.'

One corner of his mouth quirked into something that was suspiciously like a grin. 'I don't think we need go quite that far.'

Taking her hand, he linked it through the crook of his arm and together they walked towards those who were patiently waiting, worried frowns on their faces, wondering what Adeline would do, what she would say, hoping Grant had managed to persuade her. It wasn't until Adeline smiled, a smile of such radiance, that they knew he'd succeeded.

'So,' she said, laughing, 'this is why there have been so many whisperings and sudden silences when I entered a room. Shame on all of you.'

'Grant planned all this very carefully,' Lettie explained. 'But it was never intended to embarrass you.' Her eyes misted with tears. 'I'm so glad you're going to be my sister-in-law.' She was holding a little posy, which she handed to Adeline. 'This is for you.'

Adeline gazed down at it in wonder. 'Snowdrops? In December?'

'From Grant's hothouses.'

'Oh, but they're beautiful.'

'Like you, my darling,' Grant murmured.

'I would like a word with my daughter before she enters the church.' Taking Adeline's arm, Horace drew her aside.

Adeline searched for some hint of displeasure or contempt in her father's shadowed face, but only a gentle smile met her enquiring eyes. 'Father, I hope you will be happy for me?'

His reply was slow, but then he asked, 'Are you happy, Adeline? Will marriage to Grant please you after all?'

'Yes, it will please me very well. I love him—I have loved him for a long time.' Her whisper was soft and happy.

'Then that is all I ask. I shall be glad to see you properly wed.'

'But what of you? Rosehill will be a lonely place. Perhaps

you should sell it and live in London as you intended before—before Paul and I separated.'

'I have no intention of selling Rosehill—especially now.'

Adeline followed his gaze, which had fallen on Mrs Leighton, who was smiling back at him with her ever-tolerant knowing gaze. 'Oh—I see.' And she did see. She smiled delightedly. 'So *that's* the way of things.'

Horace's grin was almost boyish. 'So it is. Now, I believe Grant is waiting for you inside the church.' He offered her his arm, looking at her as he had never looked at her before. 'This is a proud moment for me. Come—you don't want to keep him waiting. Are you ready?'

Taking his arm, and holding the snowdrops to her waist, Adeline looked at the church, her heart thundering with dread, hope, uncertainty—and love. 'Yes,' she murmured. 'I'm ready.'

The day was one of immense celebration, culminating in the staff ball. But before that Grant and Adeline had found time to be alone, to seal their union in the best way possible.

Entering the ballroom with Adeline on his arm, his eyes glowed warmly into hers. Fresh from their lovemaking, ecstatic bliss glowed inside her like golden ashes, long after the explosion was over. Turning to all those present, he introduced her, immensely proud to say in a loud, clear voice, 'Ladies and gentlemen—my wife, Adeline.'

Immediately all those who had just arrived pressed eagerly forward, bestowing good wishes on the newly wedded couple. Grant's arm remained about Adeline's waist, claiming her as his possession, as he light-heartedly conversed with friends.

In a break with tradition, Cook was happy to let the newlyweds open the dancing. Grant brought Adeline into his embrace and they took to the floor, surrounded by family, friends and staff, Adeline resplendent in a gown of cream satin that bared her shoulders sublimely, and Grant darkly handsome. A thunder of applause broke and shook the rafters.

Grant looked down into the eyes of his wife of eight hours, unable to imagine a future without her by his side. She was smiling up at him, a smile that brightened the room and warmed his heart, and the closeness and sweet scent of her heated his blood.

'Happy?'

'Ecstatic.' She ached with the happiness she felt.

'Your cheeks are pink. You look radiant.'

'Because of you.'

He lifted a brow. 'I love you, Mrs Leighton, and if we were alone I would quickly prove the ardour you have stirred in me.' The heat of his stare lent the weight of truth to his words.

'The feeling is mutual, Mr Leighton. You are a wonderful man.'

'A very lucky man.' Grant looked at her for a long moment, caught up by emotions he could no longer conceal. 'I will love you until I die—and even after that, God willing.'

* * * * *

SPECIAL EDITION

Life, Love and Family

*These contemporary romances will strike
a chord with you as heroines juggle life
and relationships on their way to true love.*

New York Times *bestselling author Linda Lael Miller
brings you a BRAND-NEW contemporary story
featuring her fan-favorite McKettrick family.*

Meg McKettrick is surprised to be reunited with her high school flame, Brad O'Ballivan. After enjoying a career as a country-and-western singer, Brad aches for a home and family...and seeing Meg again makes him realize he still loves her. But their pride manages to interfere with love...until an unexpected matchmaker gets involved.

*Turn the page for a sneak preview of
THE McKETTRICK WAY
by Linda Lael Miller
On sale November 20, wherever books are sold.*

Brad shoved the truck into gear and drove to the bottom of the hill, where the road forked. Turn left, and he'd be home in five minutes. Turn right, and he was headed for Indian Rock.

He had no damn business going to Indian Rock.

He had nothing to say to Meg McKettrick, and if he never set eyes on the woman again, it would be two weeks too soon.

He turned right.

He couldn't have said why.

He just drove straight to the Dixie Dog Drive-In.

Back in the day, he and Meg used to meet at the Dixie Dog, by tacit agreement, when either of them had been away. It had been some kind of universe thing, purely intuitive.

Passing familiar landmarks, Brad told himself he ought to turn around. The old days were gone. Things had ended badly between him and Meg anyhow, and she wasn't going to be at the Dixie Dog.

He kept driving.

He rounded a bend, and there was the Dixie Dog. Its big neon sign, a giant hot dog, was all lit up and going through its corny sequence—first it was covered in red squiggles of light, meant to suggest ketchup, and then yellow, for mustard.

Brad pulled into one of the slots next to a speaker, rolled down the truck window and ordered.

A girl roller-skated out with the order about five minutes later. When she wheeled up to the driver's window, smiling, her eyes went wide with recognition, and she dropped the tray with a clatter.

Silently Brad swore. Damn if he hadn't forgotten he was a famous country singer.

The girl, a skinny thing wearing too much eye makeup, immediately started to cry. "I'm sorry!" she sobbed, squatting to gather up the mess.

"It's okay," Brad answered quietly, leaning to look down at her, catching a glimpse of her plastic name tag. "It's okay, Mandy. No harm done."

"I'll get you another dog and a shake right away, Mr. O'Ballivan!"

"Mandy?"

She stared up at him pitifully, sniffling. Thanks to the copious tears, most of the goop on her eyes had slid south. "Yes?"

"When you go back inside, could you not mention seeing me?"

"But you're Brad O'Ballivan!"

"Yeah," he answered, suppressing a sigh. "I know."

She rolled a little closer. "You wouldn't happen to have a picture you could autograph for me, would you?"

"Not with me," Brad answered.

"You could sign this napkin, though," Mandy said. "It's only got a little chocolate on the corner."

Brad took the paper napkin and her order pen, and scrawled his name. Handed both items back through the window.

She turned and whizzed back toward the side entrance to the Dixie Dog.

Brad waited, marveling that he hadn't considered incidents like this one before he'd decided to come back home. In retrospect, it seemed shortsighted, to say the least, but the truth was, he'd expected to be—Brad O'Ballivan.

Presently Mandy skated back out again, and this time she managed to hold on to the tray.

"I didn't tell a soul!" she whispered. "But Heather and Darlene *both* asked me why my mascara was all smeared." Efficiently she hooked the tray onto the bottom edge of the window.

Brad extended payment, but Mandy shook her head.

"The boss said it's on the house, since I dumped your first order on the ground."

He smiled. "Okay, then. Thanks."

Mandy retreated, and Brad was just reaching for the food when a bright red Blazer whipped into the space beside his. The driver's door sprang open, crashing into the metal speaker, and somebody got out in a hurry.

Something quickened inside Brad.

And in the next moment Meg McKettrick was standing practically on his running board, her blue eyes blazing.

Brad grinned. "I guess you're not over me after all," he said.